THE 12.30
FROM
CROYDON

THE 12.30 FROM CROYDON

Freeman Wills Crofts

With an Introduction by
MARTIN EDWARDS

This edition published 2016 by
The British Library
96 Euston Road
London
NW1 2DB

Originally published in 1934 by Hodder & Stoughton

Copyright © 2016 Estate of Freeman Wills Crofts
Introduction copyright © 2016 Martin Edwards

Cataloguing in Publication Data

A catalogue record for this book is
available from the British Library

ISBN 978 0 7123 5649 7

Typeset by Tetragon, London
Printed and bound by
CPI Group (UK) Ltd, Croydon CR0 4YY

CONTENTS

INTRODUCTION

The 12.30 from Croydon is a pleasingly crafted novel about murder and its detection, which illustrates the evolving nature of crime fiction during 'the Golden Age of Murder' between the wars. Here, one of the most admired authors of traditional detective stories changed direction, to focus in detail on the behaviour and psychology of a ruthless murderer, before pitting him against doughty Inspector Joseph French of Scotland Yard.

First, a word about the book's title. Some modern readers – especially those who know that Crofts was a railway engineer before he became a novelist, and that trains often feature in his books – may assume that it refers to a rail journey, like Agatha Christie's Miss Marple novel, *4.50 from Paddington*. In fact, the title refers to a trip by aeroplane. A small family group from Yorkshire flies from Croydon to Beauvais – but by the time the plane lands, Andrew Crowther, a wealthy manufacturer, is already dead.

The action promptly flashes back four weeks, and the setting switches to Yorkshire. We are introduced to Crowther's nephew, Charles Swinburn, who is facing ruin because of the Slump. It is sometimes said that Golden Age novels ignored the harsh realities of life in the Thirties, but although the books certainly offered readers the chance of escapism, the truth is that the economic calamities of the time often acted as the catalyst for fictional crime, with financial disaster driving ordinary men and women to the drastic remedy of murder. So it is with Charles Swinburn, whose need for money is made more urgent by the mercenary nature of Una Mellor, the woman he adores. The solution to his difficulties seems to stare him in the face:

How strange it was, Charles ruminated, that the useless and obstructive so often live on, while the valuable and progressive die early! Here was Andrew Crowther, a man whose existence was a misery to himself and a nuisance to all around him. Why should he be spared and others who were doing a great work in the world be cut off in their prime? It didn't somehow seem right. For the sake of himself and everyone else it would be better if Andrew were to die.

Charles devises a cunning plan to dispose of Andrew Crowther, and much of the appeal of the story comes from following his meticulous implementation of the scheme. Unfortunately for him, complications ensue, and his bad luck is compounded when Inspector French comes on to the scene.

This novel, the fifteenth published by Freeman Wills Crofts (1879–1957), followed *The Hog's Back Mystery*, an outstanding example of the fairly clued whodunnit. The popularity of his books had enabled Crofts to retire from engineering, and relocate from his native Ireland to Guildford to concentrate on writing. He became a founder member of the Detection Club, alongside the likes of Agatha Christie, Dorothy L. Sayers, and G.K. Chesterton, a sign of the regard in which his work was held by his peers.

But as Sayers noted in her enthusiastic review of this book, success for a novelist sometimes gives rise to a dilemma:

Among the major temptations that assail the detective author (and others) is that of writing the same book over and over again. Publishers and public encourage him to do so, because they like to know what to expect. Then, quite suddenly, they turn on the poor man and rend him, complaining that his books are all alike and that he has written himself out. The author, who is probably as heartily weary of the book as they are, but has been too timid to abandon a vein which has hitherto paid very well, is then faced with the task of starting all over again, under a heavy handicap.

Crofts had, Sayers noted, 'lately shown signs of a certain restlessness', and in *Sudden Death*, published in 1932, he had seemed to be 'groping after a new formula'. With this book, he took the plunge, undoubtedly inspired by the recent emergence of the psychological crime novel. Novels focusing on the mindset and machinations of murderers had occasionally appeared in the Twenties – notable examples are A.P. Herbert's *The House on the River* and C.S. Forester's *Payment Deferred*. But the real breakthrough came when Anthony Berkeley Cox, the founder of the Detection Club, published *Malice Aforethought* in 1930, under the name Francis Iles. His novel achieved both critical acclaim and commercial success, and Iles soon gained a number of talented disciples, including newcomers to the crime genre such as C.E. Vulliamy and Richard Hull.

Several established writers of detective fiction were also inspired by Iles' example; books written under his influence included *Portrait of a Murderer*, by Anne Meredith (a pen-name for Lucy Malleson, who usually wrote under the name Anthony Gilbert), and *End of an Ancient Mariner*, by G.D.H. and Margaret Cole. Crofts was, therefore, in good company in deciding that the time had come to try something different with the crime novel, but although his books did not delineate character in such depth as those by Iles, they benefited from his scrupulous attention to detail.

Sayers pronounced that *12.30 from Croydon* was 'an excellent book, though here and there the practised hand betrays a little unsureness in working on the unaccustomed material ... the story, as a story, is highly successful, and Mr. Crofts is to be congratulated upon his experiment'. Duly encouraged, Crofts promptly wrote another book in the same vein, *Mystery on Southampton Water*, before venturing on an even bolder experiment in 1938, with *Antidote to Venom*. That book, like *The Hog's Back Mystery* and another cleverly plotted novel, *Mystery in the Channel*, is available in the British Library's Crime Classics series. Taken together, the four novels provide an enjoyable reminder of Freeman Wills Crofts' range and ambition as a crime writer.

MARTIN EDWARDS
www.martinedwardsbooks.com

SELECT BIBLIOGRAPHY:
Freeman Wills Crofts and Golden Age detective fiction

Melvyn Barnes, 'Freeman Wills Crofts', in *St James Guide to Crime and Mystery Writers* (1996)

J. Barzun and W.H. Taylor, *A Catalogue of Crime* (1971)

John Cooper and B.A. Pike, *Artists in Crime* (1995)

John Cooper and B.A. Pike, *Detective Fiction: The Collector's Guide* (2nd edn, 1994)

Martin Edwards, *The Golden Age of Murder* (2015)

Curtis Evans, *Masters of the 'Humdrum' Mystery: Cecil John Charles Street, Freeman Wills Crofts, Alfred Walter Stewart and the British Detective Novel, 1920–61* (2012)

H.R.F. Keating, *Murder Must Appetize* (1975)

H.M. Klein, 'Freeman Wills Crofts', in *Dictionary of Literary Biography, volume 77: British Mystery Writers 1920–39* (1989)

Erik Routley, *The Puritan Pleasures of the Detective Story: From Sherlock Holmes to Van der Valk* (1972)

CHAPTER I

Andrew Takes the Air

ROSE MORLEY WAS AN EXCITED YOUNG LADY AS WITH HER father and grandfather and grandfather's servant she reached the air station at Victoria. For the first time in her life she was going to fly!

Excitements indeed had followed one another without intermission since last night, when the dreadful news had come that her mother had been knocked down and seriously injured by a taxi in Paris. Rose was staying with a school friend at Thirsk, in Yorkshire. She had gone to bed and almost to sleep, and then Mrs Blessington had come in softly and told her to get up and dress, as her father had come to pay her a late visit. Wonderingly, Rose had obeyed. She had gone down to the drawing-room to find her father there alone. He had smiled at her bravely, but she had seen in a moment that he was really terribly upset. He had explained at once what had happened. That was one thing she did like about daddy: he always treated her as a grown-up and told her the truth about things. Poor mummy had had this accident in Paris and he and grandfather were going over to see her. And wouldn't she, Rose, like to go with them and see poor mummy, too?

Rose said she would. At first she had been dreadfully distressed at the thought that her mother might be in pain, but then so many thrilling things had happened one after another that these regrets had become dulled. First there had been the run home in the car through the darkness, sitting beside daddy, who drove. Then the getting up again at half-past two in the morning – she had never before been up at such an hour; the coffee and sandwiches in the dining-room, and the long drive in the car to York. She was sleepy in the station, which was horrid, so big and empty and cold. But the train had soon come in and she had had such a delightful little room with a real bed to sleep in. Then daddy had wakened her to say that it was time to get up, and she had found that they were in London. As soon as she had dressed they had gone to an hotel for breakfast. There grandfather had rested till after a while they had had this thrilling drive across Town, and now here was the air station: and she was going to fly!

Now that the crowning excitement of the journey had been reached, all thoughts as to what might lie at its farther end vanished from her mind and she became intent solely on the present. Small wonder! Her outlook was not that of her father and grandfather. She was only ten.

Her father, Peter Morley, was a man of about forty, of medium height, thin, stooped, and a trifle dyspeptic. His face was set in a melancholy cast, as if he had little faith in the good intentions of the goddess of chance. His passion was farming, and when he had married Elsie Crowther they had bought the little estate which for many years he had coveted. Otterton Farm was near Cold Pickerby, where his father-in-law, Andrew Crowther, lived. It had a small but charming old homestead building, an excellent yard and out offices, and just over a hundred acres of good land. Peter's management was sound and he made a success of the venture: until the slump had come. Now he found himself in the same difficulties as his co-agriculturists. He had a son and daughter: Hugh, a boy of thirteen, who was also away on a visit, and this girl, Rose.

Andrew Crowther, the father of Peter's wife, Elsie, was a retired manufacturer and a wealthy man. The first impression that he produced on the observer was that of age. He was an old man; old for his years, which were only sixty-five. His hair was snow-white and his face seamed and haggard. For some time he had given up shaving, and now he wore a thin straggling beard and moustache. Always to Peter he suggested Henry Irving as Shylock, with his hooked nose, stooped shoulders and grasping, claw-like fingers. He could somehow be imagined crouching over a fire and holding out his thin hands to the blaze. Up to some five years earlier he had been a personable and well-set-up man, but he had then had a serious illness which had sapped his vitality and all but taken his life. He had pulled through, but he emerged from his sick-room the wreck of his former self. Peter had doubted the wisdom of his undertaking this journey, but Elsie was Andrew Crowther's only daughter, the only living being indeed of whom he seemed really fond, and he had insisted on coming. His heart was known to be weak, and Peter had rung up his doctor and had him specially examined as to his fitness for the expedition. Of this Dr Gregory had expressed no doubt. All the same Peter watched him anxiously, though to his satisfaction the old man did not so far show signs of fatigue.

The fourth member of the quartet was John Weatherup, Andrew Crowther's general attendant and butler. He was a thin man of middle height, with a dark saturnine face and a manner expressive of gloom. He had come to Andrew during the latter's convalescence with excellent qualifications as a male nurse, and when Andrew was as well as he was ever likely to become and no longer required a nurse, Weatherup had taken no notice of the fact, but had stayed on as 'man'. As an attendant, he was not the person Peter would have chosen, but he appeared to be a success at his job, and could effectively humour his employer.

Peter Morley was eagerly anticipating their arrival at the air station. He had arranged that a telegram with the latest bulletin of his wife's condition should be sent him there, and his anxiety grew almost painful as they drove across Town. Indeed he could scarcely contain himself till the taxi came to rest, leaping out and hurrying to the office.

As he disappeared two porters in neat blue uniforms came forward.

'Have you got reserved places?' one asked.

Weatherup explained that these had been obtained on the previous evening. Thereupon the porters seized the luggage, and to Rose's intense interest, threw it lightly into a hole in the office wall. She could see the suit-cases departing slowly and mysteriously downwards into the bowels of the earth on a series of metal rollers which stretched away like some unusual kind of flat stairway. But before she could point out the phenomenon to her grandfather, Peter reappeared, waving a buff slip.

'It's not so bad as we thought,' he cried as he came forward. 'Look at this! *Better this morning. Injuries believed superficial.* Thank God for that! Great news, Mr Crowther! Splendid, isn't it, Rose?' He was so excited that he could scarcely pay the taxisman. 'Great news, great news!' he continued repeating as they crossed the footpath to the office. 'We'll see her in four hours! And she might have been killed!'

The others in their diverse ways expressed their relief and they entered the office. It was a large room, modern as to design and comfortable as to furniture: an office-waiting-room. Along one side was a counter behind which smart young men functioned. Elsewhere were settees on which would-be passengers had disposed themselves. Andrew Crowther joined the latter, while Peter and Rose went up to the counter.

'Your tickets, please?'

'You have them,' Peter explained. 'I rang up for places last night. Mr Peter Morley.'

The tickets were found to be in order, and then passports were demanded and handed over. 'You'll get them back at Croydon,'

explained the smart young man. Then he pointed. 'Will you stand
on the scales – with your handbags, please.'

They were duly weighed in. Rose wanted to know their weights,
but as set forth in the Company's advertisement, a veil is drawn over
this intimate matter and the figures repose in the brain of the clerk
alone. They were, however, handed a map and booklet of information
about the flight. Presently there came the cry: 'All for Paris, please!'
and with varying degrees of eagerness or indifference everyone began
to drift towards the door. Outside the Croydon bus was waiting, they
all got in, and it moved slowly off.

The morning had been fine when they left York, but the sky had
soon become overcast and now a dismal rain was falling. Though
Rose remained immensely excited, her enthusiasm became somewhat damped by the miles of wet streets through which they passed
and the drab and dingy buildings which edged them. An uninspiring
drive, though as they got nearer Croydon things improved. Here it
was not raining, though it was cloudy and threatening to commence
at any moment.

At last the aerodrome! Behind the buildings fronting the road
Rose could see sheds, a tall square tower, a green field and a glimpse
of planes. They swung in through a narrow gate and pulled up at the
porch of a large building. Everyone got out. The passengers sorted
themselves into groups and passed in through the porch to a large
hall. There the passports were returned and they were shepherded
by officials to a second door leading out on to the drome.

Now the great moment had come! Here in front of them was the
aeroplane. Rose had eyes for nothing else as in a thin stream the passengers emerged on to the concrete on which the great machine was
standing, some thirty or forty yards from the building. How huge it
looked! Unwieldy too, thought Rose, gazing at the criss-cross struts

connecting its wings and its long, slightly curved body. Not in the least like a bird, but still like something she had seen. What was it? She remembered: it was a dragonfly. It was just a huge dragonfly with a specially long head, which projected far forward before the wings like an enormous snout. And those four lumps were its motors, two on each wing, set into the front edge of the wing and each with its great propeller twirling in front of it. And there was its name, painted on its head: H, E, N, G, I, S, T; HENGIST. Hengist and Horsa; she had heard of them, though she wasn't quite certain who they were.

But there was really no time to look at the strange machine. Halfway between the wings and the tail a door was open in its side, with a flight of steps leading up to it, and before Rose knew where she was, she was climbing up after her father. A step through the doorway and she was in the cabin.

It was just like the bus in which she had so often gone to school, with four seats across it and a narrow corridor down the centre. Her seat was next to the side immediately in front of the door, with her father next to her. Beside her was a window, but she couldn't see out because the door opened back across it. She therefore looked round the cabin instead.

Her grandfather was just taking his place right in front of her with Weatherup in the seat next to him. There were eighteen seats in the compartment, and in a few seconds every one of them was filled. And Rose knew that a lot more people had got in through another door to the forward cabin in front of the wings. It was to it, she supposed, that that door in the front partition led.

Everyone was settling down, putting handbags on the racks above the windows and getting out papers and magazines. No one seemed to think it at all strange that they were going to fly. How *could* they, she wondered? However, she supposed they had all done it before.

The door was now shut behind her and she suddenly found that the obstruction was gone from the window and that she could see out. The principal object in the landscape was the lower wing. It seemed simply huge from so close. From it the great criss-crosses went up to the upper wing, which she could see only by bending down and gazing up. Others of these criss-crosses went down to the landing-wheel which had a pneumatic tyre a good deal bigger than her whole body.

At each side of the wheel were large wooden wedges, and now a man came forward and pulled these away. Then an officer in a smart blue uniform made a signal to someone on board. At once the motors began to hum more loudly, and the propeller, which had been flickering, now became a round blur. Suddenly she saw that the ground was moving. They were off!

There was a stain of mud on the great landing-wheel, and fascinated, Rose watched it going round and round. The plane turned to the right, and the air buildings and the small crowd of onlookers swung round backwards and slipped out of sight. Soon they were off the concrete and on to the grass of the field. The machine ran very easily: Rose could feel the motion like that of a car, but there were no bumps. Out in the middle of the drome they slowed down and the plane was turned, to meet the wind, her father explained. Then suddenly the motors roared out loudly. There was a feeling as if an enormous hand had grasped the machine and was pulling it forward. The speed increased so quickly that Rose felt pressed immovably back into her seat. More fascinated than ever she watched the mud stain on the great wheel, going round faster and faster and always faster.

They were now racing across the field with the speed of an express train, the wheel turning so quickly that Rose could scarcely see the mud stain. She watched it breathlessly, her hands clasped with excitement. Then suddenly the wonder happened.

Without feeling anything unusual she saw there was a little space, a few inches, below the great wheel! The space increased. It became a foot, a yard, several yards. They were flying!

'Oh!' gasped Rose, delighted and yet just the least little bit afraid.

'Now we're off,' said Peter somewhat unnecessarily, but she scarcely heard him. She was too busy looking down on Croydon. As far as she could see, they were not rising: the ground instead was sinking quickly down from them in some quite inexplicable way. Two or three hundred yards below them Croydon seemed a far prettier place than it had looked on the way from Town. There were hills and hollows and the roads wound about in curves, and there was any amount of green between the houses. From the bus she had only seen streets and shops.

Suddenly her heart shot into her mouth and she gripped the back of the seat in front of her in momentary terror. 'Hengist' gave a horrid drop, as the stern of a great ship will slip off a receding wave. It was like a lift of which the rope had broken. Immediately he brought up, as if landing at the bottom of the shaft. Then for a while he was unsteady, swooping up and down quicker than the quickest lift Rose had ever been in. He didn't pitch or roll, but rose and fell on an even keel. Rose hated it. However, it didn't last long, and soon he settled down steadily again.

Now a fluffy strip of vapour floated past the window, and almost at once they were in fog. Rose could still see the great wing and its wheel, but the ground was gone. Except for the wing and wheel there was nothing anywhere but pearly grey mist.

'Fog, daddy,' she said, disappointed that she could no longer see below.

'It's cloud, darling,' Peter Morley answered. 'We've gone right up into the clouds! What do you think of that?' He leaned forward. 'How are you getting on, Mr Crowther? The motion's not unpleasant?'

'I'm enjoying it,' the old man returned. 'It's the first time I've ever travelled by air and I'm enjoying it. We might as well be in the car.'

'Yes, it's pretty steady now and not too noisy. A wonderful improvement on the early machines, when you had to get cotton-wool in your ears, and even then were half deafened.'

'They said it would be no noisier than a train, and neither is it.'

Rose guessed from her grandfather's manner that in his quiet way he was just as much excited by the experience as she was. It was not really noisy, she thought; still, there was that tremendous drone of the motors going on so steadily all the time. But after a while she supposed one would get so used to that as scarcely to hear it.

'See those little dials?' her father pointed.

There were three, side by side, like three clocks, set into the wall in front, beside the door leading to the other cabin. One indeed was a clock; the others she couldn't read.

'Those tell us our height and our speed,' Peter went on. 'You see, we are three thousand two hundred feet high and going at one hundred and twenty miles an hour: twice as quick as an express train. You see that, Mr Crowther?' and he went on to repeat his information.

Rose thought it all very thrilling, but she wished they were out of the cloud. She had wanted to see the sea, and it didn't look as if she were going to. However, long before she began to feel bored, a new diversion occurred. The attendant came round to know if they were taking lunch.

They all took it. Tiny flaps on the backs of the chairs in front were let down to make tables, and little rings, which came out like the chalk dishes of a billiard table, held their glasses. They had a four-course lunch followed by coffee, all very nice and comfortably served. Rose enjoyed every minute of it, particularly as she could still see nothing from the window but the wing with its attendant hanging wheel and the pearly grey fog.

Lunch was still in progress when she noticed a difference in the appearance of the fog. She couldn't understand it, but her father explained. They had come out of the cloud and were flying through clear air. Still they could see neither earth nor sun. Layers of cloud stretched both above and below them. Gradually they rose above the lower layer and as they did so its appearance became more and more impressive. It looked solid, like a rolling, hillocky plain, but the hillocks had soft edges like frayed cotton-wool. It stretched away as far as they could see into the distance, its valleys showing dark between its lighter crests. Above them, however, the cloud looked flat and unbroken, like the sky of a wet day on the earth.

Presently it grew lighter ahead and they saw that they were approaching the edge of the upper cloud. From a definite line on the lower cloud the sun was shining. They flew out into the sun. Above, the sky was now blue; below, the hillocks of the vast plain were more intensely white and the valleys between them correspondingly darker.

'Where are we now?' Peter Morley asked the attendant, who came to change the plates.

'Over the Channel, sir.'

Rose was a little disappointed. She had missed that aerial view of England to which she had been looking forward ever since she had heard they were to fly. However, she had seen the clouds from above, and that was something.

Presently she noticed that a large area of the cloud below had darkened in colour. For a moment she gazed at it with a rather listless attention. Then, realizing what it was, she was suddenly thrilled.

'Daddy, look, look!' she cried excitedly. 'Look at the land!'

She was right. There, three thousand two hundred feet below them, was the surface of France. Peter leant forward to see, old Mr Crowther was evidently fascinated, and even the sombre Weatherup showed a grudging interest.

It was indeed a fascinating map upon which they gazed. The land was divided up into little irregular squares like tiny crooked postage stamps in various shades of greens and browns and reds. Feathery green areas obviously represented woods. In all directions ran traces, a perfect network of lines, representing roads and lanes and water-courses. A few were straight or evenly curved, evidently main roads or railways. A darkish worm headed by a tiny white streamer made certain of the nature of one dark line. The houses showed as tiny rectangles and the villages reminded them of the relievo models so often made to illustrate dead cities. Tiny yellow circles, looking about as big as the heads of matches, at first puzzled Rose. Then she saw that they must be haystacks. Some fields had a still more mysterious appearance. They were covered with a pattern of little dots, arranged in lines as if for ornament, like tiny beads sewn on an old-fashioned mitten.

'What are they, daddy?' she asked, pointing them out.

Peter Morley was not sure, but suggested cartloads of fertilizer, laid down in the fields but not yet spread.

The most striking thing in the landscape was, however, the shad-ows. Every object had its shadow stretching away north. The shadow alone showed that objects had height. Every building, every hedge, every embankment had its shadow. Thin clumps of trees, feathery and indeterminate, stood out clearly because of their shadows.

Looking backwards from the other side of the car they were able to get a glimpse of the sea, showing up as a flat plain of dark, slaty blue.

'That,' said Peter Morley, who had been studying his map, 'is the estuary of the Somme. And that,' he returned to Rose's window and pointed, 'that straight dark line is the Nord Railway from Calais and Boulogne to Paris. The town over there is Abbeville.'

Rose gazed down. It was all very thrilling and wonderful. So that queer-looking country was France! To think that all those funny little spaces between the houses were really streets, and that people were in them, too small to be seen! It was like looking on an ant heap from the top of a high building.

'What's that white ring, daddy?' she asked presently, as a circle containing letters showed in the middle of a field far below.

'Poix,' Peter answered, again studying his map. 'It's an aerodrome, and you could see its name in the circle if we were lower. That's how the pilots know where to come down.'

Rose was still meditating over this when she noticed that little wisps of cloud were forming far below. Small and widely separated at first, they quickly grew larger and closer together, allowing mere glimpses of the land. Soon even these gaps disappeared and once again they were looking down on a world of rolling cloud. What a pity, she thought, when the view of the country had been so wonderful.

She was interested to notice that her grandfather had gone to sleep. He was leaning back in the corner of his seat with his head against the wall of the car. Asleep! she thought amazedly. Fancy anyone going to sleep in the middle of all this excitement! But old people were like that. They got tired easily. Her father noticed it at the same time.

'Having a nap, is he?' he said to Weatherup.

'Yes, sir. He generally goes off for a few minutes after lunch, so I suppose it's force of habit.'

'It won't do him any harm.'

'No, sir. This is a good deal for a man of his years and health.'

Just then the attendant came round.

'We're landing at Beauvais,' he told everyone. He did not explain why, but the whisper went round that there was fog in Paris.

Almost immediately Rose felt the plane falling, gently, like an easy lift. The motors still kept on droning as before, but the cloud layer was coming up rapidly. There was nothing unpleasant in the motion, it was so easy and gradual. Presently the motors slackened speed till Rose could see the quivering of the propeller blades. Then they dropped into the cloud and were once more surrounded by opaque whiteness, through which only the wing and wheel were visible.

They fell on and on through the cloud, the motors going on and off more than once. Suddenly they saw the ground. They were close to it now, not more, Peter estimated, than three or four hundred feet up. Once again the motors roared out and they continued flying across the fields at this height.

Expecting as they were to come down to earth at any moment, the flight now seemed endless. But at last Rose could see their objective, a large field with another white ring, this time very big indeed, and containing the word BEAUVAIS in huge letters. Still they kept up, passing nearly over the aerodrome. Now the plane seemed to want to land and made some disconcerting swoops and dives. Then it banked. The wing took up an angle of forty-five degrees with the ground, and they swung slowly round in a great circle. Suddenly they dropped, easily. The ground rushed up to meet them. They were within fifty feet of it, forty, thirty, ten.

The ground had been slipping past pretty quickly, but only now could Rose see their real speed. It seemed tremendous. The ground absolutely dashed past. It was faster than any train she had ever been in.

As they slipped over the edge of the aerodrome they seemed not more than four or five feet up, and almost at once the great wheel touched and began to revolve as it had at Croydon, so quickly that Rose could scarcely see its patch of mud. They were down; down without the slightest shock or sensation of landing! Indeed it was less steady as they taxied across the grass, gradually reducing speed. Then quite slowly they moved up to the aerodrome buildings and – the flight was over!

'Well, Rose, how did you like that?' her father queried as he got up and began fumbling for his handbag and coat.

'Oh, daddy, it was lovely!' she cried. 'Lovely! I want to go back this way.'

'I hope we shall,' he answered. 'Will you take your coat?'

She stood up and took the coat, looking at the passengers all doing the same thing. Her grandfather was still asleep and Weatherup bent over him. Then he straightened up and spoke hurriedly to her father.

'What?' Peter answered very sharply, glancing at the old man. Immediately he turned to Rose and said quickly: 'Now, Rose, out with you! Look sharp now; you mustn't keep everyone waiting.'

Rose was amazed. This wasn't the way her father usually spoke, and besides she wasn't keeping anyone waiting. But his face bore an unusual expression, and when she saw it she thought it better not to argue, but to get out at once. He helped her down.

'Wait there for me,' he went on. 'I shan't be long', and he climbed quickly back into the plane.

But he was: a long time. All the other passengers had come out and walked off before he reappeared. Then his face was very grave.

'I'm sorry to say your grandfather has been taken ill,' he said. 'We shall have to carry him out of the plane. Will you come over to the office and wait for us there.'

It was not till later that Rose learned that Andrew Crowther had been dead when the plane came to the ground.

CHAPTER II

Charles Considers Finance

S OME FOUR WEEKS BEFORE ANDREW CROWTHER'S TRAGIC AIR journey his nephew Charles Swinburn sat in his leather-covered chair in the head office of the Crowther Electromotor Works at Cold Pickerby gazing unseeingly at a Thorpe Engineering Company's calendar which adorned the opposite wall of the somewhat dingy room. Above the neatly lettered card headed 'August' was a spirited reproduction in bright flat colours and jet shadows of a titanic crane hoisting a brobdingnagian locomotive over the cliff-like side of a mammoth ship. Yet this spectacular feat did not rivet Charles Swinburn's attention as it deserved and had been designed to do. In the first place he had seen it every day for nearly eight months, and in the second he had something more pressing to think about.

Something serious surely, to judge by the harassed expression on the man's face. He was in his early prime: as a matter of fact he had just celebrated his five-and-thirtieth birthday. The skin of his pale oval face was still unmarked by lines of care and his dark hair remained free from grey. Beneath his high, if somewhat narrow, forehead his eyes, sparkling with intelligence, looked out upon the world. Good features these, as was his nose. But there was a falling off in the lower part of his face. His mouth was not firm enough and his jaw was too narrow. The face indeed showed a strange mixture of intellectual power and moral weakness.

Charles Swinburn had cause to look anxious. He had cause to look more than anxious. For he was pondering a very dreadful problem.

He was trying desperately to find a way in which, with safety to himself, he could bring about the death of his uncle, Andrew Crowther.

To murder his uncle! That had lately become his obsession. Slowly the desperate circumstances in which he found himself had forced him to the terrible conclusion that if his uncle's life were not forfeit, he would lose his own.

A fortnight earlier no thought of crime had entered his mind. A fortnight earlier this terrible solution of his difficulties had not even occurred to him. Then, as now, he had sat in his office with an equally harassed expression on his face, but his anxiety had been then the anxiety of an honourable and law-abiding man.

There was good cause for his distress then, as now. Charles Swinburn was suffering from an extremely common complaint, so common indeed as to justify the adjective epidemic. He was in fact hard up. For some months things had been growing steadily worse, and now he was actually in sight of ruin.

He was the sole owner of the works, in the private office of which he was now seated. He manufactured small electromotors for driving low-powered machines from klaxons and gramophones to the more modest forms of machine tools. When he had received the business as a legacy from his father it had been small but flourishing. It was still small, but now its prosperity had departed. With the slump had come a gradual reduction of orders, Charles's profits had diminished till at last came the unhappy time when he found himself actually at a loss on the week's work. At first he had made good the deficit from his private account, but as things continued to grow steadily worse he saw that he could not continue to carry the business. His private fortune was practically gone and he was in debt to the bank, and if things did not mend he would be faced with the necessity of closing down.

With an abrupt movement he rose to his feet, and taking a bunch of keys from his pocket, unlocked a safe which stood in the corner of the office. The room was of fair size with two tall windows, facing which was Charles's table desk, with the usual shaded light, telephone and wicker correspondence baskets. Beside the fireplace stood a deep leather-covered arm-chair, provision both for Charles's less energetic moments and for his more important clients. More humble callers were accommodated on the small chair before the desk. The furniture was good, but the paint was shabby and the walls required repapering.

Charles took from the safe a locked book bound in black leather, placed it before him on the desk and opened it with a small key. It was his private ledger, of the existence of which neither his confidential clerk nor his manager had any idea. In it were recorded the damning facts which were now giving him so furiously to think. His staff knew that things were in a bad way, but no one but himself had any inkling how serious the position really was.

For some time Charles continued working with the figures in his book, then he was interrupted by a knock at the door. Before calling 'Come in!' he slipped the book into a drawer and became immersed in the papers which had been beneath it. A thin elderly man in thread-bare black, with a pessimistic expression on his sallow face, entered and stood in a hesitating way before the desk.

'Well, Gairns?' said Charles, contriving to banish his depressed expression and to speak cheerily.

James Gairns was the chief of Charles's clerical staff, nominally confidential clerk, accountant, and general office manager, really Charles's office boy and general attendant. Charles made a show of consulting him on everything, but he actually did all the important business himself. Gairns was utterly honest and trustworthy and car-ried out his routine duties efficiently enough, but he had no initiative and could not be trusted with power. With resignation, but an obvious expectation of the worst, he followed Charles's lead in anything out-side the ordinary course. Professionally speaking, he was as old as the works themselves, having been a foundation member of the staff. For ten years he had remained a clerk, then in a moment of mental aber-ration Charles's father had promoted him chief, and he had occupied the position ever since, a matter of three-and-twenty years.

'Well, Gairns?' said Charles again.

Gairns slowly rubbed the palm of his right hand with the tips of the fingers of his left, a trick which from much repetition had got on Charles's nerves.

'I wondered, sir, if you had heard from Brent Magnus Limited lately?'

'I lunched with Mr Brent yesterday.'

Gairns continued to rub his hands. 'Oh then, there'll be nothing in it,' he went on despondently.

'Perhaps,' Charles suggested, 'you'd tell me what you're talking about?' When in Gairns' company Charles always felt at his mental and moral best.

'It's only that I saw Tim Banks.' This was the Brent Magnus Ltd head clerk. 'I had occasion to slip round to the bank; about that cheque of Fleet's: you know, sir?'

'I know. Yes?'

'On the way back I met Tim Banks. He was just going into the bank. He stopped and we chatted for a moment.'

'Well? For goodness' sake, get on, man!'

Gairns began to rub his hands again. 'He asked if we'd heard from Mr Brent yet. I said, not so far as I knew. He said, well, we would be hearing soon. I asked what was up and he wouldn't say; not at first he wouldn't. But I pressed him and then he gave me the hint. "Mind you," he said, "I'm only giving you a hint and you don't know nothing till you hear from Mr Brent."'

'What was the hint?' Charles demanded patiently.

'We've lost the contract.' Gairns shook his head sadly.

'What!' Charles exclaimed. 'You don't say so! Was Banks sure?'

'He seemed so.'

Charles made a sudden gesture. 'Damn it all, Gairns, that's pretty bad news!'

Gairns shook his head hopelessly.

'What was our tender?' Charles went on. 'Seventeen hundred and ten pounds! Good heavens, Gairns, we can't afford to lose a seventeen hundred pound contract these times. It was going to be a help to us, that contract.'

Charles sprang to his feet and began to pace the room. This was certainly very unexpected and disagreeable news. The firm of Brent Magnus Ltd was an important toy-making concern, employing a large staff. The machines for making the toys were all small, and were operated by an elaborate system of shafting, the driving of which consumed nearly as much power as the machines themselves. The directors had just decided to throw out this shafting and to replace it by a separate electromotor for each machine. They had advertised for tenders for the work, and as the largest motors made by Charles were just big enough, he had tendered. He had cut his price to the last sixpence and had been hopeful of success.

It was a blow, and Charles could not entirely hide the fact. He presently ceased his pacing of the room and threw himself once more into his chair. 'Sit down a moment, Gairns.' He pointed to the small chair. 'We must talk this over.'

Gairns seated himself gingerly on the edge of the chair and sat waiting for what was to come. Here was a difficulty, and it was Charles's part to meet it and his, Gairns's, to assist by doing what he was told. The idea of offering a suggestion did not occur to him.

It was fortunate for him that he was not called on to do so, for as a matter of fact he had none to offer. Indeed he did not even see that there was anything to discuss. The order was lost. Very regrettable, but there was nothing to be done about it.

Charles, however, had other ideas.

'I'm afraid, Gairns,' he began, 'that this affair will bring up a question which I have been thinking over for some time, and which I'd much rather not mention. Which of those two clerks, Hornby or Sutter, is the better man?'

Gairns slowly rubbed his hand. 'Hornby or Sutter?' he repeated. 'Well, they're both good young fellows enough, as young fellows go in these days, that is.'

'I asked you which was the better.'

'Hornby's better at the books. His posting's neat and he doesn't make mistakes, or not many of them anyhow. But Sutter's the best man when it comes to handling anything out of the common. If you have a message up town you send Sutter.'

Charles saw that he must get down to it. 'The reason I ask you is that I'm afraid you'll have to let one of them go.'

Gairns was appalled. He blinked at his employer. 'Let one of them go, sir? That wouldn't be easy with all the work that has to be done.' He could scarcely believe Charles was in earnest. There had always been the typist, the office boy, and two clerks, and to make so fundamental a change would alter the whole of the established routine.

'I know it won't be easy,' Charles went on. 'I hate to think of getting rid of either of them, for I know they're both good men. But I'm afraid we can't help ourselves. We simply can't afford to go on as we are doing. We've got to save somewhere. You know as well as I do that every firm's doing it.'

The old man was actually trembling. Charles, who overlooked his annoying little ways in remembering his devoted service, was sorry for him.

'We can't help it, James,' he said kindly. 'You go off now and think how you're going to manage with one clerk. There's less correspondence now than there was and Miss Lillingstone can help with the books. And that boy Maxton can do more than he's doing. Think which of those two you'd like to keep and let the other go. I don't want him taken too short. You may give him a month's notice.'

Charles was a considerate employer and hated turning into the street a man who had served him well. But for some time the dwindling work had been forcing him to the conclusion that the office was overstaffed. The loss of the Brent Magnus job had simply brought the matter to a head.

For Charles had no doubt of the truth of Gairns's story. He had been afraid of that very thing happening, and he knew that the confidential clerk, Timothy Banks, was a highly reliable man.

When Gairns left the office, the expression of worry and care settled down once again on Charles's features. This hiding of his troubles from his staff and turning a smiling face to the world was a wearing business. And yet he must go through with it. He had a special reason why no whisper that all was not well in the Crowther Works must get abroad, an overwhelming, all-compelling reason. For Charles Swinburn was in love, desperately, consumingly in love. And he knew that Una Mellor would never marry a poor man.

Six months previously Colonel Mellor had moved to Cold Pickerby, and a week later Charles and Una had met on the golf links. She played a good game and so did he, and the meeting was followed by others. For Charles it was love at first sight. Till then he had been comparatively free from attachments, and now when he caught the fever the attack was correspondingly severe. Una instantly saw what had happened – and laughed at him. But this, instead of cooling him, still further inflamed his passion, till the winning of the tantalizing young woman became the one thing he lived for. After weeks of discouragement he began to think he was making progress, and latterly he had been sure of it. But he knew that the mere suggestion of financial difficulty, not to mention bankruptcy, would remove her as far from his reach as if she lived in the moon.

For some time Charles remained sitting motionless at his desk with bowed head and despondent features. Then with a half-shrug he rose, locked away his book, took his hat and went out.

Though a big Scotsman named Macpherson served him in the nominal capacity of works manager and engineer, Charles was his own manager. The works were his hobby and his baby as well as the source of his income, and he enjoyed pottering about in them and watching what was going on. When work in the office was slack he was to be found 'down the yard'. When his thoughts in the office became too bitter he would take refuge in the same sanctuary. So it was on the present occasion.

He passed through the store, nodding to the storesman and running his eye along the shelves with their load of wire, castings, bolts, terminals, and spares of all kinds, and in another section the finished motors, stacked according to size and winding. Charles was very proud of his store, with the continuous card indicator system he had introduced by which at a glance the exact amount of everything stocked could be read off. Also it pleased him to see the neat way in which everything was stacked, and he complimented the storesman on his well-swept floor and tidy shelves.

From the store he glanced into the tiny foundry, exchanged a word or two with the solitary pattern maker, and then wandered across the yard to the winding shop. Here the armatures and the field magnets were wound. Charles rather aimlessly stopped before a small machine and stood watching it work.

It was winding a coil with copper wire of the thickness of an extremely fine hair. The fairy-like thread, after coming off its reel, was carried through a bath of insulating varnish, dried in a current of hot air, and wound on the coil, all just as if the machine was a human being. The way the coil was turned to take the successive layers fascinated Charles, and he invariably stopped to watch the operation.

'One of the distance relays for yon Dalton pit job,' a voice said presently in deep Scottish tones. 'A bonny wee machine, that.'

'I could stand and watch it all day, Sandy,' Charles admitted.

'So I've obsairved,' the Scotsman returned dryly.

'I want to see that relay scheme fitted up and tested before we make too many of them,' Charles went on, and they began to discuss technicalities.

Alexander Macpherson, after visiting most of the maritime world in the engine-room of a tramp steamer, had suddenly fallen in love with and married a Glasgow girl. Evincing a desire to settle down, he had turned in his extremity to advertisement. The Crowther Electromotor Works, being at that precise time without an engineer, had had recourse to the same medium, with the result that Macpherson became works manager and engineer, to the lasting advantage of both himself and Charles Swinburn.

'Strictly between ourselves, Sandy,' Charles said at last, 'I've had a bit of bad news. I hear we've lost that Brent Magnus job.'

The engineer stared. 'Lost it?' he repeated in surprise. He shook his great head. 'That's no' so good, Mr Charles; no' so good. We canna afford to lose a job o' that sort these times. You're sure of it, I suppose?'

'Well, Tim Banks told Gairns. He's usually pretty reliable. I've not heard officially.'

'Oh, aye; Banks is all right. Man, I'm sorry about that. I was counting on yon to keep the big slotter going.'

'I was counting on it to keep more than the slotter going,' Charles returned. 'We're going to have to reduce, Sandy.'

'Reduce?'

'Reduce hands. I'm sorry, but there's no other way.'

The engineer nodded. 'I was feared of it. Aye, I've seen it coming. And there's not a man I want rid of. They're a good crowd.'

'I know they are, poor devils. I don't want it any more than you. But we can't help ourselves.'

They had left the winding shop and were pacing up and down in the yard between the buildings.

'There's the alternative of a cut in wages,' Charles remarked.

'No good. We hav'na the war-rk. We'll have to lay some of the fellows off. That Brent Magnus job would 'a' just saved them.'

'Well, turn it over in your mind and let me know what you propose. We've got to save as much as we can.'

For once Charles found his remaining round of the works buildings irksome. He could not bring himself to watch his men and receive their salutations, knowing that a number of them would be without a job in a few days' time. He contented himself with a glance through the machine and erecting shops, then returned with a heavy heart to his office. A letter from Brent Magnus Ltd had just come in.

> *We much regret to inform you that at their meeting yesterday the directors found themselves unable to accept your tender for the proposed alterations to our works, as it was considerably above the lowest.*

Charles sighed as he pushed the letter into one of his baskets. That was that.

He felt up against it, and for a few minutes deliberately allowed himself the luxury of day-dreaming. Instantly Una Mellor filled his mind to the exclusion of all else. He dreamed about a Una who was always kind and glad to see him, about a Una who had accepted him, about a Una who had married him! Longingly he pictured Una in his home. What a heaven it would then be! He could see himself returning to it with the feelings of the parched and weary traveller who at last reaches the oasis which had so long eluded him. Una…

Presently he was brought with a jar to earth. There was a knock and Macpherson entered. He closed the door carefully behind him, came over to the desk and sat down without being invited.

'I've been thinking again, Mr Charles,' he declared. 'There's one thing would save us sacking any men, as I believe I've mentioned before. If you could raise that wee bittie o' capital and get those two or three machines, we'd beat the Parkinson crowd. Our costs are about the same as theirs now, and if we had that slotter and the two lathes we could undercut them.'

This was an old question. For several months Macpherson had been advocating replacing three of their present machines with new ones of a more up-to-date pattern. Charles had agreed with him in principle, but had made no move. He didn't see where the money was to come from.

'Talk sense, Sandy,' he said now. 'Who do you think's going to put capital into a works like this at the present time? I know all about what the machines would do, but we can't get them.'

'They wouldna cost so verra much,' the engineer persisted. 'A couple o' hundred for the slotter and, say, six for the two lathes: less than a thousand altogether, fixing an' a'.'

'I doubt if they'd have got us the Brent Magnus job all the same.'

The Scotsman twisted his head sideways to express pitying contempt. 'Would they no'?' he retorted witheringly. 'Besides,' he added, 'yon's no' the only job that's going. If our costs were a bit lower, we'd have plenty of work.'

'You may trust me, Sandy. If they can be got, I'll get them, but I don't believe there's the slightest chance.'

Still the engineer waited. 'Of course,' he said at last, 'it's no' my business, but ye wouldna think o' putting that wee droppie in yoursel'? What would a thousand be to a man like you?'

Charles winced. There was a time, not so long ago, when that remark would have been justified. But neither Macpherson nor anyone else, except Charles and his bank manager, knew how many of those thousands had been swallowed up in keeping the business going and how many still remained. He shook his head.

'I've put enough into it,' he declared. 'No, Sandy, there's no way out but what I've said. Think over who you can spare and let them go.' He paused, then went on. 'Why are you so sure we'd be all right if we had the machines?'

For the first time the Scotsman seemed satisfied. He thrust his hand into his pocket and drew out a bundle of papers.

'That's what I came in to show you,' he said. 'See here. Here's the make-up of our tender for that Hull job, total £1,275. But Parkinson's people got it at £1,250. But if we'd had those machines our figure'd 'a' been £1,190. See? And here's another case.'

Charles grew more interested. Their two heads drew together over the table. For half an hour they talked, then Charles, in a different tone, said he'd consider it further.

Just then the one o'clock horn blew. Macpherson nodded and withdrew, and Charles, after locking his safe, put on his hat and followed his workers from the enclosure.

CHAPTER III

Charles Suggests Accommodations

THE CROWTHER ELECTROMOTOR WORKS HAD BEEN ESTABLISHED at the beginning of the century by Charles's uncle. Andrew Crowther, then a young man of ingenuity, had devised a moving advertisement for the window of the electrical supplies shop in which he was a salesman. His directors were delighted with the idea and had given him leave to have the sign made. Andrew had soon done so, but when he had tried to buy an electromotor of one-twelfth horsepower to operate it, he had had difficulty in obtaining it. At once his keen mind had seen an opening. He was sure there was a latent demand for small motors, a demand which he did not doubt could be developed to respectable proportions. Inquiries in likely directions confirmed his opinion, and he decided to throw up his job and start a small factory. To obtain the necessary technical knowledge, he spent three years on a small salary in an electric works. Then he set himself to overcome his major difficulty – the lack of capital. This he found easier than he had expected. Henry Swinburn had a year or two previously married his sister, and Henry had developed a considerable respect for his brother-in-law's engineering ability. When he heard Andrew's scheme, he announced that he was prepared to come in and put up his entire capital. It amounted to less than a thousand, but it sufficed. The two young men took an old shed in a slum in York, fitted it with the mini-mum of machinery, mostly second-hand, and set to work. Andrew was a mechanical genius, but no business man, while Henry was good at figures and an excellent canvasser. They prospered, adding slowly but steadily to their plant and staff. Soon they took over a couple of additional sheds, bought more machines and increased their personnel to a dozen. Then came the War. At first it looked as if the business would close down and its owners join His Majesty's forces. But just then the War Office discovered that they required a large number of tiny electromotors in connexion with certain field signalling apparatus, and, looking round, found that those supplied by the Crowther firm were exactly what they wanted. Henceforward for four years there was no shortage of work. The great difficulty of Andrew and Henry was to obtain sufficient plant and labour to complete their orders. They gave up the York sheds and took over a factory at Cold Pickerby, which, with a little alteration, suited their purpose.

In the post-War boom they continued to coin. When it was over Andrew thought he had done enough work and would like to see the world before he died. He therefore retired from the concern, taking with him his entire capital of £190,000. He bought an old house in the neighbourhood, The Moat, went round the world, and then settled down to amuse himself with a number of hobbies, including photography and some rather amateurish attempts at market gardening.

Henry Swinburn continued to carry on the works, now helped by Charles, his only son. Charles had had a good training, having taken a degree in science in Leeds University. In 1927 Henry died, and then Charles came into the property. Mrs Swinburn had died some years earlier, so, as Charles was an only child, he found himself alone in the world. He took a small house, got a man and wife to look after him, and settled down to devote himself to the business. Under his management it had been reasonably prosperous till the world slump had come. Now, as has been said, Charles was faced with bankruptcy.

Leaving the works, Charles turned along the Malton Road till he came to the River Gayle, on which the little town was built. His mind, freed for the moment from business, became filled with its usual preoccupation – Una Mellor. He preferred taking the path along the river bank because it was usually deserted and he could indulge his day-dream with greater ease. In spite of his preoccupation, however, he could not but subconsciously admire the stretch of country presented to him, often as he had seen it. To-day it was looking specially charming, lit up as it was by the rich August sunshine. The little river, narrow and placid, wound here through open country, but a little farther on it entered a belt of trees, through which the crocketed spire of the parish church reached up a pointing finger. To the right of the trees were the jumbled houses of the town, while behind, towards the north-east, the country swept irregularly up to the higher ground of the moors.

Charles passed along the river through the trees till, reaching the church, he turned through its well-kept grounds and found himself in the Mall. Cold Pickerby was a clean and pleasant little town of some eight thousand inhabitants, situated in the triangle at whose corners were Thirsk, Easingwold and Helmsley. Its great glory was Pickerby Castle, a twelfth-century ruin covering the summit of a rocky crag just west of the town, and which, owing to certain peculiarities of construction, was the Mecca of archaeologists from far and near. The town had a sheep market, which once a year converted the streets into dusky rivers of expostulating fauna, a house in which Queen Elizabeth had slept, and an inn which had been an inn when Domesday Book was compiled.

In the Mall was Charles Swinburn's goal – the Cold Pickerby Club. Here the *élite* of the town's business men lunched, and when Charles entered the lounge he was greeted by half a dozen who had already arrived. There was Brent of Brent Magnus Ltd, Witheroe the bank manager, Crosby the solicitor, and Stimpson and Hughes, both owners of large shops. Stimpson was holding forth on some matter of finance.

'Eight per cent doesn't sound so bad,' he was saying, 'but when you remember that they paid fifteen last year, it puts a different complexion on things.'

'Who have halved their profits, Stimpson?' Charles asked as he joined the group.

'Bender & Truesett. Dividend just announced. Eight per cent.'

'They're in good company,' Witheroe declared. 'Can anyone tell me a firm whose profits are not down fifty per cent?'

Charles was startled. Here was another blow! Most of such money as remained to him was in Bender & Truesett's. It was true that his principal was now so small that the loss in actual cash would be but slight, yet in his almost desperate position every little counted.

'That's a nasty jar,' he said as lightly as he could. 'I've got a few shares.' Witheroe, the bank manager, knew he had shares, and Witheroe, of all people, must not suspect his embarrassment. Not to mention his holding would look worse than admitting the loss.

'So have I, worse luck,' declared Crosby. 'I should have thought Bender & Truesett was about the soundest firm in the north-east.'

'They're sound enough,' Stimpson returned. 'They're putting something like seventeen thousand more to reserve than last year. Considering everything, I don't think that's so bad.'

As Crosby replied, Charles felt a touch on the arm. Brent beckoned him into a corner.

'I say, old man,' he began, speaking in a low voice, 'I've just written you.' He seemed embarrassed and paused uneasily.

Charles had himself well in hand. He laughed. 'I've got it,' he admitted dryly.

Brent nodded. 'I wanted to say that we were all really sorry about it, Swinburn, really distressed; but yours wasn't the lowest tender, not by a good deal. We would have liked you to have it: we've always been on friendly terms; and we would have liked to have kept the work in the town and all that, but with things as tight as they are, we just hadn't any option.'

'Of course you hadn't, old man. That's all right. I'm not pretending I'm not sorry: I am. The work would have come in handy enough. But it'll be a good lesson. Macpherson has been plaguing the life out of me for some new machines and now he'll have to get them. If we'd had them we'd have had a better chance of your job.'

Brent seemed relieved. 'Very decent of you to take it like that,' he declared. 'I'm glad it's not going to make any real difference to you.'

'I didn't say that,' Charles smiled. 'But I don't think it'll bankrupt us.'

But that was exactly what Charles did think, and it said something for his self-control that he was able to join with apparent ease in the conversation and chaff of the lunch table. The talk, after concerning itself with the Bender & Truesett dividend, continued for a little on business topics, and then slid gradually over to cricket, where it remained. Stimpson and a couple more were going to Leeds on the following Saturday to see Yorkshire wiping Kent off the pitch – so Stimpson put it – and they discussed County fixtures like schoolboys.

Lunch over, the men adjourned to the smoking-room, and there, when the good-looking maid brought round coffee, they separated into little groups and began more intimate conversations. Charles, who had engaged in a political discussion with Witheroe, the bank manager, manœuvred him into a corner.

'I was considering calling in to see you this afternoon,' Charles said when the iniquities of the Government had been adequately dealt with. 'What I wanted will only take a moment, and perhaps it would save the time of both of us if I were to mention it now.'

'Delighted to see you,' Witheroe returned. 'But by all means go ahead now if it's more convenient.'

Charles drew slowly at his cigar. 'I'm going to have to put in three new machines at the works,' he said. 'I've been considering it for some time and I put it off as the present didn't seem the best time for launching out. But I find I was wrong. I should have done it months ago.'

'I thought your plant was pretty up to date.'

'It's not so bad, but it's just bad enough to make the difference. I'll tell you, Witheroe, between ourselves. We tendered for that reconstruction job at Brent Magnus Limited's, and I've just heard that we've lost it. That's because I didn't get those three machines. If we'd had them our tender would have been well below the winning figure.'

Witheroe murmured polite regrets.

'It was my own fault and I can't grouse about it,' Charles went on. 'Parkinson's have a very modern plant and they deserved to get it. But with these machines we could beat Parkinson's. Our transport costs are less, for one thing.'

'You've a good lot of men, haven't you?'

'Absolutely top-hole. I'd back them against any other crowd in the country.'

'I'm sorry about that job, Swinburn. Apart from yourself, I'd like to have seen the money staying in the town.'

Charles nodded. 'I'm sorry, too, of course. But I'm not really worrying about it, because, as I say, I see where we went wrong and we can remedy our mistake. But that brings me to business, Witheroe. I'd like, if it was quite satisfactory, to get the money for these machines from you.'

Witheroe looked grave. Before replying, he very slowly and care-fully pushed the tobacco down into his pipe. Then when it was settled to his satisfaction, he looked up.

'You know, Swinburn, there's no one I'd be better pleased to oblige than yourself, but you're pretty well overdrawn as it is.'

Charles nodded. 'I know that, and, of course, I'm not asking you to do impossibilities. I can easily raise the money, and more, by sell-ing a couple of my late father's pictures. But, as you can understand, I don't want to do this unless I can't help.'

Witheroe whistled an inaudible tune below his breath. 'How much will the machines come to?' he asked presently.

'About a thousand. Say eight hundred for the machines themselves and a couple more for putting them in.'

'That's not so deadly. I imagined somehow it would be a bigger thing.'

'Oh, no, it's only three machines – two lathes and a slotter. The rest of the plant's good enough. As a matter of fact, the three old machines are in perfect order, but they haven't got the latest timesav-ing gadgets, and that's what counts these days.'

Again the bank manager paused. 'And – eh – security?'

Charles shrugged. 'The same security as you've got for the present overdraft. You've got the entire works as security, and you'd have these new machines as well. They couldn't run away.'

Of this Witheroe somehow seemed unconvinced. However, he answered promptly enough. 'I'll put it up to the directors. You know that in these matters they make the final decision. I'll put it up to them as fairly as I can and let you know the result. You wouldn't like to write me a letter which I could put before them?'

Charles shrugged. 'If you think it would strengthen your hand – yes. Otherwise, I'm perfectly satisfied to leave the matter with you.'

'Well, I'll do what I can.' He smiled crookedly. 'The trouble is that everyone wants the same thing.'

'I suppose it's not unnatural,' Charles admitted, and the talk turned to other channels.

Charles kept his face as straight and his manner as off-hand as he could, but he had no illusions as to the result of the interview. His request would be refused. It would be refused in the pleasantest and least hurtful way, but it would be refused. Charles wondered if Witheroe suspected what was really in his mind: to get the money, but not to get the machines. Charles wanted the money to carry on: to carry on either till he was married, or till Una Mellor had turned him down so decisively that no possible hope of marriage remained.

That this was sailing rather near the wind in the matter of dishonesty Charles did not stop to think. He was really capable of only one idea. He wanted Una. If he won Una he would get money with her – though it was not the money he really wanted. If he lost her, then nothing else mattered. He did not care whether he himself sank or swam.

Well, he was not beaten yet. The Northern Counties Bank was not the only string he had to his bow. He looked round upon the rapidly emptying room. Yes, Bostock had gone. He would wait a little and then follow him.

Anthony Bostock fulfilled a number of rôles in Cold Pickerby. He was first and foremost a stockbroker, but to this business he added a number of minor, though possibly more lucrative, activities. He was really a commission agent. Anyone who wanted anything out of the common carried out went to Bostock. He was pleasant-mannered, efficient, and as close as wax. People felt that their business was safe with him, and there was little doubt that if his mind could be made to give up its secrets, a good many people in the neighbourhood would wish themselves out of it.

The particular sideline of Bostock which interested Charles at the moment was that of moneylender. Bostock was reputed to be willing to accommodate 'on their mere note of hand alone' all and sundry. Charles, of course, recognized the limitations explicit in this 'all and sundry', but he thought that he should prove one of the elect.

Leaving the club, he passed from the Mall to High Street, and turning the corner at the town hall, entered a narrow lane. A couple of doors down was Bostock's office, and Charles pushed open the door.

Bostock was a tubby little man with a slightly oily manner. He welcomed Charles effusively.

'I meant to have a word with you after lunch,' Charles began, 'but when I looked round you were gone. How're things?'

Bostock admitted that things might be worse, though he didn't look as if he believed it. 'That drop in the Bender & Truesett dividend is going to play Old Harry with me,' he went on. 'I have quite a lot in it: quite a lot for me, I mean.'

'I had some in it, too,' Charles returned. 'Fortunately, not a great deal. Still, these days every little counts. And that brings me to the subject of my call.'

'Glad to see you, whatever it is. Won't you smoke?' He held out a box of cigars.

'I'll have a cigarette, thanks.'

Bostock produced another box and both men lit cigarettes. 'Well, it'll be a pleasure to serve you, Swinburn. What can I do for you?'

Charles laughed shortly. 'What do you think, Bostock? Money! I want some money.'

Bostock smiled also. 'Plenty of that in the world at the present time,' he declared, 'if only we could get at it. What money do you want?'

'It's a matter of some machines,' and Charles went on to repeat what he had told Witheroe. Bostock was far from enthusiastic.

'You think these machines would enable you to beat your competitors; but tell me, Swinburn, do you foresee many jobs coming along? That's the snag as I see it. No jobs!'

Charles smiled wryly. 'You're certainly nice and optimistic,' he retorted. 'If there are no more jobs it doesn't matter what we've borrowed or lent: we'll all go down together. No, I think you're wrong there, Bostock. Jobs are bound to be coming along, though perhaps not so many.'

'It's all very well. There's nothing to be gained by not facing up to facts. You know as well as I do that the general trouble is shortage of orders.'

'I know that very well. But that's no reason why I shouldn't get what is going.'

'Of course not, and I hope you will. But seriously, Swinburn,' he paused uncomfortably, 'there's no one I'd like to oblige more than yourself, but I don't know that the state of my own finances would allow me to advance the amount you say. I didn't tell you, but I'm really very badly hit, not only by this Bender & Truesett affair, but also in several other ways. I had a good little bit in Swedish Matches, for instance. And in the R.M.S.P. Also, of course, the War Loan Conversion has made a difference. You would propose to offer your works as security?'

'That was my idea.'

'That really means mortgaging your works. Are they mortgaged already?'

'No, they're not. There's a slight overdraft to the bank, for which they're security, but that's a mere bagatelle.'

Bostock nodded. 'I don't know, Swinburn; I'm a little afraid I couldn't afford it. When must you have an answer?'

'Oh, I don't know. There's no desperate hurry, but as soon as is convenient.'

'I'll look into it at once,' Bostock replied with obvious relief. 'I'll see just exactly how I stand and whether I can manage it, and I'll let you know in the morning without fail.'

'That'll do fine. Thanks, Bostock.'

'As I said,' the stockbroker went on, 'there's nothing I should like more than to be able to meet you. You're not going to see the match on Saturday?'

After a decent rounding up of the interview, Charles took his leave. Another blank! He had no need to wait till the following morning to know what Bostock's answer would be. Turned down again! Charles felt as bitterly hurt by the rebuff as if it had been conveyed with crude directness.

He had, however, still another string to his bow. The last, definitely the last, but, if properly handled, the most hopeful. On the other hand, if bungled, the most dangerous.

There still remained his Uncle Andrew.

Andrew Crowther, as has been said, retired from the works after the boom period with a fortune of some £190,000. He was still living in the house he had then bought, The Moat, and as he lived quietly and economically, he must still be a wealthy man.

And half of this fortune would come to Charles at the old man's death. Not once but many times Andrew Crowther had told him that he was making him his heir jointly with his daughter, Elsie Morley. Charles felt sure that he could count on sixty or seventy thousand at his uncle's death. That was if things went normally.

But Charles had no guarantee that they would go normally. His uncle's very peculiar temperament had to be reckoned with. The old man was not exactly mean, but he had a very exalted idea of the value of money, and he would certainly not leave his to anyone whom he considered 'unworthy'. And in Andrew's philosophy 'unworthiness' would be proved by a business failure.

Charles knew, not only from his estimate of his uncle's character, but from the old man's actual speeches, that if he let the works down all of the money but a pittance would go to his cousin. Andrew had raised the concern from nothing to a flourishing business, and he would have no mercy on Charles if, receiving it in that state, he proved himself unable to carry it on.

It would be simplicity itself for Charles to go to Andrew and ask him to advance him a small proportion of what would eventually come to him. Under the circumstances it would be a small request and the old man could not possibly feel it. But Charles knew that Andrew would not agree without inquiring into the whole circumstances, and the effect of that on Charles's prospects would be incalculable.

Therefore everything depended on the way the old gentleman was handled. If Charles could put his case satisfactorily he might get what he wanted without a word. On the other hand, there was a real possibility that the interview might end with not only a refusal, but disinheritance as well. And, of course, that would definitely involve the loss of Una.

It was for this reason that Charles had up to the present avoided approaching his uncle, but now he felt that if both Witheroe and Bostock turned him down he must take the risk.

CHAPTER IV

Charles Advocates Matrimony

I T WAS ONE OF THOSE MINOR COINCIDENCES WHICH HAPPEN SO frequently in life, that almost the first person Charles met after coming to his decision to approach his uncle was the husband of his co-legatee, Elsie Morley.

In a sense it might almost be said that he met his co-legatee, for Elsie and Peter Morley were a devoted couple, and Charles knew that any money Elsie might get would be at her husband's disposal.

Though at first Peter had made a success of his farm, Charles was aware that in later years profits had dwindled considerably. That was even before the great British agricultural slump had set in. Now, indeed, it was generally believed that Peter was in a bad way. No outward sign of this had, however, so far become apparent, nor had the matter been discussed between the two men.

Charles did not see a great deal of his cousin's husband. In fact the two men did not 'pull'. Peter seemed to Charles narrow and misanthropic and concerned with himself and his own affairs alone. Peter, on the other hand, thought of Charles as wanting in seriousness and in sympathetic interest. There had been nothing in the nature of a breach between them; simply they were not over cordial.

On this occasion as Charles left Bostock's to go back to the works, he turned into his tobacconist's for some cigarettes and came face to face with Peter, who was just coming out.

'Hallo, Peter,' Charles greeted him. 'Haven't seen you for a month of Sundays. What's your best news?'

Peter was looking old and rather worn. He shook his head gloomily. 'Not too good, Charles. Not any too good. What about yourself?'

'Oh, struggling along.' Charles moved on into the shop and Peter turned back with him, evidently ready for a chat. 'And what's the trouble?' Charles went on.

Peter did not reply till Charles was served, then as they left the shop he remarked in a lugubrious voice, 'I've had to get rid of Thompson.'

'Thompson? Your chauffeur, ploughman, gardener, handy man, and general factotum? Why, I thought Thompson was your best man.'

'So he was by a long way. That's just the reason. Couldn't afford him any longer.'

Charles turned. 'Bless my soul, are things as bad as that?'

'Things,' Peter said hopelessly, 'are just about as bad as they can be. I declare on my honour, Charles, I don't know what I'm going to do.'

'I'm sorry to hear that, Peter.'

'This year it's worse than ever. There was a good crop. Nearly everything is above the average. But I can't sell the stuff. Prices wouldn't pay getting it to the market. I don't know what's going to happen to us all.'

'Pretty rotten, that.'

'You may thank your stars you've nothing to do with land. For years there's been talk about it, as you know, and the Government were always going to take it in hand.' He shook his head. 'They'll tinker with it till there are no farmers left in the country.'

'Industry's as bad,' Charles returned. 'Why, only now I've heard that Bender & Truesett are halving their dividend.'

Peter looked at him. 'You don't say so! Does that hit you?'

'Yes, it does. Fortunately, not badly. I have a little in it, but not much.'

'Oh, you're all right. That business of yours must be a little gold mine. But I'm in such a bad way that' – he looked round and sank his voice – 'that I've determined on a desperate remedy. I'm going to tackle the father-in-law.'

Charles strove to conceal his chagrin. This wouldn't suit his book at all. If Peter applied to Andrew Crowther for help it would probably scotch his own chance in the same direction. He wondered if he could put Peter off.

'You'll not get much out of Uncle Andrew,' he essayed.

'I don't see why not. It'll be for Elsie's sake, of course. And I don't want much – only a little of what's coming to her in any case later on.'

'Why not let Elsie tackle him?'

Peter hesitated. 'I haven't really told Elsie how bad things are,' he answered. 'I don't want to worry her more than I can help.'

Charles shook his head. 'I shouldn't touch Uncle Andrew if I were you.'

'I don't see why not. He can only refuse.'

'That's where you're wrong, Peter,' Charles returned sharply. 'If you count on that you may make a thundering big mistake. Neither you nor I can afford to upset the old fellow, because your upsetting him is the same as Elsie's doing it. He's told us she and I are to be his joint heirs, but that's not a law of the Medes and Persians. He can change his mind.'

'He'd never do a thing like that.'

'Wouldn't he? Like a shot he'd do it. Look here: you know his ideas about efficiency and all that. Well, suppose you go and tell him that you've let your farm down. What will his reaction be?'

Peter did not reply. Obviously this view of the situation had not struck him. Charles was pleased with the effect he was producing. He went on with the good work.

'Of course you might get on the right side of him, but there's a risk. He might just as easily say, "This fellow can't look after his own business and he's certainly not going to throw my good money after his bad." I don't know: if I were in your place I'd only go to the uncle as a last resource.'

'But I tell you it is a last resource.'

'Oh, come now, Peter, it can't be as bad as all that. Couldn't you get a loan on the security of Elsie's expectations?'

'Do you think I'm a fool altogether? I tried that first thing. No go.'

Charles did not mention that he knew it also and for the same reason. 'Couldn't you sell the farm and live in a smaller way on the proceeds till the rainy day is passed? The old man can't go on for ever.'

'A good scheme,' Peter admitted; 'a thorough good scheme – provided you produce the buyer. I tell you, Charles, I'd have as good a chance of selling the North Pole.'

'Well, you know more about it than I do. Still, if I were in your place I should be very chary of approaching Uncle Andrew.'

Charles thought he had said enough and changed the subject. In speaking as he had he was not swayed by unkind or insincere feelings towards Peter. He really believed that Peter was a bungler, and that if he approached his uncle he would put the latter's back up and queer the pitch for both of them. He was sure that he himself could handle the old man more tactfully, and if he succeeded not only he but Peter would benefit. If Andrew made an advance to him, there could be no possible reason for his refusing a similar accommodation to Peter.

For a while Charles was tempted to make common cause with Peter, then he saw that this would be a mistake. In the first place Peter wouldn't agree that he, Charles, could handle the affair more successfully than himself, and in the second, even to Peter it would be unwise to admit that he was in difficulties. Though he believed

Peter would never willingly betray a trust, it was very easy to give away information involuntarily, and the best way of ensuring the preservation of a secret was to keep it to oneself.

'Here we are almost at the works,' Charles said at length. 'Come to the office and have a drink and let's think if there are no other ways out.'

Peter pulled up and looked at his watch as Charles had hoped he would. 'No,' he said, 'I can't. I've got an appointment with Crosby directly. Well, Charles, I'm glad to have met you. When are we going to see you out with us?'

'Oh, I don't know. Soon as I can I'll drop out. Remember me to Elsie and the children.'

They waved adieu and Charles strode on towards his works, while Peter turned back to the centre of the town.

How far, Charles wondered, had his cautiously applied douche of cold water put Peter off his idea of applying for help to Andrew Crowther? It was a fortunate thing for both of them that they had met. With any reasonable luck he, Charles, should get in first, and if he could not sway Andrew, he did not believe that anyone else in the world would succeed.

Charles was strongly tempted to go out then and there to The Moat and put his fate to the test. But a little thought showed that this would be sheer lunacy. Besides the fact that Andrew hated to be hurried, such haste would point most undesirably to the urgency of his need. Andrew would be more suspicious and less pliable. No, the matter must be adequately prepared. The preparation, however, could be done at once.

On reaching his office he rang up The Moat, and in a moment he recognized the lugubrious tones of his uncle's man.

'Good afternoon, Weatherup. How's Mr Crowther to-day?'

Andrew, it appeared, was in his usual state of health. He was reading in the study and Weatherup was sure it would be convenient for him to speak. He would put Mr Charles through.

A moment's delay and then Charles heard his uncle's thin voice. Mutual greetings passed.

'I wanted some time to have a chat with you on a small matter of business,' Charles went on presently, 'and I really rang up to ask you when would be convenient. There's no hurry; it's simply that I want to keep clear whatever time we fix.'

This produced the reaction which Charles expected.

'I'm not particular,' came Andrew's voice. 'I'm not overwhelmed with appointments, as you know. When would suit you?'

'I can't come next week,' Charles went on, 'but it happens that I'm lunching in York to-morrow, and I could look in on the way back, if that would suit.'

The following afternoon would suit Andrew. They had tea, as Charles knew, at half-past four, and would expect him some time before that.

So far, so good. With a slight sigh of relief Charles turned to his papers, of which a number had accumulated since he went out for lunch.

That evening a big event in Charles's life was to take place, and as the afternoon dragged slowly away he grew more and more restless and excited. For three days he had not seen Una, but that evening they were going to meet. Both were invited to the Countess of Croler's charity ball, an annual affair of the first social magnitude, which was held in Croler Castle, some five miles from Cold Pickerby. How would Una greet him? The last time they had met he had fancied she was just a little cool – cooler than usual, for unhappily she was never really cordial. To-night he would know how he stood.

Indeed, Charles was sorely tempted to put his fate definitely to the test that night. He wondered if anything could be worse than the miseries of doubt which he was enduring. Better to know, even if the knowledge meant final disaster.

Then he saw that he was wrong. A definite refusal would be a thousand times worse. Now he was living on hope. If that hope were withdrawn it would be the end – the end of everything; the end of life itself. Without Una he would not wish to live.

But with Una by his side…

He finished his day's work, then just as the closing whistle blew he set off for home. Charles usually walked the short mile to and from the works, in the belief that the exercise helped to keep him fit. And a pleasant walk it was! His way led him up hill, in the direction of the moors. For a while it passed up the valley of the Gayle, then, turning at right-angles to the river, it mounted the side of the valley, winding through thick coppices of nuts and birch, which presently gave place to oak and elm.

Charles lived alone on his little estate, looked after by an elderly married couple called Rollins. The house was placed perfectly on the hillside. Before it the trees fell away, leaving a charming vista southwards of Cold Pickerby, with its rock and ruined castle and beyond the rich, rolling plain towards York. North and east it was protected from the cold winds by a veritable forest, behind which began the gorgeous open spaces of the moor. Charles loved his house and its situation, its views and the garden which he had made with such care and toil. If only its loneliness could be abolished by the coming of Una Mellor it would be paradise on earth.

As after dinner he dressed for the ball, he indulged himself by letting his imagination run riot. If Una said yes, what would be the first thing he would do? Why, get out plans for adding a wing to the house.

As it was, it was scarcely adequate. Half of it, the half containing the principal rooms, was good, but the hall, staircase, and offices were poor. An addition to that end of the house giving a larger hall and a couple of new rooms would make the place perfect.

Charles shivered as he thought of the alternatives, one of which was in store for him. A marriage with Una. Heaven! Heaven on earth, irrespective of anything else! But there would be more. There would be money: his present difficulties would be gone. Una and he – mentally he gloated over the phrase – Una and he would go abroad while the alterations were being carried out, away from the fogs and the east winds to Egypt or Cyprus or some place where there was sun and warmth and leisure. For if it were done it would be done in the winter. Then they would come back in the spring, when everything was at its absolute best, to the perfect house in its perfect setting: to the country which both he and Una loved…

And otherwise?

Otherwise, hopeless ruin and despair. Death even. Without Una, why should he want to live? There would be nothing to live for, nothing to struggle for. If he went bankrupt, what matter? He would settle the thing quickly. He would have insomnia. He would get a few sleeping draughts from his doctor. He would take the lot at one go. He would sleep – and that would be the end. It would be easy…

Charles did what he very seldom did, particularly before going to see Una. He poured himself out a stiff glass of brandy and drank it neat. It pulled him together and his morbid thoughts vanished. As he went to his garage and started up the Sunbeam he was once again cool, collected, and in good spirits for the coming festivities.

We need not follow Charles's doings at the Countess of Croler's charity ball. One charity ball is very like another, and this was no exception to the rule. But Charles's interview with Una Mellor so intimately concerned the dreadful events which afterwards took place that some reference to it must be made.

He went early so as to be there before her, and placing himself where he could watch the stream of entering guests, waited with an anxiety which even the brandy could not entirely quell. Suppose she should not turn up! Accidents did happen, unlikely events did occur, you couldn't be absolutely sure of anything till you actually had it in your hand – and not always then.

Charles found himself stammering answers to the greetings of more than one acquaintance, without having a very clear idea of what he was saying. But he did not care. What did these wretched people matter? If only they would go on and leave him alone!

The stream of arrivals was now thinning, and yet there was no sign. Charles found it impossible to stay quiet. He moved jerkily about, dodging acquaintances and shaking off as quickly as he could those whom he couldn't escape.

And then she came.

Charles's heart gave a leap as he saw her mounting the stairs. Now at last heaven would open!

But Charles was still upon earth, and upon earth Fate has a distressing habit of taking back with one hand what she bestows with the other. So it was in this case. Una, indeed, appeared, but not with her father, Colonel Mellor, though he usually accompanied her on more formal occasions like the present. Charles glared as he saw beside her the sleekly groomed head, retreating forehead and rabbit mouth of Freddy Allom.

Though at the moment Charles could not see that he had any redeeming feature whatever, he knew perfectly well that in Freddy he had a dangerous rival. Freddy, though an idler, was not really a bad youth. Well mannered and good natured, his instincts were social.

Hostesses were glad to see him, for he brightened things up and made dull parties go. And, not least of all, he would be wealthy.

For a moment Charles felt dashed. Then Una saw him and smiled, and Allom became as though he were not.

Una, indeed, was a sight to quicken the blood in any man's veins. She was tall, but perfectly proportioned. Her hair of exquisite gold lay on her head in natural waves. Her hair was her great glory and made the unbiased observer sigh with the pity that it had been cut in the modern style. Her features were good, but not out of the ordinary, though her small, firm mouth and light blue eyes showed both character and intelligence. Her carriage was superb, and there were few who did not turn to look at her as she reached the head of the stairs and passed into the room.

Charles, seeing no one else in the entire gathering, was at her side directly she had made her bow to Lady Croler.

'Hallo, Charles,' she greeted him unemotionally. 'You know Freddy Allom, don't you?'

Charles was forced to let his eyes rest momentarily on the worm. The confounded impertinence of the fellow to be smirking there alongside Una as if he had some claim to her notice! If wishes could have killed, Allom would even then have been carried out for burial.

'Una, I thought you were coming with the Colonel. There's nothing wrong with him, I hope?'

'Yes, he's got a fit of laziness. Calls it a chill. Luckily Freddy turned up, or I should have been in the soup.'

'How can you, Una, when there's a telephone? I'll take you back. Do please let me. Allom'll be a sport and divide the honours. Won't you, Allom?'

'Not unless she says so.' Allom grinned quizzically at Charles.

Una was not looking particularly pleased, and Charles passed from the subject. 'We'll form a cavalcade,' he declared, and turned to the more serious business of begging dances.

They had the supper dance, and afterwards he persuaded her to sit out in a sheltered nook in the conservatory. She made no objection, and it was during their walk to the corner he had in mind that an incident happened which completely bowled Charles over and caused him to throw all his caution to the winds.

As they turned the corner of a stand which bore large numbers of young plants in pots, Una gave a stumble. It was not a serious stumble, and she was in no danger of falling. Some previous passer-by had knocked a flower-pot off the shelf, and it was over this that she tripped. She recovered herself, or would have recovered herself, in a moment.

Charles, however, saw her give the false step and sprang forward to her assistance. But he didn't reckon on the consequences. As he touched her an electric current seemed to sweep through him. It overwhelmed him as the flood from a broken dam submerges the adjoining country. He lost his sense of time and place and became oblivious of everything but her immediate presence. In a moment she was clasped in his arms and he was covering her face with passionate kisses.

When he came to himself his heart gave a great throb. She had made no resistance. She was not angry. She was lying in his arms with closed eyes. For a moment he held her steadily, then she opened her eyes and gave a tremulous laugh.

'Are you often taken like that, Charles?' she asked. 'Let me go.'

'Never,' Charles declared. 'I'll never let you go as long as I live.'

'Then you'll have to carry me home.'

'I'll do so.'

'Don't be silly, Charles. Someone will come. Let me go.'

'Let them.'

'Let me go!' Her voice grew more imperious. 'I mean it. I won't be mauled against my will.'

Slowly he obeyed, then drew her on to the seat for which he had originally been making. Then, as if a barrier had been withdrawn, all his love and longing poured out in a very spate of words. He had loved her from the very first moment he had seen her, and every day since then his love had only grown the more. Her love was the only thing which mattered to him, and if she would not marry him he wouldn't try to go on living. What was his fate to be? He could not exist in his present agony of doubt.

Una's cool common sense poured a douche of cold water on his passion. Yes, she was fond enough of Charles, though whether she really loved him she did not know. Certainly she didn't love him up to his own standard of love. As to whether she might eventually marry him, she didn't know. No, she wasn't going to pretend she loved anybody else. What she really loved was her freedom.

It was then when they settled down to a more rational discussion of the question, that the subject came up which was to prove of such importance to Charles.

'It seems a beastly thing to say,' Una declared, 'but I may as well tell you at once that under no circumstances would I marry a poor man. This is not entirely mercenary and selfish. I shouldn't be happy without the things I am accustomed to and my husband wouldn't be happy either. To marry where there would be shortage and privation would mean misery for both of us. It would be simply foolish and I'm not going to do it.'

'Dear Una, that question wouldn't arise in my case. I'm not wealthy, but I'm not poor. You would have what you're accustomed to if you married me.'

In spite of his entreaties she would not agree to an engagement, though he believed his case was not hopeless.

But that night, or rather, later on that morning, as he lay tossing on his bed, he saw beyond possibility of doubt that all his chances of happiness in this world were bound up with his getting the necessary money to carry on his present way of life.

CHAPTER V

Charles Grows Desperate

CHARLES'S STATEMENT TO HIS UNCLE THAT HE HAD A LUNCH in York on the following day was the truth, and shortly after midday he took out his car and drove to the historic city. It was a fine summer's day and the sun brought out vividly the rich colouring of the landscape. A breeze, blowing gently from the north, prevented it being too hot and cleared the atmosphere, making the various objects, far and near, stand out distinct and sharp cut as a series of superimposed cameos. Charles, lost in thought, drove slowly. For once he missed the charm of the outlook, but the purr of his tyres on the asphalted road sounded pleasant and companionable in his ears.

Thoughts of the Chamber of Commerce lunch, at which he was to be a guest, did not enter his mind. He was accustomed to speaking in public, and though he had made no preparation, he was sure that when the time came he would think of something adequate to say. It was to more personal matters that he gave his attention. When his mind was not filled with Una, it was occupied with his coming interview with his uncle. This interview would doubtless prove momentous and he must be careful not to bungle it.

How wretched, he thought, that there should be this need for tact in dealing with the old man. How much pleasanter it would be if he could go to Andrew and put his cards on the table and ask directly for what he wanted! But to do so would be disastrous. Andrew's illness had warped his mind. He was now living in a sort of inner world, cut off from actualities, and he had failed, or had been unable, to keep in touch with recent world changes.

The lunch passed off as Charles had expected it would, and by three o'clock he had taken the road once again. Forty minutes later he drew up at the door of his uncle's house.

The Moat was a building of character. It was old, but not so old as its title suggested. For about a hundred years it had looked out over the same rolling prospect as did Charles's house, though Charles's, being higher, had the better view. The Moat showed a sturdy square front to the world. It had no graces of moulding or cornice or mullioned window, but it had proportion and line and dignity and its stone had weathered to a mellow shade which blended with the foliage of the trees by which it was surrounded. It was a restful-looking house, suggesting a retreat from the world. Why it had been called The Moat, no one knew. It did not possess and never had possessed any such appendage. But one name is as good as another, and when Andrew Crowther took it over he made no change in this respect. In front, between the house and the road, was a fair expanse of well-cut lawn with some great beeches standing singly like magnificent sentinels on a placid guard. Behind, hidden from the approach, were the market gardens with which Andrew amused himself.

The chief glory of the little estate was, however, its lake, or rather its half-lake, because the other half belonged to Andrew's neighbour. It was a fairly large sheet of water, about fifty acres in extent, and its particular charm was the timbering on its shores and its half-dozen well-wooded islands. Beech, oak, and elm surrounded it, fully grown trees, with their lower branches dipping to the water. It was supposed to be well stocked, and though no one at The Moat fished, there was a boat-house and a couple of boats.

Charles's ring was answered by Weatherup.

'Ah, Weatherup,' Charles said, gazing on the man's unsmiling countenance. 'A beautiful afternoon.'

Weatherup admitted the fact, though with an evident mental reservation.

'And how's Mr Crowther to-day?' went on Charles.

'Pretty well, sir. He's been lying down, but has just now got up.'

Charles followed the man into the hall. It was a good hall, generous in size and well proportioned, and the staircase which led up from it was simple and dignified. Andrew had furnished it with restraint and the effect was pleasing.

Andrew's study was on the first floor, and Weatherup led the way upstairs. He had a silent, cat-like way of walking which irritated Charles. As an unconscious protest Charles stamped heavily and talked in a loud and cheery voice. But Weatherup had no 'come back'. Charles's conversational efforts were still-born even as he uttered them.

The study into which he was presently shown was a small room, panelled in black oak. In one of its two windows stood a table desk, for though Andrew had long since given up the attempt to work, he liked to pretend he had not. Otherwise the furniture was homely and comfortable. The carpet was thick and mossy, the leather-covered chairs were deep and well sprung, and the few prints on the walls were treasures.

In one of the arm-chairs sat the master of the house. He seemed to Charles even more fragile than the last time he had seen him, now several weeks past. Certainly Andrew was ageing very rapidly. Like most semi-invalids, he had ups and downs. Sometimes he was able to be about and enjoyed a drive into Cold Pickerby or even a journey to Town, at others he would sit moping in his room, neither going out nor seeing callers. To-day unfortunately seemed one of his bad days.

'Well, Nephew Charles,' he said, in his thin, reedy voice, holding up his hand flabbily to be shaken, 'this is an unexpected honour to an old man, but I'm sure there's a good reason for it.'

'I hope it's not so bad as all that, uncle,' Charles said cheerily, shaking the hand. 'How are you keeping to-day?'

'It wasn't to ask me that that you came out all this way this afternoon,' the old man returned in his somewhat complaining tone. 'You don't claim it, I'm sure?'

'I don't,' Charles admitted, smiling broadly. 'I told you I wanted to see you on a little matter of business, and so I do. But that doesn't say that I'm not interested to know how you are.'

'I don't suppose it does. It's always a pleasure to meet with disinterested kindness. Well, Charles, what's it all about?'

'You haven't told me how you are yet,' Charles persisted with his ready smile.

'That's true, that's true. Didn't you ask Weatherup?'

Charles laughed outright. 'Weatherup's a good man for whom I've a lot of respect, but even you wouldn't call him informative. I could get more out of an oyster.'

'Well, well, well; I'm very well, if you must know. And while we're on this matter of health, how are you yourself?'

'Oh, me? Fine, thank you! I've just come from York; the Chamber of Commerce lunch. A lot of the men were asking about you.'

'I hope you relieved their heartfelt anxiety.'

'I said I was calling in on my way home, and they told me to remember them to you: Digby and Holt and Grainger and some others.'

'I'm deeply touched: almost as much as they must have been.'

'The old boy from Bathwick was there. Took too much and made a hell of a fool of himself as usual,' and Charles went on to describe the function.

Andrew was interested, as Charles had hoped he would be. He knew the older members of the chamber and had attended many a lunch with them himself. As Charles also had hoped, he forgot his suspicions and chatted about old times in a maudlin way. But soon he came back to the present.

'But you haven't told me what you came for, Nephew Charles,' he went on. 'It wasn't to talk about your lunch in York, now was it?'

'No,' Charles admitted. 'You're right; it wasn't. It was something a good deal more personal and less pleasant. It's about the business, uncle, and I'm sorry that it's bad news.'

Andrew was now listening carefully. He made no reply, but sat waiting with an expression half sly, half silly.

'I'm sorry to say,' went on Charles, 'that I've got into the same boat as nearly all my neighbours. Expenses are up and profits down with the lot of us. You heard about Bender & Truesett's dividend, I suppose?'

'Yes. Bender's no fool. What have they been playing at?'

Charles decided to make the most of this. 'Bender's certainly no fool, as you say,' he agreed. 'But neither Bender nor Truesett nor anyone else in the concern could help themselves. It's the slump, the slump only, and nothing but the slump.'

'Have you got this slump idea on the brain, too?' Andrew quavered. 'I can tell you, my boy, that hard work on the right lines put into a business means prosperity, and slackness means failure. That has always been so and it always will. I suppose Bender is playing tennis and golf instead of minding his business.'

'No, I really think that you're wrong there, uncle. Bender and Truesett are a hard-working pair. Practically every firm is in the same boat. Look down your paper and you'll see how receipts have shrunk in every direction.'

The old man chuckled childishly. 'It's only because nobody works now,' he persisted. 'Turning up in the middle of the day and weekends and all the rest of it. Why, when I went into business I was down at the works at six o'clock every morning and seldom went home before seven or eight at night. Do you do that, Nephew Charles?'

'I'm afraid not, uncle,' Charles returned good-humouredly. 'As you say, nobody works those hours now. But we do work hard while we're at it.'

'Playing games,' Andrew went on as if in a dream. 'That's all that seems to matter these days. Going off to Australia and the Lord knows where to play games instead of staying at home and minding their work. And then surprised if dividends are down.'

Charles made the best reply he could, but the old man had ridden off on his hobby and was not to be stopped. Presently Charles once more got command of the situation and explained his difficulties in detail.

'Now, as you can see from all this, uncle,' he went on, 'I've put a lot of my own money into the business. Most people believe that the slump is passing and that if firms can hold on for a little longer they'll be all right. That's what I'm trying to do. Those men I have are a good crowd; I don't want to get rid of any of them if I can help it. And so I've put in my own capital to keep things going. And now I want to do more,' and he told of the new machines. 'I want to put in these machines so as to have everything up to date with just the object that you recommended, to get whatever's going.'

'A most creditable desire, most creditable indeed,' the old man muttered. 'But surely a little belated? Would it not have been better to put in the machines before spending the money that was required to do it?' The story had aroused Andrew and he had got sharp and suspicious.

'It might have been wiser,' Charles admitted, 'though I'm afraid nothing would have made any difference. It comes to this really, that if I can't get some more cash to keep things going, I'll have to shut down.'

The old man seemed deeply pained. 'Never,' he declared, 'have I had such a disappointment. I put my whole life into those works, and now you come and tell me that you've let them down. It's a blow. Well, nephew, the least said's the soonest mended. At least it was good of you to come and give me this disinterested information.'

Charles swore mentally. This was just what he had been afraid of. If Andrew refused him he was down and out. He gave a wry laugh.

'I'm afraid, uncle,' he said, 'it's not so disinterested as you seem to imagine. In fact, in these very special and unusual circumstances, I've come to ask your help.'

The expression of sly suspicion grew on Andrew Crowther's countenance. 'My advice, I suppose?' he quavered. 'I'm afraid it hasn't been asked for a long time. The old man has been put on the shelf for a long time.'

'I want your advice, uncle,' Charles said good-humouredly, 'but I hope you will let me have something else as well. I hoped indeed that you would see your way to advance me a little money.'

The old man nodded childishly. 'A good idea. A good idea, indeed. You bungle your business and you want me to pay for your mistakes. A clever idea, Nephew Charles. You deserve to succeed.'

Charles with difficulty restrained his temper. 'It's not quite as bad as that,' he returned pleasantly. 'I don't want a penny that you have not already promised me. Let me explain.'

The old man chuckled spitefully. 'You want to get something for nothing, don't you? We all want that. Nephew Charles; we all want that. But we don't often get it.'

Charles forced himself to laugh. Patiently he explained his proposal.

'You're a great business man, Nephew Charles; you've shown that. And so you want the old man out of the way, do you?' He leered with a sort of sly cunning. 'If only the old dodderer were out of the way, you'd get it all.'

Charles was really annoyed. 'Now, uncle, I don't think that's fair,' he protested. 'Not a single word that I've said could suggest such a thing, and you know it's not true.'

Andrew seemed surprised. 'Perhaps not; perhaps not,' he admitted. 'But why should I pay your expenses? Can you tell me that?'

'I don't suggest that, uncle, or at least only with the money you've already promised me. The small amount I want couldn't make any difference to you.'

'Very true, no doubt, but not an answer to my question. Is it now?'

'No,' Charles returned frankly, 'I'm afraid it's not. There's no reason of course why you should, except that I'm your nephew and that as my uncle you might be willing to help me in a way that you would not do to an outsider.'

Andrew shook his head. 'Sentiment and business, Nephew Charles. They won't mix.'

'Then there is the works; your works that you built up and made so successful. You would do a little to prevent them going down?'

'I did prevent them going down – when they were mine. They're not mine now.'

'But what about the men? They're good fellows. You know most of them yourself. You would do a little to prevent them losing their jobs? Come now, uncle. It's a very small thing that I ask.'

To his intense disappointment Charles realized that the old man was getting tired. The unwonted discussion had upset him.

He suddenly seemed exhausted. His whole body sagged and he lay back helplessly in his chair. For a moment he tried to speak, while a sharp spasm of dismay passed over Charles. Then he murmured 'Weatherup!'

Charles rang the bell. Suspiciously soon the door was opened and the saturnine face of the attendant appeared.

'Mr Crowther,' said Charles quickly. 'I'm afraid he's not well. See to him, will you?'

Weatherup glanced at his employer, then, crossing to a table near the old man's chair, poured some medicine into a glass and held it to his lips. Andrew drank and in a moment recovered.

'Did you think you were going to get your money?' he sneered at Charles. 'Not this time. There's some life in the old dodderer still.'

'I admit you gave me a fright,' Charles returned. 'I'm sorry if I've tired you with my talk.'

'Oh, not at all, not at all. I'm always grateful for a disinterested visit. That'll do, Weatherup, Mr Charles wants to talk business.'

'No,' said Charles, rising, while Weatherup silently disappeared. 'I've said all I have to say. You'll think over the matter, uncle? It's the first time I have ever asked a favour, and if you can see your way to help me, it will be the last. For the sake of the men and the works, if not for my own, I ask you.'

The old man shrugged. The medicine seemed to have given him an artificial stimulus and he seemed stronger than before, while his pallid face had taken a more healthy colour.

'Sentiment, Nephew Charles; all sentiment. I know all about it. I've been stuck, not once, but many times, for money. Did I depend on my friends? I depended on myself, and that's what you must do. It wouldn't be helping you to pay that money. I won through by hard work. You do the same and you'll live to bless me.'

The stimulus of the medicine now seemed to be passing off and Andrew sank back into his chair as if exhausted again.

'Come and let me hear how you get on,' he murmured, touching the bell on the arm of his chair. Weatherup silently appeared and he went on: 'I'm tired. I'll have a little sleep, I think. Get tea for Mr Charles and tell Mrs Pollifex.' Once again he pushed out his claw-like hand. 'Good-bye, Nephew Charles; and let me know how you get on.'

Charles's disappointment was bitter as he followed Weatherup from the room. The ready way of escape from his troubles, to which he had been so hopefully looking forward, had failed him. The old man had taken up just the attitude which he had feared he would. Charles could not exactly blame him. It was old age and illness that were really at fault.

But though his disappointment was so keen, Charles did not entirely lose heart. The idea of making an unaccustomed move had come too quickly for his uncle. Andrew's natural reaction would be to oppose anything new. But there was a reasonable chance that as he thought over the situation his opposition would decrease.

It would, Charles saw immediately, be a capital mistake to show any signs of annoyance. He therefore controlled himself and told Weatherup he would be glad of tea and that he hoped Mrs Pollifex could see him.

Penelope Pollifex was Andrew's sister, the widow of a not very successful London stockbroker. When her husband had died, leaving her badly off, Andrew had offered her and her daughter Margot a home in return for running his house. The arrangement had worked well. Mrs Pollifex had carried out her part of the bargain efficiently. Andrew inhabited his own suite of rooms and was not troubled by matters domestic, while otherwise the house was to all intents and purposes Mrs Pollifex's. With the housekeeping allowance Andrew made her and her own money she was comfortably off, and entertained her friends as if Andrew no longer existed.

Weatherup led the way downstairs and threw open a door. 'Mr Charles Swinburn,' he intoned in melancholy accents. Charles passed into the room.

Like the hall, it was spacious and well proportioned, lit by three windows reaching almost from ceiling to floor, and panelled and floored in oak. In an easy chair reclined a well-preserved and elegantly dressed woman of between fifty and sixty. Though her appearance formed a striking contrast to that of the venerable wreck upstairs, there was something in the grey eyes and the set of the features which proclaimed their relationship. Mrs Pollifex suggested what Andrew might have been before his illness, looking, as she did, a woman of the world, hard-headed, resourceful, and suavely competent. As Charles entered she looked up from her book.

'Hello, Aunt Penelope,' said Charles. 'I've not seen you for a month of Sundays.'

'Not my fault, I think, Charles,' she answered with a smile. 'How are you?' Without getting up, she extended a well-manicured hand. Charles shook it dutifully.

'No, I'm afraid it's mine,' he admitted as he dropped into a chair. 'Been pretty busy lately. Things are difficult at present.'

'I suppose you're feeling it like everyone else?'

'I am rather. Can't hope to escape, you know. Everyone's in the same boat.'

'I know my dividends have dropped badly enough.' She shrugged daintily. 'However, if we go bankrupt we'll have the satisfaction of all doing it together. You were up with your uncle?'

'I was. I hadn't seen him for some time.'

'How did you think he was?'

Charles hesitated momentarily. 'Not too well, I'm afraid. In fact, he gave me quite a fright. Got some kind of attack; I thought he was going to collapse altogether. He was just able to call for Weatherup. Weatherup gave him some medicine which pulled him round.'

'He's getting those attacks more frequently. I notice a change in him. He's certainly weaker than he was in the winter; weaker both in mind and body.'

'I thought so, too. He seemed less able to grasp things.'

'He's been very depressed lately. I think it's his indigestion.'

Charles made a grimace. 'A beastly thing,' he declared. 'Enough to depress anyone. I know what it's like.'

'You, Charles? You're too young to be troubled with indigestion. What's happened to you?'

'Oh, I don't know. Not enough exercise, I expect. Uncle usen't to be troubled with it, surely? I don't seem to remember.'

'Yes, he's had it for years, but it's only lately that it's got so bad. Then someone put him on to some pills which have helped him.'

'I must find out what they are.'

'They're one of those patent medicines that are advertised every-where. The doctor doesn't know he's got them or he'd probably be annoyed. Your uncle takes them regularly, one after every meal. Says they do him a lot of good.'

'Those patent things often do for a time, but you generally pay for it afterwards. Where's Margot?'

'Gone to play tennis. She'll be sorry to have missed you.'

Margot Pollifex was Charles's cousin, Mrs Pollifex's only daughter. She was a pretty young woman of some four and twenty, with luxuri-ous tastes. Hating Cold Pickerby, she looked down on its inhabitants and its society. She wanted to live in London, and it rankled as a grievance that she had never been presented. As a result, popularity was not her strong suit locally, but the young woman had a certain caustic wit which was calculated to make a party 'go', and hostesses were therefore glad to have her at their functions.

Charles did not stay long at The Moat. With what he had on his mind small talk was an effort to him. As he started up his car the load of care which for the last half-hour he had so resolutely banished from his thoughts, descended once more upon him. With this new and bitter disappointment he felt he was becoming desperate. He did not know where to turn. Nowhere upon his horizon did there seem a ray of light.

CHAPTER VI

Charles Meets Temptation

T HAT NIGHT AFTER DINNER CHARLES'S THOUGHTS RETURNED once more to his desperate position. Not that they had ever entirely left it, but now he settled down to consider it deliberately in the almost despairing hope of finding some way, if only a temporary way, out of his difficulties.

Things were rapidly coming to a head. Before leaving the office he had had another look over his secret ledger, and he had been forced to realize that unless he could get money within the fortnight, he would be short of actual cash to pay his men.

Charles knew he should close down at once. Those men should have a full week's notice. If he delayed another week they wouldn't get it.

But now that the end was upon him, with all it entailed, he could not face it. The loss of the works, yes. The loss of his own position, unemployment for himself, poverty perhaps; yes, all these he could face. But the loss of Una he could not face. He could not bring himself to do anything which would make this inevitable. While there was life there was hope, and as long as any financial life whatever remained to him he just could not take so irrevocable a step.

His thoughts reverted to his interview with Andrew Crowther. There was the way of escape, if only the old man could be induced to change his mind. Was there no way in which he could bring pressure to bear on his uncle?

Charles felt terribly bitter towards the old man. It wasn't as if he had been continually pestering him for money. This was absolutely the first time he had ever made any serious request of him. And then, on this very first occasion, to be turned down as if he were a schoolboy asking for a holiday! It was really unbearable.

And not only that, but Andrew had been so abominable in his manner, with his jeers and his sarcasm and his puerile suspicions. Charles had no use for anyone who indulged in sarcasm. And last, but not least, there was Andrew's perfectly unpardonable suggestion that his nephew would be glad if he died. The whole thing was so unjust.

And yet, Charles thought grimly, was this last point so very unjust after all? Did he not in his heart of hearts wish the old man would peg out? Of course he did. Wouldn't anyone do so in his position?

How strange it was, Charles ruminated, that the useless and obstructive so often live on, while the valuable and progressive die early! Here was Andrew Crowther, a man whose existence was a misery to himself and a nuisance to all around him. Why should he be spared and others who perhaps were doing a great work in the world be cut off in their prime? It didn't somehow seem right. For the sake of himself and everyone else it would be better if Andrew were to die.

It was then that the dreadful idea shot into Charles's mind. *Why should not Andrew die?*

For a moment Charles scarcely realized what he had thought. Then more definitely it came again. Why should not Andrew die? He was old: he must die soon. Why not now?

Charles suddenly saw what he had really meant, and his mind revolted. At once he tried to banish the dreadful idea. Horrible, monstrous thoughts did force themselves into people's minds, and the only thing to be done was to expel them as soon as possible. Not that this idea really mattered; it was too far removed from actuality to be taken seriously.

But suppose Andrew did die. Ah, if that were to happen, what a difference it would make! That attack that he had had, that surely meant *heart*. Suppose he got one of those attacks and the medicine did not revive him. Andrew Crowther's death? What would it not mean to Charles Swinburn?

In spite of himself, Charles allowed his imagination to dwell on the prospect. In four or five days there would come the reading of the will; and once the terms of the will were known, his difficulties would be over. No longer would Witheroe hesitate to sanction the increase of his overdraft. No longer would Bostock be unable to afford a loan. The works would be saved. His credit would bound up. Una would marry him!

It was with something very like horror that Charles brought himself up with a jerk. This would never do. Even as a joke such thoughts must not be harboured. Not, of course, that there was any danger. All the same, he would put the idea out of his mind...

But Charles Swinburn did not put the idea out of his mind. Una! Una and the works. Was he going to throw up the sponge and to allow this money trouble to knock him out without making any real effort for his woman and his possessions? Or was he going to fight for what he wanted – to keep the works and marry Una?

Marry Una! The very thought of it intoxicated him. Would such a thing not be worth anything else on earth? *Anything* – even...

But no, no, no! He mustn't even think of such a thing. There must be some other way, some way of influencing Andrew. Would, or could, his aunt help him? Or Margot? Or even Elsie Morley? The old man thought a lot of both Margot and Elsie. Was it possible that he would do for them what he wouldn't do for Charles?

For a long time that night Charles tossed about, pondering his problem. There was, of course, another way out; a terrible alternative, though not so terrible as that which had been in his mind. Would the easiest way not be simply to end the whole thing – quietly to take his own life? Suicide! Was suicide not the solution of his problem?

Charles had no moral scruples on the point. He did not believe in a hereafter. To him physical death was the end of everything. He considered that he had a right to take his own life if he chose to do so. Did he choose to do so?

Then he saw that there was nothing he dreaded more. No! A hundred times no! Abstractly and at a distance the idea of suicide was not repulsive. But brought face to face with it as an immediate need, he shivered at the thought. With the whole strength of his being he wanted to live.

At last Charles fell into a restless doze, only to awake unrefreshed and unhappy. In vain he took out his mare and went for a gallop across the fields before breakfast. In vain he plunged into his cold bath and rubbed himself down with energy. He could not rid his mind of the dreadful thought which had obtained lodgement.

It was all that Charles could do that day to preserve a quiet manner and a smiling face. Till the worst actually came to the worst – if it did so – no one must know what was impending. Nothing irrevocable must be done which would prevent him taking advantage of any unforeseen circumstance which might arise.

As he continued to wrestle with his problem his mind gradually became made up as to his next step. He would go out again to The Moat and plead his case with Andrew Crowther in stronger terms. He would show Andrew his secret ledger, and make him understand that for him, Charles, the matter was one either of help or of suicide.

Accordingly he rang Andrew up. The old man was in a good mood, for he made no gibe, but said he would be glad to see Charles, and would he come out next day to lunch?

This seemed to Charles so encouraging that his thoughts that night were much more normal, and he was no longer obsessed with the idea of death, either his own or his uncle's. He slept well and woke next day in a more wholesome frame of mind. When shortly before one he drove his car to the door of The Moat, he had half persuaded himself that the end of his troubles was in sight.

On good days Andrew Crowther came down for meals, and it seemed to Charles a promising omen that when he was shown into the drawing-room he should find his uncle there. Andrew greeted him pleasantly enough, but there was no opportunity for confidential discussion, as both his aunt and Margot came in directly.

Lunch was a family party – only the four were present. On the whole it was not a happy meal. Andrew undoubtedly was a good deal changed. He did not keep up with the conversation, but made spasmodic and unrelated remarks, evidently following some ram-bling train of ideas in his own mind. Mrs Pollifex's contribution was perfunctory, and it was obvious that she also had her private thoughts and was bored with her company. Margot, except in the presence of strangers, rarely exerted herself to please, and on this occasion she made no attempt to hide her dislike of Cold Pickerby in general and her uncle's household in particular. Charles himself was not up to his usual form; his anxieties too fully occupied his mind. It was therefore with something of relief that he watched the meal draw to an end.

In due course Mrs Pollifex and her daughter withdrew, and Charles and his uncle were left face to face across the table. In a few moments they would go up to the study, and then another of the critical moments of Charles's life would be upon him.

But it happened that before they made a move an incident took place, trifling in itself, but which was to prove vastly more important to Charles than either his subsequent interview or anything else which up to then had befallen him.

As they were sitting at the table prior to making a move upstairs, Andrew Crowther took from his waistcoat pocket a small glass bottle. He unscrewed the cap and shook out on to the tablecloth four or five little white pills. Evidently more had come out than he required, for he set the bottle up on end and, picking up all but one, he dropped them back into it. Then screwing on the cap he replaced the bottle in his pocket. Finally he swallowed the remaining pill.

Charles had not been particularly interested in the operation, and though he absent-mindedly watched the old man, he made no remark upon it. He could see from the name on the bottle that the pills were a well-known patent remedy for indigestion, evidently that to which his aunt had referred on his last visit.

Andrew touched the bell at his hand, and Weatherup appearing, the old man was helped up to his study. Charles followed, Weatherup withdrew, and the great interview was launched.

Charles began by repeating a good deal of what he had said at their previous meeting. Then he went on to explain that he wanted his uncle to look at the actual figures in question, so that he might see for himself the seriousness of the position. He brought out his ledger and explained it. Finally he made the strongest appeal of which he was capable for an advance on his legacy. He stated his case well. To himself it sounded unanswerable, and as he talked he felt a growing confidence that this time his request would be granted.

It came upon him, therefore, as all the greater shock when at last it was driven in upon him that Andrew Crowther did not intend to do anything of the kind. The old man hummed and hawed, and mumbled puerilely about Charles working harder and thus wresting orders from his slacker competitors. He could not envisage conditions

being in any degree different from those to which he himself had
been accustomed.

In despair Charles played his last card. 'Well, uncle,' he said with
almost desperation in his voice, 'I must tell you that if you can't see
your way to make me this small advance, it will mean ruin – ruin
complete and absolute. I can't pay my men and I must close down
the works. I shall be like the men – penniless and without a job. I have
made up my mind that I can't face it. I have decided that, rather than
suffer this shame and ruin and bankruptcy, I shall commit suicide. I
do appeal to you to save the works and the men and my life. If you
won't consider me, consider at least the good name of the family.'

At last Andrew seemed moved. He twisted nervously in his chair
while a look of indecision appeared on his face. Charles pressed home
his advantage.

'Up to the present,' he said tensely, 'a Crowther or a Swinburn has
never defaulted. Up to now the word of a principal of the Crowther
Electromotor Works has been his bond, and that bond has always
been honoured. Uncle, you couldn't sleep restfully in your bed if the
firm's good name were to be dragged in the dust. Though I might
be primarily responsible, it would rebound on you. Your name, the
family name would be smirched. And you can save it so easily.'

It seemed strange to Charles, but this line of appeal seemed to
get home, whilst his former, to him, much stronger arguments had
made no impression on his uncle. The indecision in Andrew's manner
grew. At last he quaveringly demanded how much Charles required.

Charles suggested five thousand, the absolute minimum that
would be any use.

But the mention of this sum upset Andrew dreadfully. He had, he
explained, been expecting a request for five hundred at the very most.
Five thousand! Had Charles taken leave of his senses?

Charles produced figures to show how the five thousand had been made up. But Andrew had lost his grasp of figures. He was, moreover, getting tired, and nothing would induce him to provide such a sum.

Finally, after further argument he did make a concession. He would then and there give Charles a cheque for a thousand pounds. He would not deduct it from any monies which might afterwards go to Charles under his will. He was not going to complicate his will by any such condition. This thousand would be a free gift, made in exceptional conditions and not under any circumstance to be repeated.

Charles saw that, at the moment at least, this was all he would get. A thousand in any case was a thousand. It would not save him, but it would postpone the evil day. And it was always possible that this thousand was not Andrew's last word.

Relieved for the moment of his dreadful anxiety, Charles thanked his uncle, and said he would be glad of the money under the conditions mentioned. Half an hour later he drove away from The Moat, and just before closing-time he entered the bank with the object of lodging the money.

Just as he was crossing the space between door and counter he met Stimpson, who had told at the club about Bender & Truesett's reduced dividend. Stimpson was a small, aggressive man with a predilection for laying down the law. He loved the sound of his own voice, and never missed the chance of an argument. Charles at once saw himself buttonholed.

But Stimpson did not stop. Instead of coming forward with some extravagant statement, calculated to produce an outraged denial, he hesitated, appeared to avoid Charles's eye and, murmuring something about the day not having turned out so badly, made as if to pass on.

The action was so barefaced that, in spite of his preoccupation, Charles could not fail to notice it. It aroused his surprise and resentment. He turned round.

'Well, Stimpson,' he said in a loudish voice, 'anything interesting at the club to-day?'

The man had to stop in spite of himself. 'You weren't there, Swinburn?' he mumbled.

'I was lunching with the uncle.'

'Mr Crowther? How is he keeping?'

'Not so well as usual. Beginning to go down the hill, I'm afraid.'

'He must be a pretty old man by now. Well, 'scuse me, Swinburn – Edwards is waiting for me at the office.'

The man was civil enough, but evidently uneasy, and in moving off he did not meet Charles's eye. Charles was puzzled as well as annoyed. However, he controlled his feelings and moved up to the counter.

'Good afternoon, Handcock,' he greeted the teller. 'Lovely day.'

'Splendid, Mr Swinburn. Too hot, if anything.'

Charles wondered if he was getting super-sensitive. Was there in the clerk's manner that same element of constraint which he had noticed in Stimpson's? Certainly the man did not seem at ease, and Charles caught him eyeing the cheque which Charles had produced with evident anxiety.

But the moment he glanced at it his face cleared. Quite unmistakably also his manner changed. He smiled in a relieved way, and asked Charles how he thought next Saturday's match would go. At the same time Charles thought he saw him make a kind of signal to someone at his, Charles's, back. In a leisurely way Charles changed his position, and glanced behind him. Witheroe was there, apparently just approaching.

'Missed you from lunch to-day,' Witheroe said as he stopped at the counter. Charles explained.

'I've not seen Mr Crowther for some time. How is he?'

Charles explained further.

'You wish this lodged to current account, Mr Swinburn?' the clerk interposed.

'Yes, please; to current account.' Charles turned to the manager and became more confidential. 'I can do without that loan, after all, Witheroe,' he said easily. 'I've come to an arrangement with the old man. He'll see me through. That's a thousand to go on with, while we're fixing up the details of a proper agreement.'

The lie slipped out automatically. The meaning of the little scene was only too clear. Charles was to have been refused any further cash. The teller had been afraid of an unpleasantness, and Witheroe had advanced to the support of his subordinate. The fact that Charles had come to lodge instead of to draw had made all the difference. To both men it was clearly a surprise, as gratifying as it was unexpected. Witheroe, however, passed it off as a trifle.

'I'm glad you've arranged it,' he said with a slightly overdone casualness. 'I was sure you would. I wanted to see you, if you can spare me a moment, about this municipal-relief-work business. We were talking about it at lunch. Can you come to the office now, or would some other time suit you better?'

Charles agreed readily, though he would have taken his oath that no thought of the relief works had been in the manager's mind when he approached the counter. However, they went through the form of discussing the matter, and presently Charles took his leave.

It had been a pretty near thing, Charles thought as he started up his car. For a man in his position to have been refused cash for his own cheque would have been the beginning of the end. Though, indeed, for the matter of that, the evil day seemed merely postponed. That thousand wouldn't last for ever. And when it was done...?

Charles set his teeth. At all events he needn't think about that to-day.

As he steered his car round the corner into Malton Road his heart gave a sudden leap. There, just disappearing into Oliver's, Cold Pickerby's best drapery establishment, was no less a personage than Una Mellor. Charles parked his car outside the post office and crossed the street.

He had not seen Una since the night of the ball, but she had consented to drive with him on the following afternoon to Scarborough, dining either there or somewhere on the way home. He had imagined her agreeing to the excursion was a hopeful sign, and he was looking forward to it with corresponding eagerness.

For a young lady who could not get the simplest article of wearing apparel nearer than Paris or London, Una managed to spend a pretty considerable time in the shop. Half the cigar which Charles had lit had been consumed when she made her appearance. She was evidently somewhat taken aback when she saw him.

'Hallo, Charles,' she greeted him, and her manner was cool and off-hand. 'What brings you here at this time of day?'

'I've been paying some calls,' Charles returned vaguely. 'What a piece of luck to meet you, Una!'

'Is it? For whom?'

'For both of us,' Charles declared stoutly.

'You seem to know more about it than I do. What did you want?'

'To see you,' Charles returned, feeling pleased that he had found the *mot juste*.

'Well, now you see me, what is it?'

'Can I drive you home, or anywhere? The car's just across the road.'

'Sorry; I'm going in here to Smith's.'

'I'll wait for you.'

'You'll have to wait till dinner-time, then. I'm going to the club for tea.'

'I'll come back just before dinner.'

'No, you won't. Freddy Allom's taking me home.'

Charles lost his head. 'Oh, Una, can't I see you this afternoon at all?' he begged.

'My dear Charles, don't be such a priceless ass. Much better if you'd go and do some work. And, by the way' – she had been walking on, but now she stopped and faced him – 'I'm afraid I'll not be able to go for that drive to-morrow. We have some people coming in for lunch, and they always stay interminably.'

Charles was overwhelmed with dismay. Una was often short and unsympathetic in her manner, but this time she was positively unkind. It looked as if for some reason she had wished to hurt his feelings. She had certainly succeeded.

He had the wit to see that argument would be useless. 'I'm sorry,' he said. 'But I mustn't keep you. I'll look forward to the drive the first day that you can manage.'

She nodded curtly and disappeared into the library. Charles felt it frightfully. It couldn't be that unmentionable ass Allom? Why, the fellow was a half-wit, with the manners of a gigolo and the appearance of a cross-eyed ape. No girl in her senses could fall for such a fantastic imbecile…

Charles remembered Stimpson's manner. Was it…? Could it be that stories were already going round?… And Allom had money… Savagely Charles started up his car.

A special providence watched over the children of Malton Road that afternoon as Charles drove to the Crowther Works. He left the car outside the gates and, passing through them, walked quickly down the yard. A moment later he had found Sandy Macpherson and drawn him aside.

'Tell me, Sandy,' he said, 'are there any yarns going about this place?'

The Scotsman looked at him sourly. 'A'll no deny it,' he admitted cautiously.

'What are they saying?'

'Are ye sure ye want to know?'

'Of course I want to know. Get along, man, can't you.'

'They're saying that you're in the soup for good an' a'.'

So that was it! Stimpson had heard the same yarn, and so had Witheroe and his teller. And so had Una! And so, he supposed, had everyone else in the confounded place.

As Charles sat gazing with unseeing eyes at the titanic crane, which was still hoisting the brobdingnagian locomotive aboard the mammoth ship, he swore that such a state of things would not continue. He would either get money – somehow – and put himself right with all these people, or he would take those sleeping-draughts and forget for ever about money or people, or worry or love. Which was it going to be?

CHAPTER VII

Charles Sees His Way

CHARLES HAD THAT MORNING LEFT HIS WRIST-WATCH AT A jeweller's to have a broken glass replaced, and when the works closed he walked back into the town to call for it before going home. On his way he overtook his cousin by marriage, Peter Morley.

'Hallo, Peter,' he greeted him. 'Funny to run into you again so soon. We usually meet about once every six months. How're things?'

'I say, Charles,' Peter returned with more animation than he usually showed, 'you didn't tell me you were going to the old man.'

Charles laughed. 'No,' he said easily, 'I didn't. I hadn't thought of it at the time. In fact it was what you said suggested it to me. Have you been?'

'I have,' said Peter grimly. 'But look here, what's it all about in your case? You're not going to tell me you're feeling the draught too?'

'Everybody's feeling the draught,' Charles declared. 'I'm not stony, of course, or anything like that, but I'd be glad enough of a bit of money. Want to put in some new machines to get our costs down.'

'Bless my soul!' Peter exclaimed. 'You, of all people! And with that magnificent little business! I should have said you were rolling.'

Charles smiled. 'Everything in this world's relative,' he pointed out. 'But tell me about yourself. I gather from your remarks that you've been too.'

'Yes, I've been. And found the old boy brimming over with wrath against you. And when he heard I was coming on the same job he fairly went off the deep end. I don't know, Charles, that that was a tremendously friendly action, that of yours.'

Charles turned and faced him. 'How do you mean? What action?'

'Going to him like that. The scheme was my scheme and you might easily have spoked my wheel.'

'What utter nonsense, old man. Don't be an ass. My application had nothing to do with yours. In fact, my going to him might have helped you. I might have created a precedent. If he had decided to make me an advance, he couldn't very well have refused you.'

Peter shook his head. 'It's done now,' he declared lugubriously, 'and there's no use in saying any more about it. Did he do anything for you?'

'Nothing like what I wanted. He gave me a thousand. Better than nothing, but I could have done with more.'

Peter whistled. 'A thousand! That's none so dusty, Charles. I wish I could get a thousand out of him.'

'What did you get?'

'Nothing in cash. But he's going to consider taking up a mortgage on the farm. If he does that to a reasonable extent, it may see me through.'

'My word, I don't think you've done so badly. Did he give you any idea of the amount?'

'No. He's going to consult Crosby.'

'You bet he is. He swears by Crosby. I never could see anything in the man.'

'I don't know him well. All the same he always struck me as a good lawyer.'

'He's an old woman. Too cautious by half. If you want anything done you've got to take risks. You know that as well as I.'

'Taking risks is not a lawyer's job.'

'All right, you'll know all about it if he says the farm's not good enough security for a mortgage.'

'I was wondering if I should see him.'

Charles shook his head. 'Don't you. He'll go and tell the uncle and the uncle's back will be put up still further. Result: no mortgage. Let sleeping dogs lie.'

'Perhaps you're right.'

'When is he to let you know?'

'Nothing's been arranged. He said he would see Crosby, but he didn't say when.'

'Well,' Charles went on easily, 'you've got a pretty good argument now because of what I did. If he doesn't seem to be coming up trumps you can argue that he can't make fish of one and flesh of another. He's created the precedent you want. He's given me a thousand and he can't turn you down.'

Peter shook his head gloomily. 'I hope you're right,' he said, and the conversation turned to other channels.

When Charles reached the office next morning he found that a number of local letters had come in. These had been opened by James Gairns, the head clerk, and lay in a little pile on Charles's blotter. A sinister little pile they made!

For they were all bills.

Charles ran a number of monthly or quarterly accounts in the local shops. The largest items of material used in the works he got of necessity from outside, but where he could deal in Cold Pickerby, he did so. The bills were in respect of over half of these local accounts.

There was nothing remarkable in the bills themselves. What gave them significance was the date. To-day was only the eighteenth of the month, and none of them was due for another fortnight!

In each case they were accompanied by a personal and very apologetic letter.

Dear Swinburn [so ran Stimpson's letter, which was typical of the rest], *I have to ask you to excuse my sending on this little account before it is due, but the fact is that I have been very badly hit by the demands of a number of my wholesalers for early cash, as well as the failure of some dividends on which I was counting. I trust you will not mind helping me out of my difficulties by squaring up the enclosed. It is trifling I know, but when several of these small accounts are added together it makes a considerable difference to me. With apologies and hoping that these abnormal times may soon pass over. Yours very truly, J. C. Stimpson.*

Charles's brow grew dark as he looked over letter after letter. They varied in the reason given for the demand, they varied in the show of friendliness they attempted, but they agreed in the essential, they wanted their money from Charles while he had any to give.

Bitterly Charles wondered what kind of tales were being circulated about him. It was impossible that his real position could be known. Only he himself knew that. Even if Andrew Crowther had repeated what he had learnt from the secret ledger, which was out of the question, there would not have been time for the story to have become common property.

Charles took a pencil and began copying the amounts on to a sheet of paper. None of them amounted to a great deal. There was a ten-pound note here, twenty there, forty there. Charles summed them. The total was not overwhelming. It amounted to £345 12s. 6d.

Not a great deal in a works of the size of Charles's. And yet £345 would make a nasty hole in that thousand on which he was depending for the next two or three weeks. With a bitter thought about the rats and the sinking ship, Charles pressed his bell.

'What's all this about, Gairns?' he began, pointing to the bills, as the pessimistic head clerk entered.

Gairns shook his head lugubriously.

'All these folk haven't got suddenly hard up in a night,' went on Charles. 'Have you heard of anyone else getting their bills?'

'No, sir, I haven't. I don't know what this all means, I'm sure. It fair took away my breath when I opened the envelopes.'

'I wonder if they've been served on anybody else?'

'They haven't on Stringers, anyhow. I was talking to Caxton, their chief clerk; he was in here about that baize; and I happened to ask, by accident, as you might say. They owe to several of those firms,' Gairns indicated the accounts with a sweep of the hand, 'and none of them have sent in accounts.'

Charles nodded. 'I thought so. There are some tales going, Gairns. About us, I mean. Have you heard anything?'

Gairns hesitated.

'Come on, man, let's hear it, whatever it is,' Charles added impatiently.

Gairns shook his head. 'A most shocking and outrageous thing!' he declared. 'They're saying, sir, that Crowthers is going bankrupt. That we should ever have lived to hear such a thing whispered!' The old man was actually trembling.

It spoke well for Charles's self-control that he was able to chuckle. 'Never mind, James,' he said good-humouredly. 'We'll show them they're wrong. But tell me, how has this story got about?'

'That's what I can't think, sir. Nobody here has said anything. Not that there was anything for them to say,' he added as an urgent afterthought.

'We've been talking about cutting down the men and getting rid of a clerk.'

'There's nothing in that, Mr Charles; nothing at all. Most of the firms in the place have reduced hands and there's never been a word about it.'

'Then what is it?'

Gairns did not know. The rumours were undoubted, but what had given rise to them he had no idea. 'Oh, well,' Charles said at last, 'never mind. The mischief's done. We can't help it. That'll do, James.'

Still Gairns hesitated. 'You're not going to pay those accounts, are you, Mr Charles? Such a bit of impertinence. They don't deserve it.'

'I'm going to pay every penny by return,' Charles retorted. 'Don't you see, man, if I didn't, it would confirm their suspicions.'

Gairns nodded and went out. Charles happened to glance at him as he was disappearing. Was it possible that on the man's face there was a thinly veiled expression of relief? Charles sat back with sudden distress. So Gairns had believed the rumours! His own head clerk!

Charles smiled with grim humour as he dictated replies to the various notes. In each case he was sorry to hear his old friend was in difficulties, and earnestly hoped they were merely temporary. Of course he would do as he had been asked and with pleasure he enclosed the amount of the account. To one or two of the more obnoxious he added that if their case was really serious he might between friends be able to oblige with a small temporary loan.

But this relief to his feelings did not go very far, and when the typist left the room Charles felt more bitter than he had since his crisis began. Oh, if only that wretched old man would die!

Then suddenly into his mind flashed an idea which left him sitting rigid. Almost he held his breath as he considered it.

If he wanted Andrew Crowther to die, there was a way in which it could be managed.

There was a way! A safe way. Utterly and absolutely safe! Something might possibly be suspected, but nothing could ever be proved. Nothing could ever be found out which would connect him – or anyone else – with Andrew's death.

Charles shrank from the thought, but he could not banish it from his mind. A little effort: a perfectly safe effort; an effort which could never under any circumstances be traced to him: this little effort – and his troubles were over. His works were saved, his life was saved, Una was gained! Could he undertake that effort?

No! A thousand times, No! He was not a murderer. Charles shivered at the very idea. Murder! And what lay behind murder! No, no, he could never think of such a thing!

Not that he hadn't the nerve. He had nerve for anything. It wasn't that. It was that this deed was evil, definitely and terribly evil. If he committed it he would never be happy again.

Then he told himself that all this morality business was only an old wives' tale. He, Charles, wasn't tied up by these out-of-date considerations! What was politic was right. What was the greatest good of the greatest number? Why, that Andrew should die. What about all the men that were going to be thrown out of employment? What about the clerks? What about poor old Gairns? What about Gairns's invalid wife? Andrew Crowther's useless life could count for nothing against such a weight of human suffering.

And as to what followed murder? Nothing followed murder! It was only when murder was found out that unpleasant consequences followed. But this couldn't be found out. Besides, even if some accident occurred and the thing was discovered, suicide would meet the case. And that was the end. Charles did not believe in a life after death.

So Charles sought to convince himself, though in his heart of hearts he knew his arguments were fallacies.

His thoughts went back to the little episode he had witnessed on the day of his last visit to The Moat. Once again in his mind's eye he saw Andrew Crowther take from his waistcoat pocket the small bottle, unscrew the cap, and shake out on to the table the four or five little white pills. He seemed to see his uncle stand the bottle up on end and drop back into it all the pills except one. He imagined the old man putting the bottle back in his pocket and taking the remaining pill. And he remembered that Andrew Crowther performed these little operations regularly, day in, day out; morning, midday and evening.

It was while he had been thinking of this that his dreadful idea had occurred to him.

If one of those pills in that bottle contained poison, Andrew Crowther would die.

One pill. A pill near the bottom of the bottle, so that Andrew would not take it until several days after it had been put in. The remaining pills could be analysed: they would be found to be all right. Even if the pill was suspected, it would be impossible to prove it had contained poison. If no one knew it had been introduced, no one could prove anything about it.

Charles no longer tried to put the idea out of his mind. He found rather that the more he thought of it, the more fascinating it grew. Safe? Why, it was as safe as houses! And sure? Sure as death itself.

By a little effort, the obtaining of a poisoned pill and the slipping of it secretly into Andrew's bottle, he would achieve – everything! He need take no further action. Automatically his scheme would fructify. Sooner or later Andrew would take the poisoned pill – and Charles would be free.

He sat in a sort of dream while his busy brain grappled with the problem. There would be difficulties of course. But difficulties were made to be overcome…

As Charles continued turning the thing over in his mind, its dreadful revolting side gradually receded, and the problem, as an abstraction, grew more and more prominent.

The problem was divided of course into two main divisions: How secretly to obtain the poisoned pill, and how secretly to introduce it into Andrew's bottle. At first both these divisions seemed easy, but as Charles considered them in detail he realized that both bristled with difficulties.

He saw at once that he could scarcely buy the poisoned pill. In the first place it would have to be exactly the same in size and shape and colour as those in Andrew's bottle, and it was unlikely that such existed. Besides, a mere poisoned pill was not enough; it would have to contain enough poison to kill. Moreover, it must incapacitate quickly, so that if Andrew himself should become suspicious, he would be unable to communicate with those around him. Greatest difficulty of all, such a pill if it existed would not be on sale. Even if it were purchasable, the poison book would have to be signed, and so dangerous an action could not be contemplated.

Charles saw that if he wanted a pill, he must make it for himself. But this involved a new crop of difficulties. What poison should he employ? How much would be required? How could he obtain it, even if he knew what to ask for? If he had it, could he make it up into a pill so like the others as not to be recognized, either by appearance or taste?

And then, perhaps greatest problem of all, if he had his pill, how could he introduce it secretly into Andrew's bottle, burying it deep among the others, so that days would pass before it took effect?

The difficulties seemed insuperable.

Charles oscillated between chagrin that so perfect a method of repairing his fortunes should be impracticable, and thankfulness that he could not after all be betrayed into murder. At one moment he thought of the crime with loathing, at another he felt that he would risk anything to save himself from ruin. But all the time the scheme remained lurking in his mind.

That night Charles could not sleep and inevitably his thoughts busied themselves with the problem. His brain was vividly alive and he felt that somehow on this occasion there was nothing he could not tackle. Almost at once he saw the way out of one of his difficulties. This still further stimulated his mind and he concentrated on the others.

He had a wonderful experience that night. Never had he so triumphantly attacked a problem. Difficulty after difficulty gave way to his efforts, and by four in the morning, when he suddenly grew sleepy, he saw just how the whole dreadful scheme could be carried out. If he were to adopt it, his line of action was cut and dry.

But, of course, he would never dream of adopting it.

What Charles thought in his heart he did not admit to himself. He fell asleep assuring himself that he had reached a solution to an abstract problem, which could never affect him or his uncle in real life.

But Charles forgot the danger of playing with fire.

CHAPTER VIII

Charles Begins His Preparations

CHARLES WOKE NEXT MORNING WITH A FEELING OF OPPRESsion. He had had terrible dreams, nightmares of murder. It was with an overwhelming sense of relief that he realized that these imaginings were only dreams and that no such dreadful weight lay on his soul.

All the same he could not but admire the cleverness of the scheme he had worked out during the night. If he had wished to commit murder, no more perfect plan could possibly have been devised. It was sure, it was painless to the victim, it was not harrowing to himself, and most important of all, it was utterly and absolutely safe. Almost, he thought with grim humour, it was a pity that so perfect a bit of work should be lost.

But when he reached his office and realized anew his financial situation, doubts once again assailed him. He saw that he was face to face, not with a choice between evil and good, but between two evils. One of these evils he could not escape. Which was the worse?

His correspondence dealt with according to his usual routine – there was not much of it and none of a satisfactory type – Charles went for his customary inspection of the works. To see the machines running and the work being turned out always relieved him when depressed. But now what struck him most was the terribly small amount of work in hand. And his stock was full. He could still sell his products, but only at a loss. Should he sell at less than the cost of production in order to keep the place running? That was his immediate problem and it led straight back to that other terrible question he had considered in the night.

In the machine shop he noticed a fitter, one of his very best hands. This man had been off for a few days and now he was looking ill and worn. Charles went up to speak to him.

'I noticed you were off, Matthews,' he said kindly, for he ran his business on the old-fashioned lines of personal contact with his staff. 'What's been the trouble?'

The man looked at him dully, then with an evident effort he answered. 'The wife, Mr Charles. She had a cold, nothing to signify, we thought. And then it turned to pneumonia.' He paused, then added in a low voice, 'She was took day before yesterday.'

'My dear fellow,' said Charles, 'I didn't know. I'm sorry. Were you long married?'

'Seven years come December.'

'And there are children?'

There were three, the youngest only fifteen months. At present the man was paying a neighbour to look after the children, but that came expensive and he didn't know how he was going to carry on. He was so full of grief that he could scarcely speak.

And this man, Charles thought, good, conscientious worker as he was, was going to be turned away and have his burden increased by unemployment. He would have to give up his house, and what would happen to his children? And this was one isolated case. Doubtless there were scores more to whom the loss of the job would mean utter ruin.

And all this misery threatened because he, Charles, had not the backbone to take a remedy which he feared and hated. Well, if he didn't, he himself would be in the same boat as these men. *He* would be unemployed. *He* would be without home or means. *He* would lose his prospective wife. Could he face it?

From that moment the die was cast. Though he would not admit to himself what he proposed to do, in his secret heart he knew. It was one useless life against a number of valuable ones. Andrew Crowther must die.

Deliberately closing his mind to the awfulness of his act, Charles returned to his office and set to work on the preliminaries of his plan. Precautions were necessary, very detailed and carefully thought out precautions, if that absolute safety he required were to be achieved. He would take things slowly so as not to risk making a mistake.

All the remainder of the morning he sat at his desk developing his plans, and by lunch time he had a pretty clear idea of what he was going to do. The first part of his scheme was threefold: he had to create outside confidence in his financial stability; he had to convey the impression that he was personally overworked and not very well, so that he could go away for a holiday; and he had by hook or by crook to raise some ready money to carry him through till the event took place.

As it happened, nothing could more powerfully have helped his first object, the creation of confidence, than the two steps he had already taken. There was first the statement he had made to Witheroe when lodging Andrew's cheque for £1,000: that he had come to an arrangement with his uncle whereby he hoped to weather the storm and that the thousand was only an earnest of what was still to come. Secondly, his prompt payment on the previous day of all the small accounts sent by the local firms would undoubtedly make a strong impression. He did not doubt that the rumour of his insolvency was already in a fair way to being scotched.

That this was indeed so he felt assured when he reached the club and noticed the subtle difference in the manner of his fellow lunchers. Yesterday there had been constraint in the atmosphere. Unobtrusively he had been avoided. Members had somehow failed to meet his eye.

To-day all that was changed. Indeed a sort of forced cordiality seemed to suggest an apology for having harboured evil and unjustifiable thoughts. His words were listened to with attention and his opinion appealed to with deference.

This was a good beginning, but Charles did not let it stand there. After lunch he made it his business to have a word with both Witheroe and Bostock. To both he referred vaguely to the help which his uncle was giving him, adding to Bostock that he therefore no longer required the loan about which he had been speaking. To both he said that he was immediately ordering his new machines.

This had a further reassuring effect, and when Charles returned to the works he felt that this part of his edifice had been well and truly laid. He had now only to carry on as if unlimited money was behind him, and all would be well.

At the same time he had to simulate weariness and worry. Indeed, in this he had not to do much simulation. He really was tired and worried, and he had only to allow his genuine feelings to come to the surface. But he was careful not to overdo the symptoms.

During the afternoon he called Sandy Macpherson into the office and delighted him by there and then deciding to issue orders for the three new machines. They had always dealt with a Sheffield firm, and Macpherson wanted to place the order as hitherto. But Charles wished for an excuse to visit Town. He therefore pointed out that a Reading firm made similar machinery, and said that before coming to a decision he would see what they had to offer. If their machines seemed better than those of the Sheffield company, Macpherson could join him at Reading and they would then come to a decision.

To both Macpherson and Gairns Charles said that all reductions of staff would be postponed. To both he contrived to suggest, without actually putting it into words, that these changes of policy were due to his uncle's action. To both also he hinted that the last few weeks had been a strain, and that now that his anxiety was over he would take a short holiday.

The third preliminary was the raising of more cash, and here Charles saw his way clearly. During his later years his father had developed a taste for art, and, being comfortably off, he had gratified it by buying some pictures. They were not Old Masters, but they were good of their kind and had cost a couple of hundred or more apiece. There were fourteen in all, and Charles estimated that they were worth about three thousand pounds. He now proposed to pawn them and he thought he should get at least fifteen hundred for them.

He had, of course, during the past few weeks frequently considered selling these pictures, but it happened that Una admired them and would have at once noticed their disappearance. She would have demanded an explanation and then the fat would have been in the fire. Pawning them, however, was a different matter. She need never know they had been removed. He would be able to redeem them before having her to the house, particularly as he was going on a holiday.

Next morning was Sunday, which Charles spent in his usual way at tennis, but on Monday he carried out the first item of his programme: a journey to Town. Before starting he got Rollins to pack the fourteen pictures in his car, on the ground that he was taking them to be cleaned. He also had lunch put up, saying that this would enable him to have it when he liked, instead of having to fit in a call at some hotel. While Rollins was engaged elsewhere he secretly slipped into the car his portable typewriter, with two ribbons, its own purple and a spare black. To these he added a kitbag containing a lounge suit with black coat and waistcoat and grey striped trousers – what he called 'Town business clothes' – a pair of black shoes and a hairbrush.

Then, having given notice at the works that he would be away for a couple of days, he set off.

He had worked out an intensive programme by which he hoped to get all that he wanted done in the short time available, and had looked up the necessary firms and addresses in the directory at the club. Besides the visit to Reading, which was the ostensible reason for the trip, and the pawning of the pictures, which he wished to keep private, though not necessarily secret, he had a number of other errands. With these latter he must not under any circumstances become connected. None of them must ever be traced home to him.

From this point of view he had given the question of a disguise a good deal of thought. A proper make-up he would not attempt. He realized that a poor disguise was more dangerous than no disguise at all. But he intended at least to dress in clothes unlike his ordinary wear, put on horn-rimmed spectacles, and do his hair in a different fashion.

It was another delightful day, though there was a slight haze from the heat. The fine spell had brought out the holiday-makers, and all England seemed to be on wheels. Charles drove fast, as fast as he could without drawing attention to himself. If he could get into Town early enough he might carry through the picture negotiations that afternoon.

He was surprised to find that in spite of the terrible decision he had taken, he was feeling light-hearted and in good form. The mere fact indeed that he had come to a decision was a relief. The misery of uncertainty was gone. And if his scheme was dangerous; well, the very risk added to the thrill.

He did the run of about two hundred miles in well under six hours, arriving in London between three and four in the afternoon. He had selected the name of Jamieson & Truelove from the formidable list of pawnbrokers in the directory because they advertised themselves as dealers in objects of art. Now he stopped in a nearby park and walked round to their premises in Arundel Street.

A statement of his business brought him at once to Mr Truelove's private office. Mr Truelove was an elderly gentleman with a Jewish cast of countenance and an oily manner. He begged Charles to be seated, and, rubbing his hands, inquired what he could have the pleasure of doing for him.

Charles told him. He wished to raise some money on pictures. If that was in Mr Truelove's line, Mr Truelove might care to see what he had brought; if not, perhaps he could direct him where to apply.

It appeared that the advancing of money on pictures was Mr Truelove's heart's joy, and it would delight him to examine Mr Swinburn's property. Charles thereupon superintended the removal of the pictures to Mr Truelove's room. Truelove looked at them with an air of polite disparagement, and asked how long Charles proposed to leave them. Charles did not exactly know, but suggested six months.

'We can certainly allow you something on them, Mr Swinburn,' Truelove said at last. 'They are not valuable, as you no doubt know, but we can allow something.'

'Values are relative, as you no doubt know,' Charles returned dryly. 'What amount will you allow?'

Truelove spread out deprecating hands. Much he regretted that he was not himself a connoisseur. The pictures would have to be valued by his expert. Could Mr Swinburn come back?

Charles could come back on the following afternoon.

That, Mr Truelove explained, would do admirably. He would have a proposal to lay before, he hoped he might say, his client, and in the meantime here was a receipt for the pictures. And might he add that all their business was conducted with the utmost possible discretion?

So far as it went, this all seemed satisfactory to Charles. The offices looked large and prosperous, and he thought he would probably do as well there as anywhere else.

Charles's next business was secret, and systematically he took all the precautions he had thought out to prevent his proceedings being traced. Returning to his car, he took from it the kitbag. He left the car parked where it was, and going to Aldwych Tube Station took the train to Holborn. There he alighted and walked westwards till in one of the streets off New Oxford Street he came to a second-hand clothes shop. It was a superior sort of place, which would exactly suit his purpose.

There he bought a good though worn suit of inconspicuous brown, which he rolled up and stowed in the kitbag. In the next block there was a hat shop, and he bought there a grey Homburg hat. A third shop supplied a tie of unostentatious pattern.

His fourth purchase he dared not make while dressed in his ordinary clothes. Slipping therefore into a street lavatory, he changed his suit, tie, shoes and hat. At the same time he brushed up his moustache, eyebrows and hair into unwonted styles. Glancing at himself in a mirror as he came out, he was delighted to find his appearance was really considerably altered.

With a good deal more self-confidence he entered a theatrical supplies shop in Shaftesbury Avenue and bought a pair of plain glass horn-rimmed spectacles 'for a part he was doing at a children's show'. With these on he felt his disguise was good enough. He was ready for the first definite act of his dreadful drama.

In Charing Cross Road he drifted into a second-hand bookshop devoted to scientific works and began an outwardly desultory examination of the shelves.

He wanted a book, but his difficulty was that he didn't know exactly what book he wanted. It was a book about poisons, and it must tell not only the effects of various poisons, but the amounts required to ensure death. Also it must indicate how or where the substances in question were to be obtained. In taking his degree of Bachelor of Science Charles had worked through a fairly advanced course in chemistry. He had not, however, specialized in poisons, though, of course, he knew something about them. He felt sure that some book would give the required information, if he could only light on it.

In a leisurely way he ran his eye along the shelves. The books were classified by subject, and he was able to drift quickly past astronomical and botanical works, treatises on chemistry and daltonism, electricity, and ferro-concrete construction. He was hurrying on to the 'P's', but in passing the 'M's' he halted suddenly.

Medical jurisprudence! Was that not what he wanted?

He was only vaguely conscious of what medical jurisprudence really encompassed, and with some hesitation he began to take down and glance through one bulky volume after another. Yes, it looked as if he were on the right track. These were books about the evidence which doctors might give in cases of crime. They gave the signs for which doctors should look: the post-mortem appearance of bodies murdered in various ways, the causes which produced various results...

Charles fingered book after book, hastening though with slow outward movements, so as not to attract the attention of the assistants. The assistants, however, were busy, and as a number of other persons were standing at the shelves looking through the books just as Charles was, he was not disturbed.

Suddenly he experienced a little thrill of satisfaction. Surely this was what he required! In the second volume of Taylor's *Principles and Practice of Medical Jurisprudence* there was a huge section headed

Poisoning and Toxicology, with sub-sections on *Dangerous Drugs, The Action of Poisons* and *Diagnosis of Poisoning.*

Charles picked out the two large volumes. They were second-hand, and he thought them cheap at thirty shillings. Wrapped in paper, he took them out under his arm. The purchase had attracted no attention from the rather bored and overworked assistant who had attended to him, and Charles was certain that it could never be brought home to him.

Twice Charles repeated his manœuvre. In two other bookshops he made purchases with similar precautions. First he bought *The Extra Pharmacopoeia,* by Martindale and Westcott, which he remembered from the days of his science course as the dispensing chemists' Bible, Secondly, he picked up a good elementary book on sleight-of-hand.

In another street lavatory he changed back to his own clothes, and squeezing the books into the kitbag with his other purchases, he returned to his car and drove it openly to The Duchy of Cornwall, the hotel in Northumberland Avenue at which he invariably put up.

He met some men he knew in the hotel, and though he was on the *qui vive* to get at his book, he decided to spend the evening with them. Doing so, he thought, would enable him to account for the whole of his day: driving in a leisurely way to Town and spending the time from his arrival until bedtime in the presence of other people. So far there was nothing to suggest that he had done anything secret.

But immediately on reaching his room he seized the book and began searching for what he wanted. At once he found himself up against a difficulty. The section on poisons was so big, he didn't know where to turn for his information. He decided, however, that if necessary he would spend the entire night reading it through.

He began at Section XV, *Poisoning and Toxicology.* Sub-section A, *The Law on Poisons, including the Definition of a Poison or Noxious Thing,* did not help him. On the contrary, he was puzzled and embarrassed by finding that there were some forty or more different poisons or groups of poisons to be considered. How was he to select the one most suitable for his purpose?

He passed on to Sub-section B, *Dangerous Drugs,* which gave him no information, and then to Sub-section C, *The Action of Poisons.* Skimming rapidly through this section he came to a heading, *The Time at which Symptoms appear after swallowing a Poison.* At this he halted.

For him this was an excessively important point. It might not prove possible to get hold of Andrew Crowther's bottle of pills unknown to the old man, and the poison must act sufficiently quickly to prevent him revealing his suspicions, should any be aroused. Charles therefore read the paragraph carefully.

Immediately the sentence caught his eye: 'A large dose of prussic acid… may destroy life in less than two minutes.' This was obviously the most rapid poison. The next mentioned was oxalic acid, which killed in 'from ten minutes to an hour,' and after that the periods given were many hours.

It would seem then that other things being equal, prussic acid would best suit his purpose. Could he find out something more about it?

He turned to the index and began to run his finger down the closely printed columns. There it was: 'Prussic acid, poisoning by, page 661.' He turned to page 661.

Charles read, and as he did so his knowledge of the subject grew. Prussic or hydrocyanic acid was a medicinal drug. It did not look as if a layman could obtain it. On the other hand, the cyanides, derived from the acid, were 'Freely used in the arts… and in photography, etc.' The cyanides therefore should be easier come by, and of them cyanide of potassium seemed to be most suitable. Charles read a lot about cyanide of potassium. He learned that it was a hard white substance and one of the most formidable poisons known to chemists, that a dose of five grains had proved fatal in three minutes, that though death might not come for a few minutes, sensibility usually ceased within seconds. It killed by paralysing the nervous system and the heart. Charles assumed that in the case of a man with a weak heart like Andrew Crowther, a very small dose would suffice.

Charles sat studying his book. Could he put sufficient potassium cyanide into a pill of the size of those in Andrew's bottle? If so, how or where could he obtain the poison?

The first question he thought might be answered if he weighed one of the pills. Not conclusively, of course, because the specific gravity of the poison might be different to that of the contents of the pill. But he should get an approximate idea. The second question was more difficult.

Then it suddenly occurred to him that he had often heard that potassium cyanide was used for destroying wasps' nests, and that by signing the poison book anybody could obtain a quantity for this purpose. He wondered if this were true.

Charles was a man of resource. Two minutes' thought showed him a way by which he could find out. He decided that next morning he would put the thing to the test.

It was past three when he closed his book and got into bed. His plans for the next day were cut and dry.

Presently he slept, as easily as if his mind contained only the most altruistic schemes for the benefit of his fellow men.

CHAPTER IX

Charles Completes His Preparations

N EXT MORNING CHARLES CALLED FOR A TAXI AND WAS DRIVEN
with his kitbag to Piccadilly Circus. There he repeated his
manœuvres of the previous day. Changing to the second-hand clothes
in the station lavatory, he packed his others in the kitbag, locked it
and deposited it at the station cloak-room. Then he made his way to
the nearest chemist's.

'I'm having trouble with wasps' nests,' he explained to the assistant.
'There are two in my garden and it's as much as my life's worth to go
out there. Can you give me something to destroy them?'

The assistant suggested flooding them with petrol and setting
fire to them.

'Yes, I've heard of that,' Charles admitted. 'But petrol's rather a
nuisance to get. I don't want a huge tin of it, and it's not easy to take
out of the car. I thought you had some poison or something that one
could simply put into the nest?'

'Potassium cyanide is often used,' the assistant returned. 'But, of
course, we can't sell that to everyone.'

'I've heard of that too,' said Charles. 'I dare say it would do. What
are the formalities for getting it?'

'Well, we have to know the purchaser personally, or he has to be
vouched for to us by someone we know personally. And, of course,
he has to sign the poison book.'

'Would a letter from a doctor do?'

'Yes, if the doctor was known to us.'

Charles smiled. 'Looks as if I'd have to wait till I got home and get it from my own chemist,' he said as he thanked the man and left the shop.

For the moment he could not pursue this line of business, but there were others. A little farther down the street he saw another chemist's. He turned in.

'A bottle of Salter's Anti-Indigestion Pills,' he asked as a young man came up.

'Yes, sir. What size?'

'The smallest size, please.'

Without a word the young man parcelled up a small cardboard box and handed it across. Charles took it with a brief 'Thank you' and walked out.

It spoke volumes for the care with which Charles was playing his part, that he remembered to give his features a somewhat strained expression while making his purchase. It must not occur to the assistant that this was a very healthy-looking man to have indigestion.

He had not known that the pills were sold in more sizes than one, and he had said the smallest to avoid a discussion. Now in the shelter of another street lavatory he opened the package. The bottle was not so large as that used by Andrew Crowther. The advertisement, however, stated that the pills were sold in three sizes, and it was evident that Andrew's was the largest. Charles therefore went into a third chemist's and asked for another bottle, this time saying 'Largest size'.

Once again he received his purchase without having attracted special attention. He was satisfied that by the next day the two assistants who had served him would have forgotten the tiny transaction.

Charles had two other matters to deal with. With the help of a directory he found a chemical instrument maker's, and there he bought a working chemist's balance and weights: the smallest size. Then he turned to something more difficult.

This was his first step towards the purchase of the poison, and he felt that it behoved him to proceed with the utmost caution. He had decided to try a bluff in the hope of overcoming the scruples of some chemist more easy-going than the man he had already tackled. To do so he saw that he must adopt a personality, a real personality.

And first as to the location of his personality. After some thought he chose Surbiton. It was a big place, and yet it was surrounded by houses with gardens, many of which doubtless contained wasps' nests. A visit to Surbiton seemed indicated.

Charles, retaining his disguise, took the first train from Waterloo. On arrival he turned south, as this direction was most likely to lead to open country. Passing a bookseller's he went in and bought a directory of the town. Then he continued his walk.

He soon reached what he thought would prove the very place. Sycamore Avenue, a quiet tree-lined street of detached and semi-detached villas with small gardens. Selecting a likely looking house with telephone wires attached, he noted its name, the Dove Cot. His directory told him that it was occupied by a Mr Francis Carswell. On his way back to the station he checked at a telephone booth that Mr Carswell really was on the telephone. Returning to town, he called at a printer's and ordered a plate and a hundred visiting cards to read: Mr Francis Carswell, The Dove Cot, Sycamore Avenue, Surbiton. He explained that he was in a special hurry and the cards were promised for the following morning.

This completed Charles's morning's work. It had taken longer than he had expected, and it was now nearly lunch time. However, that couldn't be helped. Retrieving the kitbag from the Piccadilly cloak-room he changed back into his normal clothes, put the pills and scales into the bag, locked it, and drove to Paddington. There he left the bag in the cloak-room, snatched a hurried lunch in the refreshment-room and took the first train to Reading.

He had now to justify his journey to London, and he did it thoroughly. Taking a taxi to the machine tool works, he examined the products there displayed with the same care as if he contemplated an immediate purchase. Then he asked a number of questions to which in the nature of things answers could not be instantly given. Finally he left, saying that on receipt of the information he would come to a decision.

On reaching Town he found there would be just time to settle the matter of the pictures before the pawnbroker's closing time. Accordingly he took a tube back to Arundel Street.

Once more Mr Truelove received him with unction and rubbing of hands.

'Well, sir,' he beamed, 'I've had your pictures valued, and I may admit at once,' he threw out his arms with a gesture of splendid frankness, 'that they're worth more than I had thought at first. I can certainly make you an advance on them.'

'That's satisfactory,' Charles admitted. 'I've a sort of idea what they're worth. The question is, what will you lend on them?'

'Keeping them for six months?'

'I don't know exactly; about six months, I should think.'

'We shouldn't sell them for two years. If by the end of two years they were not redeemed, we should consider them our property to dispose of as we thought fit.'

'That would be all right,' Charles answered. 'By the end of two years my business will be either flourishing or dead.'

Mr Truelove became sentimentally sorry for his firm. Times were hard. The pictures would be an expense. The space they would occupy was valuable, and they would have to be kept clean and dry. Moreover, insurance on them would be heavy. In short, he could not offer as much as he would like and as he admitted the articles were worth.

'Never mind,' Charles said patiently. 'What will you offer?'

The sum, when Mr Truelove could at last be persuaded to mention it, was larger than Charles had hoped. The pictures were not all of one value, though they were nearly so. Mr Truelove proposed to offer an equal advance on each, £150 a picture, total £2,100.

Charles was delighted, though he was careful not to reveal his joy. £2,100 would cover up the deficit on the works for three or four weeks. With what he had in hand he could count on keeping things going for more than a month. And before a month was over he would be a rich man.

Truelove had prepared the necessary documents, and when Charles had signed them, notes for £2,100 were counted out to him. Very well satisfied with his progress, he left the office.

On his way back to the hotel he made certain further purchases: some envelopes of various sizes and qualities, a book of stamps, a little lampblack and an etching pen.

Charles had some bad moments that night as he thought of what was coming. In his next day's operations there was undoubted risk. There was always risk in an impersonation. Why, the chemist's assistant to whom he applied might know the real Francis Carswell. He might be a native of Surbiton, and even if he didn't know Carswell, might make some local reference which he, Charles, could not play up to. Yes, there was certainly risk.

However, the risk was not great. The odds against disastrous knowledge on the part of anyone with whom he would be brought in contact were probably some millions to one.

When he retired to his room Charles locked the door and unpacked the pills and scales. He had two principal questions to settle. The first was whether he could put a fatal dose of potassium cyanide into the compass of a pill of the correct size. The pills in each of his bottles were of the same size, there being of course fewer in the small bottle than in the large. Charles decided to use those in the smaller bottle for examination, so as to avoid fingering those in the other.

The pills were fairly large. Charles weighed a number. The average weight came to five grains. If, therefore, potassium cyanide was anything like the weight of the present contents of the pills, it looked as if he could put in about three grains. Three grains would, he imagined from what he had read in 'Taylor', be amply sufficient to cause the death of a man with so weak a heart as his Uncle Andrew.

So far, so good. He put away the pills and turned to his second question. From the envelopes he had bought he selected two of business shape and different qualities of paper. On that of better quality he typed with the machine he had brought, 'Francis Carswell, Esq., The Dove Cot, Sycamore Avenue, Surbiton', using the black ribbon. Then he put in the old purple ribbon and typed on the other, 'Mr F. Carswell', and the same address.

Next he picked out two square envelopes of different colours. Taking a couple of manuscript letters from his pocket, he set them up before him and practised copying the handwriting. Then he addressed the envelopes to 'Francis Carswell, Esq.' and 'F. Carswell, Esq.' in these two disguised hands. He was not satisfied with the first or the second attempt, but by the time he had destroyed a dozen envelopes his work looked good enough for anything.

To put on the stamps, three of threehalfpence and one of a halfpenny, was an easy matter, but his next business, to forge realistic postmarks, was the hardest thing he had yet struck. With a sample of the Cold Pickerby cancelling stamp before him he designed a similar one for Surbiton and then spent an hour making copy after copy until he had produced something really like the genuine article. He worked with his fine mapping pen and the lampblack, stippling his lines and finally, when almost dry, rolling his hand over the marks. This gave them a suitably smudgy appearance. Then, an expert from so much practice, he produced four not very clear postmarks on his four envelopes.

He now put in sheets of paper and stuck down the three envelopes with the threehalfpenny stamps, turning in the flap of the fourth. Then he kneaded and twisted the envelopes, rubbed them lightly on the carpet tore them roughly open and took out and replaced their contents. All this removed their pristine freshness and gave them the somewhat worn appearance of letters which have been through the post.

Charles was exceedingly pleased with his work. He felt that only the use of a lens could indicate the forgery. Finally he mixed the four envelopes with a sheaf of other papers and put them in his pocket.

It was now nearly three in the morning, but there was still something to be done. Picking up his Surbiton directory, he set himself to learn off the names and addresses of the doctors and a few of the principal men of the town, as well as the occupants of the houses in Sycamore Avenue immediately adjoining the Dove Cot. This occupied another hour, then he tumbled into bed and slept the sleep usually attributed to the just.

Next morning he began with a visit to Cook's. He was in need of a holiday, say for about three weeks. Perhaps a cruise… What would Messrs Cook suggest?

Messrs Cook, through the mouth of a junior clerk, suggested a cruise to the northern capitals. Charles thought he should not agree too readily. The holiday was to be the thing, not the getting away from this country. He therefore demurred about the northern capitals. He had been to most of them already. Besides he wanted the sun. Had they nothing to the Mediterranean? No, it wouldn't be too hot for him. There was nothing he loved so much as the heat. He presently left with a small mountain of travel literature, having given his name and said he would ring up when he had come to a decision.

He returned to his hotel and ordered a luncheon basket, explaining that on a motor drive he liked to be free to lunch where the scenery was good. Then he paid his bill, got out his car, and left as if on his journey north. Instead, however, he parked at the end of Waterloo Place. Then, taking his kitbag in his hand, he left the car and repeated his evolutions of the previous day. Changing in a street lavatory into the clothes in which he had ordered the visiting cards, he called for and obtained these. Then in another lavatory he changed into the suit of 'Town business clothes' which he had brought from home, and again leaving his suit-case at a cloak-room, he set off on the decisive episode of the scheme.

Starting at Waterloo, as if he had come from Surbiton, he went into the first chemist's he came to in the direction of the City.

'I'm bothered with wasps' nests in my garden down at Surbiton,' he said. 'Can you give me a little potassium cyanide to destroy them?'

The chemist hesitated. 'I'm afraid, sir,' he answered civilly, 'I can't oblige you in that. We're not allowed to sell poisons of that description to anyone who is not personally known to us. It's the law and we'd be rather seriously in for it if it were found out.'

Charles simulated mild surprise. 'I didn't know things were as strict as that,' he declared. 'I thought if I signed a book it would be all right. I suppose then my name is not enough?' He handed over one of his new cards and at the same time put his hand in his pocket and drew out the sheaf of papers he had prepared. Looking through these in a casual way, he exhibited one by one the four envelopes.

The chemist was evidently impressed. However, he was not impressed to the extent of meeting his customer's wishes. He much regretted his inability to oblige. He personally would willingly have handed over the stuff, but the law was the law and he had to keep himself right. He went on to say that potassium cyanide was not necessary to destroy wasps' nests and recommended petrol.

Charles had not thought of petrol, but he was delighted at the idea. It would save all trouble, as he had petrol in his garage. He would certainly try it and he was much obliged to the chemist for the hint. The chemist seemed relieved that the purchase had not been pressed, and they parted amicably.

At the next chemist's a similar scene was enacted. He received politeness and regrets, but no potassium cyanide. And so at the third. And the fourth. And the fifth.

Charles was beginning to think his grand scheme was doomed to failure and he began to weigh the possibilities of getting the stuff through a photographer or for photographic purposes. However, he wouldn't despair so easily. He turned into his sixth chemist's.

This was a small dark shop, more old-fashioned and less tidy than those he had previously tried. A thin old man with spectacles and a stoop came forward. He was alone in the shop and Charles judged him to be the proprietor. Charles put his question.

'Well, you know, sir,' the man returned, 'we're not supposed to sell poison to people who are not known to us. How much would you want?'

This sounded hopeful. Charles was careful to be off-hand.

'Oh, I don't know,' he said. 'A very little. Whatever you think it would take.'

As he spoke he handed over one of the cards. 'There's no question as to my identity,' he said with a smile, drawing out his sheaf of papers and exhibiting letter after letter.

The old man looked doubtful. For a few moments he hesitated and then, with a kind of would-be carelessness, asked, 'Do you happen to know Dr Davis?'

This was one of the names Charles had learnt on the previous night, or rather that morning. Fortunately he remembered the doctor's address.

'Of Eden Road?' he answered. 'Only slightly. My own doctor is Dr Jennifer of 25 St Kilda Terrace.'

The chemist had evidently some nodding acquaintance with Surbiton, and this did the trick.

'That will be all right, sir,' he said with a relieved air. 'If you will please sign the poison book, I'll give you the stuff.'

As he filled up the entries and added a bold signature, 'Francis Carswell', Charles became conversational. He talked of gardens and of wasps and of heather and of commons and of good and bad fruit years, anything to prevent a return to the subject of Surbiton, which might so easily have had disastrous consequences. Two minutes later he left the shop with in his waistcoat pocket a little tin box containing an ounce of a hard whitish compound. The box was labelled with a red label, 'Potassium Cyanide. POISON.'

'You'll please be very careful of it, Mr Carswell,' said the chemist. 'It's dangerous stuff to get about.'

'I certainly shall,' Charles returned pleasantly, 'and many thanks for your warning.'

'My worst fence!' Charles said to himself delightedly, as in a leisurely way he walked out of the shop. The getting of the poison in an absolutely untraceable way was undoubtedly his major difficulty.

As he had so successfully overcome it, he was satisfied he could easily do all the rest. With his sanguine temperament he looked upon his uncle's thousands as already transferred to his own pocket; upon his business as saved; upon Una as definitely won.

Charles found that these activities had consumed more time than he had anticipated. It was now after twelve and he wanted to be home at a reasonable time. He hurried to the cloak-room in which he had left his suit-case, retrieved it, changed into his normal attire as Charles Swinburn, and returned to the car park. Five minutes later he was threading the streets on his way to the Great North Road. Three times he stopped before he left Town – at a grocer's, a chemist's, and a garage, where he bought respectively a small bag of best quality sifted sugar, some French chalk, and a tin of petrol.

To complete his work in London Charles had now only to get rid of his tools: the visiting cards and plate, the four envelopes addressed to Carswell, the two volumes of 'Taylor', and the clothes he had worn while carrying out his secret purchases. Before he could be safe these must be destroyed.

As soon therefore as he had left the outskirts of the city behind, he forsook the Great North Road, turning into a narrow lane which wound aimlessly through the pleasantly wooded country. He wanted to reach a secluded place where he could make a fire without either being observed or endangering the vegetation.

He found it more difficult than he had expected, but at last, after wasting the greater part of one of his precious hours, he came on the very place. It was a disused sand pit and he was able to drive right into it, the car then being hidden from the road. Behind a protecting heap of sand the ground was blackened where workmen or picnickers had had their fires. Charles figuratively pounced on it.

Saturated with petrol, the cards and clothes vanished almost instantaneously. But the two large books proved a different proposition. Charles spent quite a time turning them over with sticks and opening the pages to let the air in. At last, however, they were reduced to flaky ashes.

The plate for the visiting cards now only was left. With the car screwdriver Charles scraped out the lettering, and buried the plate beneath some trees in a spot which looked as if it hadn't been disturbed for centuries. Then restarting his car, he worked his way back to the Great North Road and settled down to a spell of the fastest running of which he and the car were capable.

He managed to eat his lunch while the car was in motion, save for a few seconds at the end when he mixed himself a drink. He did without tea altogether. On all possible parts of the road he kept his speedometer needle about fifty. For one stretch of four miles it never went below sixty and once near the bottom of a long hill it touched seventy.

As he drew near his own country he gradually reduced his speed. It would not do to be seen going unusually fast by anyone who knew him. His story would be that he had spent the whole day in driving slowly down, and there must be nothing to give the lie to his statement.

With all his haste, however, he was unable to reach the works before they closed, though he got home in time for dinner. He rang up Gairns at once, explaining that he had taken it too easy along the road and asking if anything of importance had come in. There was nothing.

That evening, tired as he was, he could not resist tackling the next item of his plan. Locking the door of his bedroom, he settled down to teach himself how to make pills. This was where his Martindale &

Westcott's *Extra Pharmacopoeia* came in. There was a section on the subject and he had only to read it up.

Presently he got to work. With a little water he dissolved some of his sifted sugar into a thick, honey-like liquid. To this he added French chalk till the resulting compound grew fairly stiff. He had provided himself with a small quantity of clay. Now he rolled himself a few pellets and began trying to coat them with his compound.

He found it easy enough to get the coating on, but not so easy to give it the hard, shiny surface of the genuine pills. However, he persevered with his experiments, rolling his manufactures about on a sheet of tin which he warmed over a spirit-lamp. Gradually the coating grew harder and smoother till it really became quite like the machine-made article. At last he thought his results were good enough.

Then, drawing on a pair of rubber gloves, he took a small chunk of potassium cyanide from his precious little tin box. This he carefully trimmed with his penknife till it was the right size and shape, allowing for the coating of chalk.

The pilule shaped, he weighed it with his chemical balance. He was well pleased with the result. It weighed over three grains, which according to 'Taylor' was an ample amount for his purpose.

He next began rolling on the sugar and chalk. The mixture adhered to the cyanide as it had to the clay, and soon Charles had a realistic pill. It was perhaps not quite so glossy as those in his bottle, but he was satisfied that the difference would not be noticed.

He put it away and then opened his large bottle of pills, the one of the size his uncle used. Working with extreme care, he poured out of it sufficient pills to bring the surface of the remainder to the same level in the bottle as that he had seen in his uncle's. Finally he emptied these remaining pills out on to the table, and counted them. There were seventy-six.

It was on Thursday, the 17th, that Charles had lunched at The Moat and seen the bottle. That was six days ago, and on each of those days Andrew Crowther had presumably taken three pills. By now, therefore, the number should have been reduced by eighteen to fifty-eight. That was to say that in nineteen days from now the bottle should be finished. If the poisoned pill were put near the bottom, the old man would take it in about a fortnight.

This would suit Charles admirably. By then he hoped to be a thousand miles away from the country. A three weeks' cruise would just meet the case.

Still working in his gloves, Charles replaced a couple of layers of pills in the bottle. Then trying his masterpiece, he found it hard and dry. He therefore dropped it in, and on it the rest of the fifty-eight. Very carefully he wedged the bottle upright in his waistcoat pocket.

He realized how disastrous it would be if the remaining potassium cyanide were found in his possession. He therefore dissolved it and poured the solution down the drain of his wash-basin. The tin box he put in his pocket, to be thrown away first thing on the following morning.

There still remained one preliminary matter to be attended to – the changing of his bottle of pills with that of his uncle. His idea was that he would palm his own, distract Andrew Crowther's attention, rapidly set down his own bottle, and palm the other in its place. It was with this in mind that he had bought the book on sleight of hand. He now began to read it up.

He soon found that any attempt at palming was out of the question. It was, he learned, a difficult achievement, only to be attained by long practice. For him to try it meant disaster.

But he was encouraged by the author's next remark, namely, that palming was unnecessary except for certain small sleight of hand tricks. An open exchange of small articles could be made, if only the attention of the audience were directed elsewhere. The essence of tricks of this kind, went on the book, was in their build-up of 'business' and 'patter'. Something else should be done at the moment of the exchange upon which the attention of all would be concentrated. Then the essential movements would be lost.

For another hour Charles wearily pondered this advice, and then at last he thought he saw his way. He could now go to bed. If opportunity were afforded him on the morrow, or rather on that day, for it was long past midnight, he would be ready to act.

CHAPTER X

Charles Burns His Boats

WHEN CHARLES GOT UP THAT MORNING HE FELT WELL SATIS-
fied with his progress. He had now only to exchange the
bottles of pills and the horrible affair would be complete and he could
get away on his cruise.

Having crushed into a shapeless little block of tin the box which
had contained the poison, he threw it into the Gayle on his way to
the works. His next step was to obtain an invitation to a meal at The
Moat. With this in view he rang up his uncle shortly before lunch.

'I've got some good news for you, uncle,' he began as cheerily as
he could. But for the moment he could not go on. Unexpectedly he
experienced a painful revulsion of feeling. He had always ridiculed the
idea of conscience, but the effort to be cheery now made something
very like conscience grip him. He felt he simply could not talk in an
easy, friendly way to this old man, whose life he meditated taking.
Suddenly he got a glimpse of what he was really doing, and he felt a
little sick. He felt dirty also, somehow soiled, as if he were a traitor,
about to stab his trusting friend in the back. For a moment Charles
hesitated, wondering if this was the first tiny indication that he was
going to have to pay for his action. Then he thought of his works
and his workers, of Matthews with his motherless children, of old
Gairns without a job, of himself without a job, of Una. As he did so
he hardened his heart. In the same cheery way he went on: 'I've managed to get hold of some money. I want to tell you about it. Could I
see you if I were to come out some time?'

Andrew Crowther sounded less cynical than usual as he replied that he was pleased to hear the news. He added that, as Charles knew, he was not over-occupied, and he would be glad to see him any time. What about tea to-day or to-morrow?

Tea was not what Charles wanted. He therefore said he was occupied in the afternoons, but that if it would suit his uncle he would go out after dinner on the following evening. 'That is, if you're going to be alone, uncle. I can't talk about money if you've company.'

This produced the desired reaction. Andrew answered that they were alone and that Charles might as well come to dinner. Charles hesitated to the correct extent, then said he would be delighted.

Well, that was that. Charles must now settle about his absence from the neighbourhood. He saw that while he must not hurry away immediately, he must leave reasonably soon. To-morrow would be Friday, the 25th. Suppose he were to start on the Tuesday or Wednesday of the following week?

He turned to Messrs Cook's advertisements, which he had displayed prominently on his desk when he came in. At once he saw the very thing.

The Purple Star Line were running a twenty-one-day cruise with their 25,000-ton boat, the *Jupiter*. It was a round trip from Marseilles to Marseilles, calling at Villefranche, Genoa, Naples, Messina, Malta, Tunis, Algiers, and Barcelona. Passengers left London on Wednesday, the 30th. If he succeeded in changing the bottles next day he would go on this cruise. In fact he might begin preparations at once. If the trip fell through he could announce a change of plans.

'I'll be off on Wednesday,' he therefore said to Gairns, when a little later the chief clerk put a deprecating head round the office door. 'A sea trip for three weeks. This money business has upset me, and I feel stale. But now that things are all right again I think

I may treat myself to a holiday. As a matter of fact I hadn't one last year.'

Gairns was delighted, as delighted as if he had himself been going. Now that his ghastly dread of poverty was removed, all was well in this superlatively excellent world. Mr Charles was certainly entitled to his holiday. He had worked hard and saved them all.

Charles found that time dragged more slowly than he could have believed possible during the remainder of that day and the next. His nerves were on edge and he could settle to nothing. His reaction to his dreadful enterprise kept on altering. Sometimes he felt that he was carrying through a necessary, if not indeed a meritorious, action – obtaining the gain of the many at the expense of the one. At others he glimpsed the result to himself: that for the rest of his life he would have to carry the knowledge of his guilt, and the lurking dread that somehow something would become known. It was a relief when seven o'clock next evening came, and his period of inaction was at an end.

There were just the four of them at dinner – Charles, Andrew Crowther, Mrs Pollifex, and Margot. Andrew was in one of his good moods. He seemed better in every way – brighter, less maudlin, and with more of a grip on things. He was less lost in his own thoughts, and took a part in the conversation more in his old way.

Penelope Pollifex and her daughter were also in good form. Mrs Pollifex exerted herself to make the meal a success, and Margot for once forbore to be superior and discontented.

Only Charles found it impossible to be natural. Try as he would he simply could not behave as if nothing unusual were on his mind. In fact, he thought it advisable to call attention to his health. 'I'm off for a holiday next week,' he said when a suitable break came in the conversation. 'I didn't have one last year, and I've been feeling a bit fed-up with things lately. Three weeks I expect to be away.'

They were interested and plied him with questions. He detailed the itinerary, and the reasons why he preferred to go south rather than north.

'I envy you,' Mrs Pollifex declared. 'There are one or two places on your list to which I've never been and which I've always wanted to visit. Capri, for instance. Shall you have time for it?'

'Yes; we've three days in Naples, enough for Capri and Sorrento, Vesuvius and Pompeii, and for either the town of Naples or Baiae and Pozzuoli, whichever one likes.'

'Naples and Pompeii I know, but not Capri. Some day I must do it.'

Charles had a sudden idea. Could he manage to get his aunt to accompany him? If so, it would upset the household at The Moat and would make more reasonable the verdict of suicide which he hoped would be found.

'What about coming along, aunt?' he said with genuine heartiness; 'you and Margot? It would do you both good and you'd like it no end. There are pretty sure to be cabins left. Uncle Andrew wouldn't mind for once. Would you, uncle?'

Mrs Pollifex demurred, though he could see she was pleased at being asked. 'I don't think I could manage it now,' she said. 'I'd rather go later if I went at all. The heat knocks me up. And Margot is going to Scotland in a fortnight. Lady Skye has asked her to their shooting-lodge near Dalwhinnie. Another time, perhaps, Charles, thank you very much.'

'It'll not be so hot on the sea,' Charles persisted, 'and couldn't Margot postpone her visit for a week? It would be pleasant for me to have someone I knew on board.'

They would not agree, however. Only for the Scottish invitation Margot would have jumped at it, but the glamour of being a guest of the Countess of Skye evidently outshone a mere trip to the Mediterranean.

As dinner drew to an end and the decisive moment came nearer, Charles grew more and more uneasy and excited. He had taken rather more wine than usual, and this to some extent quieted his nerves. He believed his manner had not shown anything more than was accounted for by his plea of overwork. However, for the next hour or two he must pull himself together and keep his head. Everything depended on how he did so.

At last the ladies left the dining-room. Andrew was sitting at the head of the table and Charles at his right hand. Charles had foreseen this arrangement, as he knew that Margot sat on the old man's left. Now he filled up his uncle's glass and moved slightly nearer. They began to talk.

'I told you, uncle, that I had managed to raise some money,' Charles led off. 'It was very simple and I don't know why I didn't do it long ago. I've popped the pictures.'

'Your father's pictures? I'm sorry to hear that, Nephew Charles; sorry to hear that. I remember' – the old man leant back and became reminiscent – 'I remember your father buying the first, as well as if it was yesterday. They wanted two-fifty for it, and it seemed to him a huge price. He spoke to me about it, and I said – eh – I said: "Pay the money, Henry. It'll be an investment and it'll always be there if you want it." I was right, but – er – not in the way I thought.'

'You were – absolutely right. I was sorry about having to get rid of them, too, but it's only temporarily. With any reasonable luck I'll get them back when things improve. I don't want you to repeat this, uncle.'

'Is it likely?' Andrew returned, with more of an approach to his ordinary manner. 'I'm not so overwhelmed with pride at my nephew's actions as to wish to blazon them about the country. No, Charles, I'll keep it hidden as I would a case of cheating at cards. Not that I suggest you would do such a thing. But all the same I'm disappointed. I think you might have done better than you have.'

At another time Charles might have felt annoyed by this plain speaking, but now it acted like a tonic to him. Every word of this kind the old man uttered made his task the easier. Once again Charles felt a wave of bitterness sweep over him. If his uncle had only acted with reasonable decency, this horrible enterprise into which he had been forced would have been unnecessary. Well, Andrew had only himself to thank. Charles hardened his heart.

As he did so his attack of nerves passed away, and he became calm and cool and efficient. And it was well, for now at last the moment was upon him. Andrew was taking his bottle of pills from his pocket. He opened it, slowly and deliberately – all the better, as it gave Charles time to do his part. As Andrew opened his bottle, so did Charles open his – under the table. Charles held it in the palm of his right hand, with the stopper towards his wrist. With his left hand he took a prepared piece of paper from his pocket. He waited, talking slowly about the money.

Andrew shook out two or three pills on to the tablecloth, just as he had done before. Then he stood the bottle upright on the table, and began picking up and replacing all but one. This was Charles's moment. He must act now before Andrew picked up the bottle.

'Here are the exact figures,' he said, stretching out his left hand with the sheet of paper.

He did it with careful carelessness. His hand caught Andrew's wineglass and turned it over towards Andrew. The red wine flowed across the table and down on to Andrew's knees.

'Oh, uncle, I am so sorry,' Charles cried, and the agitation in his voice at least was genuine. He sprang to his feet, and leaning his right hand on the table near the bottle of pills, contrived with that hand to set down his own bottle and pick up his uncle's, while with the left he caught the empty wineglass and set it up on its base. In a moment Andrew's bottle was in his pocket, and with his handkerchief he was attempting to dry the wine off Andrew's trousers.

'I'd better ring for Weatherup, hadn't I?' he went on, while he continued to apologize for his clumsiness.

Andrew made light of the affair. Weatherup came in at once and cleared up the mess, wiping the old man's trousers, putting a clean napkin over the stain on the cloth, and drying the little pool on the carpet. Then when the excitement was over Andrew took up the bottle of pills and its screw cap.

Charles suddenly had a bad moment. Suppose the bottles were not made to an absolute standard? Suppose the cap would not fit?

But the cap went on perfectly. Andrew screwed it down and put the bottle in his pocket, obviously having suspected nothing. Charles gave an inaudible sigh, and surreptitiously dried some little beads of moisture off his forehead.

'You were going to show me some figures?' said Andrew, and the incident was over.

Over? Or was it just beginning?

How Charles got through the remainder of that evening he never knew. His talk with Andrew Crowther seemed to him a ghastly nightmare. And when presently they moved into the drawing-room, things were little better. It was only with a supreme effort that Charles forced himself to remain till the old man went to bed shortly before ten. Then he made his excuses and drove home.

He was now in a position to settle the matter of the cruise. When he reached his office next morning he put through a telephone call to Messrs Cook. Five-and-twenty minutes later he had reserved a single cabin on B deck, at a cost of sixty-five guineas, including shore excursions and rail fares.

That afternoon he was to have another decisive interview – an interview indeed to which he looked forward with somewhat mixed feelings. It was Saturday, and he was going to the Crosbys for tennis. There he would meet Una.

Normally a meeting with Una was a somewhat chequered slice of heaven. With Una in a 'good' mood it was heaven. Una, however, was not always in a good mood, and then the heaven was chequered. This occasion, moreover, was not normal. He had not seen her since she had come very close to cutting him outside Oliver's shop in Malton Road. He wondered how she would greet him this time.

Crosby, dressed in flannels, was standing on the steps of The Ingle, his pleasant Queen Anne house, as Charles drew up at the door. He was a man of about sixty, dry and precise, as is supposed to befit his calling. He was solicitor to most of the older families in the district. Amongst his clients was Andrew Crowther, though Charles gave his business to a more modern firm. This, however, Crosby recognized as reasonable, seeing that the interests of uncle and nephew might not always coincide. Crosby was a good fellow, straight and hard-working, and was universally liked and respected.

'Hallo, Charles,' he said with a twisted smile. 'Glad to see you. Jones and the two Hallams have cried off, and we're short of men.'

Charles grinned. 'Glad I have some value,' he returned, 'even if it's not personal.'

'Don't be so beastly conceited,' Crosby advised. 'I didn't suggest you had any value. And so you're off for a holiday?'

'Now just how did you know that? I only fixed it up this morning.'

'Ah – a little bird. One bird, little, pretty: to wit, your cousin Margot. Met her outside the office this morning.'

'I dined there last night. I mean, at The Moat, not outside your beastly office. Yes, since you mention it, I'm going for three weeks.'

'And what about the business while you're away?'

'Oh, I'll leave Gairns and Macpherson in charge. There's not such a frightful lot doing just now, worse luck.'

Crosby grew confidential and, Charles thought, questioning also.

'You'll forgive me, Charles,' he said, 'but as an old friend of your family's I'd like to say how glad I am that there was nothing in those rumours about your business.'

Charles thought rapidly. If any question were afterwards to arise, Crosby must not suspect him. He also grew confidential.

'I'm not so sure that there was nothing in them, Crosby,' he returned. 'As a matter of fact, very strictly for your ears alone, I may admit I've been approaching stony. I've wanted some new machines and I've not seen my way to get them. But I think I'm all right now. I told the uncle and he gave me a thousand. I've popped my pictures also and I'm getting the machines. The placing of the order is only waiting on getting some minor details.'

'I'm glad of that, very glad. Your uncle hasn't mentioned it to me, but I expect he will. And so the holiday? Well, I expect you deserve it.'

'I'll be glad of a change,' Charles admitted. 'I've felt a bit fed-up lately.'

Charles had come to The Ingle early so as to be there when Una arrived, but when he and his host reached the tennis-court he saw to his surprise that she was already there. A set had just been made up, and she was walking with her partner to the net. She waved her racket when she saw him, and the sight gladdened Charles's heart. It was the cheery, friendly wave he had hoped for. Heaven for this afternoon was not going to be chequered.

It was, however, largely non-existent. Whether owing to sheer bad luck or to Una's skilful contriving, he found it extraordinarily hard to get a word with her. There was only one court, and when the set was coming to an end another was made up in which he was a player. The sides were evenly matched and the new set developed into an interminable contest in which the games fell to each side alternately. When it was at last finished, Una was having tea in the centre of a large group, and Charles felt as far from her as if he had already reached the Mediterranean.

It was only when they were preparing to leave that he was able to speak to her and then it was only for a moment. But at least it was wholly satisfactory. She smiled in her old way.

'Hallo, Charles,' she said, and he hung on her words. 'So you're off to the Mediterranean? I'm so glad. You've been looking seedy and you want a change.'

'If only you were coming, Una,' he answered with earnestness if without originality. 'I'm going on living in hope that sometimes we—'

'S-h-h-h!' she silenced him. 'None of that! Perhaps when you come back we may talk about it, though I don't promise. There, go and take those Bentham girls home. Their car's broken down.'

'But what about you, Una?'

'My darling idiot, I got here without you and I can surely get home again. I have the small Austin.'

That was all, but as she turned to speak to Mrs Crosby she gave him a look which made up for everything. With his heart singing, Charles turned to offer transport to the two stout Benthams.

Though Charles had a good deal of extra work to get through in preparing for his absence, the next three days dragged interminably. Fears haunted him, nameless fears of discovery, as also the definite fear that Andrew might shake up the bottle and take the deadly pill before he, Charles, got away. He put Gairns and Macpherson in charge of their respective departments, giving them a free hand and adjuring them to consult together before taking any step. 'Here are my addresses,' he told Gairns. 'If anything crops up you can send me a wire.'

In spite of Charles's fears, nothing untoward took place before he left. Things at The Moat went on as usual, and on Wednesday morning Charles was driven to the station and took the local train for York, where he would board the London express. He reached Town in time to catch the 2 P.M. boat-train from Victoria. As the express pulled slowly across the Thames some of his dread vanished. He was at least away from Cold Pickerby. Before he returned his fate would be settled, one way or another.

CHAPTER XI

Charles Achieves His Object

THE CHANNEL SMILED ON CHARLES AS HE CROSSED IT THAT afternoon, and the blue carriages, standing on the wharf at Boulogne, seemed to him friendly and reassuring, like an ark of sorely needed refuge. With a sigh of relief, he climbed on board and settled down for his twenty-two hour run.

It was dusk when they reached the Gare du Nord in Paris, and dark when, after finishing their leisurely course round the Ceinture, they left the P.L.M. station. Charles was in bed within a few minutes of the start and asleep before they passed Fontainebleau. Once or twice he woke during the night, usually when the train stopped in some station, and for a time the whole world seemed dead. At Mâcon it was light, and when they crossed the Rhône out of the Perrache station at Lyons he thought it time to get up.

All that morning as they worked down the Rhône Charles tried to keep his attention on the passing landscape and to forget the horror from which he was flying. At Vienne and Valence he watched eagerly for the glimpses of the river which he believed he had seen on previous journeys. At Orange he recalled the great wall of the Roman theatre and tried to picture what a representation must have been like in the days of the emperors. Avignon, which he knew well, set him dreaming of medieval pomp: of jousts, of knights, of Papal splendour, and of besiegers camped outside those walls which the train was now encircling. Then came Tarascon. Once he had been in the château and he began to recall his impressions, when, suddenly remembering that it is still used as a prison, he shuddered and thought hurriedly of something else. Arles reminded him of Grecian women, of the arena with its marvellous dry stonework, its former tragedies and its present bull-fights, and of the great Roman theatre. Then they dropped to the interminable infertile Plaine de la Crau, passed the end of the Étang de Berre, and after winding through the tunnel and rocks of La Nerte, swung down the incline into Marseilles.

By four o'clock Charles was on board the *Jupiter*. She certainly fulfilled the claims of the advertisement as to super-luxury. Charles had never seen rooms of such proportions on any ship as were the lounge and great dining-hall. Indeed he had never seen longer corridors, ampler deck spaces, roomier cabins, and richer decoration. Everything, in fact, was there except the sea, of which there was nothing to suggest the presence. It was true that from the deck and certain of the port-holes it could be seen, insignificant and very far down, but it was obviously a factor which did not enter into the lives of the passengers. For the matter of that, there was nothing to suggest that these crowds of people on board were passengers. They gave Charles the impression of visitors staying in this very huge hotel.

She was not sailing, if such an expression could be applied to the *Jupiter*, till midnight, and though Charles did not care for Marseilles, he joined the trio at his table in an excursion to a music-hall ashore. It filled up the evening and kept him from thinking.

Contrary to his expectation, he slept well, and when he looked out of his window next morning – on B deck there were no port-holes – he recognized the little village of Villefranche. Villefranche he knew and loved. He thought it one of the most beautiful places, if not the most beautiful place, on the whole Riviera. As he went on deck and feasted his eyes on the view, he almost forgot that he was not there for holiday and pleasure, but as part of a scheme which he now knew that he loathed with all the strength of his being.

For two days the *Jupiter* lay at Villefranche. Various excursions had been arranged, and Charles joined those to Peira Cava and Sospel, having done the Corniche on different previous occasions and hating Monte Carlo. His incipient friendship with his table companions had grown rapidly, as they will. The leading light was a young middle-aged widow named Shearman. Mrs Shearman seemed to take a fancy to Charles, and before long he found himself telling her something of his life and his hopes of Una.

'Do you know,' she said, 'I guessed you had something on your mind. My friend, Mrs Cardew, and I agreed about it. Not that we were discussing you, but we did say that. "He's got something on his mind," I said, and she said, "Yes, I've noticed that, too. You couldn't mistake it." You wouldn't make a good criminal, Mr Swinburn, so don't ever try crime.' She laughed carelessly and changed the subject.

Charles was a good deal upset. He did not follow to the new subject.

'When you've gone so far,' he said, 'I must tell you why I'm here. I've not been well. I've had something wrong with my nerves and I've come away for a change. It's nothing serious, you know, but I want to get cured. Forgive me talking so much about myself, but you've really asked for it.'

She made a conventional reply and the matter dropped, but from that moment Charles never felt quite easy in her company. At the same time he didn't dare to break away from her party, lest this should provoke remark.

Two days later another tiny incident occurred which worried him even more. They had left Villefranche and put in at Genoa.

Charles and Mrs Shearman both knew Genoa city, though not its surroundings, and they joined three or four others in an excursion to Rapallo, Santa Margherita, and Portofino. It was at Rapallo that the thing happened.

They had finished lunch at an hotel and were sitting in its garden in the shade of some palms when Mrs Shearman gave a sudden cry. 'Sir Francis! Is that possibly Sir Francis?'

A slim man, with heavy eyelids and a tired manner, looked round and came across with outstretched hand.

'Mrs Shearman, by all that's wonderful! Where on earth did you spring from?'

'Same to you,' the lady returned, smiling.

'I? Oh, I'm here on business for my sins. At least not in Rapallo. I had to go to Rome on business, and I'd never been here, so I simply stopped on my way home. Are you staying here?'

She told him, and introduced Charles and one or two more of the party who were sitting near. Sir Francis sat down, and they smoked and chatted till it was time for the *Jupiter* party to leave.

'Do you know who that was?' Mrs Shearman asked as they turned up the gorgeous winding road over the Portofino promontory towards Ruta and Genoa. 'That was Sir Francis Smythe.' Charles wondered if she hesitated for a moment before adding, 'He's got some job in the police.'

Whether she hesitated or not, Charles thought she watched him rather closely while she made the statement. He couldn't be sure: she had looked at him, but he couldn't tell with what significance. Was there indeed the suspicion of a smile trembling on her lips? Charles wished he knew.

He was a good deal upset that his nerves should be under such poor control. He must be careful. If he began to imagine things it could only end in disaster. With an effort he pulled himself together and chatted adequately during the drive back to Genoa.

As they got nearer the *Jupiter* the great anxiety of his day began to obsess him. They had been out only four days and each evening his excitement on reaching the ship had been greater. On one of these evenings there would be a telegram. He found it hard to talk coolly and hang back as they climbed the ship's ladder. He wanted to run to see what was awaiting him.

When, as hitherto, he found there was nothing, he was filled with a strange mixture of relief and disappointment. Relief that the ghastly thing had not yet happened; disappointment that another long day of waiting was before him. For Charles was not really enjoying his delightful surroundings. For an easy mind he would gladly have exchanged them for the slums of Leeds or the wastes of Labrador.

They sailed from Genoa after dinner, watching from the deck the beautiful city slowly fade into the pearl-grey distance. The last thing they saw was the occulting eye of the Portofino lighthouse, to which they had walked earlier in the day.

Next morning they were out of sight of land, having passed Corsica and Elba in the night. Sometimes during the day they saw hills away in the distance on the port side, and occasionally there were islands, also far away. The usual games fiends put in an early appearance, and Charles for once welcomed them.

Shortly after tea they raised more islands right ahead, with above them a rather solid-looking mass of white cloud. At once people dropped their games and their books and their flirtations and went forward to the rail to look. For that big island was Ischia, at the edge of the Bay of Naples, and beneath that cloud of steamy smoke was Vesuvius.

They anchored in the harbour just as the dressing-bell went. Charles had not been to Naples before, and even his preoccupation could not prevent his being lost in admiration of the lovely bay.

In the harbour the view was obscured by piers and buildings and shipping. But just before they entered they got a magnificent panorama of the whole coast. To the left was the hill and cape of Posilipo, with its palms and olives and cypresses, screening the fine villas of the wealthy Neapolitans. In front was the city, stretching up to the heights behind, from this distance white and fair. Then to the right the great double-coned mass of Vesuvius rose, with its almost solid column of smoke thrusting fiercely up into the blue sky. It somehow suggested power, that column, white in the mass, but flecked at intervals with the yellow of sulphur and the red of flame. It poured up in seething eddies, gradually bending over as it rose and shifting slowly inland. Beyond Vesuvius the long line of the Sorrento peninsula stretched into the sea, with farther out, dead astern as they circled into the harbour, the high, jagged outlines of the island of Capri. Charles was tremendously impressed. At the same time he thought the Bay was too big for perfection. A closer view of those distant shores would have been lovelier still.

Both Charles and Mrs Shearman preferred the masterpieces of Nature to the handiwork of men. They therefore cut the visit to the city and took instead excursions to its surroundings for the whole three days of their stay. On the first they made the ascent of Vesuvius and wandered through wonderful Pompeii; on the second they visited Capri, touching for a short time at Sorrento on the way back, and the third they spent along the coast to the north of Naples, at Pozzuoli and Baiae. It was on this third day that another of those trifling incidents occurred which so greatly worried Charles.

They had gone to see the Solfatara, a dreadful place which might well have given ideas to Dante. The Solfatara is the crater of a volcano, which, though it has not been in eruption for seven hundred years, is by no means completely extinct. The crater is now floored by a lake of solidified mud, entirely infertile and destitute of vegetation. Only an extraordinarily thin crust can be solidified, for every here and there are holes or mouths in the ground, filled only four or five feet down with hot liquid mud which occasionally seethes as it reaches the boiling-point. The floor of the lake sounds hollow, and one has the impression that it shakes when one steps on it. The ground everywhere is hot and the whole place is like an evil dream.

It was while they were crossing the mud floor that Mrs Shearman made the remark which so upset Charles.

'My goodness,' she said, 'what a place! If I wanted to commit a murder, this is where I should do it. I should offer my victim a drink of some drugged wine, and when he was partly helpless I should give him a push into one of those holes! How would you commit a murder, Mr Swinburn?'

Once again it was not the words, but the possible intention which lay behind them that gave Charles a cold shock. In spite of himself he glanced at her. Were the words as innocent as they sounded? Was she testing – suspicions?

He did not see any signs of it in her manner or appearance. But, then, you never can tell. Women were the deuce. Born actresses, every one of them. With a man you would know where you were. But with women…

However, whether she was testing suspicions or not, she must not receive any confirmation. It took all Charles's resolution, but he made a joke. He changed the subject with a joke, and she made no attempt to return to it. She had, he felt sure, meant nothing.

Still there was the terribly disquieting fact that at the mere mention of murder or police or Scotland Yard, he was seized with a feeling of panic which, if not curbed, must inevitably sooner or later give him away. For the thousandth time he told himself that he *must* get over this disastrous tendency.

How he wished the thing would happen! The suspense he was now experiencing was nerve-racking. He couldn't, he felt, stand it for long. If only the thing were over and he knew where he was! And yet he needn't worry. His plan was perfect and he was as safe as if he had already been acquitted of the crime.

That last evening of the stay in Naples Charles felt the same anxiety, almost pain, gripping his heart as they returned to the *Jupiter*. This time, however, he forced himself not to hurry for his letters. He stayed on deck for quite five minutes, chatting to some people who had that day done the Capri trip. Then he went below.

It was there! A radiogram was handed to him. He thanked the officer and turned away. He would read it in the solitude of his cabin.

When he reached it his hands were shaking so that he could scarcely tear the flimsy envelope. Ah!—

Regret to inform you Uncle Andrew died suddenly yesterday while on journey to Paris. Am taking remains home.

– Peter.

Charles took his flask and poured himself out a couple of fingers of brandy. He drank it neat.

On journey to Paris! Whatever could that mean? What could have taken his uncle away from The Moat? Now Charles saw that the message had been sent from Beauvais. Beauvais! Beauvais wasn't on the way to Paris. What could have happened?

However, for the moment none of these questions mattered. Here at last was need for action. The dreadful waiting was over. He rang for his steward.

'Just got a wire that I have to leave you,' he said. 'A relative has died in France. I wish you'd shove my things into those suit-cases while I go and arrange matters with the purser.'

The man, scenting a fat tip, was anxious to oblige. 'You'll have to hurry, sir,' he advised. 'We're due to sail almost at once.'

Charles hurried. By a stroke of luck he found the purser in his cabin.

'You're just in time, Mr Swinburn, if you look sharp. Are your things ready?'

'The steward's packing them.'

'Well, he'd better look slippy. I'll let the captain know.' He telephoned to the bridge, then rapidly turned over some books. 'There are a few extras,' he went on. 'You'd better square them now and then apply to the office for a part refund.'

They held the *Jupiter* five minutes to let Charles get ashore and he had to leave without bidding good-bye to his fellow-travellers. He wasn't sorry to see the last of the ship. For all its luxury and its pleasant companionship, he had loathed it.

At the station he found that he was too late to get through to Rome by the direct line that evening, so he took a train by the old route, which crawled about the country during the entire night, arriving in the capital about half-past six the following morning. Fortunately it had sleeping coaches and he was able to get a berth.

In the train he had an opportunity of considering the news he had received. Nothing that he could think of could account for his uncle's journey, and he presently gave up the attempt as hopeless. But there was another matter which, though equally incomprehensible, seemed amazingly good news for himself.

If Peter were taking the body home, did it not follow that no suspicion that the death was otherwise than natural could have arisen? Charles knew nothing about French law, but he felt sure that in cases of doubt some inquiry would be held corresponding to an English coroner's inquest.

If he were correct, it was infinitely more than he could have hoped for. He had never imagined that the question of poison could be avoided. The most he had hoped was that suicide might be assumed, and of this he had been far from sanguine. Could Andrew really have died from natural causes after all and the deadly pill still be reposing in the bottle? Oh, how utterly splendid that would be! That his own conscience should be clear of murder! That he would be safe, *really* safe from arrest! For though Charles continued telling himself that he *was* safe, in his heart of hearts he never fully believed it.

If this amazing piece of good fortune really had befallen him, it must be his first care to get hold of and destroy that deadly bottle. Then nothing could come out and the whole hideous episode would be blotted out for ever.

Charles left Rome by the 'luxe' at 11.10. The train followed the coast route, and had he been capable of thinking of anything but his own affairs he would have enjoyed the scenery. After passing Pisa and Spezia they ran along the coast of the Ligurian Riviera, past Rapallo, where he had already been. Charming, the views snatched between the numerous tunnels along that picturesque and rocky shore. By the time they reached Genoa it was dark, and shortly afterwards Charles turned in. When he got up they were down on the plains of France near Amberieu, having passed through the Alps during the night.

At Laroche Charles was able to get the Paris morning papers and at once he received the shock which he had been half expecting since he left Naples. The poison had been discovered! He wasn't going to get off in the easy way he had hoped. The case had been handed over to the English police for investigation!

There was only a paragraph, giving just this information and no more. Charles rallied himself. It was only what he had expected. There was no reason to imagine that things from his point of view were not all right.

When he reached Paris the last day service to London had already left and he decided to wait where he was till the next day. He reminded himself that he was going home, not to learn the result of his dreadful scheme, but to pay his last respects to his uncle. To travel without a break from Naples to Yorkshire would therefore be not only unnecessary, but actually indiscreet.

He left next morning by the 8.25, and travelling in a sort of dream, duly reached London. He drove across town and caught the 5.30 express from King's Cross to the north. At York, where he changed into the branch train, he bought a local evening paper. At once he saw that things had been moving.

Under the caption, 'The Death of Mr. Andrew Crowther', appeared the following paragraph:

'This afternoon at Cold Pickerby Dr W. J. Emerson, coroner for the district and sitting with a jury, opened an inquest on the body of Mr Andrew Crowther, The Moat, Cold Pickerby. Mr Crowther will be remembered as one of the founders of the Crowther Electromotor Works of that town. The deceased gentleman died on the 7th inst. in an aeroplane while on a journey from London to Paris, and it was suggested from France that the cause of death might be potassium cyanide poisoning. After a formal identification of the remains by Mr Peter Morley, son-in-law, and the reading of the French depositions, Dr Emerson adjourned the proceedings till the 2nd prox.'

Charles reached home by ten o'clock and drove direct to The Moat. He found Peter there, looking very worried.

'I'm glad you're back, Charles,' Peter greeted him, 'though it was hard lines having to break up your holiday like that. An unexpected affair this! I should have said Andrew Crowther was the last man in the world to have committed suicide.'

So that was the suspicion! Splendid, if it were generally accepted! Charles shook his head, expressing very genuine bewilderment.

'I should say so!' he exclaimed. 'The whole thing is absolutely incomprehensible to me. First that journey to Paris, and by air of all ways! Then his death, and now the suspicion of suicide! I declare, Peter, I can't imagine a bigger puzzle.'

'Of course Charles hasn't heard anything,' Mrs Pollifex remarked. 'Tell him, Peter.'

'It's all very simple,' Peter returned, 'except the last extraordinary item. Elsie went over to Paris to stay with some American friends, whom she hadn't seen for years. Then late one evening we got a wire to say she had been knocked down in the street and was unconscious. I, of course, wanted to go at once, and then the old man said he would come with me. I tried to dissuade him: that sort of hurried travelling is no joke for a man of his health and years. But he would come. He was always pretty fond of Elsie, you know.'

'I know,' said Charles. 'It's not surprising. His only child and she's always been pretty decent to him.'

'Well, he insisted on coming. But your aunt and I were determined he should be examined first, so we asked Dr Gregory to come in and look him over. Gregory was satisfied he would stand the journey. There's some question about the height in a plane affecting the heart, you know. Well, that was all right. We decided that Weatherup should come to look after him. I also went over and brought Rose; she was staying with some friends near Thirsk. You see, we didn't know how badly Elsie might be hurt. She might have wanted to see Rose. Hugh we couldn't get. He was staying with a school friend at Northallerton.'

'Hard lines on you, Peter. It must have been a bad time.'

'It was a bad time till we got to the air station at Victoria. I had arranged for a message to be sent there, and it said Elsie was not badly hurt. However, when we had gone so far, we went on. And then it happened.'

'How?' Charles asked in a low voice.

'We don't know. We had lunch over the Channel, and the old man took a good lunch – as good as usual, Weatherup says. Weatherup was sitting beside him and Rose and I were behind. Then after lunch he seemed to go to sleep. He was leaning back in the corner of his seat with his head up against the wall of the car. I thought he was asleep and so did Weatherup, but when we landed at Beauvais we saw he was dead. I got Rose out of the plane and we sent for a doctor. He took a longer time to make his examination than seemed reasonable, and then we learned the reason. He suspected poison. It was horrible, Charles. The police were called in and there were endless formalities. However, the matter was finally handed over to the English police. An officer was sent for and Inspector Appleby of the local force here came across. I had been allowed to have a coffin made, and everything was ready when Appleby arrived. There was a day to spare while he was getting over – Beauvais is the devil of a place to get to from England; and I took Rose up to Paris and we saw Elsie. Thank God, she was little the worse, and I'm going over shortly to bring her home.'

'I'm glad of that, Peter.'

'I'm sure you are. Well, Appleby arrived in the evening and next day we brought the remains to London; we couldn't get on the same day. But the next day, that was to-day, we arrived here by an early train, and this afternoon the inquest was opened. You saw that it had been adjourned?'

'Yes, I saw that.'

'Well, that's all. The poison, I understand, was potassium cyanide. We don't know how he got it or why he took it. He seemed all right all that morning and was interested in the flying: he'd never been in a plane before.'

'Could the height have had anything to do with it?' Charles asked. 'Upset him or anything?'

'I don't know; it's a complete puzzle to me.'

'Had he been depressed before starting?'

Peter looked at Mrs Pollifex and she answered, 'Well, latterly he had been a little depressed and he certainly was so before leaving. But I don't think more than recently.'

'If he had the poison with him, it looks as if he had had the idea of suicide in his mind for some time.'

Peter nodded. 'I thought of that, Charles, it does. But what an extraordinary time to take it, just when he was looking forward to seeing Elsie! That seems to me the most puzzling point of all.'

Charles nodded in his turn. 'It's inexplicable, the entire affair,' he declared. 'How on earth could he have got the poison, to take one point only?'

'No one can make out,' Peter returned. 'It was the first question I asked myself, but I couldn't answer it.'

'He certainly couldn't have got it recently,' Mrs Pollifex added positively. 'He rarely went into town, and never by himself. Besides, no one would have sold it to him. He must have had it hidden away somewhere for a long time. At least, that's the only way I can account for it.'

'I suppose he must,' Charles agreed, 'though it certainly was not at all like him. And yet I'm not so sure. He was secretive: I suppose most men of his age are.'

Peter agreed. For some moments there was silence, which Charles at last broke. 'And there's no theory as to motive?' he said, more for something to say than in the hope of gaining information.

Peter shook his head, but Mrs Pollifex answered. 'The only possible thing I can think of,' she said hesitatingly, 'though I've never put it forward – is that Andrew might have been excited on the previous evening and that it brought on a reaction next day. That Wednesday evening Peter and Mr Crosby dined here; that is, the evening the wire came from Paris. You and Mr Crosby had some business with Andrew, hadn't you, Peter?'

'Yes,' Peter admitted uneasily. 'It was that question of the mortgage on the farm. We discussed it quite amicably, though nothing was settled about it. But as I told you before, Mrs Pollifex, Mr Crowther was not in the least upset or excited.'

Mrs Pollifex nodded. 'I know. I really only made the suggestion because I couldn't think of anything else. Besides, the dinner was a small excitement compared with the journey.'

Mrs Pollifex had spoken calmly, but her manner showed the strain the affair was causing her. Peter also seemed ill at ease. The tragedy had obviously shaken them both.

'Well, we may get some light at the adjourned inquest,' said Charles. 'When is the funeral?'

'To-morrow at two-thirty.'

'Then I'm just in time. Whom are you going with, Aunt Penelope? Can I take you and Margot?'

'Thanks, but we're going with Peter.'

On the whole Charles was relieved by what he had heard. Though he deplored the publicity due to the tragedy having occurred in the plane, on another point he was delighted. From the first he had recognized that he had to run one serious risk. Andrew might have called attention to the pills or mentioned that spilled wineglass. Though nothing could have been proved, the suggestion would have been very disquieting. But nothing of that kind could now arise. Andrew had died without making a statement. He, Charles, was safe.

And not only was he safe: he was now rich. Not rich, perhaps, as some men count wealth, but rich enough to carry on his works and get his machinery and marry Una – if she would have him. Charles's fears evaporated. Everything was going to be all right. It had been a dreadful, a *loathsome* job, but it was now over. All was well.

CHAPTER XII

Charles Becomes a Spectator

THE NEWS WHICH GREETED CHARLES ON HIS RETURN TO THE works was also good. It seemed that while he was away they had booked no less than four orders. Admittedly none was large. But they represented a fortnight's work for all hands, and though Macpherson had cut the price so that the profit could only be seen through a microscope, there was at least no loss. Charles congratulated him heartily.

'What about the new machines?' he went on. 'Got all that information in from Reading?'

'Aye, it's a' there, and from Sheffield forby.' The engineer pushed forward a little pile of papers. 'I slippit down to Sheffield to see yon,' he went on, marking the illustration of a lathe with a huge thumb. 'Man, it's a bonny tool. It'd do fine for our wor-rk.'

'Better than the Reading people's, you think?' said Charles, turning the papers over.

Macpherson thought so and lapsed into technicalities. His points were sound, as they always were, and Charles agreed with him. 'Well, get the orders out and we'll send them to-day,' he directed, and went on to discuss the new jobs. When he had finished Macpherson hesitated.

'We're a' very sorry aboot your trouble, Mr Charles,' he said awkwardly, 'though I'm thinking we're maybe going to benefit here in the wor-rks. All the same it'll be an upset to you.'

'I would like to say the same,' added Gairns, who had entered while they were talking. 'We're glad of anything that does you good, but sorry for the cause of it.'

Charles thanked them. Though it was true that they also stood to gain by Andrew Crowther's death, he knew that they would have been pleased had he alone benefited.

After an early lunch Charles drove out to The Moat. The funeral was private and only special friends of the deceased, like Crosby, were present. The weather fortunately was fine, and with this mitigation the function dragged out its melancholy course. After it was over Crosby and the members of the family returned to The Moat for the reading of the will.

For Charles there was still an element of anxiety left. Andrew had told him on many occasions that he and Elsie were to be his joint heirs, and Charles had little fear that the old man would have changed his mind. All the same he had seen nothing in writing on the subject, and he could not help being worried by dark thoughts of slips between cups and lips.

Crosby, however, had gone only a little way with his reading before Charles saw that his fears were groundless. The will began with a number of small legacies. Mrs Pollifex was to get £10,000 and Margot £2,500. Weatherup, 'in memory of kindly service', was left £500, and there were five or six other small bequests. Then came the real issue. After the forementioned legacies were paid, free of death duty, the residue was to be divided equally between Charles and Elsie. The Moat was left to Elsie and for purposes of calculation was to be valued at £10,000. Crosby estimated that when all taxes and duties were paid, Charles would get about £62,000 and Elsie £52,000 and The Moat.

Sixty-two thousand pounds! It was a little fortune. Charles could scarcely restrain his excitement. Here was the financial safety he had so terribly wanted! Now he could afford to marry Una. Moreover, all his difficulties about the works were over. Now the bank would lend him whatever he required. Well, here was justification and reward for all he had done! He had had some bad minutes, but it had been worth it. It was like everything else: nothing venture, nothing win.

Charles, glancing across the room, was a little surprised by Peter's manner. Peter did not seem at all impressed with his good fortune – for Elsie being the heiress really meant that he would have the handling of the money – and this was the more remarkable because of the straits he had been in. On the contrary he was looking extraordinarily anxious. Charles now remembered that he had been looking anxious on the previous evening. Ah well, Peter was a queer fish. You never knew how he would take anything.

Charles was excited for a reason other than the money. After dinner he was going to see Una. Now, as he put it to himself, would come the tug-of-war. Now the barrier which had been separating them had been swept away. How would she react? Would she accept him and agree to name the date, or would she find some other excuse for postponing the decision? Or would she turn him down?

Anyone who had seen Charles as he left Dehra Dun, the Mellors' luxurious bungalow, could have guessed the answer to these questions. His face was shining, lit up with an overwhelming delight. Una had not agreed to name the day, but she had given Charles to understand that she would soon do so. For the moment everything seemed to Charles just right. Once again, here was the reward for his courage! Once again, nothing venture, nothing win!

Next day Charles found that he had regained more than all his former popularity in his native town. At the club everyone was commiserating and congratulating him in a breath: formal commiserations given conventionally; real congratulations both from genuine well-wishers and from those who wished to be friends with an influential man. At all events, whatever the motive, it was all very pleasant. In the congenial atmosphere Charles's spirits rose still further.

'We must celebrate,' he declared, sending the waitress for some bottles of champagne.

After lunch he had a telephone call from the local police station. 'Could I see you, sir, if I called at your house to-night?' Inspector Appleby asked. 'I'm trying to get some details about the late Mr Crowther.'

In spite of himself some of Charles's exhilaration evaporated. However, he told himself, he had nothing to fear. As Andrew Crowther's nephew it was obvious that the police would interrogate him. All he had to do was to keep his head, to answer as immediately and as truthfully as he could everything they asked him and to volunteer nothing. Moreover, he must show no nervousness. Well, he could do all these things. There was no reason why he should be nervous.

Nevertheless he could not help some quickening of the pulse when that evening there was a ring and heavy steps sounded in the hall. The door opened. Rollins announced, 'Inspector Appleby.'

'Good evening, inspector,' Charles said cheerily, and yet with the slight solemnity suitable to the occasion. 'Good evening, sergeant,' for Appleby was followed by a policeman in plain clothes. 'Can you find chairs?'

'Thank you, sir. I'm sorry to trouble you, but I'm making inquiries for my report on this matter of Mr Crowther's death. I'll not be very long.'

'That's all right, inspector; I'm at your service.' Charles held out his cigarette case. 'You'll have a drink before you begin?'

'No, sir, thank you very much. I don't drink when I'm on duty. But I'll take a smoke with thanks.'

Charles felt a certain relief. He believed police officers would not accept even a cigarette if their purpose was inimical. He passed over the matches and an ash-tray, then sat waiting.

'You've been away, sir?' Appleby began, while the sergeant settled himself at the table with his notebook open and pencil poised.

'Yes, I was away for a holiday. I'd been feeling a bit run down and I decided to take three weeks.'

'I envy you there, sir. Someone said you went to sea?'

'Well, I did and I didn't. I went on a cruise round the Western Mediterranean: the *Jupiter,* a Purple liner. You live on board all right, but you're not really much at sea. You're ashore at different places each day.'

'So I've read. You weren't able to complete your cruise?'

'No. I got my cousin's radiogram at Naples and came home to attend the funeral.'

'Quite so. When did you see your late uncle last?'

'Just before I went away. Let's see.' Charles took his engagement book from his pocket and looked it up. 'I started for the cruise on Wednesday morning, the thirtieth of August. I dined at The Moat on the previous Friday. Mr Crowther was fairly well that evening and came down to dinner. That was the last time I saw him.'

'I'm afraid then, sir, you won't be able to give me much useful information. But still I might as well know what you thought of his condition?'

'I thought him rather feeble, since you ask. Not exactly ill, he didn't seem to have anything special wrong with him, but he seemed to be growing old too quickly, if you know what I mean.'

'What was his condition of mind? Was he depressed or worrying about anything?'

'He was slightly depressed. I put it down to the indigestion which my aunt, Mrs Pollifex, told me he was suffering from. So far as I know he was not worrying about anything.'

'You didn't think his depression would lead towards suicide?'

'I certainly didn't. Such a thing never entered my head, though now, in the light of what has happened, I'm not so sure.'

The inspector nodded slowly. 'You had seen him a number of times recently?' he asked.

'Twice; no, three times,' said Charles, looking up his book.

'Was that usual, sir? I mean, to see him three times at short intervals?'

'Well, no, it wasn't.' Charles hesitated for a moment, then spoke more confidently. 'As a matter of fact I had a little business with him.'

'Any objection to mentioning its nature?'

'None whatever, provided you keep it to yourself. I don't want it all over the town. I wanted him to give me some money.' Inspector Appleby nodded. 'You understand, sir, that you're not obliged to tell me this unless you like. But if you've no objection, did he give it to you?'

'He gave me part of what I wanted, and I think he was going to give me the rest, though he hadn't actually said so. He gave me a thousand pounds. I wanted it to put in three new machines at the works, and the thousand covered that.'

'You say, sir, that that thousand was only part of what you asked for. How much then did you want?'

Charles smiled. 'As much as I could get,' he declared. 'As a matter of fact I mentioned five thousand, hoping to get two. My uncle gave me a thousand right away, and this, as I say, covered the matter of the machines. He hadn't actually promised the second thousand, but I was satisfied from his manner that he would give it.'

'I understand, sir. Did you put your machines in?'

'Not yet, but they're on order.'

The inspector nodded and remained silent for a few seconds. 'Quite so,' he said slowly, and then: 'Your cousin, Mr Peter Morley, was also asking the deceased for money?'

Charles shrugged. 'I heard so. I heard that my uncle was considering taking up a mortgage on his farm. But I know nothing of it
first-hand. You'll have to see my cousin.'

'I'll do so, sir.' Inspector Appleby gave a powerful representation
of a man thinking, then asked: 'Well, sir, I think that's about all I
want. Except one question. Can you suggest any way in which the
old gentleman might have got the poison?'

Charles made a gesture of helplessness. 'I can't form an idea,' he
answered earnestly. 'As Mrs Pollifex was saying, he seldom went into
the town and never alone. And it's certainly not a thing anyone would
bring him. Mrs Pollifex suggested that he might have had it hidden
away for a long time, and that's the only thing I can think of either.
But I don't give it as an opinion.'

The inspector rose. 'That's all, sir, at last. I'm much obliged.'

'Not at all, inspector. You have your work to do like the rest of us.
Now you're off duty, would you have something?'

The inspector was again obliged, but unhappily he wasn't yet
off duty and couldn't break his rule. Ponderously he and his satellite
removed themselves.

Charles wiped his forehead. It hadn't been at all bad and yet he
was glad it was over. He fancied he had done well. He had not kept
back that business of the thousand pounds. That was wise: probably
the inspector knew about it already. And that remark that he believed
Andrew was going to give him more, was a stroke of genius. Even if
it wasn't true, no one could prove that he hadn't thought it was. And
it removed any special motive. He had certainly done well.

The next few days passed more rapidly for Charles than any within
the last three months. For one thing he was busier at the works. The
four jobs which had been obtained during his absence meant work
for him as well as his staff, and he was also occupied in getting out a

tender for a big job near Darlington. But the chief reason was the ease to his mind which had come since his dreadful plan had succeeded. If only the inquest were safely over, he might dismiss the whole horrible affair from his thoughts, marry Una, and live happily ever after!

Peter had decided to try to sell Otterton Farm, move to The Moat, and carry on Andrew's market gardening on a larger scale. He had asked Mrs Pollifex and Margot to stay on with his own family, but they had refused this offer and were going to move to Hove. It would, of course, be some time before these changes were put into effect.

At last the day of the adjourned inquest arrived. It was to be held in the old town hall of Cold Pickerby at half-past ten, and at a few minutes before that hour Charles entered the building. The room was already packed, not only because the case had aroused unusual interest, but also because so many of the unemployed saw in it a means of escaping for one morning the tedium which pressed so heavily upon them. Indeed, there was in many instances a more personal motive than that. Several of these men had known Andrew Crowther, and not a few had actually worked for him.

Sergeant Bray, who had visited Charles with Inspector Appleby, now showed him to a reserved seat, and there a few minutes later he was joined by Mrs Pollifex, Margot, Peter and Elsie, who had returned from Paris, while Weatherup and some of the other servants slipped in behind them. Peter was still looking worn and anxious. Charles was surprised at his appearance. Surely the man wasn't ill? He decided to ask Peter when he got an opportunity.

The coroner was Dr Emerson. Charles knew him by reputation as a clever man with a good knowledge of law in addition to his medical qualifications.

The preliminaries were quickly carried out. The jurors answered their names and then Dr Emerson read a brief résumé of the evidence already taken. Peter Morley had identified the deceased as his father-in-law, and stated that he had died in his presence while travelling from Croydon to Beauvais in an Imperial Airways liner. The French doctor at Beauvais had given a certificate that he had examined the body of the deceased and could find no natural cause of death, recommending that a post-mortem be carried out. Finally Inspector Appleby had stated that he had gone to Beauvais, where the French authorities had handed him over the remains, which he had brought to Cold Pickerby. The coroner then reminded the jury that he had adjourned the inquest to enable further inquiries to be made by the police. 'I will now,' he continued, 'call Dr Claude Ingram.'

Dr Ingram was a big man with a determined manner. He strode forcefully into the box and took the oath with whole-heartedness.

'You are the police surgeon of this district, Dr Ingram?' the coroner went on.

'Yes,' the witness answered pugnaciously, as if daring anyone to dispute it.

'Did you make a post-mortem examination of the remains of the deceased?'

'Yes, I did, with the help of Dr Harrington.'

'And with what result?'

'I sent the stomach and certain other organs to Mr Grant of Messrs Grant & Colby, the analysts. I understand he found potassium cyanide present, but I see Mr Grant in court and no doubt he will give you this information.'

'I shall call Mr Grant presently. Now, doctor, did you find anything else which might have caused death?'

'Nothing; the organs, if not entirely healthy, were not dangerously diseased.'

'And you do not think that death could have resulted from the unusual height or from excitement?'

'I do not think so.'

'Now, without prejudice to what Mr Grant may tell us later, will you tell the jury the effect of potassium cyanide?'

Dr Ingram shook himself importantly. 'Potassium cyanide is one of the most deadly and rapid of known poisons,' he declared with the air of a professor lecturing to a class. 'Death has occurred within three or four minutes of taking it, and unconsciousness within a few seconds. Of course its effects are not always so rapid as this, but it is usually a matter of minutes. The symptoms,' and Dr Ingram became highly technical, as also when the coroner asked him as to the quantity of the poison required to ensure death.

'I shall remind you of these figures,' went on Dr Emerson, 'when we come to take Mr Grant's evidence.' He looked at his jury. 'Any questions?' he asked, including Inspector Appleby, who was seated with his chief, Superintendent Lucas.

No one wishing to obtain further information from Dr Ingram, he left the box, and Peter Morley was recalled.

Peter looked more worried and anxious than ever as he settled himself for the interrogation. It proved to be slow and extremely detailed. In answer to the coroner's numberless questions the whole story of the ill-fated journey came out: the visit of Elsie to Paris, her accident there, the decision to go to Paris as quickly as possible, the deceased's insistence on being of the party and the decision to include Weatherup and Rose. Peter described his and Mrs Pollifex's anxiety as to how the deceased would stand the journey, the calling in, late at night, of Dr Gregory to make a special examination of the old man, the doctor's favourable report, the start in the middle of the night and the journey to London. Then he told of the rest which Andrew had

had in London, of the departure from Croydon, of lunch during the transit, and of Andrew's apparent good health and enjoyment of the flight. Finally he recounted how the old man had leant back in the corner, supporting his head against the cabin wall. He had believed the deceased had gone to sleep, and he had been horrified when at Beauvais it was found that he was dead.

'Was he dead or only unconscious when the plane landed?' the coroner asked.

'I think dead, but I am not sure. He was certainly dead about twenty minutes later when the doctor arrived.'

'How were you sitting in the plane during lunch, Mr Morley?'

'The seats are arranged across the cabin, two at each side of the corridor, as in a bus. The deceased and his attendant, Weatherup, were sitting together, the deceased next the side of the plane and Weatherup next the corridor. My daughter and I were immediately behind, she behind the deceased and I behind Weatherup.'

'Both the seats were facing forward?'

'Yes.'

'Did you speak to the deceased during the flight?'

'Oh, yes, several times.'

'Did you stand up to do so?'

'No, I leant forward and spoke over his shoulder.'

'And he seemed perfectly well?'

'Perfectly, but, of course, when I saw him, as I thought, go to sleep, I didn't speak to him again.'

The coroner nodded slowly. 'I understand,' he agreed and paused for some moments. Then, after a look over his notes, he started off again.

'Now, Mr Morley, prior to the journey to France, when did you last see the deceased?'

'On the evening before the journey. I dined that evening at The Moat. I was actually there when the message from Paris was forwarded from my house.'

'Were there any other guests?'

'Mr Crosby, the solicitor.'

'Quite so. Now was that a purely social meeting or had you some business with the deceased?'

'I had some business with the deceased.'

'What was the nature of that business?'

'I had applied to Mr Crowther for some financial assistance and it was to arrange the details of this.'

'You were – eh – in difficulties financially?'

'No,' Peter answered, 'it wasn't as bad as that. But farming has not been very profitable lately and I should have been glad of some ready money.'

'Quite so. You had applied to the deceased previous to the evening before his death?'

'Oh, yes, I had asked him if he could do something for me and he had agreed to do so. The exact details of how it was to be done were not settled. That was what our meeting was for on that last night. My father-in-law – the deceased – wished to consult Mr Crosby on the matter.'

'And that consultation took place?'

'Yes.'

'And was the matter settled satisfactorily?'

'No. Various ways of settling it were discussed, but no decision was reached. Mr Crowther favoured taking up a mortgage on my farm, but he had not absolutely decided to do so.'

'But he had definitely decided, one way or another, to give you the help you required?'

'Quite definitely.'

Dr Emerson then questioned Peter on the deceased's health. Peter said that Andrew was getting rapidly feebler, though he had seemed no worse on the day of his death than at other times. It had never occurred to Peter that his father-in-law was a likely subject for suicide. He was depressed at times, but not unduly, and certainly not enough, in Peter's opinion, to make him take his life. He, Peter, was completely puzzled by the whole affair. He could not see why the deceased should have wished to commit suicide, particularly at such a time. Nor had he any idea how the old man could have obtained the poison.

No one wished to ask a question and when Peter had signed his deposition he stood down, relief struggling with anxiety on his somewhat melancholy countenance. Interest in the proceedings had become very keen and some of those present appeared to think Dr Emerson's questions had thrown an entirely new light on the case.

Dr Emerson had buried his head in his notebook, but now he raised it and looked round as if unconsciously seeking for applause. None came, however, and he went on: 'I will now call Mrs Penelope Pollifex.'

Mrs Pollifex stepped forward to the box. She looked grim and plain and was dressed quietly in black. She was quite collected and answered the questions in a clear though low voice.

The coroner was gentle with her. 'I'm sorry, Mrs Pollifex,' he began, 'to have to call you to-day. I can only say I shall be as quick as I can. You are the deceased's sister?'

She was the deceased's sister. She had lived at The Moat for some years, running the house for her brother. She was asked a few other questions about herself and then Dr Emerson turned to Andrew.

Mrs Pollifex somewhat amplified the evidence Peter had given. Her brother, she said, was sixty-five years old. He had been a fine figure of a man and had enjoyed excellent health until same five years previously, when he had had a severe illness. That had left him a comparative wreck. He had remained a semi-invalid, and though he was able still to take an interest in various hobbies, it was in a much feebler way. Latterly he had been failing more rapidly. He did not seem to have any organic disease, but he was just going slowly down the hill. The doctor could perhaps tell more about that.

Dr Emerson assured her that the doctor's testimony would not be overlooked, but he now wished to have her views. Had she noticed any more sudden recent deterioration in his health?

Mrs Pollifex couldn't say that she had. He was slowly and steadily getting worse, but there had been no sudden change. She didn't think his depression would account for suicide. Yes, photography was one of her brother's hobbies. Oh, yes, he had worked at it on and off up till the end.

This, it appeared, was all. Dr Emerson politely thanked the witness, asking her not to leave in case some other point might crop up. Then he called Weatherup.

Weatherup had entered the deceased's service some five years previously. He had come as a male nurse during his illness and had stayed on as butler and attendant when Andrew grew better. Before that he had had experience in a mental home near Dunstable. Yes, he was a fully qualified nurse. He agreed with the opinions expressed by the last witness as to the deceased's health. It was undoubtedly failing and he, Weatherup, believed his employer would not have lived for very many months. He had not, however, become suddenly worse at the time of his death.

Dr Emerson then took his witness over the events of the journey to France, Weatherup simply confirming what Peter had said. At last Emerson came to the lunch in the plane.

'What did the deceased have for lunch?' he went on.

'Just what the rest of us had, sir: clear soup, cold tongue and salad, cheese and biscuits, an apple and coffee.'

'And what did he drink?'

'Whisky and soda; a very little whisky.'

'Was that everything he had?'

'He took a pill after the meal, same as always. Except for that, he had nothing.'

'What sort of pill?'

'Salter's Anti-indigestion Pills.'

'Well, that wouldn't kill him. You say he took one after every meal?'

'Yes, sir.'

'For how long had he been doing so?'

'Oh, several weeks.'

'You've just said you sat beside him at lunch. Are you sure he didn't take anything from his pocket and put it into his mouth or his food?'

'I didn't see him do so, sir.'

'Ah,' said the coroner, 'that's just what I want to get at. Would you have seen him if he had?'

'I think so, sir.'

'But you can't be sure?'

Weatherup hesitated. 'I couldn't be absolutely positive, sir, but I think I should have seen it, and I certainly didn't.'

'Could anyone else have slipped anything into his food unnoticed by you?'

'I should say certainly not, sir.'

Dr Emerson leant forward. 'Tell me, did you at any time during the meal look at the other side of the cabin or out of the opposite window?'

Again Weatherup hesitated. 'Well, yes, I did. I was admiring the effect of the sun on the cloud.'

'Only once?'

'I may have looked more than once.'

'Then why shouldn't the deceased have taken something out of his pocket while you were looking away?'

Weatherup uneasily admitted it would have been possible.

The coroner was evidently dissatisfied. He paused and then had another shot.

'Now can you explain how the deceased could have got the poison?'

This was, however, unproductive. Weatherup disposed of it with a curt 'No, sir.'

Dr Emerson paused again and glanced over his notes. The hall was very silent. All were sitting motionless as if hypnotized. Then the coroner raised his head.

'Any gentleman wish to ask the witness any question?' He looked at the jury, but no one moved. 'You, Inspector?' Appleby shook his head. 'Then that'll do, thank you, Mr Weatherup. James Bradley!'

An energetic looking young man came forward and took the oath.

'You are an attendant in the service of Imperial Airways and were on duty in the liner which left Croydon for France at 12.30 on the 7th of September?'

'Yes, sir.'

'Do you remember the last and a former witness as well as the deceased and a little girl having lunch?'

'Yes, sir.'

'Did you collect the soiled plates, glasses, and so on from the tables?'

'Yes, sir. They were all packed together and taken out of the plane to be washed.'

'Then no chemical analysis was made of the food or drink remaining?'

'No, sir, the washing was in progress before I heard anything of the possibility of poison.'

'Did you search the plane afterwards?'

'Yes, sir, I searched it with the French police officer.'

'What were you looking for?'

'Some kind of box or bottle in which the poison might have been brought, I think, the officer specially wanted.'

'But you didn't find it?'

'No, sir, we found nothing.'

Dr Emerson looked across to the jury. 'You will remember, members of the jury, that the French police officer's report, which you heard read, stated that he had searched the body also and had found no such box or bottle on it either. Any questions?… Thank you, Mr Bradley. Oh, by the way, why did your plane come down at Beauvais instead of Le Bourget?'

'Fog at Le Bourget, sir.'

Dr Gregory was the next witness. He stated that he knew the deceased well, having attended him for many years. He had specially examined him on the night of the 6th of September and had come to the conclusion that he was strong enough to undertake the journey to Paris. Yes, the deceased was suffering from indigestion. He was treating him for it, but not with the pills which had been mentioned. Yes, indigestion frequently produced depression, and he thought it had done so in this instance. He could not say that the deceased's depression was sufficient to have led to suicide, but, of course, depression tends in that direction. There was no doubt that the deceased's health was failing, though he agreed with the previous witnesses that there had been no sudden change for the worse.

Inspector Appleby then gave evidence. He had taken charge of the remains of the deceased in France and had conveyed them to Cold

Pickerby. He had found in the pockets a bottle of pills, which he had personally handed to the analyst. After consultation with the doctor and the analyst he had removed certain bottles from the deceased's dark-room and also conveyed these to the analyst.

Gavin Grant, of Messrs Grant & Colby, analysts, was then called. He had received from Dr Ingram the stomach and other portions of a human body. He had analysed their contents and had found potassium cyanide present. He became technical as to the quantity, but explained that there would have been sufficient to have killed an ordinary man in normal health, but not very much more. He was quite satisfied that there was enough to have killed the deceased.

He had received from Inspector Appleby a bottle of pills. He had analysed all of these and had found no trace of poison in any of them.

He had been questioned by the inspector as to how the poison might have been obtained, and when he heard that the deceased was an amateur photographer he asked the inspector to look if there were certain bottles in his dark-room. The inspector brought him certain bottles, saying he had found them in the dark-room. He, witness, had analysed the contents of these bottles, and in one of them he had found potassium cyanide. Yes, it was used in photography for intensifying weak negatives. He was satisfied that had the deceased taken a certain quantity of the contents of this bottle, the effect would have been what actually obtained.

'Was that potassium of which you speak in solid or liquid form?' the coroner went on.

'In liquid form.'

'Then it could not have been conveyed in the plane otherwise than in a bottle?'

'That is so, if you are referring to what was shown to me.'

'I was referring to what was shown to you because I didn't under-stand there was any other. Am I now to understand that more poison was found than that one bottle?'

'No, sir, not so far as I am aware. What I mean is this: potassium cyanide is sold in the solid, and unless the deceased made a special arrangement with his chemist to dissolve it for him, he would have received it in the solid and dissolved it himself.'

The coroner nodded. 'I follow. You mean that he may not have dissolved all the solid he presumably obtained?'

'I did not say so, sir. I was of opinion that you should know of the possibility, that's all.'

'Quite. That is very interesting. Then your suggestion is that he may have had some solid cyanide which he could have carried in a scrap of paper in his pocket?'

Mr Grant disclaimed all intention of making any suggestion whatever. He had simply thought that the point should be brought to the coroner's notice. It was not for him to make deductions. Dr Emerson agreed dryly and then complimented him on the correct-ness of his attitude.

The last witness was Mr Crosby. He corroborated Peter's state-ment about the business talk which had taken place after dinner on the last evening of the deceased's life. As solicitor to the deceased, he had been called in to advise. Nothing had been settled, but it was his impression also that the deceased intended to make a grant of some kind to Mr Morley.

Yes, he had drawn up the deceased's will. The provisions were as followed, and he enumerated them. No, there had been no secret about these provisions. Everybody concerned, with the possible exception of the servants, knew quite well what he or she had to expect.

This completed the evidence, and for a moment there was silence in the court while the coroner looked over his notes. Charles had found the proceedings a terrible ordeal, even though he had no doubt as to the verdict. He was rejoiced beyond measure at that suggestion of the poison having come from the photographic bottle. This would meet the only real difficulty to the suicide theory – where Andrew could have got the poison. Strange that he had never thought of that himself. He remembered now having seen in 'Taylor' that potassium cyanide was used in photography.

Once again Charles deplored the unlucky chance which had made the old man take the poison while on the journey. If the tragedy had occurred within reach of the dark-room the photographic explanation would have been more convincing, and the absence of a receptacle in which the poison could have been carried would have mattered less.

But the coroner had arranged his notes and was beginning to speak. He set off with a little homily about the duties of the jurors and the need for a verdict founded on the evidence and on that alone, and delivered without fear or favour of any man. Then he became more concrete.

They had first, he declared, to determine whose were the remains they had seen, and what was the cause of his death. That was their primary duty. But they had a secondary one also. If they considered blame attached to anyone, whether to the deceased himself or to some other person, they were to say so. With that their duties ended.

Now, in the present case he thought they would have no difficulty in finding that the deceased was Andrew Crowther of The Moat and that he had died as the result of taking potassium cyanide. That seemed clear from the evidence. But the question of possible blame was not so clear. Unless this was an accident, blame attached, and they had first to consider whether or not it was an accident. He did not wish to direct them, but he thought they would have little difficulty in deciding that no case for an accident had been put forward.

If they took this view, then someone was to blame. Who was that person? Was this a case of suicide, in which the blame must lie on the deceased himself, or was it murder?

The case for suicide, as he saw it, was that the deceased was old and in feeble health and had been suffering from depression due to indigestion. In this connexion it must be remembered that none of the witnesses who had testified to the deceased's depression had believed that that depression was severe enough to cause suicide. When weighing this evidence the jury would consider how far these witnesses were qualified to form such an opinion. Then they must not rule out the possibility that the deceased might have been in an abnormal condition after lunch. He was subject to indigestion and it was not impossible that something in the lunch might have disagreed with him, producing more acute indigestion, and thereby greatly increasing his misery and depression. Admittedly there was no evidence for this, but the jury were entitled to consider such possibilities in the light of their own common sense.

They had heard what he, the coroner, might call the photographic evidence. The deceased was an amateur photographer, and as such had potassium cyanide in his dark-room. Unless some special arrangement had been made with his chemist, of which there was no evidence, he would have purchased that potassium cyanide in the solid. It was required in liquid form, and some of it at all events had been dissolved. It would be for the jury to consider whether it had all been dissolved, or whether a certain portion might not have been retained in the solid. In the latter case they might consider whether this solid portion might not have been carried – perhaps in a scrap of paper – in the deceased's pocket. In this connexion he would remind the jury of the evidence of the attendant, Weatherup, who admitted that, unobserved by him, the deceased might have taken something from his pocket and eaten it. Such, in the coroner's view, was the case for suicide.

On the other hand, a case could also be made for murder. A large number of persons had an interest in the deceased's death: the jury would remember the evidence Mr Crosby gave about the will. It was for the jury to consider whether the poison could have been introduced into some article consumed during the lunch. If they thought so, they might, if they considered there was sufficient evidence, indicate the person whom they suspected of having done this.

They would see, Dr Emerson concluded, that there was some difficulty in accepting any of the theories put forward, but they must weigh the evidence as they would weigh evidence in the ordinary affairs of their daily lives. If they believed that this death was due to accident, suicide, or murder, they would say so, but if they did not think there was sufficient evidence to enable them to reach a conclusion on this point, they would find that while the deceased died from potassium cyanide poisoning, there was no evidence to say how the poison was administered.

He would now ask them to retire and consider their verdict, and if there was any help he could give them in reaching a decision, they had only to ask for it.

They were not long away. In less than ten minutes they returned. Yes, they were agreed on their verdict. They found that Andrew Crowther had committed suicide while temporarily insane.

CHAPTER XIII

Charles Has a Caller

T HOUGH CHARLES HAD EXPECTED NO OTHER VERDICT, HIS
relief when the inquest had become an accomplished fact was
overwhelming. Now at last the death of Andrew was definitely a
matter of history. The verdict had, as it were, pushed it authoritatively
into the background, as no longer of interest or importance. Never
again would he, Charles, hear of it.

At the same time there were one or two things to be done before
he could banish the whole tragic episode from his mind. There were
those pictures, for example. Una might now at any time come to his
house, and on the walls of his house were fourteen blank spaces. She
would miss the pictures and would ask questions. Those questions
must not be asked.

It happened that on the third evening after the inquest a dinner
of the old boys of Charles's school was being held in Town.
Charles had occasionally attended these functions, though this
time he had refused. Now he rang up the secretary and said
that his refusal had been due to the fact that he had believed
that on the date in question he would have been cruising in the
Mediterranean. Owing to the death of his uncle he had had to
return unexpectedly, and he would like to change his mind and
be present at the dinner.

On the morning of the day Charles once again drove up to Town.
Once again also he drove fast, with the result that he arrived in the
comparatively early afternoon. By four-thirty he was in the office of

Messrs Spiller & Morgan, of Bedford Street, off the Strand. He had obtained their name from a directory and had telephoned from Cold Pickerby that he was going up. Mr Spiller was expecting him and received him immediately.

'You desire to be accommodated with a loan,' Mr Spiller began after impressive courtesies. 'I hope we shall be able to meet your wishes. How much did you think of, and for how long?'

'I want to know first whether we can do business,' Charles inquired. 'Unfortunately, I am unable to offer you proof of the genuine nature of my security. The fact is, I have just been left an estimated sum of sixty-two thousand pounds, free of death duties. The will has been read, but probate has not been granted.'

Mr Spiller bowed. 'So, sir, I understand. I may say,' he went on with a discreet smile, as Charles looked surprised, 'that in my business I have to have ways of assessing such matters, and on receipt of your telephone message I got in touch with my agent in your district. He gave me such information as he could obtain. It was, of course, not fully satisfactory, but I am prepared to act to a limited extent on the strength of it.'

'I'm glad to hear it,' Charles returned. 'What I want, then, is a loan until probate is granted, or rather, until I actually receive the inheritance. You probably know better than I how long that would take. I imagine three months, but I'm not sure. I may say that there are no legal complications in the matter.'

'Quite so, Mr Swinburn. Three or four months should meet the case. And the amount?'

'Five thousand.'

Mr Spiller bowed again. 'That should be easily managed,' he repeated. 'When did you want the accommodation?'

'Now,' Charles returned. 'At least, if possible tomorrow morning.

Would that give you time to make any further inquiries you may desire?'

Mr Spiller made a gesture as if sweeping the idea of inquiries from the discussion. 'No further inquiries are needed for a loan to Mr Charles Swinburn,' he said grandly, 'but, sir,' he smiled deprecatingly, 'we require to be assured that you are Mr Swinburn. You will excuse the obvious precaution?'

'Of course,' Charles agreed. 'I'm glad it's only that. Let's see. I would suggest the manager of the London branch of my bank, whom I know fairly well, but the bank is closed now. What about the manager of my hotel, or the officials at my club?'

'Either would be satisfactory. Perhaps, however, I might make a suggestion. You want the money tomorrow morning?'

'I should like it, but it's not essential.'

'There will be no difficulty whatever. Suppose tomorrow we go along to your bank, you and I, see your manager, obtain the formal identification, and I then and there write you the cheque and you can cash it in the bank?'

Charles hesitated. 'I don't like that idea, Mr Spiller,' he said presently. 'You may put it down to false pride if you like, but I'm not particularly anxious to blaze it abroad that I'm negotiating a loan. No, come and see my bank manager by all means, but let it be in connexion with an insurance or something of that kind. Then let us return here and you give me the money in cash. It doesn't seem very polite, but I'd rather not have my dealings with your firm passing through my own bank.'

Mr Spiller appreciated the point and would be delighted to oblige. Many of his clients felt as Mr Swinburn did, and there was nothing in it to call for apology. What time would be convenient in the morning?

The appointment made, Charles drove to Messrs Jamieson & Truelove. About those pictures which he had deposited some days previously. No doubt Mr Truelove had heard that he, Charles, had come into some money since they had done their business? No? Well, it was so, and the result was that he wished now to redeem the pictures. Could they be packed for conveyance in his car and he would call for them on the following morning?

The remainder of Charles's visit worked out according to plan. He drove from Messrs Jamieson & Truelove's to his hotel, attended his dinner, where he made the speech of the evening, and next morning carried through his two pieces of business. After a satisfactory interview with his bank manager, to whom Mr Spiller was introduced as a manufacturer of electromotors with whom Charles wished to do business, Charles received notes for five thousand pounds, a four months' loan at four per cent per month interest. Then he went on to the pawnbrokers, paid up his money and received his pictures. Finally he made another quick run north, arriving at a reasonable time at Cold Pickerby.

About this time Mrs Pollifex and Margot left The Moat. A small house at Hove which they had admired during a previous visit was still vacant, and they secured a lease on favourable terms. As soon as they were gone Peter and Elsie moved into The Moat. By a stroke of extraordinary luck Peter had received an offer for Otterton Farm, provided immediate possession could be given. Though the actual amount was small, he had jumped at it, and the sale had been put through.

Somewhat to Charles's surprise, Elsie got rid of the two women servants she had had at the farm and took over Andrew's staff. This consisted of Weatherup, who would now act as butler, and two women servants, a housemaid and a cook.

For Charles life looked like settling down and becoming once more normal. It was true that at intervals he was seized with dreadful fits of remorse, during which he would have given everything he possessed to undo the past. But these he was sure he could overcome, and that he would soon succeed in banishing all thoughts of his late uncle and of the dark period surrounding his death. Una was undoubtedly growing more friendly, and if she did not seem to be getting nearer the idea of matrimony, at least nothing occurred to upset Charles's happy anticipations.

At the works the new machines had arrived and Macpherson and Charles were having the time of their lives in getting them erected on their new foundations. They had missed the Darlington job, but had got two or three more small ones, and so far no dismissals had taken place.

Charles fell back into his old routine of lunching at the club and settling the affairs of town, state, and world with his acquaintances. Everything, in fact, became as it had been before the crisis, except that now Charles had an easy mind about money. He was losing on the business, but not a great deal, and he could stand the loss almost indefinitely.

And then, just as things seemed to be settling down, he received some information which rudely shattered his dream of security and brought him for a time up against actual stark panic.

It was mid-October. All day the atmosphere had been heavy and the sky lowering and everyone was expecting a storm. It came while Charles was walking back to the works after lunch. The street, which had been fairly crowded, cleared as if by magic, and Charles, following the general example, turned into a shop. It was Mullins', the booksellers, and there he found Peter.

'Hallo, Peter,' Charles greeted him. 'Doing a bunk from the rain?'

Peter's face was drawn into that same expression of worry which it had worn during the period following Andrew Crowther's death. Charles was the more surprised, because latterly this had given way to Peter's usual look of slightly resigned melancholy. Evidently something pretty serious was weighing on his cousin's mind.

'As a matter of fact, I came in for some books,' said Peter, taking Charles's remark seriously.

'Didn't think you were a reading man,' Charles rallied him.

'A man must read something,' Peter returned, adding inconsequently, 'They're books about market gardening.'

'Oh!' Charles shook his head. 'You're looking worried, Peter. The garden not going well?'

Peter glowered at him. 'Of course it's going well. I wish to heaven you'd control your imagination, Charles. Things are bad enough without your constant sneering.'

Charles was surprised. He went closer and spoke more confidentially. 'Look here, Peter, there's something up. What is it?'

Peter looked round. They were alone in a corner of the shop. 'Don't you know?' he asked in a low tone. 'No? Well, we can't talk here. I'll go to your office when this infernal rain's over.'

Charles, mystified, nodded, and Peter moved to the back of the shop to complete his purchase.

The storm had been sharp, but it was short. By the time Peter had finished, the worst was over, and in a couple of minutes the cousins walked on. Till they reached the works Charles asked no further questions, but as soon as Peter was smoking in the leather-covered arm-chair, he said: 'Now, go ahead!'

'Do you mean to say you've heard no whisper of anything, Charles?' Peter began.

Charles made a gesture of impatience. 'Nothing to put a face on me like that,' he retorted. 'What's it all about, for heaven's sake?'

Peter glanced round at the door, then leant forward and sunk his voice. 'The inquiry about Mr Crowther is reopened!'

Charles's heart missed a beat. For a moment he felt almost sick. This was utterly unexpected, and as terrifying as it was unexpected. It surely couldn't mean that the authorities suspected – anything? And yet it must! Besides, there was Peter's manner. Why should Peter speak to him in that way about it? Peter couldn't suspect?… No, impossible. It couldn't be that.

Charles hastily employed a trick he had learned at school: he sneezed. Then he blew his nose, slowly and carefully. It gave him two or three seconds. By that time he had pulled himself together.

'Good Lord, Peter!' he said, and he flattered himself that his manner was no more abnormal than the situation demanded. 'How do you mean, the inquiry? Has the coroner started another stunt?'

'No. It's worse than that. It's the police. And it's worse than that, Charles.' Again Peter sunk his voice. 'They've got a man in from Scotland Yard.'

Then it was that for the first time for weeks absolute sheer panic gripped Charles. He could not indeed speak, in spite of all his efforts. Motionless and sweating, he sat looking at Peter.

But Peter was not looking at Charles. He was gazing vacantly down on the desk with an expression of extreme anxiety. Charles once again pulled himself together. Slowly he got to his feet and began to pace the room.

'That's astounding news, Peter,' he said as soon as he could trust himself to speak. 'Scotland Yard! How do you know?'

'How do I know? Because the man's been with me. Very nice and very polite and all that, and asking questions world without end.'

'Good Lord!' Charles exclaimed again. 'Tell me.'

Peter shrugged. 'That about covers it,' he declared. 'He came to The Moat last night, the Scotland Yard man, he and a sergeant. It was after dinner and he sent in an ordinary visiting card – "Mr Joseph French". I asked Weatherup what he was like and Weatherup said he didn't know; he thought they were business men of some kind. I went into the study, and then the first one gave me another card – "Detective-Inspector French, Scotland Yard". I was surprised, as you can imagine; but I was more surprised when what he wanted came out. "I've been sent down, sir," he said, "to make certain inquiries in connexion with the death of the late Mr Andrew Crowther."'

'"His suicide?" I said.

'"Well, sir," he answered, "that's just the point. A question has arisen as to whether it really was or was not suicide, and that's what I've been instructed to inquire into."'

'Good Lord!' said Charles for the third time. He was rapidly recovering his normal frame of mind. This was a terribly regrettable affair, this inquiry. It would lead to worry and annoyance and anxiety. But that would be all. As he thought over the precautions he had taken, he *knew* that he was safe. But he must keep his head. Only his own self could give him away.

'Then he began to ask questions till I scarcely knew whether I was standing on my head or my heels. All about my circumstances, all about the meals I had had with the old man shortly before he died. Every question under heaven you could think of, and a lot more besides. I'm sure he was there the best part of two hours.'

'And what then?'

'What then? Isn't that enough?'

'Well, I admit it's a nuisance and all that, but what harm can it do? We have only to answer what he asks, and that's the end of it.'

Peter shook his head gloomily. 'Is it, Charles? I hope you're right.'

Once again Charles was filled with panic. It couldn't be that this inspector had indicated that he, Charles, was suspected? He must at all costs find this out.

'How do you mean, is it?' he asked with some appearance of exasperation. 'What I say is so, isn't it? Have you any reason to doubt it?'

Peter looked more worried than ever. He jerked about on his chair, glanced again at the door, and gave every indication of uneasiness. As Charles watched him his panic came on again in great waves. He *was* suspected, and Peter couldn't find words to tell him! In spite of himself, Charles's voice had an edge as he went on uncontrollably: 'For heaven's sake, man, get on and say what you have to say. What is it?'

Peter seemed slightly surprised at this outburst. 'You're feeling it too?' he queried, then went on in a burst of confidence: 'I'll tell you, Charles, what I've never told to mortal, and what's troubling me now. That evening I dined there; you know, the night before he died?'

'Yes, of course; go on.' Charles was sweating with a sudden relief. Whatever it was, it had nothing to do with him.

'You remember the question of the pills?' went on Peter. 'Weatherup said at the inquest he had taken one after lunch. And so he had. I saw him take it myself. I leant forward to speak to him and saw him take it.'

'His indigestion pills?' said Charles with renewed misgivings. 'What about them?'

'It didn't seem to occur to anyone that the poison might have been in a pill.'

Charles snorted. 'How could it? Those pills are sold by the hundred thousand. Besides, they were analysed and they were all right.'

'The rest were analysed, but not the one he took.'

Charles's anxiety was welling up again. What was Peter after?

'For heaven's sake, Peter,' he burst out, 'let's have it and be done with it. What are you getting at?'

Peter moved uneasily. 'Well, don't you see? Suppose someone had wanted to murder the old man. All one had to do was to put a poisoned pill in the bottle.'

'Rot! How could he get the bottle? Or the pill, for that matter?'

'I think it might have been done.'

'Was that what the inspector suggested?'

'No, of course he didn't. What do you take him for? But he might have thought it.'

'Hell!' Charles cried testily. '*Might* have thought it! He *might* have thought the old man was bitten by a rattlesnake. I don't know what you're trying to get at, Peter.'

Again Peter hesitated. He seemed most unwilling to go on. Then at last he took the plunge. 'Something very unfortunate happened that night,' he explained. 'A matter of absolutely no importance in itself, but now, since the old man's death, no one knows how important it mayn't become. I'll tell you.'

Again he glanced at the door and still further lowered his voice. 'After dinner, when the old man, Crosby and myself were sitting over our wine, Crosby went out to the hall to get some papers from his coat-pocket. He was out of the room for two or three minutes. The old man seized the opportunity to take his pill. It happened that absent-mindedly I picked up the bottle of pills to read the label. You know how one does those sort of things, without any real object. I didn't want to know what they were, but I did it the way one sketches on one's blotting-paper. You know?'

'Of course. But I don't see. What matter if you did?'

'None in a sense, but it just happened that when I had it in my hand Weatherup passed, and he saw me holding it.'

Charles gasped. So that was it! Peter was afraid of being suspected. Charles almost laughed in his relief. He did not, in fact, entirely repress a chuckle.

'Why, you cuckoo,' he cried, 'you're not imagining you'll be suspected?' Peter didn't answer. 'Peter, you're not? You're not really such an almighty fool?'

'It's not so foolish as you seem to think,' Peter said gloomily. 'Look at it this way. The old man was in a normal frame of mind at the time of his death. Weatherup swore he was neither upset nor depressed nor unduly excited, and I had to agree. He took his lunch normally, and he was keen to get to Paris to see Elsie. Well, from all that it can be argued that he wasn't very likely to do himself in.'

'All that was known to the coroner's jury, and yet they brought in suicide.'

'I know, but it was because they couldn't account for the thing in any other way. Supposing now you add to all that, that the poison could have been put into one of those confounded pills, and supposing that on the evening before he died I was seen actually handling the bottle – what about that?'

'Nothing about it. You weren't the only one. Anyone in the house could have tampered with that bottle.'

'Yes; but no one in the house was hard up and had been trying to get cash out of the uncle, which up to then he had refused.'

'You said – and Crosby confirmed your statement – that he intended to give you some.'

'Ah, yes – intended. But he hadn't done so. Besides, what would I have got for a mortgage on the farm compared to what Elsie would have got if the old man had pegged out?'

'But, man alive, you mustn't deliberately *make* a case against yourself. All that's biased.'

'It's the case that the police may make. I have to admit it's reasonable from their point of view, and so must you. There's no use in sticking your head in the ground, Charles. Everything I've said is a fact. They may take that view.'

'Well, damn it, suppose they do? What matter? They can't prove anything.'

'They can prove all that. Will they need to prove anything more?'

For the second time the cold hand of fear descended on Charles's heart. Was Peter right? Would they need to prove anything more? And if they didn't, where would he, Charles, come in?

Here was a contingency he had never in his wildest moments foreseen. That his scheme should succeed so completely that not only he himself should not be suspected, but that his cousin's husband be brought in guilty! Beads of sweat broke out on Charles's forehead. If this ghastly thing really happened, what would he do?

He couldn't, he *couldn't* let Peter suffer – what he would suffer. But if Peter didn't, then he himself... Una...

But they couldn't bring Peter in guilty on such evidence! And yet could they not?

Charles shivered. The more he thought over the situation, the less he liked it. And the fact that this inspector had asked Peter about his movements that evening did certainly look as if he had something of the kind in his mind.

But wait a minute. They couldn't prove that Peter had any poison. Charles turned with some eagerness.

'You had no poison,' he suggested.

'No,' said Peter, nodding his head. 'I thought of that. It's good as far as it goes. But you know, Charles, it doesn't go very far. They might argue I had gone upstairs and got the stuff from his dark-room.'

'Were you upstairs?'

'Not then, but I have been upstairs.'

'Nothing in it, Peter. You couldn't have been guilty because you hadn't any poison. And since you really hadn't any poison they can't prove you had.'

Peter seemed mildly comforted. 'You really think so?' he insisted with a kind of wistful eagerness.

Charles reassured him as best he could when his own mind was a quaking morass. 'What you've got to do,' he told him, 'is to think up all the reasons you can why you must be innocent. If they accuse you, why not Crosby, why not Weatherup, why not Aunt Penelope, or even Margot? Why select you?'

'That's no good.' Peter shook his head mournfully. 'Motive. No one but I had any real motive. None of the others were hard up.'

'You don't know. Inquiries might show that Weatherup, to take the first name that comes, was stony. Why, for all we know to the contrary, he might have slipped something into the old man's food in the plane. You see what I mean. If they go for you they must produce proof.'

'They know I was hard up. They can find out from my bank just how hard. No, Charles, that cat won't jump. Of course the inspector never hinted that he thought anything of the kind, but then he wouldn't.'

'No,' said Charles slowly, 'I don't suppose he would.'

For some moments silence reigned, then Charles went on. 'But what gets me is – what has raised the confounded thing now? Has anything new come out?'

Peter shook his head despondently. 'I'm damned if I know. I've a sort of idea they were never satisfied at all; that they just let the coroner go ahead because they weren't ready to do anything else. A lot of these police don't care two hoots about a coroner.'

Charles absently agreed. Peter ground out the stump of his cigarette and got up.

'There's no use in worrying overmuch,' he said, though his looks belied his speech. 'You'll come and dine as soon as we've settled down?'

'Thanks, I'd like to.'

'Right; I'll let you know. Don't come out, Charles. I can find my way.'

When Peter had gone, stark fear once again settled down on Charles. How beyond words ghastly if Peter should really be arrested! What should he, Charles, do? Dare he risk waiting to speak till after the trial? Then of course…

Charles resolutely put the dreadful idea out of his mind. It was all nonsense. A thousand to one nothing would come of it. He was giving himself all this anxiety and disquietude without any real need. They couldn't prove anything against Peter.

And if they did?… But no, he wouldn't think of that. It couldn't happen.

At the same time Charles's face was pale and his knees shaky when he left the office to go home. He felt that this interview with Peter had given him the most terrible shock of his life.

And yet it was not long before he came to look upon it as his salvation, and to feel that without it he must inevitably have been lost.

A few nights later, as he was sitting after dinner over a glass of port, Rollins brought him a card bearing the words, 'Mr Joseph French'.

Charles's heart gave a sudden leap. He took the card and bent over it to gain a second or two. Then he answered as calmly as he could: 'Show him into the study, Rollins, and say I'm just finishing dinner and I'll be with him in a moment.'

Charles listened to the footsteps in the hall as though they were the tread of Fate itself. Now was the time for him to show his courage and self-control! At least he was forewarned. That tale of Peter's! If he hadn't met Peter, this ghastly visit would have come on him as a surprise. Unsuspecting, he would have given himself away. Now it wasn't so bad. He knew what was coming.

When the footsteps had died away he crossed to the sideboard and poured himself out a stiff peg of brandy. Then, feeling normal again, he went to the study.

A stoutish man of slightly below middle height was sitting near the fireplace, while a second, evidently a policeman in plain clothes, sat near the door. They got up as Charles entered. The stoutish man revealed a pleasant, clean-shaven face and a pair of shrewd but kindly blue eyes. Charles took comfort at his appearance. He did not look as formidable as he had somehow expected.

'Good evening, sir,' the newcomer began. 'We're sorry to trouble you at this hour, but our business is our excuse. You know my name, but I should tell you my calling.' He took another card from his pocket and handed it over. 'And this,' he indicated, 'is Sergeant Carter.'

'I know your name,' Charles answered. 'You're the inspector, aren't you? I met my cousin, Peter Morley, a day or two ago, and he told me you had called on him.'

'Yes, sir; that's right. I saw him last Wednesday. Then he told you what I was here for?'

'He did, and I was never more amazed in my life. Do you mean to tell me that there really is a doubt that my late uncle committed suicide?'

'I gather, sir, that it's the local chief constable who thinks there may be a doubt. The local police appear to have been satisfied enough. At all events I happened to be in this neighbourhood, and,' he smiled slightly, 'I was seized and pressed into the service.'

'And what do you think yourself?'

'I'm afraid I've not yet learnt enough about the affair to form any opinion. That's what I'm now trying to do, and I've come round to ask you to kindly give me any help you can.'

Charles felt surprised and somewhat reassured. This was not like the opening he had expected from the police. There was no attempt here to browbeat or to intimidate by a loud voice and boorish manners. This man seemed reasonable, if not considerate. On the other hand, he certainly didn't look a fool.

'I'm at your service, inspector,' he answered.

'Thank you, sir.' The man took out a notebook, opened it, and laid it, together with a fountain pen, on the table beside him. 'First I may ask you the general question: can you tell me anything that may help me in this inquiry?'

Charles moved uneasily. 'I don't know that I can,' he answered. 'I take it that you mean what I know of my own knowledge, not, for example, what came out at the inquest?'

'I mean anything that you may know of your own knowledge.'

'I'm afraid there's nothing. You see, I never for a moment suspected this theory that you've put up.'

'I've not put it up as my own theory,' French reminded him. 'Perhaps I'd better go into details. What was your opinion of your uncle's health? Did you think him predisposed to suicide?'

Charles, perhaps over-sensitive, scented here a trap. If he had definite opinions about this, it would show that he had considered the matter.

'I thought his health was failing rather rapidly,' he replied. 'He was certainly growing weaker, both in mind and body, during the last few months. As to a predisposition to suicide, I never suspected it for a moment. I presume you mean before the inquest?'

'Before the inquest – yes, sir.'

'Before the inquest I never suspected it. After the inquest I assumed that it was suicide, surprising though this seemed. Certainly, till my cousin spoke to me to-day I never considered any other possibility.'

Inspector French nodded. 'When did you last see your uncle?' he went on.

Charles took his engagement diary from his pocket. 'On Friday, the 25th of August. On that evening I dined at The Moat.'

'And how did he seem then?'

'Just as I have described. Weaker in every way, though it was what we called a good day with him.'

'I understand. And had you seen him shortly before that date?'

'Yes, I had seen him' – Charles searched back in his book – 'on the previous Thursday, the 17th of August. On that day I lunched with him. He was not so well on that day – in fact he got some kind of attack which scared me stiff. I thought he was gone, and called Weatherup, the attendant. He gave him some medicine and it revived him.'

French appeared interested in the attack. He got the fullest details Charles could give him.

'If you don't care to answer this question, you needn't,' he went on. 'I should like if possible to know what your conversation was about. I should like to know whether it could have upset him at all?'

Charles wondered if another trap lay here. At all events, honesty was his obvious policy. 'I'm afraid it might,' he said with some appearance of regret. 'I blamed myself afterwards, at all events. As to the subject of our conversation, I've already told Inspector Appleby all about it. All I asked him was that it shouldn't be made public unless unavoidable. I wanted some money from my uncle,' and Charles repeated what he had told Appleby, and what was indeed the truth. French noted it, then for some moments seemed lost in thought.

'Well,' he said at last, 'that seems to be all about that. Now let's see if I've got these dates right. You lunched with your uncle on the seventeenth and then dined on the night of the twenty-fifth. That was eight days between your visits. Doesn't that seem a long time to have let such a matter hang fire? I'm not questioning your statement, you understand, but only clearing up my own mind.'

'I don't think so,' said Charles. Really the interview was being much easier than he had anticipated. 'There were several reasons. In the first place the matter was not immediate. It was urgent, but not as urgent as all that. A week or two one way or another didn't matter.'

'I see, sir. And you got the money for the machines at that first call on the seventeenth?'

'Yes. It wasn't the first call on the subject, you understand, but it was the first of the two we are considering.'

'Quite so. And there were other reasons, you said?'

'Yes; another was that I didn't want to hurry or to seem to be hurrying the old man. But the chief reason was that I was busy. I had to go up to Town. Or perhaps I should say, I did go up to Town; to look into the purchase of the machines.'

French nodded. 'I think that answers my question. Did you stay long in Town?'

'Two nights only.' Charles thought he should be lavish with information this inspector could easily get for himself, and about which there was no secret. He therefore went on: 'I drove up on the Monday, slept at the Duchy of Cornwall in Northumberland Avenue, went down to Messrs Endicott Brothers, of Reading, to inspect the machines on the Tuesday, and drove back on the Wednesday.'

French shrugged. 'I didn't really want to know all that,' he declared, 'though I'm not sorry to have it. It'll make my report look more complete, as if I was really doing good work. Always worth while that, you know, sir.' He smiled. 'Yes,' he went on, 'I'm afraid we Yard inspectors get asking questions just out of habit. There's some excuse for it, of course, as we're seldom doing anything else.' As he spoke, he was slowly putting away his notebook and pen. 'You were from home at the time of Mr Crowther's death, Appleby tells me.'

'Yes, I was on a cruise in the Mediterranean.'

'I envy you that, sir. I've never been beyond San Remo. Some day I hope to get down as far as Rome.' He got up.

'Well,' said Charles, getting up also, 'I'd advise you to go either earlier or later than I did. It was too hot.'

'I'm afraid,' French returned, 'I needn't worry about that. Well, sir, I'm much obliged to you. Some other question may occur to me later, but that's all I want at present.'

Charles was doubtful as to whether he should offer the men drinks. Then he thought not. They were not village constables. Then it was too late. With a respectful 'Good evening, sir,' they had withdrawn.

Charles, while terribly worried that the main question should have been reopened, was at least thankful as to the result of the interview. These police officers were all the same, at all events they asked the same questions. This interrogation had been practically identical with Appleby's. And the best of it was he had told neither of them anything. French in particular he had told absolutely nothing: nothing that he couldn't have found out for himself and nothing that there was any reason he shouldn't know. His questioning had been indeed amazingly perfunctory; indeed it might be called actually inept. Why, Charles himself could have done better! And the man seemed absolutely satisfied with Charles's replies. Obviously so far he suspected nothing, and equally obviously there was no reason why he should. It was a false alarm. Charles was safe!

CHAPTER XIV

Charles Meets a Criminal

THERE'S AN OLD SAYING IN USE IN CERTAIN PARTS OF THE country: 'It never rains but it pours.' It is the crystallized thought of the ages on the question of how misfortunes come. Before he was much older Charles was to experience the truth of the adage.

In spite of the way in which his interview with French had passed off, Charles had had a severe shock from Peter's disclosure. He was just rallying from it when he received a second of an even more alarming character.

It occurred about three weeks later, when Charles fulfilled his engagement to dine at The Moat. All that day he had been restless and miserable, with a premonition of evil weighing heavily on his mind. But he could not tell what he feared. Sometimes it was that suspicion of himself would be aroused, sometimes that Peter would be arrested. This latter possibility absolutely staggered him. How in his perfect scheme he had come to overlook anything so vital as that suspicion might fall on someone else, he didn't know.

The long hours at the office dragged through at last, and Charles went home to change. He felt he wanted exercise, and as there was a nearly full moon, he decided not to take his car, but to walk the mile or more to The Moat. His way led him through the trees to the west of his house and out on to a narrow lane running up towards the moor. From this lane a footpath diverged westward towards a hamlet a mile or so away. The path skirted The Moat grounds not far from the lake, and a branch path led through the woods to the shrubbery surrounding the house. It was an impossible route in wet weather, but to-night the ground was hard and dry.

As far as was possible with the shadow resting upon himself and Peter, Charles enjoyed his evening. Peter, though apt to be gloomy and depressed, was at heart a good fellow, and his wife, Elsie, Charles had always liked. She was short and stout and a great talker, and one of the kindliest and best-natured people in the world. Peter had evidently not confided his fears to her, and she rattled on cheerfully about nothing in particular, apparently oblivious of the men's preoccupation: an alleviation for which Charles was profoundly thankful.

About eleven Charles thought he had had enough of it, and a few minutes later he left the house and started off on his homeward walk. The sky had clouded over, but the moon was still shining, and he had no difficulty in finding his way. It was very calm and very silent as he passed into the shrubbery, and there was a cold bite in the air that suggested frost before morning.

He had not gone more than a few score yards when he heard a sound behind him. Swinging round, he saw a man approaching. He stopped and a voice came softly. He recognized Weatherup's melancholy accents.

'Excuse me, Mr Charles,' the voice said, 'but if you're not in a hurry could I have a word with you?'

'Weatherup, is it?' Charles answered. 'Of course. What's the trouble?'

'Perhaps, sir, I might walk along with you for a few yards. It would save your time.'

'I'm afraid my time's not so valuable as all that. However, by all means come along.'

'Thank you, sir.' They fell into step, walking slowly beneath the trees. 'It was a matter that I thought you ought to know of, in case you didn't.'

Charles waited for more, but Weatherup seemed unable to proceed.

'I can't say whether I know about it unless you tell me what it is, you know,' Charles said at last.

'No, sir, I'll tell you. It's about the master; the late master, I mean, Mr Andrew.'

Charles instantly grew wary. 'Yes,' he answered, 'what about him?'

'I suppose you know, sir, that the inquiry has been reopened?'

'Yes, of course I do. What then?'

Weatherup hesitated. 'A Scotland Yard man has been making inquiries,' he went on presently.

'Inspector French? Yes, I know. Again, what then?'

Weatherup shifted his ground. 'That inquest, sir. I should like to ask you a question about it.'

'What about it? Get on, man. What's worrying you?'

Weatherup still seemed to find a difficulty in proceeding. 'Were you satisfied with it, sir, might I ask?'

'Satisfied with what?' Charles sounded a little testy. 'Do you mean with the way it was carried on, or with the verdict, or what?'

'Both, sir; but principally the verdict.'

Charles was very wide awake now. He didn't like this beginning. A sense of impending danger took possession of him. He steeled himself to reply without faltering.

'I don't know what you're getting at,' he declared. 'If you mean, did I think the verdict was the right verdict, I did. What about it?'

Again Weatherup hesitated.

'I rather fancied, sir, that the police didn't.'

'It looks like it now. But they didn't say so at the time.'

'They couldn't get proof.'

Charles's nerves were wearing thin. 'Well, once again, what about it?' he said irritably. 'I wish you'd come to the point, Weatherup, whatever it is.'

'It has occurred to me since then that I possibly could give them the proof they wanted.'

'You could?'

'Yes, sir.'

'Then why don't you?'

Weatherup seemed taken aback. Presently, however, he went on: 'It might prove inconvenient in other ways. Perhaps, sir, I'd better tell you what they thought.'

'That's what I've been waiting for.'

'They thought, sir, that one of the master's pills had been poisoned.'

In spite of Charles's iron control he shrank back as if he had been struck. He felt he was giving himself away, but he could not help it. Then with a sudden instinct of self-defence he got himself in hand once more.

'And you think you can give proof of that?' he asked quietly.

'I think so, sir.'

'How?'

'It was one evening several weeks ago now,' Weatherup said slowly. 'We had a caller to dinner, a gentleman. After dinner the ladies withdrew, and he and Mr Andrew were left alone in the dining-room. As usually happens, sir.'

'Well?'

Charles grew angry. Here was this business coming out of Peter's handling the bottle. But why should Weatherup tell him? Was he going to attempt blackmail? If so, Charles told himself, the man had come to the wrong shop.

'Well, sir, I don't know if you are aware that in the wall of the dining-room opposite the fireplace there's a serving-hatch. It leads through from the pantry. That evening after dinner I happened to enter the pantry. The hatch was almost but not entirely closed. I glanced up and couldn't help seeing through it into the dining-room.'

'You were spying, you mean?'

'Oh, no, sir, not at all. It was purely accidental. When I saw it was open I put out my hand to close it. I would have closed it then and there if it had not been for what I saw. I admit I was interested. I did close it immediately afterwards.'

Suddenly a dreadful misgiving shot into Charles's mind. 'And what did you see?' he asked, and in spite of himself his voice sounded hoarse.

'I saw the visitor, sir, suddenly knock over Mr Andrew's wine.'

For a moment there was a tense silence. 'Well?' Charles asked again in that curiously hoarse voice. For the life of him he couldn't speak in any other.

'I was naturally surprised and remained motionless, watching. Then I saw him do a strange thing. He put his other hand, his right hand, on the table, picked up Mr Andrew's bottle of pills and set down another in its place. Mr Andrew didn't notice.'

Now that Charles was really up against a danger that he could see, his nervousness dropped away and his courage rose to meet it.

'You saw all that, Weatherup, and you didn't report it to the police? Don't you know that you're now guilty as an accessory after the fact?'

'No, sir. I couldn't imagine what it was done for.'

'I said *after* the fact. When the old gentleman died of poison you knew what had been done.'

'I might have guessed it. I didn't know.'

Charles laughed harshly. 'If you imagine any jury would take that view you're a bigger fool than I took you for.'

'No, sir.' Weatherup spoke with assurance. 'I would get off. I would go to Inspector Appleby and say that I have been most dreadfully unhappy; that I had seen this and that I'd been trying to argue to myself that there was no real connexion; that I felt I could not do so any longer, and that there was the information. I would say that I admitted being weak for not going before, but I hoped the affair would come out through some other agency. I might get at most a few months. On the other hand, sir, the visitor would be hanged.'

'Well,' said Charles, 'I'll tell you what to do, if you want my advice; and I suppose you do or you wouldn't have spoken to me about the matter. Go with your story in the morning to the police, or to-night if you like that better. See if they take your view or mine about your action.'

'I agree, sir, that I would run a trifling risk of getting a month or two. On the other hand, if I once made a report my mind would be easy for the future.'

'Then why not ease your mind? Why consult me about it?'

'I'll tell you, sir. I'm hard up for money. For money I would take the risk of keeping that evidence back.'

'Oh, I see. Blackmail?'

'If you like, sir. I'm not particular about names. I call it a matter of business and values. I'd like to explain my position. I've got a sister married in the States. Her husband's a farmer in Missouri and he's just about ruined. If he could get some money to tide him over the present trouble he would do well: he has the best of rich land and all that: I needn't go into details. The point is that if I had some money to put up he'd take me into partnership. It would give me a better start and save my sister and her husband. That's what I want the money for, and the question at issue now is simply this: is it worth money to the visitor to have the evidence kept back? It either is or it isn't, and it seems to me that's an end of it.'

'The visitor would have no guarantee that you would do your part.'

'No, sir. He would have to take my word for it. He would have the hold that I had received money, if he could prove it. But, of course, it would be one of my conditions that I should receive the money in a way that couldn't be traced. And, of course, the fact that I hadn't reported the matter at the time would make it less easy for me to do so later: for reasons which we've just discussed. Besides, I would go to the States: I'd never be heard of here again.'

'And what sum would you ask for this accommodation?'

'Sixteen per cent of monies that the visitor has recently obtained. Ten thousand pounds, sir.'

Charles laughed harshly. 'Why not say a hundred when you're at it?'

'Because, sir, he couldn't pay a hundred. He could pay ten, I don't say without feeling it, but practically without feeling it. He got an inheritance of sixty thousand pounds. My proposition means that he would have got one of fifty instead. And fifty thousand pounds is a comfortable sum.'

'Why,' said Charles in a very cold, hard voice, 'should not this visitor do you in, same as you imagine he did Mr Andrew in?'

'I'll tell you, sir.' For some reason which Charles could not fathom, Weatherup persistently retained his butler's tone and attitude of respect. 'I foresaw that some such reception might be awarded my proposal and therefore guarded against it. I'll tell you how.'

Charles was putting a bold face on it, but slowly his courage was dying. Weatherup was evidently very sure of himself. The fact that he spoke so moderately showed his strength. He did not need to bluster. Once again Charles saw panic approaching and once again he fought it back.

Weatherup paused for a moment, but Charles not replying, he went on: 'I've written out a detailed account of what I saw, giving dates and times and names. I've sealed the account in an envelope and handed it to Mr Peter. I've told him that it refers to a family matter; that it contains valuable certificates which in the event of my death should go to my son and daughter. I may say, incidentally, that I've got neither, but Mr Peter doesn't know that. I've asked him to keep the envelope safely for me, but if anything should ever happen to me to open and deal with the contents. I think that, sir, should do the trick, as besides the death of Mr Andrew, it would give the motive for doing me in.'

Charles wondered was this truth or bluff. He determined to find out if he could.

'Oh, don't be an ass, man,' he exclaimed. 'You don't mean to tell me Mr Peter would stand for anything melodramatic like that?'

'He stood for it all right, sir.'

'I bet he's lost the blessed thing by now,' Charles sneered.

'No, sir, you're wrong. He has it all right. I watched him lock it away.'

Charles's brain was now working keenly. It looked like a true bill after all. If so, the letter must be in Peter's study. And if so again, he, Charles, was in danger. If he didn't want arrest, trial, and what would inevitably follow trial, he must deal with this matter boldly.

'And for ten thousand you would forget what you know? I dare say that forgetfulness would be worth ten thousand to the visitor, if only he knew he could buy it. Look here, Weatherup,' he turned closer to the other and still further lowered his voice, 'suppose I give you ten thousand, how do I know that you'll keep faith? Answer that and the money's yours.'

Weatherup seemed a little taken back by the direct question. 'I can't, Mr Charles,' he said with some hesitation. 'I can't see that there's any way in which you could be sure. I should give you my word, of course, but I don't suppose that would satisfy you. I would like to meet your difficulty, but I don't see how I can. Do you, sir?'

'I should want to be guarded against two things,' Charles went on. 'First, I should want to be sure that when I had paid you the ten thousand you really would keep your mouth shut about what you saw. Second, I should want to be sure you wouldn't come in a few weeks or months and want more money. Now, Weatherup, you're a clever man: your action has just proved it. Surely it's not beyond your power to devise a scheme which will satisfy us both?'

'I'm afraid, sir, it's a take-it-or-leave-it proposition for you. All the same I want to be reasonable. If you can suggest any way out of the difficulty, I'll be glad to go into it. I'm really genuine in saying I don't want more than the ten thousand, and that, as far as you are concerned, I'd disappear in America.'

'You're a wise man; you're not going to try me too far. Well now, would something like this do? I've not thought it out: it's only the rough idea. You've got a hold on me about those pills. I admit that because there's nothing else I can do. Now if I pay you hush money about that and it can be established that I've paid you hush money about it, you definitely become an accessory after the fact. You see? There's no way out for you. Now I can't tell about you, because the essence of the whole affair is that I changed those bottles of pills. You can't tell about me, because you've taken money to hush up a murder. Some scheme of that kind I'd agree to. You shouldn't object to it. You'd get your ten thousand and it wouldn't affect you unless you tried to act crookedly. Now I know you, Weatherup, and I don't for one moment believe you're contemplating acting crookedly. Therefore, as I say, I see no reason why you should object to it.'

'But I'm entirely clear of it at present, Mr Charles. You're asking me to give up my privileged position, so to speak, and run my head into a possible noose. The thing might come out by accident or through someone else. Surely, sir, you will see that we needn't discuss that?'

'You're not clear of it at present: that's where you're making the mistake. All that about what you would say to the inspector is just a bit of blether. You're not clear, and you know it. Without an agreement with me you can't spend a penny of that money, and what good will it be to you then?'

'I can spend all I want of it at any time.'

'No, you can't. Suppose you do and suppose we fall out and you give me away. I then give you away. The police go into your affairs. They soon find you've been spending more than you ever made out of butlering. They ask you where you got it. You tell them some yarn. They go into your reply: and that's the end for you. No, my friend, you're for it without a chance of escape if you begin to spend. Come now, Weatherup. You've got me over this, I admit. But I'm not going to have my life spoiled over it. I've thought it all out before this, and if there's going to be trouble I'll commit suicide. So there you have it. If you'll act in a reasonable way, I'll hand you over ten thousand pounds sterling. If you don't, I admit you can make me commit suicide, but you'll not get a farthing yourself.'

Weatherup, to Charles's surprise, seemed impressed. He was evidently trying to assess the value of this argument. Charles hit again while the iron was warm.

'I'll tell you what we'll do. We'll both think over the affair for a day or two. We must do so in any case, as I don't happen to have ten thousand pounds in my pocket. Think over it and I'll do the same. Let's try and meet each other's views. I'm always for compromise, as perhaps you know. We can have another meeting later and settle it. What do you say, Weatherup?'

'That seems reasonable, sir. I agree except for one thing. Suppose this Inspector French comes to me in the meantime. If he asks me awkward questions I must know where I stand.'

'Very well, I'll tell you. If you meet my views about safeguards I'll pay you the ten thousand. If you don't, I won't; and if you give me away I'll commit suicide. So there you have it and you can take your choice.'

'I understand your position. When can we meet again?'

Charles thought. 'I can't say off-hand. How can we communicate?'

'Perhaps, sir, you could ring me up? You could give me some incidental message at the same time that I could pass on to the family.'

'Very well, I'll do so. By the way, don't let us mention our names over the telephone. You be Jeffries and I'll be Audinwood. That all right?'

'Yes, sir. Good night, sir.'

Weatherup faded away like a shadow in the gloom of the trees and Charles pursued his way homewards, walking as an automaton, unconscious of his surroundings. This was a ghastly, an appalling blow! The house of cards he had been living in had crashed. He was now in infinitely worse case than before he began to plot for Andrew's life. Then his business and position were threatened: now it was his life. If Weatherup were to give away that fatal piece of information, he, Charles, was as good as hanged. He sweated at the thought.

Would Weatherup give it away? Charles did not know. He realized that all that he had said to the man was the merest bluff. Weatherup could quite easily go with his story to the police and admit openly his fault for not going before. As he said, at the most he would get a few months, though he might well get off without any penalty. And it was true what he had said, that no reciprocal hold could be devised upon him. He would not be such a fool as to agree to leaving traces of his receipt of the money, and in no other way could Charles have any hold at all. In any case what would such a hold be worth? Nothing! As long as Charles's life was at the butler's mercy, nothing that he could have on Weatherup would weigh in the balances.

No, so far as Charles could look forward, he would be in the man's power for the remainder of his life. Always he would be in fear that either deliberately or by accident the truth would be made known. Always he would be open to fresh demands for money, which he dared not refuse. It looked as if Weatherup really did mean to clear out of the country with his ten thousand, but suppose there was another pinch when that was spent? Would he not come back then for more? Of course he would!

All the same, Charles began to consider schemes for raising ten thousand pounds in notes of small value. He had already two thousand in the house, the balance of what he had got from the moneylenders on his recent visit to Town. Weatherup would have to take that to go on with. The man seemed not unreasonable. He would understand that some months must elapse before he could get the larger sum.

As in a dream Charles let himself into his house, had a couple of stiff pegs and went up to bed. But not to sleep. It was only as he settled down in the silence that the true horror of his position swept over him. His life, and more than his life, at the mercy of a man of whom he had always been distrustful! Could he face it? Could he really settle down to live his life with this horror hanging over him? Would he not go mad? Wouldn't death itself be easier?

He tried to rally himself. It was certainly true, on the other hand, that every day which passed would make it more difficult for Weatherup to inform. Suppose by lavish payments the disclosure was staved off for a year. How could the man then go to the police? Would he have the slightest chance of escaping conviction as an accessory?

Charles thought so. He had only to go and express penitence, as he had himself suggested, to get off with a nominal penalty. He could easily explain that he had intended to report before, but had weakly put it off in the hope that the information would come out through some other channel. Unless, of course, the taking of the bribe could be proved. That would fix him all right.

In any case, whatever might or might not happen to Weatherup, there would be no doubt about Charles's own end. He turned actually sick with dread as he pictured it...

Then another idea flashed into his mind and he lay sweating in sheer horror. He had forgotten that Weatherup drank!

The man didn't often exceed, but every now and then he had a break and got drunk: not helplessly drunk, but what might be called jolly. Just drunk enough to loosen his tongue!

Here was another side to the affair. No matter what Weatherup agreed to; no matter how he were tied up; could there be any safety? No matter what his intentions might be, might he not give the thing away when tipsy?

For this there was no way out, *but the one.* From the first moment of Weatherup's revelation that way had been lurking deep down in Charles's mind, though he had earnestly tried to banish it. Now if he were to be safe, Charles must once again take that desperate remedy. Once again it was his own life or another's. Before, when he had taken that remedy, it had been his life only very indirectly. There was no such indirectness this time. Charles saw looming terribly clear before him that hideous shed, that noose, that square outline on the floor. It was that, and all the horrors that led up to it, or it was Weatherup's life. Which was he going to face?

Then he thought of the letter! Weatherup had foreseen that if a man commits murder at one time he may do it again. Weatherup had provided against that.

Charles settled down to consider this matter of the letter. Suppose Weatherup had really written it as he had said, and the whole story was not merely a bluff. Suppose Peter really had the letter, what then? Was there no way out of the difficulty?

Charles thought there might be. He thought that if the major difficulty of the removal of Weatherup could be overcome, he might be able to surmount this also. As a matter of fact the letter – if it existed – must be dealt with in any case. Suppose Weatherup were to be knocked down in the street and killed. Would not Peter then open the letter? And if so, where would he, Charles, be?

But the more Charles thought about the letter, the less inclined he was to believe in its existence. It would be a double-edged weapon. If by some accident it were unintentionally opened – and how easily such a thing might occur – Weatherup's goose was cooked. The whole thing would come out, not only what the man had seen, but that he had been deliberately keeping it secret. Charles rather doubted that he would have taken such a risk.

If, then, Weatherup had been bluffing, it made his removal easier. But even if he were not, and the letter was there, Charles thought he could deal with it.

But could he deal with Weatherup himself? For hours he lay awake thinking, and gradually a scheme formed itself in his mind. It was a simple scheme, easier to work than that of the poisoned pill, possibly not quite so watertight. But Charles had no choice. Inaction or delay would be alike fatal. Better to take the risk while he could, and fail – when he would turn to suicide – than to do nothing and live, if he did live, in hell.

Before Charles fell asleep Weatherup's fate was sealed.

CHAPTER XV

Charles Shows the Strong Hand

W HEN CHARLES AWOKE NEXT MORNING, THE MAIN OUTLINES of his plan were settled. Details had still to be worked out, but these would be easy. The only danger now was that Weatherup might speak before he was able to carry it out. But he did not think Weatherup would. Ten thousand pounds was a tremendous sum to a man of the butler's class.

In considering this pressing danger Charles had almost lost sight of that other sword which was hanging over his head: the question of Peter being suspected. But in that he could do nothing. Peter would be all right unless Weatherup told what he saw. Was Weatherup, Charles wondered, blackmailing Peter also? He might well be. Could this, in fact, be the reason why Weatherup had been kept on at The Moat?

Charles wondered if he could do nothing in the matter of Peter also.

Suddenly he marvelled at his denseness. Of course he could! He could make Peter as safe as he was himself. And how? Why, in the very same way! Peter's danger came from the same source as his own. The proof that Peter was alone with Andrew in the dining-room on the night before the old man's death and during that time was handling the bottle of pills, depended on Weatherup's testimony. If Weatherup didn't give that testimony, no one would know of the incident. Weatherup simply must not be allowed to give it.

To Charles with his fatal gift of imagination it now began to seem a sacred duty to save Peter by removing Weatherup. At worst the affair didn't now bear the same dreadful stigma of evil. Once again, so Charles told himself, it was not a choice between evil and good, but between two evils. It was not life against life, but two lives to one. And of two evils must not one always choose the less?

That day in the office he settled down to complete the working out of the details of his new plan as he would have settled down to work out the wiring of an electromotor. He took each problem in rotation, thought out a solution, and checked up the result. When he had finished he was satisfied. If he were careful, the thing would be as safe as the other.

The first thing was to get Peter away from home for a night: Peter's presence might hamper his operations. This was perhaps the most difficult part of the whole affair. Charles must not appear in it. Peter had grown very suspicious and he must not be allowed to suspect.

By lunch time Charles had not settled exactly how this was to be done, though the remainder of the plan was cut and dry. And then occurred a very astonishing coincidence, a coincidence so remarkable that had Charles still been doubtful as to his course, it would certainly have forced his hand.

As after lunch he was walking along High Street, intending to pay a couple of calls before returning to the office, he met Peter hurrying in the direction of the station.

'Just running for my train,' Peter explained, halting for a second. 'I'm going to Town for the night.' He glanced round and sank his voice. 'To tell the truth I can't stand this nightmare I'm living in. I want to see if I'll be stopped or followed.'

Charles could scarcely believe his good fortune. He must not, however, overdo his approval. 'It's not a bad idea, Peter,' he admitted. 'I'll bet your fears are groundless, but this scheme of yours will certainly put them to the test. Yes, it's a good idea. When will you be back?'

'Oh, to-morrow. I don't really want to go to Town. It's only for a test.'

Charles nodded. 'A good idea. Well, you're in a hurry. Cheerio and best luck.'

Only that Charles, with the queer streak of superstition so often exhibited by evil-doers, did not wish to be blasphemous, he would have said that here was a heaven-sent opportunity. It was an opportunity at all events which he dared not miss. He would put his plans into operation that night.

The only thing required to do so was to arrange the necessary meeting with the victim. Stepping into a telephone booth in a side street, he rang up The Moat. As he had hoped, Weatherup answered.

'Don't say yes or reply at all, Jeffries,' he said quickly. 'It's Audinwood speaking. Can you slip out and meet me at two o'clock to-morrow morning in the boat-house? Bring the key as I have something to give you and we shall want to be in some building where we can have a light. If you understand and can do so, reply, "Sorry, you've got the wrong number."'

'Sorry, you've got the wrong number,' came Weatherup's voice: a safe phrase if overheard. It was followed by the click of his ring off.

That afternoon was a desperate nightmare to Charles as he sat in his office trying to concentrate on anything which would keep his thoughts off what was before him. He was afraid to go down to the machine shops, lest his obvious nervousness should be noticed. For the same reason he could not bear a discussion with Gairns. When the man came in with a pile of papers he told him to bring them in the morning instead, as he was engaged with some private letters.

At last, however, the afternoon drew to a close, and at his usual time Charles packed away his papers and left the office. So far he was satisfied that no one had noticed anything unusual in his manner. Now he had only to consider his man Rollins, and he would be careful to keep him at a distance.

Charles did not dress when he was alone, and there was a little time between his arrival home and dinner. He employed it in making the one or two final arrangements he required. Going to his workshop, he sawed a foot off a piece of heavy lead pipe which had been left after the last visit of the plumber. Round one end of this he wrapped a piece of softish canvas, tying it on tightly with cord. This made a formidable weapon which he thought could be used with the same effect as a sandbag. He hid it in a drawer in the workshop, together with the remainder of the lead pipe, a piece about three feet long. To these he added thirty yards of strong cord off a ball, a small crowbar with a fine chisel point like a cracksman's jemmy, and a powerful electric torch. Next he took a piece of strong rope some twenty-five feet long, and winding it round his body beneath his coat, he slipped up unseen to his bedroom. There he hid the rope in his wardrobe, locking the door. In his pocket he put the rubber gloves he had already used in working with the pills. Then folding a bit of newspaper into a thick wad, he pushed it into his pocket-book.

All was now ready. He went downstairs and sat with a paper in his hands till he heard the gong, when he began dinner as usual. Rollins did not stay in the room, but came in to change the plates when Charles rang. It was Charles's habit to chat with him on these appearances, and though it took an effort, he was careful to do so on this occasion also.

The evening dragged interminably. Charles sat in his study, ostensibly reading, but really too much excited and on edge to attend to anything. This terrible adventure on which he had embarked was of a very different type to that of his previous essay. Then he merely set causes in operation which after a long delay produced the desired effect. He was not present when the climax came and he saw nothing distressing. Now the affair would be personal and direct. He would actually have to commit violent murder with his own hands. They might be bloodstained literally as well as figuratively. Charles writhed as he thought of it.

At half-past ten Rollins came in with the usual drinks to find Charles writing busily at his desk. Charles murmured good night without raising his head. He had already been to the dining-room for a stout peg, and now he had another. It steadied him, and his outlook became more normal. At his usual time he went up to bed.

But not to sleep. He did not even undress. Instead he went on with his preparations. First he locked his bedroom door. Then taking the rope from his wardrobe, he began tying knots on it a couple of feet apart. Next he opened two adjoining sashes of his window and tied the rope round the dividing mullion. He then paid it out till the end lay on the ground below.

Charles had decided to leave and enter the house by his bedroom window because he did not dare to use the stairs and front door. The former creaked and the latter had a noisy spring bolt. A passage through the house would almost certainly be heard by either Rollins or his wife, both of whom were light sleepers. Charles hoped indeed that the converse argument might be used: that as no such sounds had been heard, no one could have left the house. Obviously such an argument would not constitute an alibi, but he thought it would have a certain weight.

Charles was in the habit of reading for a short time before going to sleep, and for this time he kept on the light. Then he turned it off and lay – waiting.

If time had gone slowly in the study, it now crawled. Over and over again in his mind's eye he pictured the scene which lay before him and rehearsed the actions he would have to perform. Over and over again he considered the various contingencies which might arise and the methods he would adopt in such cases. Twelve had struck on the hall clock before he put the light out, and now half-past twelve came floating up with muffled reverberations; then one; then half-past one.

At last! Charles turned on his torch, crept on tiptoe over to the window, mounted the sill and swung himself out. Then he slid down, knot by knot, to the ground.

It was a suitable night for his purpose: fine and dry. Then and for some days past the ground was hard and would leave no footprints or other traces. There was unfortunately an almost full moon, but the sky was heavily overclouded, and in any case most of his work had to be done beneath trees. A slight breeze rustled through the branches and would cover up any faint sounds that he might make.

Halting for a moment to make sure that he was unobserved, Charles crept round to his workshop. There he picked up the two pieces of lead piping, the cord and the bar, and with the torch and the rubber gloves in his pocket, he set off for the rendezvous.

He pushed on as quickly as he could over the route which he had followed some thirty hours earlier. He passed through the trees surrounding his own house, reached the lane leading up on to the moor, and branched off along the footpath which skirted The Moat grounds. From this he turned into the wood surrounding the lake. It was dark and eerie among the trees and not easy to keep on the ill-defined track. However, his eye presently caught the faint shimmer of water and the black mass of the boat-house loomed up in front of him.

The door was round the opposite corner, and very silently Charles laid down the bar and cord and the longer piece of piping. The shorter piece with the tied-on canvas he hid beneath his coat. Then he moved round to the door. As he reached it the illuminated dial of his watch showed just five minutes to two. He called softly. There was a movement within and a voice answered.

'That you, Weatherup?'

'Yes, sir.'

'No difficulty about your getting out?'

'No, sir. Mr Peter has gone up to London and it worked in handy. He might have heard a movement.'

'I knew he was going. That's why I rang you. I thought you'd find it easier to arrange.'

'Yes, sir. Have you come to a decision, sir?'

'I have,' said Charles, moving into the boat-house and shutting the door. 'We shall want a light presently and we don't want to be overlooked. Yes, I've thought the thing over carefully and I see that what you said is reasonable. No matter how you may wish to do so, there is no way in which you can assure me of your good intentions other than by pledging your solemn word of honour. I am, therefore, going to trust you – I admit, because I can't help myself.'

'You may do so, sir: I assure you most earnestly that directly I get the money I will take my passage for America and you'll never hear of me again.'

'Well, I've got some money here. Not all of it, of course. You'll understand that until probate is granted I won't be able to lay a finger on what's coming to me. What I've got here is all the ready money I could lay my hands on at the present time. It amounts to close on two thousand pounds.'

Even in the dark Charles believed he could sense the butler's little movement of greed and satisfaction. His voice was certainly a little strained and husky as he answered that he was glad of that.

'Well, we don't want to be here all night,' went on Charles. 'Have you a torch?'

'Yes, sir.'

'Very well, then; just have a look over those notes. I'm not sure if they're in small enough denominations. Better not turn on your torch where we're standing. Let's go into the corner where there's no window.'

As Charles spoke he pushed into the butler's hand his pocket-book, swollen with folded newspaper. Both men turned towards an area of still greater blackness, away from the blue-grey parallelograms of the windows. Charles managed to take his place on Weatherup's left and half a step behind him. Weatherup eagerly clasped the pocket-book and moved forward. As Charles followed he took the pipe from beneath his coat. Then directly Weatherup switched on his torch, he silently swung it up, and brought it down with all his force on the head of the unsuspecting butler.

Weatherup collapsed without a cry and lay motionless in a tumbled heap. Charles turned his torch on the body. Yes, he had made a job of it. The man was obviously dead. His skull was crushed. But thanks to the canvas and his hat, the skin was scarcely broken, and there was practically no blood.

Charles wiped his forehead. That had been a bad moment. However, now the thing was done. He had burnt his boats and he could not stop to commiserate with himself. Now was the time for coolness and courage. Well, he told himself, he had them both.

His first care was to remove his pocket-book from the dead fingers. After a quick look to make sure there was no blood on it, he thrust it back into his own pocket. Then, fighting down his distaste, he began to search the pockets.

Ah, here in the trousers pocket was what he had hoped to find: a key. Charles was not quite sure what key it was, but thought it was that of the french window of the study. If so, it would suit his purpose admirably. The study was away from the sleeping-rooms at The Moat, whereas the hall door was just beneath them.

But there should be another key; of the boat-house. He went to the door. Yes, it was in the lock. He went out, brought in the bar and the cord and the long piece of piping, and locked the door from the inside.

It took all Charles's courage to carry through what next had to be done. First he completed his search of the pockets to make sure that if the remains were found, nothing incriminating would be there. Then he put the hat inside the coat, buttoning the latter upon it. Next with the cord he tied the two pieces of lead piping to the body, lapping and re-lapping the strands to make quite certain the piping could not break adrift. Lastly he carried the remains down to one of the two boats which were lying moored in the water basin.

Having untied the painter, he pushed silently out on to the still water. Moving his oars in the quietest possible way, he worked gradually out into the middle of the lake. Then he unshipped the oars and set himself to get rid finally of the dreadful evidence of his act.

It was not easy to get the remains overboard without upsetting the narrow skiff. However, he managed it. With the utmost care he worked the body out over the stern, till suddenly, as if once again alive, it jerked itself out of his arms and plunged in with a soft splash. For a moment a bubble appeared, then all once again was still.

The sweat was running down Charles's face as, after a careful examination of the bottom of the boat, he pulled silently back to the boat-house. There he tied up the boat as he had found it, and after swabbing up the oars with his handkerchief to make sure they would not drip on the floor, he replaced them on their rack. Then with a look round to make quite certain he had left no clue, he picked up the bar, let himself out of the boat-house, locked the door behind him and put the key in his pocket.

His night's work was not yet over. The letter had still to be dealt with. While now he scarcely believed in its existence, he must put the matter beyond doubt.

Creeping silently along the path to The Moat, he presently reached the french window of the study. The key fitted and with the utmost precautions he opened the window, tiptoed in, and closed it behind him.

His first care was to steal across the room and, passing through the door to the hall, to hang the boat-house key on the nail on which he knew it was kept. He hoped in this way to prevent suspicion arising that the boat-house had figured in the affair, and so to avoid attention being directed to the lake.

Returning to the study, he locked the door from the hall. Then he settled down to search. If that letter of Weatherup's was in the room, he must find it.

He worked unhurriedly and systematically, starting at one corner of the room and moving gradually round until he had examined every piece of furniture and every piece of paper he could see. Fortunately there was no safe. Most of the drawers were unlocked and slid out easily enough, in fact only the writing-desk was fastened. The desk, however, was the most likely place, and when he had completed the rest of the room, he turned again to it.

Inserting the chisel point of his bar between the shutter-lid and the desk table, Charles slowly prised. This gave him a powerful leverage and the wood dinted and the internals of the lock slowly gave. Nothing could have worked more satisfactorily until just as the lid came clear, the wood split with a crack like a pistol shot.

'That's torn it,' he thought, in more senses than one. 'They must have heard that.'

Quickly he pushed the lid back to its place, crossed to the door and unlocked it, opened the french window, slipped out, drew the window shut after him and locked it.

He *had* been heard! A light had sprung up in the window of Elsie's room. Charles's nerves were tense. If his scheme broke down now his fate would be sealed. If he had left Weatherup's letter in that desk, he was as good as hanged.

For an eternity he waited, then a light showed in the windows of the drawing-room. Charles moved cautiously along the path till he reached the window. The curtains did not fit tightly and he was able to see in.

At the door Elsie was standing, in a dressing-gown and mules. She looked frightened and was gazing round the room. Decent, plucky little woman, thought Charles. She had imagined there were burglars in the house, and had aroused no one, but had gone herself to see!

Completing a somewhat cursory inspection, Elsie left the room, switching off the light. Charles hastened back to the study window. As he reached it, the light went on. Now his fate was in the balance! Would she see the dint of the jemmy on the wood of the desk? He held his breath as again he watched through the curtains.

After a quick glance round Elsie came forward into the room and stood looking at the walls. It was evident she thought the sound she had heard was a falling picture. To Charles's overwhelming relief she did not examine the desk and obviously saw nothing amiss.

He had now only to wait till she returned to bed. He would see the light going off in her room.

If time had dragged before Charles started on his expedition, it now stood still. For endless ages he waited, watching that light in Elsie's window shining on steadily and relentlessly as if there for eternity. It was not till he had become sunk in the depths of despair that it went out. Then he found he had been waiting only fifteen minutes. He decided, however, that he must give Elsie time to settle down and that for another thirty he would not make a move.

To put away that half-hour took all his resolution. The night was cold and silent and a raw mist was forming, but he noticed none of these things. His mind was full of terrors and he spent the minutes fighting them one after another. He would be late. It would be light before he had finished. If he entered that ghastly study again Elsie would certainly hear him. If he escaped himself, the letter would remain. The letter mightn't be hidden in the study at all. Peter might have sent it to his bank. In fact, there was no possible disaster that didn't suggest itself as inevitable.

He would have given a good deal for a couple of fingers of brandy. A mistake, he thought, not to have brought a flask. Brandy would have just made the difference. It would have banished all these morbid fears and steadied him. He said to himself that he would remember it next time, and then the very thought of repeating this hideous experience made him sick.

At long last the half-hour he had set himself passed and his vigil was over. With the coming of action his nerves steadied somewhat. Once again he opened the french window, passed through, locked the door leading to the hall, and returned to the desk. The lock was broken and he was now able with infinite pains to push up the shutter. This released all the drawers and he sat down to go through them.

He was soon satisfied that he had at least reached Peter's private papers. Here was his cheque and bank books, his private account books, and all kinds of personal papers. If the letter was in the house, it would be here.

But Charles could not find it. His search was rapid, but thorough, and when it was over he was positive that it was not in the study.

Charles grew more and more satisfied that Weatherup had been bluffing. There was no letter. At all events, whether there was or not, he, Charles, could do no more. He knew of no other likely place in the house and he could not search Peter's bank.

But though he didn't find the letter, he came on something else which gave him furiously to think. This was a roll of bank-notes, and when Charles counted them he found they amounted to £135 10s. After a moment's hesitation, he slipped them into his pocket.

Closing the desk as carefully as he had opened it, Charles reversed all his other proceedings. He unlocked the door into the hall, left the room by the french window, locked the window behind him and slipped the key into his pocket. Then he set off to walk home, burying the key on the way.

He was fairly satisfied with what he had done. If he had not found the letter, he had at least left no traces, having kept his rubber gloves on all the time. Moreover, he saw with increasing satisfaction that the roll of bank-notes was going materially to improve his scheme. Yes, he thought things were going as well as he could have hoped.

Reaching his workshop, he put back the bar in his rack. He would have liked to have hidden it, but Rollins knew of its existence. In his little fireplace he burnt the bank-notes, carefully crumbling the ashes to dust. Then he returned to his rope, took off his shoes, tied them round his neck, and began to climb. He found it a terrible job, but his neck was the penalty for failure, and at last he reached his window. He pulled in his rope, untied the knots, coiled the rope and locked it once more in his wardrobe. Ten minutes later he was in bed.

CHAPTER XVI

Charles Assists Justice

ON THE WHOLE CHARLES WAS SATISFIED WITH HIS NIGHT'S work. He had carried out a loathsome job with skill and courage. He had kept his head and he had effectively hidden his traces. Granted that the thing had had to be done, it could not have been done better.

Indeed, those bank-notes had enabled him to make an even more perfect job of it than he had believed possible. Their disappearance, he believed, would supply what had been before missing: the motive. Would it not be argued that Weatherup, wanting money, had burgled Peter's desk and decamped with the spoils?

How he wished he could have removed Weatherup's clothes and suit-case and small possessions! This would have practically proved a voluntary disappearance. He had thought of it when he found the notes, but he hadn't dared to risk it. He wasn't positively sure which was Weatherup's room, and in any case it must be close to the rooms of the women servants, either of whom might have heard him.

He realized that this next day or two would be nerve-racking, and while he was dressing he kept screwing his courage up to the sticking point.

The first thing to be tackled was the single item of his scheme necessarily left over till then – the return of the rope to the workshop. This did not present any difficulty. He had merely to wait till Rollins and his wife were out of the way and carry it down. In a few seconds it was hanging in its usual place: where it was known to hang by Rollins.

Breakfast passed uneventfully and Charles went in due course to the office and settled down to his day's work. He was surprised not to have heard from The Moat, and was dreadfully anxious to know what was happening there. He was sorely tempted to make some excuse and ring up, but restrained himself.

About eleven the message arrived which he had been so eagerly expecting. Elsie rang up. She was rather troubled about Weatherup. He had disappeared and had left no message. Peter was away and she didn't know whether she should do anything about it.

Charles asked for details and then mildly pooh-poohed the whole thing. It was certainly strange, but the man would turn up. He had gone out on some business of his own and had been delayed. Had he ever done it before?

He had never done it before and Elsie couldn't imagine him doing it at all. She sounded quite upset.

All this was just what Charles had hoped for. He made light of the affair again, but said that as Elsie was evidently worried, he would come round presently and discuss it with her. She was sorry to trouble him, but was evidently relieved. He told her he wouldn't be long.

He knew that sooner or later the police would have to be sent for, and he wanted to be the one to advise and carry out this step. Also he wanted, if possible, to have a look in Peter's dressing-room before the police arrived, in case by some unlikely chance the letter might be there.

To demonstrate his belief in the unimportance of the matter, he delayed for half an hour before setting out for The Moat. Elsie was obviously glad to see him. She was a good deal worried and poured out the details at once.

Weatherup, she said, had seemed just as usual on the previous night. His bed had been slept in, but that morning he had not been seen. Nor had any news come from him since. It was quite unprecedented, and altogether unlike what Weatherup might be expected to do. What did Charles advise?

Charles for the moment didn't advise anything. He asked questions. Had Weatherup really said or done nothing which would throw light on his action? Had he had any unpleasantness with Peter? Had any letter or caller or message come for him recently? Was anything known of the man's relations or family?

Nothing helpful of course came out, though Charles was glad to note that his telephone call did not appear to have been overheard. He gradually became more impressed.

'Has anyone looked in his room?' he asked.

'Yes, the maids looked. His bed had been slept in.'

'Could they say what clothes he was wearing when he left and also whether he took away his things? It might indicate whether he went away deliberately.'

'I asked that. He was wearing his ordinary butler's dress except that he had taken his usual off-duty tweed jacket instead of the tail coat. His hat was gone, but the girls missed nothing else.'

'What about looking in the grounds?'

'We did so.'

Charles allowed himself to become still more impressed.

'When will Peter be home?' he asked.

'Not till the evening.'

'Well, I suggest that we have a more careful look through the house and grounds and if we find nothing I think we should ring up the police. What do you say, Elsie?'

Elsie wrung her hands. 'Oh dear,' she cried, 'as if we hadn't had enough of police! But I agree, we must tell them. Let's do what you say, have a good search round, and then if we find nothing we'll ring them up.'

This was Charles's opportunity. The two maids were called and he organized the proceedings. He did it skilfully, slipping away quite naturally from the party to make his own investigations. These proved easier than he had anticipated. Not only was there no letter in the dressing-room, but there was no place where one might have been hidden.

The house complete, they went out into the grounds. The search here was equally thorough and equally unproductive. They returned to the sitting-room. Charles walked up and down.

'It's getting on to lunch time, Elsie,' he said presently. 'I'm not at all sure that we shouldn't ring up Lucas. Shall I?'

'Yes, Charles, if you will.'

Superintendent Lucas heard the news without comment save that he would send a man at once. Would Mr Swinburn kindly wait till he came, so as to give him the details?

Sergeant Bray and a constable arrived in a few minutes. Charles met them and explained what he had been told. They took his statement and Elsie's and the maids, then disappeared to examine Weatherup's room.

'You'll stay to lunch, Charles?' Elsie invited.

Charles was sorry, but he wanted to get back to his office. If, however, there was anything he could do, he would come out again. In fact, he would come back in the afternoon in any case, for Elsie must not be left too long alone.

Elsie said it was good of him. She would be glad to see him.

As a matter of fact Charles had stood just about as much as he was able. There was his constant dread lest he should say or do something, or omit to say or do something, which might give himself away. That in itself was nerve-racking. But there was more. There was the memory of the night. Wherever he looked he seemed to see that dreadful, motionless shape on the boat-house floor; at all times rang in his ears the soft yet hideous sound of the lead pipe falling on the skull and the faint sucking splash when the remains disappeared over the stern of the boat. Charles was beginning to think he would never be able to blot those sights and sounds from his memory.

He could not face lunch at the club, so he drove to an inn some five or six miles away and had some bread and cheese and a whisky and soda. Then he returned to his office.

Nothing of importance had come in and he spent an hour smoking and resting. Then, a good deal recovered, he drove out once again to The Moat. Elsie herself opened the door.

'I saw you coming up,' she explained. 'Oh, Charles, isn't this dreadful!' she went on, wringing her hands. 'Fancy what they've found. He had broken open Peter's desk and stolen a lot of money!'

'No!' answered Charles in shocked tones. 'Weatherup! I shouldn't have believed it. I never liked him, but I always looked on him as absolutely honest. You amaze me!'

'It amazed me, I can tell you. Oh, it's utterly horrible! But do come in.'

Charles followed her into the sitting-room. 'There's no news of him, of course?'

'No, none. The sergeant's still there in the study. You know, I heard Weatherup in the night.'

'You heard him?'

'Yes, about three this morning.' She sat down and pointed to a chair. 'I heard a crack like a pistol shot from somewhere downstairs. I was awake at the time. I thought probably a picture had fallen: I've been frightened at night in that way before. So I went down and had a look, but I couldn't see anything wrong and I supposed it was just the woodwork cracking. But now the sergeant says it must have been the forcing of the desk.'

'My goodness, Elsie, that was plucky of you! It was a mercy you didn't come upon him in the act. He might have attacked you.'

'He must have been there at the time, so the sergeant says. He must have been either behind the desk or outside the window. See him and he'll tell you.'

'I certainly shall. It's just about the most astonishing thing I've heard for years! And Weatherup of all people! That's what I can't get over.'

'Nor I.'

'Was much money taken?'

'I don't know exactly how much. I think over a hundred pounds.'

'Oh, well, it might have been worse.'

Elsie wrung her hands again. 'It's not the money,' she declared, 'though that's bad enough. It's the whole thing. Oh, Charles, it's terrible, coming so soon after the other! Really I'm beginning to feel as if I couldn't endure the sight of this place for another day.'

'I'm so sorry, Elsie. And I'm afraid it will worry Peter, too.'

'Peter! I don't like to think of it. He was worried enough as it was. And he'll hate not having been here; you know what I mean. My being alone and all that.'

'I expect that was the reason of it, you know,' said Charles, having hastily thought out the bearings of the remark. 'If Weatherup was going to – do what he did, he would choose a time when Peter was away; naturally.'

'I suppose so.' She shook her head again.

'Have you had lunch?' Charles asked.

'No; I couldn't think of eating.'

'Now look here, Elsie, go and have some lunch,' Charles said with decision. 'Have some coffee or a whisky and soda if you can't eat.

There's no use in your getting knocked up as well. You go and I'll speak to the sergeant.'

'What about yourself, Charles?'

'I've had it, thanks.'

Charles surprised himself, so well in hand were his nerves as he crossed the hall and, tapping on the study door, pushed it open and entered. Sergeant Bray rose from the desk.

'Well, sergeant,' said Charles, 'I hear you've made a discovery?'

'Yes, sir, and it's a bit surprising too. I shouldn't have thought the butler was the man for this job.'

'Nor I,' Charles answered. 'What's the meaning of it all?'

Bray shook his head.

'Is that the broken desk?' Charles gazed with interest. 'Mrs Morley says she heard him breaking it open.'

'She heard a sound which we attribute to that cause,' Bray returned more accurately. 'You knew the man, Mr Swinburn?'

This was more like the police. Questions, no information, was their line.

'Oh, yes,' Charles answered. 'He was with my late uncle for a number of years. I'd seen him many times.'

'Did you ever hear anything about his relations or family?'

'Not a word.'

'Or if he was going after any woman?'

'No.'

'Or, I suppose, of any secret in his life?'

'Nothing of the sort.'

'He made no previous breaks while with the late Mr Crowther?'

'None; at least so far as I know. Have you been through his room?' Charles didn't see why all the questioning should be on one side.

'Yes, sir, but I found nothing.'

Bray was not communicative, and after a little further conversation Charles left the study. He found Elsie having coffee in the dining-room.

'Glad to see you doing that,' he assured her, then with a change of tone, 'Do you know what train Peter's coming by?'

'The one that gets in just before dinner.'

'I'll meet him,' Charles declared.

He stayed on at The Moat for an hour or more discussing the affair with Elsie, or rather letting her talk about it while he sat with the appearance of listening. At the end of that time he felt himself at the end of his tether and pleaded a business engagement. He wanted terribly to be alone, but to go off anywhere by himself would look suspicious, and that he could not risk. However, at the works he was next thing to being alone, and somehow the afternoon dragged away.

Peter was a surprised man when at the station Charles told him the news. Eagerly he asked for details. Charles, considering carefully what he knew and what he didn't know, gave them to him.

'I have the car here,' Charles went on. 'Get in and I'll drive you home.'

Peter was obviously a good deal puzzled as well as distressed by the affair. 'What could have gone wrong with him?' he asked more than once. 'He never gave any hint of being short of cash. And then to go and risk prison for that amount! And look here, Charles, here's another thing. How did he know that I had the money there? I never told him. I told Elsie, but she would never have repeated it.'

This was a point Charles had not foreseen. 'He must have overheard you telling her,' he suggested.

'I suppose he must,' Peter agreed doubtfully.

Charles was relieved by the admission. Peter evidently accepted the man's guilt.

'Frightfully hard lines on Elsie, this upset,' Charles went on, 'especially following so close on the last,' and he began to talk generalities.

That evening passed for Charles like a nightmare. What he wanted more than anything else was information. What were the police doing? What had they discovered? Had they any reason to suspect the affair was more serious than it appeared? More vital still, had they any reason to connect him, Charles, with it? So terrible was the craving to know how he stood that more than once he contemplated going down to the police-station to inquire of Sergeant Bray how the case was progressing, in the hope that from the man's manner he would be able to read the answer to his real question. Indeed, only the utter madness of such a proceeding prevented him.

The next day it was the same. Oh, if he only knew! Of course he rang up The Moat, but what Peter could tell him was not what he wanted to hear. As a matter of fact Peter had little news. With the single exception that the key of the study french window was missing, nothing had been discovered.

And so it was the next day and the next. Nothing fresh learned! Charles's anxiety had by this time passed its peak and every hour that now elapsed was an ease to his mind. If anything dreadful had been discovered, he would have heard of it. Instead of being upset, he should be thankful that everything was going so well. This second terrible crisis in his life had passed, as had the first, leaving him unscathed. He needn't have been afraid. His scheme was good. As before, he was safe!

Then on the fourth day he received a dreadful shock.

It was a Sunday. On Sundays when he could not play tennis, he usually played golf. Now as he was about to start for the links, Peter rang up. From his voice Charles could tell that something was wrong.

'I've got some bad news, Charles,' Peter said. 'This affair is much worse than we had any idea of. Sergeant Bray has just been here and what do you think? They're going to drag the lake.'

Charles felt suddenly cold. Drag the lake! His knees began to tremble. Then savagely he pulled himself together.

'Drag the lake, Peter?' he repeated to gain time. 'Whatever do you mean? They don't suppose…?'

'Yes,' Peter answered, 'they do. They think he's dead. They think he's in the lake. They're starting now to drag. It's perfectly dreadful!'

'But I don't understand. How…? What do they think has happened?'

'I don't understand either. They came for the keys of the boat-house and whatever they found I don't know, but they came back and asked for the use of the boats.'

Charles was getting himself more in hand. 'Peter, I'm so sorry,' he said, 'and also particularly on Elsie's account. If there's anything in this, it'll be a nasty shock for her.'

'Yes, she's pretty much upset as it is. This coming on the top of the other, you know. I'm not surprised. I feel it myself.'

'I'm sure you do. But I can't bring myself to believe such a thing could have happened. Why should anyone – commit such a crime?'

'I suppose to get the notes; how do I know?'

Presently Charles said that he would go over to The Moat to discuss the affair, and rang off. He was terribly upset. As he drove he went over again in minute detail what he had done in the boat-house. The more he recalled that dreadful time – and every moment of it was seared into his memory – the more convinced he became that he had left no trace of his presence. And yet a trace of some kind must have been found. The overwhelming question was: did the trace, whatever it was, point to him personally or only to the fact that someone had been there? At all costs Charles must find this out. The suspense, if he didn't, would kill him.

But he mustn't show more interest than the occasion ought to warrant. Could he face Peter and Elsie and the police and act as an interested outsider? Yes, he must. Any mistake now might be fatal.

He soon saw that so far as Peter was concerned, he need not have worried. Peter's own manner was strange. Peter had undoubtedly taken the affair very much to heart and so had Elsie. After some talk the two men walked down to the lake. Three boats were in use, the two from The Moat boat-house and one belonging to Peter's neighbour. In each were two men, one at the oars and one manipulating the large rake-like drag. Bray was in one of the boats. A constable stood at the boat-house and saluted respectfully as Peter and Charles approached.

Peter engaged him in conversation, but without result. The dragging was the authorities' idea, and the constable did not know what had made it necessary. No, they had not found anything so far, but of course they hadn't much more than started. He did not know what they had found in the boat-house, if anything. He could not say how long they would keep up their efforts. In fact the constable was an excellent police representative.

For some little time the three men stood watching the sinister operations. The police were working systematically and Charles felt sure that if they continued as they had begun, they would find the body. At present they were keeping to the shore, but each new path they swept was a little farther out. To reach the middle of the lake was a mere question of time.

The day dragged interminably. Charles could settle to nothing. He cancelled his golf and hung about The Moat with Peter. He was longing to go home and be alone, but he could not tear himself away from the chance of news. When night came and nothing had been found he could scarcely have told whether he was the more distressed or relieved.

The next day was the same. Indeed it was almost worse. He knew that the boats would by this time have crept a good deal nearer to that ghastly spot in the centre of the lake. He would have given a lot of money to know just how far they had still to go, but he dared not exhibit that kind of interest. No, there was nothing for it but to get through the day as best he could, showing pressing interest in nothing but his business.

That evening his body was aching all over from sheer weariness. For almost the first time in his life he was drunk when bedtime came.

On the following morning a splitting headache was almost a relief. It gave him something to think of, or rather it took his mind to some extent off the lake. He tried to concentrate on business. Almost he succeeded.

Then in the middle of the morning the news came. Peter rang up to say that the body had been found.

CHAPTER XVII

Charles Attains Security

P ETER DID NOT SEEM TO HAVE OBTAINED MUCH INFORMATION beyond the mere facts that the body had been discovered and that the case was one of murder. He asked Charles to go over to lunch and discuss the situation. Charles, fighting his fears, agreed.

Charles found both Peter and Elsie still very much upset when he reached The Moat. Already Peter had been warned to remain at home for the next day or two, as he would be wanted at the inquest.

'As if we hadn't had enough of that sort of thing,' Elsie complained. 'I'm terribly sorry for poor Weatherup, though he was a man I didn't really care for. But I'm also sorry for ourselves, having to go through all this police business again and so soon. I don't think we'll be able to stay here. This place has become utterly hateful.'

Charles asked for details of the discovery.

'There's not much to tell,' Peter returned, and Charles soon found that this was the case. Peter, however, had two items of information, one of which Charles found disquieting and the other reassuring.

'Did you know,' went on Peter, 'that the Scotland Yard man was here still and all this work at the lake has been done at his request? He's been here asking questions and I found him at the lake yesterday. I went down to see how they were getting on and he was there talking to Bray. Bray was deferring to him in the most obsequious way.'

This was an unexpected blow. Charles, however, managed a creditable reply.

'I thought – what's his name? – French had gone back to town? hadn't heard anything of him lately.'

'I thought so, too, but we were wrong. I wonder what he thinks he's getting at.'

Charles shook his head vaguely. It was what was so terribly agitating himself.

'You say,' he went on, 'that it was definitely a case of murder. How did they know that?'

'His skull was fractured. He had evidently been hit over the head with something heavy, and Bray thinks it may have been a piece of lead pipe. Two pieces of lead pipe were tied to the body to weight it down. It shows the affair was premeditated, doesn't it, if the murderer had provided himself with weights.'

Charles agreed. 'Makes it more mysterious than ever,' he commented. 'In the first place, if Weatherup was murdered for the money, how did the murderer know he had it on him?'

'I don't know,' Peter returned. 'I saw that difficulty myself. Indeed, I put it to Bray.'

'What did he say?'

'He said he had been puzzled by the same thing. The police are not giving much away.'

'I thought you believed they agreed with me?' put in Elsie.

'Well, I did,' Peter admitted slowly; 'I thought so, but I'm not sure. I had precious little to go on.'

Charles turned to his cousin. 'You had a theory, Elsie? What was it?'

'I suggested,' Elsie answered, 'that some unknown person had burgled the house and that Weatherup had heard him and gone down. Perhaps he had followed him out and challenged him and the burglar had turned on him and murdered him to save himself being caught.'

'That's ingenious, Elsie,' Charles declared. 'To me that sounds the most likely theory yet. And you say you think the police accept it, Peter?'

Peter moved uneasily. 'I thought so, but I couldn't be sure. As I say, I mentioned it to Bray, and he seemed impressed. I agree that it would explain a lot. But then it assumes that the burglar knew the money was in the desk, which doesn't seem possible.'

'Does it assume that?' Charles queried. 'Might the money not have been found simply by accident?'

'Then what was the burglar looking for?'

'Anything valuable. It would have been a reasonable enough assumption that there might be money there. But if not there would almost certainly have been something valuable.'

'The dining-room was full of silver. Why didn't he take some of that?'

'Silver's bulky and hard to get rid of. Money is what he'd look for. At least, I think so. What do you say, Elsie?'

They agreed that while not entirely satisfactory, this theory was the best so far put forward. 'I'd be glad if it turned out to be true,' said Elsie. 'I hate to think of that man after all these years being just a common thief.'

'Yes,' Peter agreed, 'I feel that, too. Weatherup wasn't a bad soul. The old man liked him and indeed Weatherup was very good to him.'

'Tell me,' said Charles. 'You said the key of the study window was missing. Was it found on the body?'

Peter hadn't heard. He had forgotten to ask and Bray had not volunteered the information.

They continued discussing the affair during lunch, and then Charles went with Peter to the study to smoke a cigar.

'There's one thing, Peter,' he said as they settled themselves with a decanter of port on the table between them; 'I wonder has it occurred to you? This affair may make a considerable difference to your peace of mind. Have you realized that there is now no evidence that you were handling the old man's bottle of pills on the night before his death?'

Peter nodded several times. 'I thought of that,' he answered, glancing meaningly at his cousin. 'In fact in a way I've scarcely thought of anything else since the body was found. I've felt ashamed of myself, because I found myself actually glad that it had happened. Still, I suppose I had some excuse.'

'Of course you had,' Charles said warmly. 'I don't see how you could be anything else but glad. Not that I ever believed you had anything to fear. But now you won't have it on your mind any longer.'

Peter seemed relieved. 'I declare, Charles, it's a comfort to hear you say that. Though I'm glad the way it has worked out, you understand I'm sorry about Weatherup. Poor fellow, it was a horrible death to die; and yet I suppose in a way it was an easy one. He couldn't have felt anything, at all events.'

As soon as Charles could manage it, he took his leave. Talking about the affair was a terrible strain, and though he thought he had acquitted himself well, there was always the danger of making some slip. It would be so desperately easy to know a little bit too much, and once he had shown undue knowledge, nothing on earth could explain it away.

The rest of that day was a torment. Suspense! That was what tried him so desperately. Though his reason told him he was safe, his imagination kept on suggesting all sorts of possibilities.

Late that evening there was a telephone call from Peter. The police had just advised him that the inquest was to be held in the town hall at half-past ten on the following morning. Peter supposed that Charles would like to be present.

'Yes, I'll be there,' Charles answered. 'How's Elsie keeping?'

'Oh, all right. She's not looking forward with much pleasure to to-morrow.'

'She won't be called, will she? I should have thought they'd take evidence of identification and adjourn.'

'The constable who came round wasn't sure. She's been summoned on chance, at all events.'

To his surprise Charles slept like a log all that night. All the same he woke in a very depressed condition and with the thought of what he had done heavy on his mind. He had first the impression that he had just been dreaming a dreadful nightmare, and then he experienced the contingent feeling of relief that he was not really in the appalling position he had supposed. For a moment he lay luxuriating in the belief that the horror was non-existent. Then he remembered! The nightmare was real. The horror was actual. He was doubly a murderer. Moreover the knowledge would always be there. Nothing that he could do would blot it out. And there was not only this dreadful moral weight on him. He was in danger physically. He was in danger of death and of worse than death.

However, breakfast and strong coffee steadied his nerves and when he reached the town hall he felt cool and sure of himself. To-day at all events would not be so bad. He was not even to be called as a witness. All he had to do was to sit tight and say nothing.

History seemed to be repeating itself as he pushed his way into the crowded room. Once again Sergeant Bray showed him to a seat, where presently he was joined by Peter and Elsie and the two maids from The Moat. Once again the unemployed formed the larger part of the audience. Once again the interest was keen.

The coroner was the same Dr Emerson who had presided at the first inquiry. He settled down to the preliminaries with the same quiet efficiency as before. As murder was suspected, he was sitting with a jury and the members were now called.

The police were unusually strongly represented. As well as Sergeant Bray and his constables, both Superintendent Lucas and Inspector French were present. Charles's anxiety was somewhat increased when they took their places, then he told himself that in any murder case they would come. It meant nothing to him.

Peter was the first witness. Peter had pulled himself together, and, while grave, he was quite collected and apparently free from nervousness. He listened to the coroner's questions with attention and replied to them quickly and fully. To Charles he seemed a model witness.

First he stated that he had inspected the remains and that they were those of John Weatherup, his butler. He sketched Weatherup's career so far as he knew it and testified to his excellent character. He had always found him strictly honest and he would be very much surprised indeed to learn that the man had stolen his money. He knew nothing of the deceased, however, prior to the latter entering the service of his father-in-law, the late Mr Andrew Crowther. Nor did he know anything of the man's family; he had never heard the subject mentioned. He had no reason whatever to suppose the deceased was carrying on any intrigue. Weatherup was a somewhat secretive man and he, witness, knew really nothing of his private life. No, he certainly had not known of his being in any financial or other trouble. Had such circumstances obtained, he would have been glad to help Weatherup out, and he believed the man would have known this and applied to him. He had noticed nothing unusual in his manner prior to his death.

The coroner then asked about the money. Peter said that he had been going to an auction of agricultural machinery and he had obtained some cash as he wished to purchase on a fairly large scale. He had used some of it, leaving a balance of £135 10s. It was mostly in single notes, though there were a few fives. He locked the roll in his desk, there being no safe at The Moat. He mentioned that he had done so to his wife and to no one else. He did not think he could have been overheard in doing so, but of course he could not be absolutely certain. On the night of the robbery and tragedy he himself was in London. No, he was entirely puzzled by the affair and could not suggest any theory of what might have happened.

In reply to a juror Peter said that so far as he knew there was only one key to his desk and that he kept that on his ring in his pocket. The desk was certainly left open at times, but he had been careful to keep it locked while the money was there. No one therefore could have opened it accidentally and learnt of the notes.

Elsie was next called. She generally corroborated Peter's evidence about Weatherup's character and manner prior to his death and declared her ignorance of his family or private affairs. Then she told of the night of the tragedy. She had been lying awake. About three in the morning she had heard a loud report from somewhere downstairs. She had once heard a picture fall during the night and she thought this sounded much the same. She went down and had a look through the lower rooms. Everything however seemed normal and she supposed the sound must have been caused by a creaking board. No, she had not called the servants. Why should she, since she had been satisfied there was nothing wrong? Next day the police had shown her the split in the wood of the study desk. She was sure that split was fresh. The sound she heard might have been that wood splitting, but of course she could not say so definitely.

Next morning Weatherup had disappeared. She asked the maids and found that his bed had been slept in. She did nothing for a while, thinking that he had gone out and would presently return. He did not come however and about eleven she rang up her cousin, Mr Charles

Swinburn, to ask his advice. Mr Swinburn went over to see her and they made a rough search of the house and grounds. When they found no trace Mr Swinburn advised informing the police. She agreed and asked him to ring them up and he did so. The police turned up in a few minutes.

No, she couldn't understand what could have occurred. She had always found the deceased perfectly honest and she also would be very much surprised to learn it was he who had stolen the notes.

The maids were the next witnesses. They deposed that when the deceased had not appeared in the morning they had looked into his room. They had found that his bed had been slept in, and that the deceased's ordinary clothes had gone: his dress waistcoat and trousers and an old tweed coat which he used to wear if he went out about the place in the evening. His manner had been quite normal on the previous evening and neither could imagine what had occurred. So far as either knew he had not received any letter or message during the day.

A slightly increased show of interest passed over the assembly when the next witness was called: Detective-Inspector French of Scotland Yard. He looked a pleasant, rather kindly and very ordinary man as he stood in the box and took the oath. He spoke quietly and courteously, but gave a good deal less information than his hearers would have liked.

He explained that as he had been at Cold Pickerby at the time of the disappearance and had actually investigated the death of the former owner of The Moat, the local authorities had asked London to allow him to go into this case also, and he had received instructions from headquarters to do so.

'Very good, inspector,' the coroner went on. 'Will you just tell the jury in your own words what you can about this case.'

'I began, sir, by going to The Moat and making certain inquiries. Acting on information received I asked Superintendent Lucas to have the lake adjoining The Moat dragged. This dragging was done, with the result that the body of the deceased was discovered. It was taken from a point near the middle of the lake, and appeared to have been submerged for about five days, just the period which had elapsed since the disappearance. I was able personally to identify the remains, having come across the late Mr Weatherup in connexion with the earlier inquiry.'

Charles would have given a good proportion of his inheritance to know just what the 'information received' actually amounted to. But it was obvious that he was not to have enlightenment. French was continuing in his pleasant unhurried way.

'I examined the remains and at once I saw evidence of foul play. The skull was obviously fractured from a blow, the back of the head having been actually driven in. The head was bare and the hat was buttoned inside the coat. To the body were tied two pieces of three-quarter-inch lead pipe, one piece fourteen inches long and the other thirty-five inches, with the obvious intention of preventing it floating after decomposition set in.'

'Are you satisfied that it was a case of murder?' asked the coroner.

'Yes, sir. In my opinion both accident and suicide are out of the question. I examined the clothes and the objects in the pockets, but without finding anything of interest.'

'No letters or papers?'

'None, sir.'

'Nor any of the missing bank-notes?'

'No, sir.'

'Very well. Go on, please.'

'I think, sir, that all the further information I have has already been placed before the jury. With the exception of the broken desk in the study I found nothing in the house or in the deceased's room which threw any light on what had taken place. I found that the desk in the study had been burst open with the aid of some tool like a burglar's jemmy. I also found that the study french window was locked and the key missing. The key had been there on the previous day.'

'You didn't find any footprints or marks on the ground approaching the window?'

'No, sir, but the ground was hard owing to the dry weather. On examining the desk I found that the table portion was cracked or split along the line of the lock keeper, evidently caused by the pressure of the jemmy. It occurred to me that this would not have cracked without giving a loud report, and I assumed that it was this sound Mrs Morley had heard. Of course there is no proof of this.'

'Yes? Is that all you have to tell us?'

'Yes, sir. That covers everything.'

'You are not then in a position to explain to us just what occurred?'

French smiled slightly. 'No, sir,' he said dryly.

The coroner paused. 'The reason I asked that question is this,' he said slowly. 'Here we have a man of, so far as is known, exemplary character, found dead in circumstances which suggest that one of his last actions may have been to help himself to his employer's money. Now it would be a deplorable thing if such a stigma should lie unjustly on a dead man. I therefore wondered if there was any other way of explaining the facts.' He paused and leant forward. 'Tell me, inspector, do you know any reason why the following theory should not be true?'

Again Dr Emerson paused, while French waited respectfully. Interest had become more tense and the silence was complete.

'Suppose,' Dr Emerson resumed, 'the deceased heard or saw something during the night which aroused his suspicions, and suppose he went down and found someone burgling the study, or perhaps leaving the study after having burgled it. Suppose it proved impossible to capture the burglar – the man might for instance have been armed. Suppose the deceased therefore decided to follow him with the idea of finding out where he went. Suppose that in doing so the deceased attracted the burglar's attention, a scuffle ensued, and the burglar murdered the deceased to avoid subsequent identification. Now, inspector, from your knowledge of the facts, do you think that this or some similar theory, which would acquit the dead man of theft, might be the truth?'

French moved uneasily. 'Nothing, sir, that I have learned is inconsistent with such a theory, but I must point out that I have no proof of its truth.'

'Oh, quite, I understand that. I only wanted to know whether it was possible to account for the facts on the basis of the deceased's innocence of theft.'

'I think it possible, sir, but entirely unproven.'

'I understand. That's quite interesting, inspector.' The coroner paused, glancing over his notes. 'I think that's all,' he said slowly, then, after a further pause, gave his usual invitation to the jury.

This time the foreman availed himself of it. 'I should like to ask the inspector if he looked for the jemmy the desk was broken open with, and if so, whether he found it?'

On the coroner nodding, French replied: 'Yes, to the first part of the question and no, to the second. I made a search for the tool, but didn't find it.'

This was all the foreman wanted to know and the inspector stepped down.

Dr Gregory was then called. He repeated in more technical language what French had said about the dead man's injuries, and confirmed his opinion that these injuries could not have been inflicted otherwise than through murder.

This completed the evidence and Dr Emerson summed up, beginning with the same little homily on the duties of the jurors which he had given at the Crowther inquest. As before, he told them they had to state the identity of the deceased and to say how death was caused. Also if they thought that anyone was to blame for what had occurred, they were to say so, and if further they were of opinion that such blame had been incurred by any particular person or persons, they might express that opinion. He thought they would have little difficulty in arriving at a decision on all these points. They had before them definite evidence as to the deceased's identity and as to the cause of death, and if they believed that evidence they could have no hesitation as to their finding.

So far as he was concerned, he did not see that any evidence had been offered incriminating any person, and if they agreed with that view they would bring in a verdict of wilful murder against some person or persons unknown. They would now retire and consider their verdict.

After seven minutes' consultation the jury found as the coroner suggested.

Little voices were singing in Charles's mind as he heard their announcement. At last definitely he was safe! The police suspected nothing. So far as he, Charles, was concerned, the whole ghastly affair was closed. Not only was he safe in this Weatherup case, but he was safe in the original Andrew Crowther case as well. And what was more, Peter was now safe also. What Charles had now to do was to forget this dreadful period of his life, and to fill his mind once again with the normal ideas and pursuits which had been so long interrupted. He had been so terribly worried that he had scarcely been able to think even of Una. Now that was past. He would see Una that very day and try to get her to agree to an early date for the wedding.

Peter interrupted his thoughts. 'We can't find that he had any relations,' he said. 'I don't know whether to advertise or not. I'm settling the funeral, of course.'

'I shouldn't advertise,' answered Charles, who wanted the affair to be forgotten as quickly as possible. 'It's not as if he was a millionaire. That's good of you about the funeral, but I'm sure you're doing the right thing.'

Peter shook his head. 'I won't advertise if you don't think it's necessary. Well, we must be getting along. Come out and see us soon, Charles.'

Charles said he would, then getting his car from the park, drove to the works.

Safe! All nature conspired to shout the word at him. The wheels of his car droned it to him, the klaxons in the street barked it at him; in the meaner streets near the works it came up in the cries of the children at play. Through the open window of his office a bird was singing it: even the muffled rumble of Miss Lillingstone's typewriter seemed to breathe peace and security. Nothing suspected! With the rolling away of this terrible black shadow which had been darkening his every moment, Charles felt like a boy released from school.

Then came a slight reaction. Of course, in a way, neither case was over. It was said that the police never entirely dropped any case. Further investigations might be made...

But, he asked himself again, what if there were? What could come out? Nothing! No: definitely for him the thing was over! And Una? That very afternoon he would go to see her. Oh, blessed thought! She would understand his apparent neglect. She would see that he had not been to blame. She would perhaps complete his cup of joy by agreeing to fix the date of the wedding.

But in the afternoon Charles received a sharp disappointment. Una was from home. She had gone on a visit to some friends in Gloucester and would not be back for a week. However, he got her address and in the evening wrote her a satisfyingly voluminous letter.

As day succeeded day Charles picked up one by one the threads of his former life. The look of anxiety gradually disappeared from his face and its old expression of easy good humour took its place. The dark episode was being successfully banished from his mind.

Things at the works seemed to have taken a slight turn for the better. The new machines had arrived before the contract date, had been installed, and were now running. Charles was delighted with them, while Sandy Macpherson's 'Man, they're fine,' showed real enthusiasm. It was a day of excitement when the first costs from their working were available.

'They're bringing down the machining on the Standard A model from two-and-threepence to one-and-fivepence-farthing; say ten dee every set up,' Macpherson declared rapturously. 'That would 'a' meant seventy-two pounds knocked off our estimate for that Northallerton job. We'd 'a' got yon if we'd 'a' had the machines.'

That very evening the post carried away a revised estimate for a largish job near Leeds, an estimate with nearly a hundred pounds knocked off the previous figure. Some days later the entire staff were overjoyed to learn that they had got the contract; Charles afterwards learned by a margin of some five and twenty pounds.

'It looks as if you were going to be right about the machines, Sandy,' commented Charles, who always made a point of giving his subordinates their due.

'Aye, it's no' looking so bad,' admitted the Scot.

Another thing which gave Charles a new interest in life was a visit paid by an architect to his house. Plans materialized for the addition of another couple of rooms, an enlarged hall, and the installation of all kinds of improved appliances. A landscape gardener also arrived and produced suggestions to improve the surroundings of the improved house. Charles gloated over the thought of laying these plans before Una. Their existence would at least prove that she had not been out of his mind – if such proof were necessary.

Peter also seemed happier than for many months. He had engaged a new butler and was laying plans for market gardening on a larger scale. This new interest was good for him and was shown in his more cheerful outlook upon the world.

In fact, Charles felt that he had entered upon a new chapter of his life, in which all seemed propitious and in which he would have the same chance of happiness as the next man.

Then an incident occurred which brought him up with a jerk and rudely dispelled all his hopes of having left behind this dark period of his life. Once again he was gripped by doubt and distress, while actual panic hovered closer and closer.

CHAPTER XVIII

Charles Experiences Panic

I T HAPPENED THAT THE QUARTERLY DINNER OF A CERTAIN MANU-facturers' association was taking place in Newcastle, and as there was an important business meeting before it, Charles went up to attend it. He travelled by train, leaving on the Tuesday morning, sleeping the night and returning the following day. The function proved as interesting as he had expected, and it was in a very good humour that he reached the works after lunch on the Wednesday.

Settled down once again in his office, he rang for Gairns to bring the correspondence which had been received during his absence. This was disposed of satisfactorily, and then Gairns administered the shock.

'That Scotland Yard officer – French, his name is,' he said, 'was here yesterday looking for you. He said you had told him you had gone to London shortly before leaving for your holiday, but that he had mislaid his note of the dates, and that he wanted them to complete his report.'

Charles was completely taken aback. Inspector French still here? What could it mean?

'Oh, that's right,' he said, though in spite of all his efforts there was a little tremor in his voice. 'He's welcome to the information. You were able to give it to him, I suppose?'

The old man shook his head. 'No, sir, I knew nothing about it. I told him he'd better ask yourself.'

Charles actually succeeded in producing a laugh. 'Think you might give me away to the police, did you?' he chuckled. 'I hope it's not so serious as all that. That all he wanted to know?'

Gairns wasn't sure. Charles had seldom known him sure of anything. It seemed the inspector had stayed for a considerable time
chatting. What about? Oh, everything: bad trade, how the district
was weathering the storm; how he, French, compared the conditions
in Yorkshire and Lincoln, where he had just been working; whether
the works had avoided reductions of staff or wages; whether such had
been threatened; when these reductions had been threatened, and
when the threat had been removed.

Charles's heart sank during this recital; however he resolutely
concentrated on getting rid of the clerk. 'That's what most people
talk about nowadays – unfortunately,' he said as lightly as he could.
'Well, James, that all? You'll send that quotation to Armstrong's by
the afternoon post?'

Gairns gathered up his papers and withdrew, leaving Charles to
face this terribly upsetting news. French had undoubtedly left Cold
Pickerby; everyone was agreed as to that. What had he come back
for? Surely, surely the case couldn't have been reopened? And the
Crowther case; not the Weatherup case. That question about the dates
of his going to London: that was a bit thin. Was it likely that a Yard
inspector would mislay his notes? Coming when Charles was away
for the day and asking a question like that. Yes, it was thin. The man
was after something else.

But what? There was nothing in his questions about the works. It
couldn't be about shortage of money; he, Charles, had made no secret
of the fact that for a while he had been short. What, then, was it?

The indefiniteness of the peril terrified Charles. Or was there really
any peril? Could it not simply be true what the man had said, that he had
to complete a report for filing, and that he really had mislaid his notes?

Charles tried to reassure himself on these lines, but when he went
home that night his anxiety grew acute once again. French, it appeared,

had been there also. He had interviewed both Rollins and his wife, and with the same story. Rollins, unlike the cautious Gairns, had at once given the information. But French had not seemed satisfied. As at the works, he had remained chatting in an apparently aimless way about Charles and his affairs; asking if he was much from home, to what extent he entertained, and even if he saw much of Una Mellor. He had professed a great admiration of the situation of the house and asked if he might walk round it and see the view from all sides.

Charles could make nothing of it, though the whole thing was excessively disquieting. However, he heard no more from French. Once again the man appeared to have left the town. As the days passed he found himself growing increasingly satisfied that French's statement about his report had been the literal truth. He, Charles, need not have been so much upset.

Everything indeed did seem to be going well in the days that followed, with one exception: he could get no further with Una. She was pleasant, she let him see her as much as he wanted to, she played golf with him, she looked at the plans for the house and garden, but she would come to no decision. She wouldn't fix the date for the wedding; indeed, she said once or twice that she had not yet decided whether she would marry him or not. She admired the proposed alterations to the house, but she would not allow them to be put in hand. In a word, she was most tantalizing and unsatisfactory. But Charles had no redress. She intimated that if he forced an answer it would be 'No'. He had to be content.

Then one evening a dreadful and totally unexpected blow fell.

Charles had had a tiresome day at the works. Owing to the non-delivery of certain materials an important job had been held up and it looked as if it could not be completed in contract time. Everyone was working at high pressure, and worry and frayed nerves were the result. Charles had brought home with him the relevant papers, intending during the evening to draft out a statement of his claim against the defaulting contractor. The matter was not straightforward, and he foresaw trouble and possible litigation.

Charles dined and read the evening paper while he smoked a leisurely cigar. Then about nine he settled down with his papers in the study.

He had the faculty of concentration. Soon he drafted out the main heads of his argument and then turned to give the detailed proof of each. He got on better than he had hoped, and at ten o'clock he thought that another half-hour should see him through.

A few minutes later he heard the rolling sound of a car and a ring at the door. Charles listened to Rollins passing down the hall. Then came the murmur of voices. There were heavy steps and the study door opened. Rollins announced, 'Superintendent Lucas and Inspector French.'

One glance at their faces told Charles that his hour had come. Both were looking grave and troubled, as if engaged on a distasteful errand. Moreover, though they didn't seem to move across the room, they were there at his side instantly. Charles stood up uncertainly. Rollins disappeared, closing the door.

Till then neither spoke, but as the door shut the superintendent broke the silence.

'We're both sorry, Mr Swinburn, to come on distressing business, but it is my duty to tell you that I hold a warrant for your arrest on a charge of murdering your uncle, Andrew Crowther, and his man, John Weatherup. I must also warn you that anything you say will be taken down and used in evidence. I have a car here and if you will come with us quietly I promise you shall not be inconvenienced more than is necessary.'

The strength seemed to leave Charles's knees and he sank back into his chair. His heart seemed to be beating in a queer way and he found it hard to breathe. What was this incredible thing that he had heard? They couldn't arrest him on mere suspicion surely? And they couldn't, they *couldn't* have any real evidence against him. No, no; it was not possible. He had left no loopholes. They were making some ghastly mistake. Or was he asleep? God, this wasn't real. It wasn't real!

Confusedly he was conscious of movement. Then a tumbler was before him and he heard French's voice. 'Drink some of this, sir.'

Charles gulped down the brandy which had been taken from the decanter on his side-table. It was what he had wanted. Suddenly his nerves grew steady. He put down the glass with a firm hand and actually smiled.

'Yes, I don't deny you gave me a fright. I'm afraid, superintendent, you've made a pretty bad mistake, though I know there's no use in my telling you that. If I have to go with you, I'll do so, of course. The matter'll be quickly put right.'

'I hope so, Mr Swinburn,' Lucas answered. 'You'll be able to see your solicitor at once and make whatever arrangements you think best. In the meantime, sir, will you please come along.'

Charles got up. 'I'm quite ready. I'd like to get a coat.'

'Certainly, sir.'

To Charles's surprise they did not touch or hold him in any way, nor was he handcuffed. But he could not but realize that both men kept so close to him that any movement he might make could be instantly checked. They went, a compact trio, into the hall. Charles made for his coat.

'I'll get it for you, sir,' said French. He took down the coat and held it. Charles slipped his arms into it, put on his hat, also handed to him by French, and turned towards the door. Then he stopped.

'We'd better tell Rollins,' he said, 'or will you do that?'

'As you like, Mr Swinburn.'

'Then touch the bell, there, will you?'

The speed with which Rollins appeared showed that he had appreciated what was taking place. His face wore an expression of absolute horror.

'I'm going with these gentlemen,' Charles said as lightly as he could. 'I expect to be back in a day or so.'

Rollins achieved a tolerable 'Very good, sir,' and Charles passed out of the hall into the night. In spite of his brave front, his heart sank. The doubt assailed him as to whether he should ever see that hall door again. Was this a mere episode, a momentary police error, or was it the end? Then Lucas's voice came: 'Will you step in, sir?'

French had got into the waiting car and Charles, feeling numb, followed. The superintendent got in after Charles, the three of them squeezing into the back seat. A policeman in plain clothes, who had been waiting outside the door, mounted in front with the driver, and the vehicle moved off.

During the drive no one spoke. Charles was conscious only of horror. He could not think connectedly. He could not believe that these men really could have anything against him, and yet he knew that police will not arrest unless they have obtained what they consider pretty convincing evidence. Well, there was time enough to think of all that. What he must now concentrate on was to get through this immediate present without doing or saying anything to give himself away. He had heard of these police inquiries. They were not exactly unfair, but there were the wits of several keen, practised and unperturbed men against the single and often terrified individual. However, thanks to the brandy and the excellence of his scheme, he would be able to hold his own.

The drive seemed interminable. It was dark, but Charles could make out the black masses of the trees surrounding the house, then the open country and the bridge over the Gayle, the isolated houses, the streets, and finally the turning in through a gateway into a courtyard and the closing of the gate behind them. Charles had no time to think of the significance of that closing gate, but its clang remained in his memory, heavy with hideous suggestion. They quickly dismounted, and still in a compact trio, entered a bare room with a desk in the corner. The superintendent's manner became more businesslike and events moved so quickly that Charles could scarcely keep pace with them.

First he was formally charged with having, on the 25th of August and the 1st of November, respectively, feloniously murdered Andrew Crowther, of The Moat, Cold Pickerby, and John Weatherup, butler at the same address. He was then asked if he wished to make any statement, being told that he need not do so, but that if he did, what he said would be used in evidence. Charles answered that beyond declaring that a mistake had been made, he had nothing to say at the moment.

This completed the business side of the affair, and he was taken to another room. There he was searched with the greatest thoroughness. Finally, his clothes were returned to him minus several of the articles he had had in his pockets, such as his knife, folding scissors, and one or two other sharp metallic instruments, and he was led to a cell and locked up.

He was a little surprised at the kindly way in which everything was done. There had been no attempt to question him, still less to browbeat him or trap him into some unintentional admission. The men who had searched him had been almost friendly, and had certainly tried to save him humiliation. The constable who locked him up wished him good night civilly. Both French and the superintendent had treated the whole matter as a regrettable but impersonal piece of business routine. Lucas had undertaken to inform Charles's solicitor, Alec Quilter, of what had taken place, and to arrange for him to have an interview with Charles in the morning. Charles could not have expected better treatment.

It was not till he settled down on his hard mattress, with that locked door between him and everything he valued in the world, that real panic swept over Charles. He thought he was safe; but so had many another who had gone to that unthinkable end. Crippen must have felt quite sure that all was well when he had not only hidden the traces of his crime, but successfully left the country. Smith, Mahon, Rouse, did one of these, or a score of others, doubt their own safety? Why should Charles fare better than they?

Somehow, alone there in the semi-darkness, the excellence of his own plans seemed less convincing than ever before. Stories he had read recurred to him in which the guilty had made perfect plans, but in all cases they had broken down. Those double tales of Austin Freeman's! All the criminals had been so sure of their safety and the perfection of their schemes, and in every case these watertight schemes had been like sieves; just honeycombed with errors and oversights and clues.

Charles, for not the first time since he had embarked on his desperate remedy, knew real anguish of mind. He simply could not look forward to the horrors which might be in store for him. For hours he tossed, then at last he fell into an uneasy sleep. Hideous dreams pursued him till he was wakened by the friendly constable, who presently brought him some breakfast.

'Mr Quilter'll be here at half-past nine,' said the constable. 'You'll go before the magistrates at eleven, but that'll be only formal: won't take five minutes. You can see Mr Quilter before it.'

'Thanks,' Charles answered. 'Will Mr Quilter be brought here?'

'Yes; here.'

Though Charles was still terribly upset, his extreme panic of the night had passed off. He could now at least think collectedly, and by the time the solicitor arrived he was almost cheerful.

Alexander Quilter was a big man, with a rugged face, and the reputation of being better at court work than on questions of intricate law. His partner, Dunsfold, was the authority on the latter, the two of them making a formidable combination. Quilter had a boisterous manner, and his greeting of Charles was loud and hearty.

'My dear fellow,' he exclaimed before the door had well opened, 'this is a terrible business. But we'll soon have you out again. What has the super been thinking of?'

'How are you, Quilter? Good of you to come so promptly.'

Quilter replied in kind. For a few moments he continued to talk encouraging platitudes, then, lowering his voice, he turned to business. 'Now,' he said, 'tell me exactly what has occurred, and don't you, as you value your liberty, keep anything back. Let's have it all, whatever it is. Then we'll know where we are.'

Charles began. He told of his financial difficulties, of his visits to The Moat, of his late uncle's reactions to his requests, all exactly as the incidents had occurred. Then he spoke of the machines for the works, the attempt to borrow from the bank and from Bostock, and of his raising money on the pictures. He described his visit to London, mentioning the business of the pictures and the machines at Reading only. He explained about his feeling run down and his deciding to go on the Mediterranean cruise, recounted his receipt of the message at Naples, his journey home, and his arrival in time for the funeral. Finally he told of the purchase of the machines and the improved position of his firm. Everything he said was true, except when he denied point-blank knowing anything about the deaths of either his uncle or Weatherup.

'That sounds all right,' Quilter said when he had finished, 'though I admit one or two things are a bit unfortunate. But we'll have no trouble with them. By the way, you knew what was coming to you under the will?'

'Yes, of course I knew it. Everyone knew the old man intended to divide the bulk of his money between Mrs Morley and myself. He had said so again and again.'

Quilter now began asking questions – shrewd questions, some of which gave Charles a good deal of trouble to answer. However, he acquitted himself well. He was pleased with the story he was able to put up, and when he had finished his case seemed watertight and his innocence unquestionable.

'That's about all we can do at present,' Quilter said at last. 'You'll be brought before the magistrates at eleven and there'll be a remand. Then we can go seriously into the question of defence.'

'I suppose nothing can be done before the magistrates now?'

Quilter shook his head. 'Nothing. There's certain to be a remand. The police always get it. No, you'll have to put up with that. And there'll be no bail. I'm sorry, old man, but you needn't expect it. It's never granted on such a charge. But you'll be all right. A bit irksome, I admit, but it'll soon pass. We can't really do much till we get the prosecution's case. Then we'll know where we are. We can discuss counsel and all that sort of thing later.'

Charles did not know whether to be elated or depressed as a result of the interview. Quilter evidently believed the case would go to trial, that was, that the police had a case. On the other hand, he was cheerily certain of the result. But was that only his manner? Charles felt once more a sinking horror come over him as he thought of the possibilities.

But he hadn't much time to brood. He was presently brought into court. There on the bench were four of his own friends in the town. They looked embarrassed and sorry for themselves and him. They were very businesslike, listened to the superintendent giving evidence of arrest, and granted the remand without discussion. In a few minutes Charles was back in his cell.

Then Charles began to learn something about the length of time. The hours dragged interminably. He could not complain of his treatment. He was allowed books and the food was not too bad. No one was unpleasant to him. But he could not escape from his own thoughts.

He had, moreover, a terribly disquieting suspicion that Quilter seemed more and more grave about the case upon each successive visit. Occasionally also he asked some extremely awkward questions. He asked, for instance, whether Charles had ever bought any potassium cyanide? He was quite emphatic about it. 'Now, look here, Swinburn,' he had said, 'tell me the fact: did you or did you not buy it?' and when Charles declared he hadn't, he went on, 'Then, if the prosecution allege you did, you'll be able to contradict them?' Charles, inwardly quaking, had given the required assurance.

Time dragged slowly on. At the final proceedings before the magistrates, when he was committed for trial, Charles was rendered almost speechless with horror at the strength of the case against him. Quilter, however, seemed less impressed, merely saying that the defence was reserved. Quilter had worked hard, both before and after this hearing, till at last, a fortnight before the trial, everything was ready. Mr Lucius Heppenstall, perhaps the most eminent K.C. at the bar, had been briefed for the defence, and he was to be assisted by Mr Everard Byng, also a man of the highest standing in his profession. Conferences had been numerous and everything that money and skill

could do had been done. Charles was bearing up better than he had
expected, though periods of optimism and hope were usually followed
by others of depression and a cold fear. It was at night that he suffered
most. Often he could not sleep and then he sweated in sheer terror.
He had in the last month grown thin and pale, and streaks of white
were showing in his hair.

And then, at long last, but inexorably, came the day of the trial.

CHAPTER XIX

Charles Attends Court

DURING THE NINE WEEKS OF HIS INCARCERATION CHARLES had lost a good deal of his cheery optimism. While he still clung desperately to his belief in the impossibility of an adverse verdict, at times he was the victim of dreadful doubts. He would have given a large sum to know what Quilter and Lucius Heppenstall really thought. They never said anything despondent; always they spoke as if the trial were the merest formality, an unpleasant ritual certainly, but one which could not under any circumstances have a sinister result. But always Charles wondered... Those nine weeks had added nine years to his life.

He woke on that Tuesday morning overshadowed by the vague weight of some impending calamity. Then, as he realized what it was, panic once again submerged him. He had frequently felt that he would be glad when the trial had come. Terrible as the ordeal would be, it could scarcely be worse than this frightful suspense he had so long borne. But now he saw that the loss of hope would be worse even than suspense.

He was indeed faced with a twofold ordeal. He would be tried separately, so Quilter had told him, on the two charges: first, the complete Crowther case would be taken, and then that of Weatherup. Charles was bitterly resentful of this arrangement. He considered that not taking them together was an unnecessary aggravation of his suffering. Quilter, however, explained that it was the invariable custom and could not be altered.

Charles was given a quite good breakfast, but he found it hard to eat. The journey to the court was a nightmare. In a sort of dream he reached it and was taken to a room off a stone passage. Here there were benches, and between two warders he sat down to wait.

But not for long. There was a sudden movement, a call at the door, and the warders sprang to their feet. 'Now his lordship's in,' said one. 'Come after me up these stairs.'

Charles stepped up after the first warder and was closely followed by the second. Then in a moment he was in court. The sudden change from the silent and gloomy waiting cell to this thronged and brightly illuminated room was upsetting. Charles blinked, and then felt – yes, *felt* – the eyes all round him. The court was filled to overflowing, and of all that crowd of people every one was staring at him. What *beasts* they were to stare like that! He glanced round, but couldn't bear those eyes. He dropped his own, moved forward to the front of the dock as the warder motioned, and stood waiting. For a moment nothing seemed to happen and he glanced round him again.

He remembered the court, in which he had once been to give evidence in a case of theft. Down below him, in a sort of well, was the table at which the barristers engaged on the case sat with their advisers, while a little farther away were the pressmen. Beyond the well were court officials and behind them was the raised tribune or bench, on which was seated a little old gentleman in a wig and red gown. On the wall behind him, symbolic, was a representation of the Royal Arms. To the right was the empty jury-box, to the left the witness-box, and behind at each side were rows of thickly packed seats.

So much Charles observed in his hasty look, and then his attention was attracted to a movement in front. A court official in front of the judge's bench was standing up and speaking. With a shock Charles realized that he was addressing him.

'Charles Hargrave Swinburn, you stand here indicted that on the 25th of August, 1933, you did feloniously and of malice aforethought murder one Andrew Crowther, of The Moat, Cold Pickerby, Yorkshire. How say you? Are you guilty, or not guilty?'

Now that the peril was here Charles was suddenly cool and collected. He surprised himself by the steadiness of his voice as he answered, 'Not guilty!'

The plea was entered and slowly, but relentlessly, the business of the court proceeded. To Charles this commencement, awaited by everyone present with tense excitement and involving his own life or death, seemed extraordinarily tame and wanting in drama. Indeed, before he realized that a beginning had been made, the case was under way.

The jury was first called. Neither side challenged any of the members and the business proceeded smoothly. Charles eagerly tried to picture the mind of each of its members, nine men and three women, as his or her name was called and as he or she moved into the jury-box. First came the foreman, a thick-set man with greying hair, a determined manner, and the appearance of an upper-class trades-man or small shopkeeper. A man who would know his own mind, this foreman, but it would be a terribly limited mind. Charles was sure he belonged to the hard-headed 'practical' type, a man without imagination and who would pride himself on accepting the obvious solution to every problem, and ruling out metaphysical or psychologi-cal considerations as 'tommy rot'. His name was Jinks.

However, he was counterbalanced by the second person to be called. This was a tall, lanky individual, with dark, dreamy eyes, pale cheeks, and long, thin fingers like claws. A man, this, who would instantly feel himself in opposition to the views of his chief, who would instinctively reject the 'practical' view and found his opinion on what he would call psychological considerations, but which would really be his own prejudice. He followed his leader into the box.

As one by one the other ten came forward, Charles had to admit they were as representative a crowd as he could well imagine. There was the small man with the receding chin, who would always hold the opinions of the previous speaker, and his opposite, an individual with an expression of overwhelming stupidity, whose opinions no speaker on earth could move. There were ordinary commonplace decent-looking men, who, while trying to be fair, would be anxious to temper justice with mercy. Of the women, two looked over at Charles with a kindly sorrowful glance, but the third was thin and acid-looking, probably dyspeptic and probably a shrew. This third woman completed the tale of the jurors, and they were then sworn with due ceremony.

Presiding over this activity, but not taking part in it, Mr Justice Herriott sat motionless like a little dried-up old sphinx. In his expressionless face showed nevertheless an immense age and knowledge of life. Charles knew that he had the reputation of being a hard judge; scrupulously fair, but hard. His knowledge of law was believed to be as profound as his knowledge of life, and a successful appeal from his decisions was practically unknown.

But events were again moving. The preliminaries were by this time complete, and leading counsel for the prosecution stood up to deliver his opening address.

Charles had heard a great deal about Sir Richard Brander. His reputation was that of the judge, a hard fighter, but scrupulously fair to those unfortunates whose life or liberty it was his unhappy duty to seek. A big, broad-shouldered man, his gifts ran to cold reason and argument rather than to moving eloquence. He pinned his faith to the mercilessly clear setting out of cold facts, and no one more than he could by a few dry sentences more completely annihilate the effect of an impassioned plea for the defence.

He began to speak in a gentle voice while still bending over the table, arranging his notes. As it was not easy to hear what he was saying, this had the effect of producing immediate silence and ensuring the fullest attention. Then having achieved this end, he straightened himself up, put his left hand on his hip, a characteristic gesture, and allowed his rich voice to reverberate to every corner of the court.

A few tactful preliminary words about the gravity of the case and the importance of the duty of the jury, and he was into his stride.

'The main features of this unhappy case are not new,' he went on. 'Probably as far back as history goes we could find parallels, and as long as human nature remains what it is, it will doubtless continue to be paralleled. It belongs to the type of murder for gain. The prisoner, I shall show, was embarrassed financially. He was also heir to a considerable sum. He is charged with murdering the testator to obtain that sum of money and so to relieve himself of his difficulties.

'Charles Hargrave Swinburn who stands here in the dock to answer this charge, was born in 1898, making him now thirty-five years of age. He was educated at public schools in Buxton and York and his boyhood was full of promise. In 1913 he graduated at Leeds University. Then came the war, and in 1916 he joined up. He had two years' honourable service in France, being twice wounded. On demobilization he returned to Leeds University to complete his studies, eventually taking his degree in science. In 1921 he entered the Crowther Electromotor Works, then the property of his father and uncle, but of which he afterwards became the sole owner.

'In the following year, 1922, Andrew Crowther, the prisoner's uncle, and joint owner of the motor works, retired from the business. He broke completely adrift from it, taking out of it all his money.

The works then belonged absolutely to the prisoner's father, Henry Swinburn. The accused thereupon became a partner. Five years later, in 1927, Henry Swinburn died, the accused then becoming sole owner of the property.'

After this beginning Sir Richard described the vicissitudes of the works, showing that after Charles took over the management it had first enjoyed a period of prosperity, and had then got into difficulties. Almost figure by figure he traced the gradually increasing financial embarrassment Charles had suffered since the slump set in. This information, Charles recognized unhappily, must all have been obtained from his private ledger, the book which up till then no eye but his own had ever seen. 'These figures,' declared Sir Richard, 'will be put before you in evidence, and you will see from them that by the middle of last summer the accused's position had become intolerable. Ruin, in fact, was staring him in the face. He was going to have to take some drastic step to save himself, or else go under.

'It may be thought that his state of affairs supplied a sufficient motive for the crime which it is alleged he afterwards committed, but it happens that the prisoner had a further incentive to retain his existing mode of life. Whether that second motive was or was not more powerful than the first I cannot tell you, but you will all agree that it must have been extremely powerful. The prisoner was, in fact, in love,' and Sir Richard went on to develop this line of argument. Charles groaned as Una was mentioned by name, and the history of his attachment to her was set out in cold and dreadful detail.

'Money, then,' went on Sir Richard, 'must be had if utter ruin was to be avoided. Where might it be obtained?

'The accused tried the usual methods. Evidence will be put before you that he had overdrawn his bank account by £6,000, and that on the 14th of August he approached the manager for a further overdraft.

On the same date he attempted unsuccessfully to borrow £1,000 from a moneylender.

'Ordinary means had failed him, but there remained one source of supply still untapped. His uncle, Andrew Crowther, was a rich man.' Briefly Sir Richard described Andrew Crowther's affairs; his money, his will, his health, his peculiar temperament. 'Swinburn decided to appeal to his uncle, and he did so on the 15th, the 17th and the 25th of August. As a result of this appeal Andrew Crowther handed him a cheque for £1,000, and there is doubt where a further sum was or was not to follow. The accused's own statement is that he got £1,000 and hoped to get a second. But, members of the jury, a thousand pounds or even two would have been little use to him. The figures taken from his own private ledger will show that nothing less than £6,000 or £7,000 could have saved him.

'Where, then,' said Sir Richard in his incisive voice, 'might the necessary money be obtained? There was only one source. Swinburn was aware of his uncle's will. It was obvious to him that if Andrew Crowther were to die his own future would be assured.'

Sir Richard paused, ostensibly to consult his notes, but really, even Charles could not but see, because his orator's instinct told him that a pause was necessary to drive home his point. The audience had settled down to silence and intentness. Charles tried to rally his courage. Under this pitiless *exposé* his motive was standing out clear and unquestionable as the beam of a lighthouse on a dark night. Of course, he reminded himself, there never had been any question of his motive. He had always admitted it himself. It was his action that they could never prove.

'Now,' Sir Richard continued, 'it happened that Andrew Crowther suffered from indigestion and that for this complaint he took three times a day after meals a certain pill. These pills, Salter's

Anti-Indigestion Pills, are a patent medicine and are sold in identical bottles of standard sizes. You will hear that Swinburn knew of his uncle's ailment and of his habit of taking one of these pills after each meal. Now it must have been obvious to him that if poison could be inserted into a pill, and if that poisoned pill could be introduced into Andrew Crowther's bottle, he would sooner or later take that pill and die, though the person who put it there might be far away from the place at the time. I shall prove to you that the poison was in point of fact inserted into one of these pills, and the pill introduced into Andrew Crowther's bottle, and that the deceased did take that pill, and that he died as the result.'

Once again one of those ghastly attacks of fear drove down on Charles. He had, of course, known that this would be part of the case against him. All the same, to hear it announced in that definite unquestioning way somehow seemed to make it infinitely more deadly. Sir Richard seemed so sure... But of course that was his business. He was paid to seem sure. It was all right. Charles rallied himself.

'I have mentioned that the accused had interviews with his uncle on the 15th and 17th of August,' went on Sir Richard. 'This second interview on the 17th was the one at which Andrew Crowther handed him the cheque for £1,000, and we may take it, I suggest, that the accused left that interview knowing that his application had failed. He had got a thousand and might get a second, but he wanted six or seven. I submit that at that time he had decided on his course of action and that his uncle's fate was sealed.

'On the 21st, four days after that interview, the accused drove to London, where he stayed for the nights of the 21st and 22nd. His ostensible reason for the journey was a call on a Reading firm relative to some machinery which he was contemplating buying for his works. He did pay that visit to Reading, but I shall prove that he did some other business besides: two other pieces of business.

'The first was this. If Andrew Crowther were to be murdered, several weeks, if not months, must elapse before the prisoner would be able to handle the actual cash. Money must therefore be provided with which to carry on till the larger sum became available.

'Now, on that visit to Town I shall prove that Swinburn took with him in his car fourteen pictures which had been collected from time to time by his father and which had a total value of about £3,000. He took them ostensibly to have them cleaned, but they were not cleaned. Instead he pledged them for a sum of £2,100. This money was not paid into his bank, but he received it in notes. You will hear further that he estimated the time during which he would leave the pictures pledged at six months, which, I suggest, indicates that he knew that by the end of that period he would be in funds.

'The second piece of secret business done during that visit to London was more sinister. I shall prove that on that day, the morning of the accused's return from Town, he went into a certain chemist's shop in a street near Waterloo Station, and there, under a false name and on the excuse of wanting to destroy a wasps' nest, he purchased an ounce of potassium cyanide, the poison from which Andrew Crowther died.'

At this statement a little movement passed over the court, as if in involuntary recognition of its significance. The speech was having its effect. With a dreadful eagerness Charles searched the faces of the jurors, wondering how it was impressing them. The foreman looked as if his mind was already made up. His expression said 'Guilty!' and Charles imagined that if he had had his way he would have stopped the case and given his verdict then and there. The weedy-looking man beside him looked doubtful; but then Charles could scarcely imagine

him otherwise than doubtful on any question. The others appeared
to think it a clear case. Even the expression of the two comfortable
women had changed. They still looked sad, but to Charles it now
seemed as if they avoided his eyes. The thin woman looked almost
pleased. As Charles watched them his heart sank.

Sir Richard's finely modulated voice continued to rise and fall
musically as his speech dragged on and on. Charles gazed at him with
horror. In his eyes the man's very appearance had grown hateful and
sinister. His face was so implacable, so relentless, with his strongly
marked features, his big nose, his square chin, his thin lips and his
forceful expression. A dangerous man! And he was Charles's enemy.
He was fighting for nothing less than Charles's life.

For a moment Charles was so carried away by this picture that he
missed a few sentences. Then his attention swung back.

Sir Richard was now discussing Charles's visit to The Moat on the
25th of August – the last visit of the three.

'Now why, let us ask ourselves, did the accused pay that visit to The
Moat? As I have said, I shall prove that the accused bought potassium
cyanide in London on the 23rd of August. I shall prove also that the
deceased died later from taking a pill containing potassium cyanide. I
shall prove that this visit to The Moat was the only occasion on which
the prisoner saw the deceased between these two months. Therefore,
if the accused *did* put the poison into the deceased's bottle, it must
have been done on that occasion.

'Let me again ask the question: why did the accused pay that
visit? I shall prove that he had been there twice in the previous few
days, so that it could scarcely have been a mere social call. Similarly, it
could scarcely have been to borrow money: he had already done his
utmost in that direction. I shall suggest that that visit was paid, and
could only have been paid, with the object of putting the poisoned

pill into the bottle. Whether this suggestion is the truth will be for you to say.

'In this connexion I wish to call your attention to an important point about this visit. After dinner on that evening I shall prove that when the ladies withdrew the prisoner remained alone with the deceased. During that period when the two men were alone, a glass of wine was spilled on the tablecloth. Here again it will be for you, when you have heard the evidence, to say whether this was an accident, or whether it was done purposely by the accused to distract the deceased's attention while he placed the deadly pill.'

Sir Richard then turned to the cruise. 'An essential feature of the scheme which, it is submitted, the accused carried out was to provide himself with an alibi. When Andrew Crowther died the accused must be far away. As a matter of fact he was in Naples.' Then followed a description of Charles's booking of his ticket, of the cruise itself, of the radiogram received at Naples, and of Charles's return to Cold Pickerby in time for the funeral.

'Now,' went on Sir Richard, 'there are two points about the cruise to which I want to direct your special attention. The first is the relationship of two dates. I shall prove that the accused booked for his cruise on the morning of the 26th of August. And, members of the jury, it was on the night of the 25th, the previous evening, that he dined with his uncle and, it is submitted, changed the pills. It is submitted that he was waiting till the pills were changed before deciding to go, and that once this was done he took the first cruise which offered.

'The second point is this. Evidence will be put before you that while the accused was on that cruise he was the whole time in a nervous and excited state; that his first care on returning from excursions was to ask for letters, and that his unease was very noticeable when radiograms were taken round the deck. A Mrs Shearman, a fellow-passenger, will tell you that she noticed his state of mind and commented on it, when the accused explained that he had not been well and had come away for a change. I shall suggest that this uneasiness cannot be explained otherwise than on the assumption that he was expecting news of his uncle's death.

'One other point, and I have done. When the tragedy took place fourteen of the accused's pictures were under pledge in a dealer's in London. There were, therefore, fourteen blanks on the walls of the accused's house, and it is obvious these blanks were calculated to lead to questions which might reveal the true urgency of the accused's financial straits. So great a danger must necessarily be avoided, and the accused endeavoured to avoid it. I shall prove...' and Sir Richard went on to give full details of Charles's loan of £5,000 from Messrs Spiller & Morgan.

This was the last point to be made by Sir Richard. With a few brief words of peroration he sat down, and his junior, Mr. Lionel Coppard, rose and called 'Percival Crosby!'

Then for what seemed the first time since the proceedings opened, his lordship moved. 'It's so nearly time for lunch, Mr Coppard, that I think we'd better adjourn now. Two o'clock, please.'

A warder at once touched Charles on the arm and signed to him to follow down the stairs to the waiting cells below. As Charles turned he had the vision of the court rising, to stand respectfully while the judge passed out.

Charles felt utterly stunned at the strength of the case which had been urged against him. He had, of course, heard the evidence at the proceedings before magistrates, but somehow, as put by Sir Richard, the whole thing seemed worse than he could have imagined. For the first time the possibility of conviction became real to him. Quilter, however, when he came round to say a word or two of encouragement, seemed quite unmoved by the speech. 'Wait till Heppenstall gets at them,' was all he would say. Comforting so far as it went, but it went such a meagre distance!

Charles could not eat, in spite of the rough kindness of one of the warders, who adjured him to keep his pecker up, adding that the food would stand to him. But he felt he could drink the sea dry. He drank and then sat waiting numbly.

When the court reopened there was no delay in getting to business. Crosby was at once called, and Coppard rose to examine him.

Crosby, as might have been expected from his profession, was a good witness. He replied in a clear voice concisely but fully to the questions he was asked, but volunteered nothing. Coppard was very quiet and courteous with him.

After obtaining his position and qualifications, Coppard led his witness through the histories of the Crowther family and of the Electromotor Works. Crosby had been Andrew Crowther's solicitor for many years, and he described what had taken place at his client's retirement and the drawing up of his will. He, Crosby, knew of his own knowledge that the accused was aware of the provisions of the will and how they affected himself. When he had finished Charles's motive had been established beyond possibility of question.

When Coppard sat down, Mr Everard Byng rose to cross-examine. He also was very polite and gentle with the witness. To Charles he did not seem to make much of his job. He appeared half-hearted, and Charles could not see that his questions led anywhere. He repeated a good many of the questions Mr Coppard had already asked, but he did get Crosby to say that all the other beneficiaries under the will, with the possible exception of Weatherup, had also known just what sum was coming to them. He also brought out that Crosby and Peter had dined at The Moat on the evening before Andrew's death, and had discussed Peter's application for financial assistance and the possible taking up of a mortgage on Otterton Farm.

'Now, Mr Crosby, on that evening did you have any confidential talk with the deceased?'

'No.'

'Do you mean to say that you were not alone with him even for a single minute all the time that you were there?'

'That's what I mean. I was not alone with him.'

'Very well. Now, so far as you know, had Mr Peter Morley any opportunity for a confidential chat with the deceased?'

For the first time Crosby hesitated. 'I don't think so,' he said presently. 'I—'

Byng interrupted more sharply than he had yet spoken. 'Did you at any time during the evening leave the room and leave them together?'

Coppard was on his feet. 'I submit, m'lud, that this is quite irrelevant.'

'It's not irrelevant,' Byng retorted swiftly to his colleague. Then he turned to his lordship. 'I wish to learn whether on this last evening of his life the deceased had an opportunity of making any confidential remarks indicative of suspicion or otherwise.'

There was a short argument, the judge finally allowing the question.

'Now, Mr Crosby,' went on Byng with righteous indignation in his voice, as if at a base attempt to defeat justice, now happily overcome, 'will you answer my question: did you at any time during the evening leave the room and leave them together?'

'Well, yes, I did,' Crosby answered, 'but only for two or three minutes. After dinner I left them in the dining-room while I went into the hall to get some papers out of my overcoat pocket.'

Byng continued asking what Charles thought were entirely point-less questions, and he did it without any appearance of conviction or interest. Presently he gave up even this effort, and sat down.

It disappointed Charles bitterly. All this talk had led nowhere. If his counsel didn't do better than this, he was lost indeed.

Peter was the next witness. He was examined by Sir Richard himself. First the whole circumstances of the journey to France were brought out, and the details of Andrew Crowther's death, including the fact that Peter as well as Weatherup had seen Andrew take his pill after lunch. Then Sir Richard became more personal. Peter repeated a good deal of what Crosby had already stated. He, Peter, also was in financial difficulties, and he had discussed those difficulties with the prisoner. His wife and the prisoner were the principal beneficiaries under the late Andrew Crowther's will, and he knew it and he believed the prisoner knew it also. He confirmed generally Crosby's evidence as to the state and history of the family, and the history of the works. In fact, he had little to say that was interesting and nothing that was new.

Nor was his cross-examination by Mr Everard Byng productive of anything of the slightest importance. Byng scarcely mentioned the journey. He also became personal. Asked the direct question, Peter admitted that he himself would have been ruined if no money had been forthcoming. He admitted further that his father-in-law had been unwilling to assist him, on the quite mistaken grounds that his difficulties were due to his not having worked sufficiently hard on his farm. Just, however, when he appeared to be about to get something of value, Byng threw up the sponge. He sat down, leaving Charles quivering with bitter fury. Charles wrathfully told himself he had paid these men their huge fees to do some work for him, not to slack about like that. So far the defence had done nothing. Charles had never felt so utterly helpless, and so alone and so up against it in his whole life.

James Bradley, the attendant on the *Hengist,* was then called to describe the flight from Croydon to Beauvais and the lunch on the plane. Deceased had eaten of each course and also had coffee, and witness had cleared away the used plates and cup. Affidavits from the French doctor and police were also put in. Inspector Appleby described the bringing home of the remains, the handing over of the pills to Mr Grant, and the finding of Charles's secret ledger. He read Charles's original statement to himself at the beginning of the inquiry, produced the secret ledger and was taken through it figure by figure, and dealt with a number of other matters of a technical and routine character. Nothing of importance was obtained from the cross-examination.

Wilfred Witheroe was the next witness. He deposed that he was manager of the Cold Pickerby branch of the Northern Counties Bank. He gave details of the gradual change in Charles's finances from prosperity to debt. He told of Charles's overdraft, of his application for the loan of another thousand (which he admitted would have been refused if pressed), and his paying in the deceased's cheque for £1,000.

This time Lucius Heppenstall himself rose to cross-examine, and Charles at once became more eager. Surely something helpful should be brought out now?

But Heppenstall displayed the same easy-going half-heartedness that his junior had shown. He got nothing helpful. He didn't even seem to try. He got Witheroe to admit that Charles had afterwards told him his uncle was helping him, and that he didn't therefore need the additional overdraft, but that was all.

When this farce, as Charles called it in his now almost despairing mind, was over, Bostock stepped into the witness-box. His evidence was short. He described Charles's application to him for a loan of a thousand and his own regret that he was obliged to refuse it. To

Byng he admitted that Charles had afterwards told him he no longer wanted the accommodation, owing to help which was being given him by his uncle.

The next witness sent Charles's heart racing with sheer misery. Una Mellor stepped into the box. Charles had not seen her in court, so her appearance was a double shock. She was very pale, but otherwise looked but slightly discomposed. Charles knew that no matter what the outcome of the trial might be, he had lost her irrevocably.

Sir Richard Brander, who rose to examine, was politeness itself. He regretted having to ask painful questions, but he had no alternative. Under his suave inquisition Una said that Charles had wished to marry her, and had proposed to her on several occasions. She had not given him a definite answer, as she had not at that time made up her mind. No engagement had therefore existed, and none existed now.

Heppenstall then rose, said he did not wish to cross-examine, and sat down again. To Charles this seemed the last straw. He could have screamed. Were these men going to do *nothing* for him? Was that the idea of a barrister – to take money in huge amounts and do nothing to earn it? Panic settled down on Charles once more. If nothing was going to be done, he was lost! Vainly he tried to catch Quilter's eye.

But now Una had vanished, and a discussion took place as to the desirability of adjourning. Crosby's evidence on the family history had taken a long time, as had Peter's and Witheroe's. It was after five. Finally his lordship decided that it was time for the adjournment. In a state almost of collapse from weariness and dread and want of food, Charles suffered himself to be led listlessly back to his cell.

His motive had been proved – up to the hilt. What would happen to him to-morrow? He groaned aloud at the thought.

CHAPTER XX

Charles Endures Despair

F OR ONE THING CHARLES HAD REASON TO BE THANKFUL: HE slept all night through. So tired that his limbs were actually aching, he threw himself on his bed at the first possible moment, and fell at once into a heavy slumber. It was as if he were drugged. He did not dream. He was conscious of nothing till his cell was opened next morning and his breakfast brought to him.

He was feeling much more optimistic than he could have believed possible after the shocks of the previous day. He told himself that invariably, as the case for the prosecution draws to an end, a spectator at a trial assumes the guilt of the prisoner. Almost equally invariably, when the defence have completed their case, he sees that the prisoner must be innocent. Until he had heard what Heppenstall had to say Charles would not despair. Heppenstall had a tremendous reputation. And he was doing better than Charles had realized. Charles now saw that he had been right not to cross-examine Una. To have made things more awkward for Una than they were would have alienated sympathy. Heppenstall had known what he was about.

This morning the same dreary wait took place in the cell under the court as on the first day, followed by the same sudden spurt of activity when the judge had taken his seat. But this morning there were not the same preliminaries to be gone through. The names of the jurors were called, they took their places, and the case was resumed.

The first witness was Penelope Pollifex. Like Una she was pale, and she gave evidence with reluctance. Yes, she had told the accused about his uncle's anti-indigestion pills, mentioning that he took them three times a day after meals. Yes, the accused had lunched at The Moat on the 17th of August, and dined on the 25th. On each occasion the ladies left the room on the conclusion of the meal, and he remained alone with the deceased.

'Now tell me, Mrs Pollifex,' went on Coppard, 'did you keep control of the linen cupboard at The Moat?'

'Yes, I did.'

'Do you remember the night on which the accused dined with you?'

'Yes.'

'The 25th of August?'

'Yes.'

'On the next day, the 26th of August, did your late butler, John Weatherup, make any request to you in connexion with linen?'

'Yes, he did.'

'What did he ask?'

'He asked me for a clean tablecloth.'

'For a clean tablecloth. On what grounds did he ask for it?'

'On the grounds that after dinner on the previous night a glass of wine had been spilled on the old one.'

'Did you see the old tablecloth yourself?'

'I did.'

'And was it stained as alleged?'

'It was.'

Beyond obtaining the admission that, so far as the witness herself knew, the wine might have been spilled by Weatherup rather than by either of the diners, Byng did not press his cross-examination. He did, however, make one point. The witness swore positively that Charles's manner had betrayed no unusual excitement on the night on which he dined – the night on which he was accused of changing the pills.

Rollins was next called. With evident regret he told about Charles taking the pictures to be cleaned and bringing them back, in each case giving the dates.

On the call of Samuel Truelove Charles saw that the whole of the picture episode was coming out. How the police had found Truelove he could not imagine, or indeed how they had got on to the question of the pictures at all.

The oily gentleman whom he had met in Arundel Street seemed more at home in the box than had the previous witnesses. He described, very fairly, as Charles had to admit, their interview. Charles had brought the pictures, saying he wished to raise a loan on them for about six months. He, witness, had had them valued, and he had been able to offer £2,100 on them. Charles had agreed to this figure, and the money had been paid over in notes, in order, he had said, to avoid the transaction passing through his bank and becoming known.

Byng cross-examined with the easy-going slackness which made Charles so furious. The accused had mentioned a period of six months as the probable time during which he would require the loan. Was this strictly so? Had no other period been mentioned?

In reply, Truelove said that at first Charles had not known how long he might want to be accommodated, then had mentioned six months as a basis of discussion. He had, however, ascertained that the firm would keep the pictures for possible redemption for a period of two years. He had remarked that this would suit him, as before the end of two years his business would be either flourishing or dead.

With regard to Charles's precautions to secure secrecy, Truelove admitted that this was a usual accompaniment of business done with his firm. It meant nothing except that clients did not wish the public to know they were in low water.

This was not so bad, but at sight of the next witness Charles shivered. He was a thin old man with a stoop, blinking through his glasses, and like a rather draggled old bird. He gave his name as Ebenezer Peabody.

Sir Richard Brander rose to examine him. He was, he stated, the proprietor of a chemist's shop in Stamford Street, near Waterloo Station, in London. He remembered the 23rd of August. On that date a gentleman had come to his shop and asked for some potassium cyanide to destroy a wasps' nest. He, witness, had demurred and pointed out that he was not allowed to sell poison to strangers. The gentleman had thereupon said that he understood that, but that there was no doubt of his identity. He showed a visiting card with the name 'Francis Carswell, The Dove Cot, Sycamore Avenue, Surbiton', engraved upon it. He also took some letters out of his pocket and passed them over. They bore the same address and had been through the post, as the stamps were cancelled. He, witness, was satisfied as to his caller's identity, but before handing over the cyanide he made two further and, as he thought, conclusive tests. He knew Surbiton himself, and some of the doctors there, and he asked the caller if he knew one of them, a Dr Davis? The man said, 'Of Eden Road?', giving the correct address, and then further mentioned another doctor as being his own, again with the correct address. This quite convinced witness that all was right, but even still, to be on the safe side, he took occasion when going for the cyanide to look up the telephone directory, and he found Mr Carswell's name there, given under the correct address.

'So,' went on Sir Richard, 'you gave him the poison?'

'Yes, sir, I gave it to him.'

'How much?'

'A tin containing one ounce – the usual amount for the purpose.'

'Did you get him to sign your poison book?'

'Yes, sir.'

'Is that the book?' Sir Richard took a book from his junior and passed it over.

'Yes, sir.'

'Is that the man's signature?'

'Yes, sir. That's what he wrote, anyhow.'

'Quite. Now, Mr Peabody,' Sir Richard became dramatic, 'look round you. Do you see in court the gentleman who gave his name as Francis Carswell, and to whom you sold the cyanide?'

The old man blinked short-sightedly at Charles. 'Yes, sir.'

'Who is it?'

'The prisoner, sir.'

'You're quite sure of that? Remember you're on your oath.'

'I'm quite sure, sir.'

Sir Richard sat down. Charles, sunk in a trough of hopeless despair, could not but see the effect this evidence had had upon all present, and particularly on the jury. After this there could be no doubt as to the end. What was the good of going on? Let the thing be finished up at once and get the end over as soon as possible. He was lost!

But Heppenstall was on his feet, careless, nonchalant, apparently a little bored. Before beginning his cross-examination he stooped to whisper something to Byng, and laughed – actually *laughed* – at the younger man's reply. Only that nothing mattered any more, Charles felt like getting up and screaming with impotent fury. To take his money and to do nothing to earn it, and actually to *laugh* at such a point in the proceedings! Charles had no language to describe his feelings.

'Now, Mr Peabody,' Heppenstall began in a pleasant, courteous tone, 'you say you saw the accused in your shop on the 23rd of August, when you sold him some potassium cyanide. When did you next see him?'

The man thought. 'May I look at my book?' he asked, and when permission was given he went on: 'On Tuesday, the 31st of October.'

'Tuesday, the 31st of October,' Heppenstall repeated. 'Quite so. And where did you see him?'

'At Cold Pickerby.'

'Now how did you come to think of travelling to Cold Pickerby?'

'The police asked me to.'

'Did they tell you why?'

'Yes, sir, they did.'

'And what was the reason?'

'They wanted me to see if I could recognize the man to whom I sold the poison.'

'Quite so.'

Heppenstall had an eyeglass with which he made great play, taking it out to consult his brief and screwing it in again to gaze at the witness or the jury. Now he screwed it in, and in his quiet, pleasant voice asked his next question:

'How long was this customer to whom you sold the poison in your shop, Mr Peabody?'

'How long?' The man thought. 'Three or four minutes, I should think. Perhaps five. I didn't watch the clock.'

'Of course not. All I want is an estimate, and you estimate the time as from three to five minutes. Now tell me, is your shop well or poorly lighted?'

'It's not so bad,' the man began in a hesitating way, but Heppenstall cut him short.

'Not so bad? That's no answer, Mr Peabody. I ask you, is your shop well or badly lighted? Remember that many of us have been there and know.'

The man appeared crestfallen. 'It's not too well lighted, I'm afraid,' he said apologetically. 'I've wanted to make some alterations to improve it, but times have been bad and I put it off.'

'Quite. Don't think I'm criticizing you. I'm simply trying to get the facts. The shop was not well lighted. How is that? Is the light obstructed in any way?'

'The windows are rather small for the size of the shop.'

'The shop is badly lighted because the windows are too small. Now another point. Can you tell the jury whether the purchaser of this poison stood with his face or his back to the light?'

The old man hesitated, then admitted: 'With his back.'

'He stood with his back to the light. What kind of hat was he wearing?'

Again Mr Peabody hesitated. Heppenstall repeated the question a little more sharply.

'I didn't just rightly take notice of that,' the chemist answered with a certain sullenness. 'I was thinking of my business and not what he was wearing.'

Heppenstall was urbanity itself. 'You were thinking of your business and not of the appearance of your customer. Very natural, Mr Peabody. As I said before, you mustn't think I'm criticizing your conduct. I simply asked if you had noticed his hat, and you hadn't. Was he wearing glasses?'

Peabody was clearly about to reply, then his eyes swung round to Charles as he sat in the dock, and he hesitated.

'Was he wearing glasses?' Heppenstall repeated.

'I thought he was,' the old man said, instantly correcting himself to 'I think he was.'

'You thought he was, but on looking at the accused and seeing that he has none, you are now doubtful. Is that it?' Heppenstall's voice was more severe.

Sir Richard Brander was instantly on his feet to protest against this imputation of unworthy motives.

'I impute no motives, worthy or otherwise,' Heppenstall retorted. 'I ask the witness if his customer was wearing glasses, and he tells me in effect that he doesn't know. Is that correct, Mr Peabody?'

Peabody moved uneasily. 'No,' he returned. 'I remember now. He was wearing glasses.'

'Oh,' said Heppenstall; 'on second thoughts you believe he was wearing glasses. Did you notice if they were pince-nez or spectacles?'

'Spectacles, I think.'

'You think? Do you state on your oath that they were spectacles?'

Peabody did not. He wasn't sure. Nor could he say whether the glasses were rimless or had gold or tortoiseshell rims.

Charles, realizing what Heppenstall was trying to do, was now listening with a painful intensity.

He saw that he had been wrong about Heppenstall. The man was earning his money all right. He knew what he wanted and he was getting it with consummate skill. Once again Charles believed there was hope.

Under Heppenstall's courteous but persistent interrogation, Peabody was getting flustered. Systematically Heppenstall took him through his customer's dress. The man swore his caller had a fawn-coloured overcoat or waterproof, though he couldn't tell which. He didn't know if he wore gloves, nor had he seen rings on his hands. On the other hand, he could not swear there were none. When Heppenstall turned from the subject his credibility as a witness had been shaken.

Heppenstall then asked him as to the law of supplying poison to customers and made him admit that in the instance in question he had broken it. Peabody, however, admitted his fault so readily that the point did not discredit him as it otherwise might, and Heppenstall slid gently away from it.

'Now, Mr Peabody,' Heppenstall went on, 'look at this plan.' He passed up a drawing. 'Have you seen it before?'

'Yes, I have.'

'What is it a plan of?'

'Of my shop.'

'Of your shop. Do you see two points on it marked respectively "A" and "B"?'

'Yes.'

'What do these points indicate?'

'They're supposed to show where the customer and I stood when I sold the cyanide.'

'Do they as a matter of fact show these positions correctly: approximately correctly, I mean?'

'Yes, they do.'

'Which point indicates the purchaser?'

'Point "A".'

'Then does Point "B" represent where you stood?'

'Yes.'

'I'll prove the plan later, m'lud,' Heppenstall remarked as the sheet was handed up to his lordship.

This completed the cross-examination and a Mr Horace Drinkwater was called. He was, he said, a handwriting expert. He had obtained samples of the prisoner's handwriting and had compared these with the entries in the previous witness's poison book. In his opinion, the two sets of writing were by the same hand.

His cross-examination by Heppenstall was very short. In fact, he only asked him three questions.

'You say, Mr Drinkwater, that the two sets of writing were, in your opinion, done by the same hand. Do you swear that they were?'

'No,' the witness returned, 'no expert would do so. I say they were to the best of my opinion and belief, but I naturally can't swear it.'

'Quite so. Now, have you had much experience of comparing and judging handwriting?'

'I've been doing it for more than twenty-five years.'

'Now, tell me, Mr Drinkwater.' Heppenstall's manner had got suddenly sharper. 'In all that long period, have you ever known your opinion to be incorrect?' He leant forward and transfixed the witness with a hard, frowning stare.

Drinkwater hesitated. 'Why, no,' he said at last, 'I don't think so. Not very often, at all events.'

'*Not* omniscient,' Heppenstall murmured *sotto voce* and sat down.

A Miss Isobel Cumming was then called to prove the purchase of the Francis Carswell visiting cards. She said the accused was like the purchaser, but admitted to Byng that she could not say they were the same.

The real Mr Francis Carswell deposed that he had not visited Mr Peabody's shop on the 23rd of August, had not purchased potassium cyanide from him or any other person, and had not ordered visiting cards from the previous witness. The defence did not cross-examine.

Mrs Shearman, with evident reluctance, described Charles's excitability and anxiety during the cruise, stating that she had commented on it, and that he had explained it by saying that he had not been well, that something had gone wrong with his nerves, and that he had in consequence gone away for a change. She was followed by a clerk from the *Jupiter,* who gave evidence as to Charles's eagerness in applying for letters and telegrams.

In each of these last two cases Byng tried to obtain an admission that the alleged facts were the mere opinions of the witnesses, unsupported by definite actions on Charles's part. Charles thought this fairly satisfactory, the evidence apparently not appealing strongly to the jury.

A clerk from Messrs Cook's gave evidence as to Charles's purchase of the tickets for the cruise. His cross-examination was unproductive.

Mr Spiller, of Messrs Spiller & Morgan, gave evidence about the loan of £5,000 which his firm had made to Charles. As in the case of the previous witness, little was gained by the cross-examination.

Dr Gregory was then examined at considerable length. He repeated the evidence which he had given at the inquest about the deceased's health and his fitness to travel in an aeroplane. He described the effect of potassium cyanide and stated that the presumption that it had been taken in the pill would in his opinion account for all the facts which had been observed.

Mr Gavin Grant, the analyst, added somewhat to his former evidence. He had found potassium cyanide in the organs sent him, which, it had been stated in evidence, had been taken from the deceased's body. Moreover, the amount – about three grains – was just about the quantity which could be introduced into a pill of the size of those taken by the deceased. This would have been quite sufficient to cause death.

'Now, Mr Grant,' went on Brander, 'did you analyse the pills which remained in the deceased's bottle?'

'Inspector Appleby handed me a bottle of Salter's Anti-Indigestion Pills which I understood were found on the deceased. I analysed them.'

'You need not go into details, but you found they contained certain substances?'

'Yes, I prepared a complete analysis.'

'Now, tell me, did you find in the deceased's organs these same substances?'

'No, I found no trace of them.'

'From that, are you or are you not in a position to say the deceased did not take one of these pills after lunch in the plane?'

'Assuming he died shortly after lunch, as has been stated, I am prepared to swear he did not take one of these pills. If he had done so, I should have found traces.'

'We have Mr Peter Morley's evidence that the deceased did take a pill after lunch. If this evidence is correct, can you account for the discrepancy?'

'If a pill was taken, it must have contained something other than the indigestion remedies.'

'Quite so. That is what I want.'

Once again Charles thought the cross-examination extremely perfunctory. A show was made of trying to trip up the witness, but nothing really was gained.

When Grant left the box Sir Richard Brander got up and said that that was his case. It being past one, the court immediately adjourned for lunch.

As he went down the stairs from the dock Charles thought that at last he knew the worst. It was bad, a hundred times worse than he could have had any idea of. How the police had discovered that awful fact about his buying the cyanide, he could not imagine. Even now he couldn't see the loophole he must have left.

He was so filled with misery and despair as to have become almost apathetic. He seemed to be existing outside himself, looking down upon himself as from some great distance. The whole trial began to feel impersonal. He could wonder what, if any, chance he had, without seeming to realize that it was his own life that was at stake.

Mechanically he forced himself to eat and then mechanically ascended that tragic stair down which so many had passed to despair and death. Perhaps before night he would have joined their ranks.

CHAPTER XXI

Charles Regains Hope

I T WAS WITH A SENSE OF UTTER WEARINESS THAT CHARLES ONCE
again reached the dock. How he loathed the court and everyone connected with it! Sir Richard Brander, with his large nose, his
square chin, his thin lips, his look of implacable determination. Mr
Heppenstall and his eyeglass. The downright 'practical' foreman of the
jury and his weak, fanciful neighbour. The two comfortable-looking
women and their thin, spiteful companion. His lordship, with his
tired, dried-up face. A clerk with a cast in his left eye. Oh, how he
hated and loathed them all!

But he had little time to consider these matters. Directly he had
taken his seat Heppenstall rose to open the case for the defence.

'Members of the jury,' he began, in his deep but pleasantly modulated voice, 'as I am only going to call four witnesses, and none will
occupy the time of the court for long, I am going to break away a
little from precedent and call these witnesses before I put before
you the case for the defence. But there is one thing which I wish
to say now, and that is that I do not propose to call my client to
give evidence.

'The right of the accused to go into the box and testify on his own
behalf has been recognized by the law for many years. This recognition was not granted before it was due. It was a terrible thing that the
true explanation of apparently suspicious circumstances could not be
given by the accused, who so often was the only person capable of
giving it. That injustice has now fortunately been removed.

'But, like every other good thing, this power of putting the accused into the box has its drawbacks. One very unexpected and very unfortunate result has followed. It has actually began to tell against the accused if he is not put into the box. That, members of the jury, is an extremely unfortunate state of affairs, because many persons, innocent and guilty alike, are not constitutionally able to stand a grilling cross-examination without showing signs of distress, and unhappily these signs are often – though wrongly – taken as indicating guilt. For this reason I at least have decided to make a stand against this practice which has grown up, and in no case will I put the accused I may be defending into the box unless I am satisfied that he could give material evidence which could be obtained in no other way. In the present instance we have, in my opinion, all the evidence from other sources which my client could give us, and I do not therefore intend to call him. I have made this somewhat tedious digression simply in order that you may not misunderstand my motive.

'With this preface I shall call my witnesses. Mr Godfrey Anderson!'

Charles, who had never heard of Mr Godfrey Anderson, felt a sudden quickening of his interest as an alert young man entered the box and was sworn.

'You are engaged in the Meteorological Office as a record clerk?' asked Byng, when he had ascertained the witness's name and qualifications.

'I am.'

'Have you there with you the records of the weather in London on the 23rd of August last?'

'Yes.'

'Will you tell the jury what it was like between eleven and twelve on that morning?'

'A deep depression centred...'

'Never mind that, Mr Anderson. What was the weather like in London in everyday language that we can all understand?'

'Well, the barometer stood at twenty-nine point…'

'Even that is more technical than I want. Tell me, was it fine or wet at the time?'

'It was not actually raining, but it was heavily overcast and precipitation was…'

'It was heavily overcast. That's what I want. Was it, in other words, a dark day or a bright day?'

'It was a dark day.'

'Quite! It was a dark day, heavily overcast with clouds.' Byng sat down.

The prosecution satisfied themselves by extracting from the witness the admission that the darkness was the ordinary dullness of a day on which the sun was not shining and not something abnormal.

'Arthur Higginbotham!' called Heppenstall, and another man unknown to Charles entered the box. He was small and sharp-featured and had the eager, deprecating manner of a young fox-terrier.

He was, he explained, a photographer, and he had taken certain views of Mr Ebenezer Peabody's shop. Yes, these – Exhibits 73, 74, 75, and 76 were handed up – were the photographs in question. The exhibits were passed to his lordship and the jury. Mr Higginbotham admitted that the pictures were poor – far below his usual standard – but he had found the shop very dark and had had to give an exceptionally long exposure to get any results at all. He had taken the pictures by daylight at about midday on a bright day, No, he had not used any artificial light.

Still another stranger to Charles was the third witness. Maurice Barlow said he was an architect. He had made a plan of Mr Peabody's shop. (The plan Heppenstall had shown to Peabody was once again produced.) Yes, this was the plan, and to the best of his knowledge and belief it was correct. He had marked upon it certain positions, A and B, which had been pointed out to him by Mr Peabody. He had tried an experiment in the shop. He had placed Mr Peabody in position A, in which, as had been given in evidence, the purchaser had stood at the time of the purchase; and he had himself taken up position B, in which it was similarly stated Mr Peabody had stood. He had found that he could not see Mr Peabody's features clearly owing to his having his back to the light.

He had also made a professional examination of the shop. It was dark – for two reasons. First, the windows were much too small for the area of the room. Here Barlow gave figures comparing the actual area of glass with that required by normal architectural practice. Secondly, such glass as there was, was much obstructed by the window display. He might point to photograph, Exhibit 75, in proof of his evidence. Again Exhibit 75 was examined by judge and jury.

For once Charles thought the conduct of the case by the prosecution was perfunctory. Mr Coppard cross-examined, but even Charles could see that he did not make much out of it. Indeed, after what seemed a mere formal effort, he sat down.

'Arthur Newport!'

The fourth witness for the defence was known to Charles. He was a small, stooped old man, with a peering expression and a dry manner. He said he was a scientist, that was to say, a handwriting expert. He had certain qualifications and had held certain positions, all of which he detailed. Byng handed him a paper.

'Have you seen that paper before, Mr Newport?'

'I have.'

'What is it?'

'It is a sample of the accused's handwriting. He wrote it in my presence.'

'Hand up Exhibit 57.'

Mr Peabody's poison register was passed to the witness.

'Do you see the entry purporting to be signed by Francis Carswell and dated the 23rd of August?'

'Yes.'

'Can you say whether or not it was written by the accused?'

The witness moved uneasily. 'It is not possible to be absolutely sure, but to the best of my opinion and belief it was not.'

'You think it was not written by the accused. Thank you.' Byng sat down.

Lionel Coppard jumped up.

'You say that it is not possible to be sure whether this entry was written by the accused or not?'

'It's not possible to be absolutely sure, but it is my opinion that he didn't write it.'

'You can either be sure of a thing or you cannot be sure of it. You say you are not sure.' Coppard sat down with the righteous air of the man who has defeated an attempt at equivocation.

Byng was on his feet again immediately.

'While you admit it is not possible to be *absolutely* sure the entry was not written by the accused, are you or are you not reasonably sure to the best of your opinion and belief?'

'Yes: I'm sure to the best of my opinion and belief.'

There being no further witnesses, Mr Heppenstall stood up to make his closing speech.

A little shiver passed over Charles. Now for it! This was his last chance. If Heppenstall made a good speech, a really good speech, there was still hope. If he bungled it – Charles knew he was done for, down and out, finished... He settled himself with a painful eagerness to listen.

He could not bear to look at the jury. Their faces told him how desperately thin were his chances. All seemed to have made up their minds. They were going to listen, because it was the custom and their duty, but not even the lanky man seemed to have any doubt left as to the issue.

Heppenstall began to speak in a quiet, pleasant conversational tone, and his manner suggested that he was confiding some interesting secret to old and well-trusted friends. Taking the jury into his confidence: that was it. Helping them to cope with their heavy duties, particularly helping them to avoid being imposed on by the representatives of the Crown...

'May it please Your Lordship, members of the jury,' he began, after a good deal of play with his eyeglass, 'I now have an opportunity of putting before you the case for my client, Mr Charles Swinburn. I need not remind you of the terrible position which he occupies. His all is at stake: his happiness, everything that he has or is, his very life itself. You cannot, and I know you will not, deal lightly with so weighty a matter. You will, I know, consider all that can be urged on his side as well as the evidence which seems to be against him. For, as his lordship will tell you, you have a double duty: a duty to him as well as a duty to the State. That you will do your duty to the very best of your ability, no one in this court doubts.

'Now you are all familiar with the phrase which tells you that you must give the accused the benefit of any doubt which may be in your mind as to his guilt, and, subject to his lordship's correction, I shall ask you to consider for a moment just what that phrase really means. It does *not* mean that you cannot convict unless there is absolute certainty of guilt – there seldom is that absolute certainty which juries would no doubt like. No, it means something much more commonplace than that. It simply means that you must exercise your powers of judgement on the question of the defendant's innocence or guilt in just the same way that you exercise them in the ordinary affairs of daily life.

'Let me put it to you like this. Suppose someone claims something from you which would involve a considerable sacrifice. Naturally, you investigate that claim to satisfy yourself whether it is or is not valid. The proof of its validity may not be absolute, but if you are reasonably satisfied that it is just, you will make the sacrifice; if not, you won't. Now it is just the same in the present case. If you are so satisfied that the accused is guilty that on similar evidence you would make a considerable sacrifice, then you will bring in a verdict of guilty. But if you feel that the evidence would not be sufficient to induce you to make the sacrifice, then you will bring in a verdict of not guilty.

'Now there is one definite case which, I put to you, must necessarily involve sufficient doubt of the accused's guilt to require an acquittal, and that is the case in which all the facts adduced by the prosecution can be explained equally well by assuming the guilt of some person other than the accused. In other words, the case that the police have got hold of the wrong man; and that, in a nutshell, is the defence I am going to put up in this case. I now hope to show you that while the evidence to which you have listened may or may not be proof of guilt, that guilt is not the guilt of my client. If I succeed in doing so, I shall be able, with every confidence, to ask for a verdict of acquittal at your hands.'

Charles's heart had begun to beat painfully. Was this really so? Was there a defence after all? If Heppenstall could prove anything like this, he was saved! Charles felt the tension almost more than he could endure. He clenched his hands till the knuckles showed white.

'Now I admit in the fullest way,' Heppenstall went on, 'that the case against my client looks very black. It could not have been conducted by my learned friend Sir Richard Brander and look otherwise. Fortunately for my client, however, that is a superficial appearance only. Its black appearance is caused by placing one arbitrary interpretation on the facts. Fortunately there are others – two others – entirely compatible with his innocence. It is my duty as well as my privilege to put them before you.

'Of all the evidence put forward, you will see as clearly as I do myself, that only one item is really conclusive of the accused's guilt. If he really went into a chemist's shop, and by impersonation and forgery obtained potassium cyanide, for the innocent use of which he is unable to account, then I say, let him hang. If I believed he had done that I would not have appeared here to defend him. But this evidence, I repeat, is the *only* evidence which is conclusive. All the rest can be explained equally well on the assumption of the guilt of another person. I'll show you that in detail presently. Let me first concentrate on this item: did the accused buy that poison or did he not?

'Now someone bought it. Moreover, someone bought it through trickery and fraud. Mr Peabody's evidence, coupled with that of Mr Francis Carswell, is perfectly clear upon that point. The question which you have to answer is simply this: was the man who bought the poison the prisoner, or was it some other person?

'You will tell me that Mr Peabody has testified definitely that it was the prisoner. I suggest to you that Mr Peabody was mistaken. Now in this I am not for a moment questioning Mr Peabody's *bona fides*. You saw him in the box and so did I, and I'm sure we're all agreed that he spoke as a perfectly honest man. But Mr Peabody suffers from the same handicap that you and I do: he is human. Like the rest of

us, he can make honest mistakes. Now will you please consider the
conditions under which this identification was made.

'Firstly, Mr Peabody's sight is not of the best. Your own observation
of his glasses will tell you that. They have very thick lenses, showing
short sight. Secondly, Mr Peabody's shop is a dark shop. He told you
that himself, and you have had overwhelming evidence upon the
point. Thirdly, the day on which this poison was bought was a dark
day. You have heard that at the time the purchase was made the sky
was heavily overcast. Fourthly, the purchaser stood with his back to
what light there was. Members of the jury, please picture this in your
minds: a short-sighted man in a dark shop on a dark day looking at
a customer who stands with his back to the light! You must realize,
as I do, that it was physically impossible for a satisfactory identification to be made under those conditions. As a matter of fact it's not a
question of whether we realize it or not. There is actual proof that
Mr Peabody did not in point of fact observe him closely. He did not
know – you heard him say so – he did not know what kind of hat the
man was wearing. He did not know whether or not he wore spectacles, or gloves, or rings. He didn't know because he hadn't observed
him closely; and he didn't observe him closely because it was too
dark. Doesn't that come out quite unmistakably from his evidence?
Of course it does. I say without hesitation that when the unknown
left the shop, Mr Peabody did not retain a clear conception of his
appearance. Why? Because he had never received it.

'Now you must not overlook another very important point. The
total time the unknown was in the shop was from three to five minutes: say, four minutes. Now during that four minutes Mr Peabody
was engaged in several operations during which he could not have
been looking at his customer. He was examining the visiting card. He
was examining the four envelopes which were presented as a forged

identification. He had to retire from the shop to get the poison, and while he was away he tells us he stopped to look up Carswell's name in the telephone directory. How long, I ask you, was he actually looking at his visitor? It could not have been more than for a minute, or two minutes at the very outside.

'Now consider! How much time elapsed between that one or two minutes' interview in the semi-darkness and the identification at Cold Pickerby? Mr Peabody has told you. No less than sixty-nine days; nearly ten weeks! Members of the jury' – Heppenstall leaned forward and spoke very persuasively – 'you don't really believe that Mr. Peabody *could* be sure under such conditions. You know as well as I that he could be nothing of the kind. It's not physically possible.'

Heppenstall stood upright again and made a little pause before continuing. 'Why then, you will ask me, does Mr Peabody, whose motives are admittedly beyond question, why does he believe he can make the identification? I'll tell you. It's due to a universal trait of human nature. It's due to the fact that we all, you and I as well as Mr Peabody, tend to see what we expect to see. Consider how this identification was made.

'Mr Peabody was interviewed in London by the police, who asked him to go down to Cold Pickerby to see whether he could identify the man who had been in his shop. I am not accusing the police of using improper methods; there was nothing else they could do. But the fact remains that Mr Peabody went down expecting to see the man. He saw a man who seemed like him. He took it subconsciously that this was the man in question. It was only human.

'Now, members of the jury, please remember that you're not being asked to give a mere opinion on this identification. You're being asked to hang a man on it. I put it to you that you can't do it. There's a great deal more here than a reasonable doubt. For a triviality you might accept such evidence. For a man's life, no! There's a doubt here so huge that not to give the benefit of it would be – I say it with all respect – it would be a responsibility neither you nor anyone else dare face.

'Particularly if the man who bought the poison *was like the accused*. Have you thought of that, members of the jury? If you haven't, think of it. You've got to have no reasonable doubts. I tell you, no one would hang a cat on such evidence, and you know it!

'Now I am making no accusation of any kind whatever, but there were two other persons, either of whom might easily have been made up to resemble my client, and either of whom might, for all the evidence that has been put before you to the contrary, have committed this murder. You know to whom I am referring: Mr Peter Morley and the late John Weatherup. I am very far indeed from saying either of them did so, but you have to go on the evidence alone, and the evidence points equally to the accused and to those two men. You have been told nothing – I say it with the utmost deliberation – you have been told nothing to enable you to decide which of the three it was.

'But there's another point, a highly important point, to which I would direct your most earnest attention. What proof is there that the purchaser of this poison was any one of the three I have mentioned? What proof is there that he had any connexion whatever with the murder? Someone purchased poison – how do you know that he used it to kill Andrew Crowther, or that he even knew of Andrew Crowther's existence? How, for example, do you know that he didn't use it to commit suicide?

'I submit that on the evidence put before you, you have no reason whatever to connect the purchase of the cyanide with this murder. There is only Mr Peabody's own testimony, and I have shown you that, without questioning Mr Peabody's *bona fides,* in the nature of the case that testimony could not be convincing.

'So much for the identity of the purchaser of the cyanide. My case here is that this purchaser has definitely not been identified with my client: more, that there is no real reason whatever to suppose it was my client. Now let us glance very briefly at the remainder of the evidence brought against him.

'I do not propose to say anything about the handwriting of the purchaser as recorded in the poison book. It has been examined by two experts, and as you know, one of them says it is the handwriting of the accused and the other says it isn't. Now, members of the jury, this doesn't mean that one of these experts is a truthful man and the other a liar. They are both, I'm quite sure, perfectly honourable men. What it means is that the question they were asked is a difficult question and that there is no real way of reaching certainty in the matter. You must have noticed that neither of them was dogmatic, each distinctly pointing out that he was giving an opinion only. I put it to you that the only possible conclusion that you can reach from their evidence is that grave doubt exists as to whether or not the accused made the entry.

'Another piece of utterly unconvincing evidence was that of Mrs Shearman and the clerk from the *Jupiter*. These two persons, while admittedly quite honest and well intentioned, actually profess to be able to tell you my client's thoughts! If you are acquainted with a person and know his moods, you can say with reasonable certainty when he is excited or upset. But my client was a stranger to these two persons. How could they possibly tell whether his manner was abnormal when they didn't know what his normal manner was like? And why shouldn't he have been anxious to get his letters? Wasn't his business in a bad way? Wasn't he keenly interested in its welfare? I submit that to found any opinion on such vague generalities is impossible, and I ask you to dismiss this so-called evidence as irrelevant.'

Hope, incredulous hope, was once again buoying up Charles. He had thought Heppenstall wasn't taking any trouble with the case and that he wasn't being worth his fee. Now Charles saw that nothing he could pay could discharge his debt to Heppenstall. Heppenstall was going to save his life: that was all he was going to do. The intensity of his concentration on Heppenstall amounted to actual pain.

The speech unquestionably was having its effect on the jury. Except in the case of the foreman that dreadful expression of a mind made up had gone from their faces. They now looked, most of them, open to conviction. Two or three looked doubtful and puzzled. Charles hugged himself. Things indeed were going well.

'Now,' went on the persuasive voice, 'the prosecution went to a great deal of trouble to prove that the accused had a motive for murdering his uncle. They might have saved it all. How did they get to know about this motive in the first instance? Was it from police inquiries or clever detective work? It was not. It was from the accused himself. In his original statement which you heard read, he *volunteered* it. He admitted in the fullest way that he had an adequate motive for the crime. But that's a very different thing to saying he committed it.

'I'll prove that for you in a few words. In addition to the accused, four other people had a similar motive for the crime. Mr Peter Morley had an even more powerful motive. Both he and the accused had asked the deceased for help, but whereas the accused got the help, Mr Peter Morley did not. Therefore his motive was actually greater than that of the accused. Mrs Pollifex and Miss Pollifex and the late John Weatherup, the butler, had also a motive for the murder. They stood to gain by Mr Andrew Crowther's death, and though they didn't stand to gain so much as the other two, for all we know to the contrary any one of them may have been in greater need.

'Now here are five persons who had a motive for murdering the deceased. They can't all have done it. Therefore some of them – four of them if not all five – are innocent. My point is that those four who are innocent had, equally with the guilty one, a motive for the crime. Therefore motive alone is no argument for guilt, and I put it to you that you may dismiss the question of motive from your thoughts. It cuts in too many ways. Let us therefore come to the next point: the administration of a poisoned pill.'

Mr Heppenstall here made an effective little pause. He stooped to consult his brief, had a perfect orgy of manipulation of his eyeglass, glanced in a friendly way at the jury, and resumed:

'Now on this point I confess to some surprise at the attitude of my learned friend, the leader of the prosecution. It is not like him to put up such an entirely baseless piece of assertion as that the accused put the poison into a pill and administered it to his uncle. That is a fundamental of the case; in fact I might fairly call it *the* fundamental of the case. I'm sure you were as much surprised as I was to find that on this fundamental point not one single iota of evidence was given. What does my learned friend say about it? I quote from his speech. "It must have been obvious to him – that is, the accused – that *if* poison could be inserted into a pill and *if* that poisoned pill could be introduced into Andrew Crowther's bottle, he would sooner or later take that pill and die." There,' cried Heppenstall in ringing tones and with a striking gesture, 'there is what you are asked to convict this man on! The mention of a possibility, without the slightest supporting evidence! For though my learned friend went on to say that he would prove that the poison was inserted into one of these pills and the pill introduced into the deceased's bottle, and that the deceased took that pill and died as the result – though he said he could prove all these, I submit that he did not do so. He did not prove a single one of these statements.

'Because please remember that the fact that the deceased may have taken *a* poisoned pill does not in any way connect my client with his death. Members of the jury, I ask you would you convict a dog on such evidence? To take a human life on it is unthinkable.

'It is argued that because the accused was alone with the deceased after dinner on the 25th of August, that he must have put the poisoned pill into the deceased's bottle, or changed the deceased's bottle for another containing the poisoned pill. I ask you to examine this argument and I ask you to disregard it for two reasons. In the first place it is logically unsound. If it were sound it would follow that everyone who had been alone with the deceased must have put a poisoned pill into his bottle – an absurd conclusion. In the second place, the accused was not the only one to be alone with the deceased. You heard in evidence that on the night Mr Peter Morley and Mr Crosby dined at The Moat, Mr Crosby left the dining-room to get papers, leaving Mr Morley alone with the deceased. Why not argue, therefore, that Mr Morley put in the pill? And we may be certain from the nature of the case that the butler, John Weatherup, and the other inmates of the house, Mrs and Miss Pollifex, were also, or could have been, alone with the deceased after his meals. That, however, is no reason for supposing them to be guilty of his murder. Here again I put it to you that you cannot say that my client was the guilty person, rather than one of these other persons.

'My learned friend tells us that the spilling of the wine is an argument for supposing my client changed the bottles. It might conceivably tend in that direction if my learned friend had proved that the accused spilled it. He did not do so. No evidence connecting my client with that spilled wine has been put before you. How much more likely that the wine should have been upset by the deceased, who was old and feeble and in poor health, and whose hand was probably pretty shaky? For the matter of that, how do you know that the wine was not spilled by Weatherup?

'I needn't worry you with further details. The matters of the pictures and of the further loan for five thousand, of which so much was made, are quite beside the point. As I have said, the accused never made any secret of the fact that he was short of cash. The same applies to his holiday. Why should he not have had a holiday if he wanted it? It shows to what straits the prosecution were reduced when they made a point out of the date on which he booked. Just consider. He got information about cruises on the 23rd of August. He booked on the 26th. What more natural? Did any of you, members of the jury, ever book on a cruise without getting information as to the possibilities before making up your mind? My client wanted a holiday, he had the opportunity, and he took the holiday, just as you or I would have done in similar circumstances. I submit also that Miss Una Mellor's evidence was quite irrelevant to the case, and I deplore the fact that the prosecution thought it necessary to give her and the accused so much unnecessary pain.'

Once again Heppenstall made an impressive pause, but only for a moment. Then he continued:

'Allow me, members of the jury, to summarize my case. It is, in a word, that the prosecution have failed to connect my client with the murder. Someone bought cyanide, but there is no proof that it was my client. Mr Peabody's evidence – the *only* evidence on this vital point – is unreliable from its very nature. All the other evidence is beside the question, as it cuts in several directions.

'That, members of the jury, is all I have to say to you, except confidently to ask you for a verdict of not guilty.'

Mr Heppenstall sat down and the hearing was adjourned for the night. Charles once again was wholly optimistic. This case for the defence was unanswerable. No jury could possibly get over it. So great was the reaction from his former despair that he wanted to get up and sing and shout and wave his arms. He was safe! They couldn't convict against that! The remainder of the proceedings would be merely formal.

CHAPTER XXII

Charles Learns His Fate

W HEN CHARLES CAME INTO COURT NEXT MORNING A GOOD deal of his optimism had evaporated. He was thankful that the end of his terrible period of suspense was approaching, but at the same time little waves of fear kept sweeping over him as he realized what that end might involve. Then he rallied himself. After such a defence there could be no doubt of the issue. That evening would see him cleared at least of this charge. Unless… But he would not allow himself to think of that alternative.

He had not time, however, to think very long about anything. Immediately on the reopening of the proceedings Sir Richard stood up to deliver the closing speech for the Crown. Like Heppenstall he also spoke quietly and addressed the jury as if they were his oldest friends, of whose good-will and cordiality he was profoundly assured.

'May it please Your Lordship, members of the jury,' he began, 'I am sure you are as greatly impressed by the brilliance of my learned friend's speech for the defence as I am. Only those who do that kind of work can appreciate the amount of thought and time and skill which that speech represents.

'At the same time, members of the jury, you must remember that my friend's recognized object was not to put before you an unbiased view of the case. It was his business to clear his client, if he could. While at all times strictly fair, the view he gave you was intentionally one-sided. It is now my business to examine how far his arguments are convincing and to give you the other side of the case, when his

Lordship will hold the balance between us. I shall be very brief in my remarks.

'Now my learned friend admits that if Mr Peabody's identification of the prisoner as the man who bought the potassium cyanide in his shop is accurate, you must find him guilty. Necessarily therefore he was bound to throw doubts upon that identification. And extraordinarily well, if I may say so, he did it. But you, members of the jury, who have to found your verdict upon your own interpretation of the facts and not upon Mr Heppenstall's or mine, you must not allow yourselves to be misled by these brilliant but specious arguments. Let us for a moment consider them.

'Now first of all, my learned friend says the day was dark and Mr Peabody's shop was dark. Let us admit both statements. But, members of the jury, will you please remember what Mr Heppenstall omitted to point out to you, and that is that our eyes have the power of adjusting themselves to their surroundings. In dark surroundings the pupils open wider and admit more light. So that on going into a dark room from the light we see little, whereas if we remain all day in that dark room we see very much better indeed. Mr Peabody had been in that shop since early morning. His eyes had become accustomed to the light. He was accustomed, moreover, to work there. All his dispensing, the delicate weighing and measuring of small amounts, was done in the same light. The writing on a visiting card was not too easy to see, yet Mr Peabody had no difficulty in reading that handed over by the purchaser.

'Then Mr Heppenstall told you that Mr Peabody was short-sighted, but he didn't point out that that short sight was corrected by the very spectacles to which he drew your attention. From the witness-box to the dock in this court is a distance of about twelve feet. At that distance Mr Peabody told you that he could clearly see the accused.

Now if his short sight allowed him to see clearly at a distance of twelve feet, would it not have allowed him to see across a counter in a shop? Of course it would.

'Mr Heppenstall has argued that because Mr Peabody could only have seen the purchaser of the poison for one or two minutes, he could not recognize him again. Members of the jury, your own experience will tell you that a few seconds' glance at a face is all that is necessary to fix its features in the memory. Think of your own experience and you will agree that I am right.

'When we meet a person for the first time, it is at his face that we look. We do not at first examine his coat or his hat or his gloves. We look at his face. That was what Mr Peabody did on that morning in his shop. He looked at his customer's face, and the fact that he was not sure of the shape of the hat and so on is no argument whatever that he had not seen the face. This also you know from your own experience.

'In fact, members of the jury, no real argument has been adduced to disprove this identification. But what I want to call your attention to is this: no argument of this kind really affects the question at all. Mr Peabody is the authority as to whether he did see this man's face or whether he did not. He tells you that he did. He tells you that he saw the man clearly in his shop, and he looks at the prisoner and he tells you that he is the man.

'Now, Mr Peabody is either telling you the truth or he is telling you a lie. If you think he is telling you a lie, then you will no doubt conclude that the accused is innocent. If you think he is telling you the truth, I do not see how a verdict of guilty can be avoided.

'And you must not be misled by the suggestion that Mr Peabody made a mistake. He knows his liability to make a mistake under the circumstances, and he tells you he did not do so. He knows the seriousness of the consequences which may result from his evidence, and still he tells you he did not do so. Here you have to consider his statement and decide for yourselves as to its reliability.'

As Charles listened to this measured discourse a cold weight of horror crept gradually down on his mind. Gone was his brief period of optimism. Why, there was nothing in Heppenstall's argument after all. Oh, if the case could have stopped at the end of Heppenstall's speech! It had left the jury in doubt, but already Charles could see that look of doubt disappearing from their features, and one of determination taking its place. Oh, if only this man with his quiet, relentless voice could be stopped!

'Now I must also ask you,' went on the voice, 'to put out of your mind entirely the suggestion that the identification which was carried out in Cold Pickerby was in any way unfair. If the police had said to Mr Peabody, "There is the man we suspect. Was he in your shop?" I agree that what Mr Heppenstall suggested might have taken place. But you know as well as I, that the police never do anything like that. Always the accused is brought into the presence of the witness with a number of other persons, and the witness has to pick him out. The process is perfectly fair. And, in any case, here again it is a question of believing Mr Peabody's statement or not believing it.

'Now, Mr Heppenstall has chosen the objectionable method of trying to divert suspicion from his client by throwing it on two other persons, a particularly objectionable method in the case of John Weatherup, who cannot defend himself. Now surely my learned friend does not think the jury don't know that before bringing such a charge against the accused, the police would have explored these obvious by-paths. You may be very sure that if evidence existed against Mr Peter Morley, he would now be standing in that dock.

'My learned friend tried to discredit the evidence as to the accused's state of mind while on the cruise. Naturally he did so, because this evidence is disastrous for his case. I leave it to you, members of the jury, to say whether Mrs Shearman and the clerk could or could not have noticed signs of eagerness and anxiety on the part of the prisoner. In their places could you have done it? I think there can be no doubt that you could, and that they could, and did.

'But if the prisoner was perturbed and anxious, what could have caused that anxiety? Not the condition of his works, as Mr Heppenstall so cleverly suggested. If he had been as anxious as all that about his works, he would not have left them for three weeks. No, I submit he was upset and anxious because he was awaiting news of the death of Andrew Crowther. I submit, moreover, that this was the only thing which could have accounted for his condition.

'Just one word more and I have done. Mr Heppenstall stated that we had failed to connect the prisoner with the pill, and that we didn't even know how the pill could have been administered. I am sorry if I did not make this part of the case for the prosecution sufficiently clear. I thought I had done so. However, I shall now try to remedy that error.

'Let me begin by reminding you of the reasons why we know that the deceased died from taking a poisoned pill. They are four in number.

'First, he was seen by Mr Peter Morley to take a pill after lunch in the plane. You heard Mr Morley describe how he leant forward to speak to the deceased, and saw him do it.

'Second, Mr Gavin Grant has told us that the remains contained none of the substances composing the Anti-Indigestion Pills, and that it therefore followed – as you can see for yourselves – that the pill taken was not one of these.

'Third, the deceased died from taking just the amount of potassium cyanide which could be put into one of these pills.

'Fourth, Mr Morley told you further that the deceased took his pill after lunch was over. This poison, you have heard from the doctor, acts with great rapidity, so that it is unlikely in the extreme that it could have been contained in any substance taken at lunch. If it had been, we may be sure that the deceased would have been unable to take the pill.

'I put it to you that the only reasonable explanation of these facts is that the pill the deceased took contained the poison.

'I admit I cannot prove to you exactly how the poisoned pill was introduced into the deceased's bottle: if I could, there would have been no need for this trial to have lasted three days. But I can suggest what was done. I suggest that the accused bought a second bottle of pills into which, near the bottom, he inserted the poisoned pill. I suggest that on that evening of the 25th of August, when he was last at The Moat, he changed the deadly bottle he had brought for the harmless one belonging to his uncle. This would have been easy. Andrew Crowther took the pills after meals, and he doubtless took one after that dinner. At that time the two men were alone in the dining-room. What easier than to distract the old man's attention, and while he was thus occupied, to exchange the bottles?

'Now, in this connexion I wish to draw your special attention to the spilling of the glass of wine. The spilling of a glass of wine is a most uncommon event, at least at a quiet dinner where no question of rowdiness or of taking too much could arise. It is difficult to see how under ordinary conditions it could have happened. But if that wine had been upset to distract the old man's attention while the bottles of pills were exchanged, the occurrence is immediately explained. Members of the jury, I admit again that I can't prove that these bottles were changed in this way. How could I? It isn't very likely that the accused would do such a thing in the presence of witnesses. But I ask you to consider again the following facts:

'First. The evidence of Mr Peter Morley and the analyst proves that the deceased died from potassium cyanide poisoning, administered in a pill.

'Second. Two days before this dinner the prisoner bought potassium cyanide in London by a fraudulent trick.

'Third. At this dinner he had an opportunity – and the only opportunity – of introducing the poison into the deceased's bottle of pills and while he and the deceased were alone, the wine was spilled.

'Fourth. The accused had no reason for paying this visit to The Moat, other than to substitute the pills.

'Fifth. On the morning following he arranged to start on the first available cruise.

'I submit that these facts are overwhelming evidence that the accused did put the poisoned pill into the deceased's bottle. It is for you, members of the jury, to say whether or not my submission is correct.

'Summarizing, my case is that the accused had a powerful motive to carry out the crime; that he had an adequate opportunity; that several of his actions can only be explained on the hypothesis of his guilt; and that no other explanation of the deceased's death can be suggested.'

Sir Richard made a short peroration pointing out the necessity for the jury to do their duty without fear or favour if human life was to be safe 'in this grand old England of ours', and then sat down abruptly.

Once again a ripple of movement passed over the court. Here was the completion of another stage of this endless terrible drama. Once again Charles was sunk in an agony of doubt and fear. The issue now would depend on the kind of lead the judge gave in his summing up. And Mr Justice Herriott, though fair, was known to be hard…

But the little old gentleman was moving. He was turning slightly sideways, the better to address the jury. Without haste, but without delay, he began to speak, his low but clear voice penetrating to every corner of the room.

'Members of the jury,' he said, 'the indictment in this case is that of this man for wilful murder. Before coming to the actual details of the evidence, I wish to say a few words to you on the question of your duty in the matter.

'You have in point of fact two duties, the duty of convicting the guilty and of acquitting the innocent. These duties are equally important. I need not tell you how important it is that if this man is innocent, he should be cleared of this dreadful charge and leave this court without a stain on his character. But I must remind you that it is equally important that if he is guilty he should suffer for his crime, for if guilty persons were not detected and punished, crime would abound and neither life nor property would be safe. So, as counsel for the defence has rightly said, you have your duty towards the accused and your duty towards your country. I am certain that you will consider very earnestly and carefully the evidence, so that you may not fail in either of these duties.

'I come now to the circumstances of the case. This man, Charles Hargrave Swinburn—' and once again the whole wearisome business was gone through; the history of the Crowther family and of the works; the financial difficulties of Charles; the possible way of escape therefrom; the purchase of the poison; the theory of the pills; Charles's holiday...

Mercifully Charles himself was beginning to feel numb. For him horror was mounting on horror. He was astonished at the irrelevant details which filled his mind, sometimes even to the exclusion of that low voice with its sentences of life and death. There was a crack in the sheeting of the railing before which he sat, and he followed this crack from one end of the board to the other, as indeed he had followed it on previous occasions during his two days of trial. A second crack joined a few inches down the board, and lower still it curved wildly round a knot. Charles knew every curve and irregularity of those cracks. There was a tiny spider crawling on the same board, which became almost more important to him than the case itself. He watched it approach the crack. Would it cross it? Almost breathlessly he watched. It did! It hesitated when it came to it, but it crossed it. It went on and disappeared between that board and the next…

Still the low voice droned on. It was all extraordinarily fair, extraordinarily impartial. There was no lead given to the jury. They were going to have to make up their own minds without help from anyone. Hope and despair alternated in Charles's mind.

'Both prosecution and defence,' went on the calm thin tones, 'have rightly stressed the importance of Mr Peabody's evidence. Whether you accept Mr Peabody's statement that the man who bought the poison was the accused, or whether you think it was some other person, will influence you a good deal in your verdict. Now to settle this point you will depend rather upon your own common sense and knowledge of shops and persons and life, than upon the arguments of the two distinguished leaders to whom you have listened. Picture yourself, each one of you, in that shop of Mr Peabody's under the conditions described, and consider whether you yourself would have been able or unable to identify the customer nearly ten weeks later. It's a matter of common sense and experience rather than of argument.

'If you are satisfied that the accused really did purchase the poison, you will probably find that you will be forced to bring in a verdict of guilty, because if the accused bought it, intending to use it for some other purpose, this would almost certainly have been brought out by the defence. If, on the other hand, you are doubtful whether the accused did buy the poison, you will then have to consider all the other facts and decide whether they are or are not sufficient to lead you to a conclusion.

'You will now retire and consider your verdict, and if there is any point of law on which you should desire further guidance, I shall be pleased to give it to you.'

At this the jurors filed out and Charles was led once again down the sinister staircase.

He had received but little comfort from the judge's charge. It had not been against him. Everything which could be said for him had been pointed out. He felt he had no grievance in the summing up. But equally it had not been in his favour. Every point which told against him had been relentlessly brought forward. None had been stressed: either for him or against him.

Nor had he learned much from the faces of the jurors. The foreman still looked as if his decision would be Guilty, but the others were not so easily read. If the foreman were a strong man it looked badly. And narrow-minded men often were strong for that very reason.

Since Charles had first conceived the idea of murdering his uncle, he had learned on occasion after occasion how appallingly slowly time can crawl. But never had he experienced anything like that time in the waiting cell under the county court-house. Again and again he found himself almost wishing for any verdict, even an unfavourable one, if only this awful suspense could be ended. Then he would once more realize what an unfavourable verdict would really mean, and be filled with panic and loathing and dread.

The warders in a somewhat rough way were kind to him. They gave him tea, which he drank thirstily, avidly. They told him to keep up his pecker and that all was not lost: that even if the verdict went against him he'd have an appeal.

As time dragged on and nothing happened, Charles sank into a kind of stupor. Once again he had that curious feeling of being outside his own body – as if from a distance he was looking down upon himself and as if his experiences were those of some other person. His thoughts went back to certain incidents in his life. Now he would give everything he had if he could have lived them differently. How thankful now would he not be if he could have a clear conscience, his freedom, and poverty! And Una! He had sacrificed himself for Una, and at the first breath of trouble she had let him down! To think of Una was only adding to his pain.

Endless hour passed after endless hour and still no move was made. The warders discussed the possibility of the jury being locked up for the night and sentence being postponed till next day. Charles felt that if this were to happen he should go mad. He did not believe that his mind could stand the suspense all night.

Then suddenly he was once more climbing the staircase. The jury were coming back!

One glance at their faces told Charles the truth! He was lost!

Mercifully the numbness settled down on him, and he felt himself only partially conscious of what was taking place. The fateful question was asked. The jurors were agreed on their verdict. That verdict was Guilty.

In a sort of dream Charles heard someone asking him – or was it someone else standing there in the dock? – had he anything to say why the sentence of the court should not be passed on him? Were they speaking to him? He hardly knew: he hardly cared. He didn't answer. What did it matter? They were going to hang him. Nothing that he could say would matter. There was a pause. He heard the awful sentence. It was over! The warders were pointing to that staircase. They were supporting him. Half unconscious, he was helped down.

CHAPTER XXIII

French Begins His Story

O NE EVENING A FEW WEEKS AFTER THAT LAST TRAGIC DAY OF the trial a little party met in a private room in a London hotel. It consisted of five persons: Julian Heppenstall, Everard Byng, Alexander Quilter, Superintendent Lucas, and Inspector French. It was not a purely social function. It had indeed been engineered by Byng for his own purposes.

The Cold Pickerby case had gone swiftly to its appointed end. There had been the usual appeal, but it had been dismissed, and Charles Swinburn had met the fate he had tried so desperately to avoid.

Interest in the affair, other than of the mere academic kind, was now confined to Byng. Byng in his spare time was a writer. Under a *nom de plume* he wrote works on criminology. Four of the Famous Trials series were from his pen, and he had been commissioned by his publishers to do a similar account of this Cold Pickerby case. It was to collect matter for this book that he was now anxious.

He had had a brain-wave which had received the enthusiastic approval of his publishers. He proposed, if he could manage it, to add a chapter to the book, which should contain a short history of the detection of the case. The entire affair would be described as it presented itself to the police. It would begin with the facts which first raised suspicion of foul play, go on to give the lines of inquiry which presented themselves, then the results of those inquiries, and finally the conclusions reached therefrom. It might be impossible for various reasons to make public every fact which had entered into the police calculations, but the general evolution of the affair from suspicion to certainty could be described. It would in fact be a detective story from real life. Byng did not know how far the thing would prove possible, but he wanted to see what he could do.

The first thing was to obtain official permission, and with this in view Byng had seen Sir Mortimer Ellison, Assistant Commissioner of New Scotland Yard. Sir Mortimer had agreed to the proposal, subject to the right of revision of all proofs. Then Lucas and French had to be approached, and when it was made clear that the successes of these officers would be given under their own names, opposition to his scheme faded away. Quilter, asked for his help, had become interested and had taken advantage of a visit of himself and Lucas to Town to invite the party to dine at his hotel. Heppenstall, also interested, begged to be included in the invitation.

The great moment had now come. Dinner was over. It had been a good dinner with good wine, and the essential guests were feeling that the world was not indeed so bad a place and that if people wanted information about things it should be given them. The private room was comfortable. The chairs were easy and the fire bright. Whisky had been set out, with port for those who liked it, and Quilter produced a box of fine Corona-Coronas. In fact, he was doing all in his power to help Byng. Perhaps not entirely without reason.

'Well,' said Quilter tactfully to Lucas and French, as he made sure that everyone was comfortable and had drinks and smokes, 'you gentlemen were too much for us at Cold Pickerby. Never mind, we'll turn the tables on you next time. I confess I'll be very much interested in what you tell us, for to me it seems an absolute miracle how you found out what you did. Even now I can't see what you had to go on. What do you say, Heppenstall?'

The big man nodded solemnly. 'It was a good piece of work,' he declared, evidently anxious to give Byng a leg up; 'just as good as ever I've heard of. I congratulate you, superintendent, on your good sense in calling in the Yard before it was too late and in helping French as you must have helped him, and with that you must let me connect Inspector Appleby's name. And I congratulate Inspector French for rising to the occasion in the way he evidently did. Yes, it was a good piece of work, and I for one am very anxious to hear just how it was done.'

'Hear, hear,' said Byng, proceeding with the mystic operation of leaving no stone unturned; 'and there is something that I may perhaps mention at this point.' He grinned at French and looked round mysteriously at the others. 'It's no longer a secret, but it is possible that all of us here may not have heard it. You spoke, Heppenstall, of Inspector French. You won't be able to a month hence. Then, we'll all be glad to know, you'll have to speak of Chief-Inspector French!'

'Bravo!' cried Quilter. 'I'm delighted to hear it. Fill up, gentlemen. I give you the toast of Chief-Inspector French, and may he live long to enjoy his well-earned promotion!'

French was evidently delighted though somewhat embarrassed. He explained that in three weeks Chief-Inspector Mitchell was retiring and that he was getting his job. He thanked them all very much for their kind words. Everyone clapped. All was peace and amity and the atmosphere just what Byng wanted.

'You have this book stunt on, Mr Byng?' said Lucas after a pause. 'What do you want us to do?'

Byng made a gesture as if abandoning frivolity and getting down to brass tacks.

'I want you, if you will, to tell me how you did the trick. First, I would like to ask you, superintendent, what made you suspicious and why you decided to call in the Yard, and then I would like to ask French how the case struck him on arrival and just what you all did right from that point up to the trial.'

'Well,' Lucas returned, 'I'm a bit surprised that such matters should be made public. However, the chief constable has agreed and I have personally no objection to telling you anything I can. I understand you've got authority from Sir Mortimer, French?'

'Yes, he's quite agreeable.'

'It's this new stunt of popularizing the detective service by letting the public know what it can do,' said Heppenstall; 'at least, I understand so. It's the answer to that silly criticism of our police forces which has obtained for so long. The authorities are at last waking up to the fact that if the public only knew what is done, they would criticize no more.'

'Shouldn't have given the authorities credit for so much sense,' declared Lucas, which showed how the atmosphere of the room had relaxed.

'Nor I,' Heppenstall agreed. 'Well, Byng, pleasant as all this is, we can't sit here for more than a month or two. Suppose you get going.'

Byng opened his notebook. He was an expert shorthand writer. 'Perhaps, superintendent, you would go ahead then and tell us why you got suspicious and why you called in the Yard?'

Lucas made the small preparations to be expected under the circumstances. He drew his cigar up to a bright red, took a sip of whisky, cleared his throat and settled himself once more comfortably in his chair. Then he began.

'It's very easy to tell you that. In the first place here was the death of a wealthy man for which the French doctor who was called in could find no natural cause. Apart from his suggestion and the suggestion of the French police, it was obvious that a post-mortem was required.

The post-mortem was held, and that gave us the fact that poison had been administered, and the equally obvious question then arose as to whether the death was due to accident, suicide, or murder.

'Now on the face of it, accident seemed unlikely. The same lunch had been served to something like thirty persons and none of the rest had complained of illness. Therefore the affair had a personal connexion with the deceased, not shared by the other passengers. Then potassium cyanide is a more or less rare poison, not in common use and comparatively difficult to obtain. It could only have been brought to the plane in a deliberate way. On a balance then, the affair looked like either suicide or murder, though admittedly this was not proven.

'Turning to suicide, it was obvious that this theory had three objections. Of these two were slight and one was serious. Of the slight ones, the first was that the deceased had no real motive for suicide. He was depressed, but no one suggested his depression was bad enough to lead to suicide. On the contrary, he had a motive for living; he was particularly anxious to see his daughter. He had undertaken a tiresome journey for the purpose, and this was almost over, so that it was unlikely he would not at least complete it. Then secondly, there was nothing in the deceased's manner to suggest suicide; neither depression nor excitement nor sense of strain, some one of which would surely have shown if he had contemplated anything so drastic.

'But the third objection was the really serious one. If the deceased had brought that poison, he must have brought it in something, some box or bottle. No such receptacle was found. It looked like murder.'

'What about the coroner's suggestion that the receptacle might have been lost when the body was being lifted from the plane?' asked Quilter.

The super shrugged: 'Possible of course,' he admitted, 'but the French police were on the job, and I ask you, is it likely? They're pretty good, those French fellows.'

'I expect you're right, super.'

'At the same time,' Lucas went on, 'I got Appleby to have a look over The Moat. Among other things he told me that the old man had been an expert photographer, and I had a sort of idea that potassium cyanide was used in photography, so I had that gone into. Mr Grant, the analyst, confirmed that the stuff was used, we made a search, and as you know, there was potassium cyanide there.'

'That was what the coroner went on at the inquest,' said Byng.

'Yes,' Lucas rejoined, 'but between you and me, the coroner—' He winked very slowly; an admirably non-committal expression of disparagement. 'Well, there was nothing in it, but we thought the coroner's views would help us by lulling the murderer to sleep, so we didn't put him wise to his mistake.'

'Now, superintendent, you're going too quickly for me,' Byng protested. 'I don't follow all that. Will you make it clearer. Words of one syllable, please, for a little one.'

'You couldn't have followed it, because I didn't tell you what Appleby found. There was thick dust all over that bottle of poison and there were no finger-prints on it. It hadn't been touched for long enough.'

'Good,' exclaimed Byng. 'That settles that. But how did you get out of telling the coroner?'

'He didn't ask. One would have thought that the first question would be, "Were there finger-prints on this bottle?" But he didn't ask it. If it hadn't been such a useful mistake we'd have told him, but nothing better for us could have happened. We could then carry on our inquiries with the murderer off his guard.'

'That's very clear. Then right at the beginning of the inquiry you knew that murder had been committed?'

'We thought so. We weren't absolutely sure, because though unlikely, it was still *possible* that the deceased had some solid cyanide and that the paper he'd had it in had got lost. However, we knew enough to know we must go further. Then when the will was read we thought we had got the motive.'

'Right. How did you find out its terms?'

'From the legatees. This was before the adjourned inquest, you understand, and we were supposed to be still making inquiries for that. None of the legatees dared to put us off, as this would have looked fishy on the publication of the will.'

Byng nodded without speaking and Superintendent Lucas after a slight pause went on.

'I confess that at this time we hadn't thought of the pills as a vehicle for the poison, and therefore our possible suspects were Peter Morley and John Weatherup only. I was personally inclined to bank on Morley, believing he had leant forward over the deceased's shoulder, attracted Weatherup's attention elsewhere, and dropped the poison into the food. But of course there was no proof. Then we thought of the pills and we saw that they enlarged the scope of the affair to include almost anybody.

'Things had reached this stage when the question of calling in the Yard arose. That was not settled on the merits of this case. It was settled by the fact that we were short-handed. Appleby was busy on those Chislefield burglaries, and I had no one else I should have cared to trust with it. So we got French down, and I'm glad we did. He has pulled off this case, while Appleby pulled off the burglary one. Hornby and Simmington, who broke into that house at Chislefield, were sentenced at the same assizes.'

'That's really very interesting, superintendent,' Quilter declared. 'That's to say that you asked French to come in to investigate a case which you believed was murder, though the public thought it suicide? That statement should be clear enough for you, Byng?'

'Exactly what I wanted,' Byng played up. 'Now,' he looked at French, 'if you, inspector, will continue on the same lines, I'll be able to work up a fine story.'

French having in his turn carried out the preliminaries of speech, took up his parable.

'The first thing I did when I got down here was to check everything I had been told.' He grinned across at Lucas. 'You see, Mr Byng, I didn't know the super or Appleby then. So I took nothing they said for granted, but checked it all over for myself.'

'Naturally,' Byng murmured. 'Knowing the police, I should have done the same, eh, super?'

'Isn't that life?' Lucas appealed to the heavens. 'Here we supply him with his whole stock-in-trade; make his job possible, in fact; and that's what we get for it! Go on, French. You checked your information?'

'I checked it.' French grinned again. 'I was started on what was probably a case of murder, and the first thing I had to do was to make sure of whether it was or not.

'I thought the best way was to assume murder, and see where it led, and I began by considering not who had done it, but how it had been done.

'Now, so far as I could see, there were only three possibilities; either Weatherup had slipped the poison into the old man's food, or Morley had done it, or it had been contained in a pill.

'It was obvious that to drop the poison into the food would have been dangerous. It might easily have been seen, if not by some third person, then by the deceased himself. On the other hand, if a poisoned

FREEMAN WILLS CROFTS

pill could have been introduced into the bottle, the murderer would have considered himself absolutely safe. The balance of probability – I put it no higher than that – the balance of probability seemed to me therefore in favour of the pill.

'There was another point. I knew that potassium cyanide was a very rapid-acting poison, and I looked it up in my "Taylor". I found that it was quicker even than I had supposed. Complete insensibility had always occurred within minutes, and often within seconds. This suggested that the poison had been taken at the end of the meal, which again pointed to the pill.'

'Ingenious,' Heppenstall commented.

'Next,' went on French, 'I went to see the analyst. He told me some rather interesting facts.

'First of all he agreed that a pill was a suitable vehicle for the poison. Further, the amount of poison found in the body could just have been contained in a pill. Moreover, this amount would have been about sufficient to kill a normal man, and more than enough in the case of a man with a weak heart. So that was all right so far.

'But there was a stronger point still. Potassium cyanide, he reminded me, is normally a solid. A pill would therefore be an absolutely ideal way of administering it, whereas in ordinary food it would probably have been found like a bone or a pebble and ejected from the mouth.'

'Good,' exclaimed Byng. 'I hadn't thought of that point.'

'I thought the argument was fairly convincing. I could scarcely see Morley or Weatherup in that public place pouring liquid out of a bottle on to the old gentleman's food. If they didn't, a solid was probably used, and if they used a solid they would scarcely put it in ordinary food, hence probably the pill. This was not of course conclusive, because there was the possibility of powdering the solid. But the pill seemed the easiest way.

'Then another thing struck me. The use of the pill would enable the murderer to establish what he would consider an invincible alibi. If the poisoned pill could be inserted in the bottle, the murderer could be miles away when the death of the victim took place.'

'That looks a more conclusive alibi than it really is,' remarked Quilter.

'That's so, of course, sir. But all the same it's a thing which would appeal a lot to the ordinary mind. How, a man would feel, could he be suspected when he wasn't there? And the farther and more completely away he was, the safer he would feel. It's human nature, even if it isn't reason.'

'That's true,' Heppenstall agreed. 'I should feel it myself under the same circumstances.'

'Well, there's a lesson to you not to depend on it,' Byng advised. 'This is going very nicely, inspector. Yes?'

'There was still another thing on the same lines,' resumed French. 'Owing to the deceased's habit of keeping the bottle in his own custody there would be difficulty in introducing the poisoned pill. This difficulty would also appeal to the murderer – he wouldn't believe he would be suspected of doing anything so nearly impossible. I don't know if I've made myself clear?'

The others reassured him.

'Well, it seemed to me that if a man was ingenious enough to think up the whole scheme, he was ingenious enough to meet this minor difficulty. At all events, rightly or wrongly, I had by this time come to the tentative conclusion that the poison medium was a pill.

'I had also taken a note to look for anyone interested who had an unusually good alibi at the time of the death.'

'Bless me,' exclaimed Quilter. 'You mean that the safeguard upon which the criminal depended most was what actually led you to him?'

'That usually happens, sir. The more ingenious and elaborate the shifts to cover up suspicion, the more obvious it usually is that they are shifts. My experience is that if criminals weren't so clever they'd be harder to catch. What do you say, super?'

Lucas nodded. 'I agree. From their own point of view they can't let well alone. Lucky for us, all the same.'

'I then dropped that side of it,' went on French, 'and started making a list of all the people whom I thought might be guilty. This was a tedious job and not very interesting, so I need only tell you my conclusion. The list included: Mr Peter Morley, Mrs Morley, Mr Charles Swinburn, Mrs Pollifex, Miss Pollifex, Weatherup, the two maids, Mr Crosby, as well as some possible unknown. These names were obtained by general inquiries, which gave me the persons who benefited under the will, and also those who might have had access to the pills.

'On the grounds of general probability I tentatively eliminated the ladies and Mr Crosby, leaving as the most likely suspects Morley, Swinburn, and Weatherup. It was understood, of course, that this list was not final, but was open to revision at any time. I also noticed with a good deal of interest that Swinburn was on a cruise to the Mediterranean at the time of the death. Was this, I wondered, the alibi I had been expecting?'

'Net beginning to close?' remarked Heppenstall.

'Well, hardly that, sir. Let us say, a path for investigation mapped out. I next interviewed Weatherup and got as complete a statement from him as I could. He told me that Morley and Swinburn had been both calling on the deceased more frequently of late than formerly, and he believed that there was "some business on between them". Of course, both had admitted what that business was. Swinburn had been to lunch and dinner before he went away on his trip, and Morley had

also been to lunch and dinner, that dinner being on the night before
Mr Crowther died. I pumped Weatherup as to whether either had
been alone with the deceased and I learned that Swinburn had been
alone with him for a considerable time after both lunch and dinner,
and that Morley had been alone with him for a considerable time after
lunch only, Mr Crosby being present on the evening when he dined.
But from Mr Crosby I learned that Morley had been alone with him
for three or four minutes when Mr Crosby had left the room to get
some papers from his overcoat.

'It was during the course of this questioning that Weatherup
made a statement of which I thought nothing at the time, but which
afterwards seemed to me to be significant. I asked him how he was
sure on what evening it was that Swinburn had dined, and he said it
was because the tablecloth got stained on that night, and he had to
change it a day earlier than usual. I asked how it had got stained and
he told me of the spilling of the wine.

'It was in bed that night when the possible significance of this
struck me. I had been puzzling over the question of how the poisoned
pill could have been introduced into the deceased's bottle. From
what I had been told, Mr Crowther kept the bottle in his waistcoat
pocket, and it was never therefore out of his possession. Moreover,
at night he was a poor sleeper and would certainly have awaked if
anyone had gone into his room to tamper with it; unless of course
he was first drugged. But no hint of his having been drugged had
come out, and with an elderly invalid I doubted if such a matter could
have been hidden. Now it occurred to me that if the wine had been
spilled when the deceased was taking his pill, his attention might have
been sufficiently distracted to allow the pill to have been slipped into
the bottle. I was not quite satisfied about this, because if it had been
merely dropped in, the old man would have taken it within a day or

so. The pill seemed to have been put low down in the bottle. Then suddenly I saw how it might have been managed. If a second bottle of pills had been obtained, and the pill had been inserted beforehand into it, the bottles could easily have been changed. A moment would do it, and the spilling of the wine would have been amply sufficient to distract the old gentleman's attention while it was being done. This, of course, was pure guesswork, but it was all tending in the same direction.'

French paused. There was no question of the completeness with which he was holding his hearers' attention. All were listening with the keenest interest; Quilter, however, not to the extent of forgetting his duties as host.

'Fill up your glass, inspector,' he said to French. 'Talking's dry work. And you, Byng, you're ready for more whisky. Superintendent, the cigars are just behind you.' He threw a pine log on the fire and beamed at the others.

'A great entertainment you're giving us, Quilter,' Heppenstall declared, taking another cigar and passing the box to Lucas. 'I wish we had something of this kind after every case.'

'Same here,' Byng agreed.

'Well, inspector, did you find out if you were right about the spilling of the wine?'

'No,' French answered, 'I'm afraid that remained a theory. I noted it and went ahead. From my conversations with Weatherup I was gradually coming to the conclusion that he was innocent. For this I had no definite reason, therefore I did not accept it, merely noting it as an opinion. But it had just enough influence on my mind to make me take the cases of Morley and Swinburn first.

'I fully realized, as you, sir, pointed out at the trial, that Morley had a stronger motive for the crime than Swinburn, for the simple reason that his uncle had given Swinburn part of what he had asked for, whereas Morley had got nothing. Therefore I took Morley first. I tried to find out if he had bought any cyanide.

'It was obvious that he would not attempt to buy it locally. He would go to some distant big town. But I could not find out that he had left home within the four weeks previous to the old man's death.

'Then I asked the same question of Swinburn, and at once I felt I was on the right track. He was very open about the whole thing – suspiciously open, indeed, making no secret of his movements. I suppose he felt quite safe. He told me that he had had some negotiations with his uncle before the 17th of August. On that day, it was a Thursday, he lunched with the old man, and I had already learned that he was alone with him after lunch. Then on the following Monday, the 21st, he went up to Town, stayed two nights in order to visit a machine-tool works at Reading, and returned on Wednesday, the 23rd. Two days later, on Friday, the 25th, he dined at The Moat, and after dinner was again alone with his uncle. I may mention that it was on this occasion that the wine was spilled.

'When Swinburn told me all this, he had no idea what a give-away he was making. My theory was now beginning to take shape. It seemed to me that on Thursday, the 17th, when he lunched at The Moat and when he got the cheque for £1,000, he must have come to the conclusion that his uncle was not going to stump up to an extent that would be any good to him. I believed that he then decided to commit the murder. On that occasion of lunching he undoubtedly saw the taking of the pill, and his idea for the method probably occurred to him then or shortly after. His problem would be to get the poison, and he would appreciate what I have been saying about the impossibility of getting it locally. What better place to get it could there be than London? So off he goes to London. I presumed he had succeeded in obtaining the stuff in London, and he returns, makes his pill, slips it into a bottle he has bought, dines at The Moat two nights later, spills the wine and during the excitement changes the bottles.

'Such was my new theory. Obviously it was only a theory, but I determined it was worth testing before I went any further.'

Once again French paused, while the others made appropriate murmurs of interest.

CHAPTER XXIV

French Completes His Story

'I DID MY BEST AT THE INTERVIEW WITH SWINBURN TO DISPEL any fears that he might have that I suspected him,' French went on. 'I was not ready for an arrest, and I didn't want to have the labour and expense of shadowing him. I believed he felt himself safe after that interview; indeed, I imagined he thought me a bit of a fool who would give him no trouble.

'Obviously my next step was in London, and next day I went back to the Yard. I began by checking his statement, though I had no doubt I should find it accurate. And so I did. Swinburn had spent the nights of the 21st and 22nd August at the Duchy of Cornwall Hotel in Northumberland Avenue, and on the 22nd he had gone to Reading and interviewed the manager of Endicott Brothers about three machine tools for his works – all just as he had said.

'But there was one fact which emerged from my inquiries at the hotel. It seemed clear that he could have done a deal more in London than pay his visit to Reading. On that second day, for instance, the 22nd, he left the hotel after an early breakfast and didn't return till dinner-time, so the porter told me. He was only in the Reading works for half an hour, so that the entire visit shouldn't have taken more than about three hours. Where was he all the rest of the day? Of course he might have had perfectly legitimate engagements, but then again, he mightn't. At all events, my discoveries were still working in.

'Now I had been pretty continuously considering how he might have got the poison. There were a number of possibilities. He could have bought it openly in his own name at any chemist's at which he was known, on some pretext such as wanting it for photography or electro-gilding or silvering, or for chemical experiments or research, or for destroying wasps or some animal which had to be made away with. I thought this so unlikely as not to be worth consideration. But by impersonating someone else, real or imaginary, and going where he was not known, he might have got it on some similar pretext. Or he might have stolen it if he could obtain access to a doctor's or chemist's store. Poison has often been stolen from a doctor's car, and some trick to get a doctor to take it in his car and leave it for a moment unwatched should not be beyond the bounds of possibility.

'No cases of theft had been reported, however, and as I thought, of all the remaining ways, that of impersonation was the most probable, I decided to work first on this assumption. This scheme meant buying the stuff at some chemist's, and that involved signing the poison book. I thought I could get what I wanted through the poison book.

'I drafted a circular at the Yard and had it sent to every chemist in London. In it I asked for a copy of every entry of purchases of potassium cyanide under the dates of the 21st, 22nd and 23rd of August. There were only seventeen in the whole of London, and I began by telephoning for confirmation to the whole seventeen purchasers. Sixteen confirmed the entries and one denied all knowledge of the affair.

'This seventeenth was Mr Carswell, of Surbiton, and the chemist who had supplied the entry was Peabody. I went off and saw Peabody, and when I found that he had failed to carry out the regulations and had not personally known his purchaser, I felt I was on the right track.

'As a precaution I arranged a meeting between Carswell and Peabody, and Peabody confirmed that Carswell was not the man who had bought the stuff. It seemed to me that the only question then remaining was whether this man was or was not Swinburn.

'To settle this point I asked Peabody to come down here to Cold Pickerby. In spite of your insinuations, sir,' French grinned across at Heppenstall, 'I wanted to be careful not to give Peabody a lead on the matter. I—'

'That was only in the way of business, inspector,' Heppenstall interrupted. 'I never thought you would do anything unfair. In fact, I said so in so many words.'

'You did, sir. It was cleverly done all right.' French grinned again. 'However, as I say, I didn't want to give the man a lead. So I fixed it this way. I borrowed a canvas hut from the Electricity Works and set it over a manhole on the street near the club. Just before lunchtime I got inside with Peabody and told him to tell me if he saw Swinburn pass along the street. He recognized him at once going into the club. I didn't take that as an identification but stayed there till Swinburn came out again. Swinburn was this time facing the hut and he passed within four or five feet. Peabody swore he was absolutely sure. So that was that.'

'Yes, there was no getting over that. You were satisfied then as to his guilt?'

'Perfectly satisfied. All the same – wrongly, as it turned out – I delayed making an arrest till I should have some further evidence.'

'Why do you say wrongly?' Byng interrupted. 'I should have thought you were wise in that.'

'I took a risk which I ought to have foreseen, but didn't. If I had acted at once I should have prevented another murder.'

All four men stared. 'Another murder?' repeated Quilter. 'Oh, you mean Weatherup's. 'Pon my soul, for the moment I forgot Swinburn had been charged with that also. We've heard so much of the Crowther case, it put the other out of my mind. You're sure he was guilty of the second?'

'Absolutely certain. The proof is even more convincing than in the case he was convicted on. If by any unlikely chance he had got off in the first case, we'd have had him over the Weatherup affair.'

'Well, I shall be interested to hear about that,' said Quilter.

'And I,' Byng added. 'You'll tell us, inspector?'

'Certainly, sir. But I hadn't quite come to that yet.'

'Well, for heaven's sake, carry on as you're doing. This tale is just what I wanted.'

'Yes, it's making a good story,' Heppenstall agreed. 'I'm enjoying it.'

'Well, gentlemen, as I say, I made a mistake in not arresting Swinburn at once. However, I thought he was safe and that all would be well, and I went on trying to get confirmatory evidence. I started with the handwriting. That was all right. Our expert seemed satisfied the poison-book entry was in Swinburn's hand. Then I went on to the cruise. If Swinburn were guilty he would be on pins and needles all the time till Mr Crowther died, while, if he were innocent, he would be enjoying himself with an easy mind. I thought I'd try and find this out.

'I went to the Purple Line people and learned that the *Jupiter* was cruising in the Mediterranean and was due three days later to call at Barcelona. So, with the advice of the chief, I went to Barcelona and had an interview with some of the officers. I found that when Swinburn got back on board from an excursion, his first care was to ask for letters. I found that when telegrams or radiograms were taken round the deck, he always hung about to make sure they were not for him. I got a note of his particular friends on board and followed them up. This brought me to Mrs Shearman, and you remember her evidence about his uneasy state of mind during the cruise. All this information helped to confirm the theory in my own mind. Then there was the date on which Swinburn had booked. That was more valuable.

'The booking had come through Cook's, and from them I got the dates. You remember the point? As soon as Swinburn decided he was going to commit the murder he saw he would want the alibi, so he obtained information about trips. Then directly he got the pill into his uncle's bottle he phoned Cook's to book on the first available cruise.'

'There's not such a lot in that, inspector,' Heppenstall objected. 'If he had been innocent he might still have acted exactly as he did.'

'That's true, sir. At the same time, it also worked in. The evidence was cumulative.'

'I see your point.'

'Well, gentlemen, when I got back from Barcelona I heard about Weatherup's disappearance. It was obvious that there might be a connexion between this and the murder, so, after discussion, the super asked me to treat it as part of the same case and look into it also.'

French paused; then, as no one spoke, went on again.

'There is just one other matter connected with the Crowther murder which I might perhaps mention at this stage, though, as a matter of fact, it was not until after Swinburn's arrest that I dealt with it. Do you mind if I take it out of chronological sequence?'

'By all means take it now,' Byng invited.

'Very well. After Swinburn's arrest I searched the study in his house. As a matter of ordinary routine I took away the blotter on his desk and photographed the blottings. Among them I found some addresses. These I followed up, but without learning anything important. But there was one address I couldn't read. It ended in W.C.2, which suggested something in the nature of business, and I thought I should try to find it. The full address, so far as I could reconstruct it, was this.'

French took a paper from his pocket and handed it across. The others crowded over it. It read:

> Messrs J
>
>   treet,
>
>   d,
>
>   ndon, W.C.2.

'The writing where standing alone was quite clear,' French resumed. 'It was where it was covered by other blottings that it became illegible. The first thing was to get the lengths of the lines. This, of course, was approximate, and I reached it in the following way.

'"Messrs J" was clear, and the length of the following name was clear, though not the letters. The lengths of none of the other words could be seen, but I estimated them as follows:

'The last line obviously began with "London". I wrote in the "Lo", spacing it as correctly as I could. Then I drew a straight line from the "M" of "Messrs" to the "L" of "London" and assumed that this would give me roughly where the second and third lines started. This gave me a length for the third line, which would just make "Strand", and as "Strand" was the only third line I could think of of that length ending in a "d", I took it I was right so far.'

'Very good,' Quilter commented.

'No, sir, it was quite easy,' French declared. 'This reconstruction, then, gave me a new problem: to complete the following.' He handed over a second sheet on which was written:

> Messrs Jxxxxxxxxxxxxxxxxxxxxx,
>
> xxxxxxxxxxxx Street,
>
>   Strand,
>
>   London, W.C.2.

'I spent long enough trying to get the name of a street with about a dozen letters, and that just shows the stupid things one'll do. Fortunately, I couldn't find it, because it would have been wrong if I had.'

'Forgot the number?' Heppenstall queried.

'It's just what I did,' French admitted. 'When I allowed for the number, it cut down the length to six or eight letters. This covered a lot of streets – Bedford Street, Surrey Street, Norfolk Street, Arundel Street, and a lot more. There was nothing, then, for it but to get a directory and to go through all these possible streets, noting all names which began with "Messrs. J". It didn't take so long as you might think, and it only gave seven possibles. You see, not only had I the "Messrs J", but I had also the approximate length of the name.'

'Quite,' said Byng. 'I've got that.'

'I looked down the seven in the hope of learning something from their various businesses. There was a publisher, an artists' supplies shop, two solicitors, a pawnbroker of a highly superior type, a chemist and a shoemaker. The pawnbroker seemed to be the most likely, and I tried them first. They were Messrs Jamieson and Truelove. I had no difficulty in getting answers to my questions. I had struck oil; it was with this firm that Swinburn had dealt. It seemed that he had pawned fourteen pictures at the same time that he bought the poison, saying he wanted the money for about six months. They were worth about three thousand, and Messrs Jamieson and Truelove had advanced him two thousand one hundred. Shortly after the Crowther inquest, on the 6th of October, Swinburn had redeemed them. From a paper in his desk I found that on the previous day, the 5th, he had approached Messrs Spiller and Morgan, of Bedford Street, the moneylenders, and borrowed five thousand on the strength of his expectations. With part of this money he had evidently redeemed the pictures, and his reason was obvious. He didn't want the pictures to be missed from his house, as it would show he had been harder up than he wished to be known.

'You see how all this works in. He is on his beam ends before the murder. He decides on the murder as his only chance of keeping above water. Once his uncle's will is known he will be all right. But he hasn't enough ready money to keep him going even till his uncle dies. He therefore pledged the pictures. That gets him two thousand of cash, which carries him on until the death takes place. With his prospects reasonably assured, he is able to borrow the £5,000, and thus to redeem the pictures.'

'That,' said Byng, 'was the case you put up to the Crown? It's no wonder they pulled it off. It left us no chance at all. What do you say, Heppenstall?'

'I never thought we had any chance,' Heppenstall declared.

'Can't make bricks without straw,' Quilter pointed out cheerily.

'Can't make them without clay, at all events,' Heppenstall returned. 'Well, inspector, that's very interesting about the Crowther case. Now we don't want you to stop. We're all interested in the Weatherup case also. What about it?'

'A pause for refreshments seems indicated,' Quilter suggested. He pushed the whisky over to French. 'Help yourself, inspector. A bit of lubricant in the throat makes it work easier.'

Talk became general for a few moments, and then French resumed his story.

'The first thing that occurred to us all on hearing that Weatherup had disappeared was to wonder whether or not the disappearance could be connected with the Crowther murder. You remember, super, that's what you thought?'

Lucas drew slowly at his cigar. 'Yes,' he answered, 'it seemed not unlikely. I don't say there was a definite reason for believing it, but it would have been a coincidence to have two cases occurring at the same time and place and among the same people unless there was some connexion between them.'

'It was the obvious thing to think,' Heppenstall declared, and Byng agreed with him.

'Well, on the chance of a connexion, Superintendent Lucas asked me to have a look into the affair. I heard what Sergeant Bray had found out and then started off.

'You remember, gentlemen, what he reported? Weatherup had disappeared, the desk in the study had been broken open and over a hundred pounds in notes had been stolen, and the key of the study french window was missing?'

'Yes, that's clear.'

'The first question I considered,' French resumed, 'was the obvious one of whether Weatherup had or had not disappeared voluntarily, and with this I thought was connected the second question of whether he had or had not robbed the desk. There were two possibilities: either he had robbed the desk and vanished with the money, or a burglar had robbed the desk and he had tried to capture him and been prevented, and perhaps murdered.

'I began then with the help of the super and his men the ordinary investigations usual under such circumstances, and I soon obtained information which seemed to settle this first question. Three items, in fact.

'Of these, the first was that Weatherup had not taken his suit-case and belongings. These belongings, while perhaps not valuable intrinsically, would be an important item to a man in Weatherup's position, and that he had left them suggested he did not mean to go for good.

'But we found something a good deal more convincing than that. In a locked cash-box in his suit-case was a little hoard of money:

fifty-three pounds in notes. Now, it was clear that if the man had intended to disappear he would not have left that money behind. That was the second item.

'The third was not so convincing, but still it weighed. Detailed inquiries along the roads and at stations and of bus conductors and so on revealed no trace of him. He might, of course, have slipped out of the country without being seen, but it wasn't likely.

'For these three reasons, but particularly the second one, I concluded that the man had intended to return. Then had he stolen the money?'

'It was possible, of course, that he had, and that he intended to say that he had found a burglar at the desk, had given chase, and that the burglar had got away. But it seemed to me more likely that this was the actual truth. It was, indeed, the only theory I could think of which would meet the facts.

'This theory admittedly didn't work in with our original idea that the Weatherup and Crowther cases were connected. That didn't matter. I had been given the case and it was up to me to find out the truth, no matter what that was.

'I thought over this idea of Weatherup giving chase to the burglar, and the more I did so the more sure I grew that if he had really done so he must have been murdered. If he was chasing the burglar he would not voluntarily disappear, and he could scarcely be kidnapped. Murder seemed the only solution.

'You will understand that this idea of murder was largely guess-work. At the same time it was sufficiently likely to need going into.'

'I don't see what else you could do,' Heppenstall agreed.

'So I think,' Quilter added. 'The finding of that money in Weatherup's room seems to me to prove it.'

'If it was murder,' French continued, 'the murderer's obvious difficulty would be to get rid of the body. Could I get him on this?

'I considered all the places where it could have been hidden. First and most likely, it could have been buried. In the woods around The Moat there were places where no one might penetrate from year's end to year's end. This meant a search. We made it, but we could find no grave. Nor was there a quarry hole, well, mine, pit, or any other hiding-place that I could think of.

'My thoughts naturally turned to the lake. If a body could be weighted and sunk the difficulty would be met.

'A walk round the lake showed that it was so shallow at the edge that a body could not be hidden from the shore. A boat seemed indicated, and I had a look over the boat-house.

'At once I saw that I was on the right track. There were two boats in the boat-house and two pairs of oars. On one boat and on one pair of oars there was a fairly thick coat of dust. On the other boat a great many patches had recently been wiped clean, and the same applied to the other pair of oars. Moreover, this second pair of oars was slightly damp.'

There was a little movement of appreciation among French's audience.

'Pretty conclusive,' said Heppenstall warmly.

'It was, sir, because inquiries showed that no boat had been taken out for legitimate reasons. There seemed nothing for it but to drag. The super arranged this, and as you know, we found the body.

'With the body we learned three interesting facts. First, the stolen notes were not on it, second, the key of the study window was not on it, and third, Weatherup's watch had stopped at two twenty-four.

'These facts seemed to me suggestive. From the absence of the notes and key it seemed fair to conclude, firstly, that Weatherup was not the burglar, and secondly that the burglar was also the murderer. If not, it meant introducing a third person, which so far at least didn't seem reasonable. But the hour at which the watch had stopped was more interesting still. It suggested the hour at which the murder took place, or rather the hour at which the body was thrown into the water – probably some little time later. But Mrs Morley had heard the desk being burst open about three. Therefore the murder had been committed before, not after, the burglary. Therefore my idea that Weatherup had heard the burglar and had been on his track was not the truth, and I had to form some other theory.'

'Very good,' Byng approved. 'This is really very interesting, inspector. It also definitely proved Weatherup's innocence of the theft?'

'Yes, sir, quite definitely. It was now beginning to look as if Weatherup had come out to keep some appointment: I couldn't see any other reason for his leaving the house. As I was worrying over this, the question of the keys occurred to me. If Weatherup had come out to keep an appointment, he would have intended to return, and he would therefore have had the key of the study window in his pocket. Obviously the murderer had taken it from him in order to get in himself. Then I wondered whether as a further corollary he could have brought Weatherup out simply with the object of getting the key.

'On the whole I thought this last was not a tenable idea. No one would have committed a murder simply to have obtained a key. No, there was more in it than that.

'Then something very significant struck me. How had the murderer obtained access to the boat-house, which is normally kept locked? Here again it was easy to guess. The meeting had been arranged to take place in the boat-house and Weatherup had therefore brought out the key. This seemed good enough to go on with.'

'It seems to me quite likely,' Quilter remarked as French made a slight pause.

'Yes, sir, but see what followed from it. The murderer, going to The Moat to commit his burglary, took back with him the key of the boat-house. He would naturally do so in order to divert attention from the boat-house and lake. But what did he do then, that is, if I'm correct so far? He hung it on its nail in the hall, the proper place where it was kept.'

The others were listening with gratifyingly close attention. No one spoke, and French went on:

'Now that would have been a splendid move if attention had not been directed to the boat-house. As it was, it proved the most complete give-away that can be imagined. How did the murderer know that the key was kept in that place? At once – always if I was right so far – at once I saw that the murderer was intimately acquainted with The Moat.'

Once again a little ripple of movement passed over French's hearers. This was a point they could appreciate, and they said so with no uncertain sound. French paused and Quilter once more filled up the glasses. Byng took a fresh pencil from his pocket.

'As I explained before,' French went on, 'I was at this time fairly well convinced that Swinburn had murdered old Mr Crowther, though I hadn't as yet got all my proof. At once I naturally thought: were we right at first, that this murder of Weatherup was connected with the Crowther murder, and was Swinburn guilty of this one also? He, at all events, I learned from casual inquiry, knew where the boat-house key was kept.

'Then came the inquest on Weatherup, and by arrangement with me the coroner put up the theory that Weatherup had heard and followed a burglar, who had then murdered him. This was to prevent Swinburn from imagining we suspected him, and it seemed to have that effect.'

'Wily birds,' Heppenstall commented.

'You couldn't be up to them,' agreed Byng.

French grinned. 'The assumption of Swinburn's guilt enabled me to form a provisional theory of what might have happened on that night. Swinburn and Weatherup have some secret business. They decide to discuss it at night and Swinburn chooses the boat-house. Perhaps it is something which requires a light, and he can therefore suggest the interior of a building without raising suspicion. They meet in the boat-house – the only such building available – and there Swinburn murders the butler. He then takes from him the key of the study window, sinks the body in the lake, goes to The Moat, burgles the desk and replaces the key of the boat-house. I'm leaving the motive out of account for the moment and considering only what might have happened.'

'It's certainly very convincing.'

'I thought so, sir. I was sure I was on the right track, and I turned next to see if I could get any proof.

'I had three clues: I am not giving you all the things I thought of and rejected: only what led to results. I had a pretty good impression of the heel of the jemmy in the softish wood of the desk, I had the two pieces of lead pipe, and I had the cord with which these were tied to the body.

'I made inquiries and found that Swinburn was going to Newcastle, and when he was away I went up to his house and had a look round with his servant on the excuse of asking for some dates. I saw then that Swinburn had a workshop. I presently left, but when the servant had disappeared I slipped back to the workshop and had a look round. At once I got what I wanted. There was the jemmy, and even without a magnified photograph I could see that the irregularities on its heel fitted the impression on the desk. I found a ball of string of identical kind to that used to tie the pipe to the body, and I got convincing proof about the pipe also.

'I should have explained that of the two pieces of pipe the shorter had been sawn off the longer. Lines across the end had been made by a saw, and the rough edges of the tiny arc that was not sawn but was broken off coincided. Now, in Swinburn's workshop I found a hacksaw with lead in the teeth, and also some lead sawdust below the vice.'

'You wouldn't want much more than that,' said Heppenstall. 'You'd have got a conviction without the least trouble.'

'I think so, sir. However, I may mention here that after the arrest when I was going through Swinburn's papers, I came on an account from a plumber for work done at the house. I called on the plumber, and he was able to identify the lead pipe as being over from a job he had done in Swinburn's house. At one end were certain cuts he had made himself.'

'Excellent! I don't know when I've heard a more convincing exposition,' Heppenstall declared. 'Now, there is only one thing left that you haven't explained.'

French shrugged. 'I know, sir: the motive. Well, there I'm afraid I fall a good deal short. I can't prove the motive. I can give a suggestion, but I can't prove it.'

'Let us have the suggestion.'

'You remember that Weatherup reported to me that Swinburn spilled his wine on the night he dined at The Moat? Now, I suggest that Weatherup may have seen more than he told me. Suppose he saw Swinburn actually changing the bottles, or something equally vital. Suppose he thought he would make something out of it and began to blackmail Swinburn. If this had happened the whole of the rest of the facts would be accounted for. Swinburn would know that to murder him would be his only real safeguard, and he could easily ask him to come to the boat-house to receive the money, accounting for the choice of the boat-house on the ground that the light required to count the notes would not be seen from there.'

'But that doesn't account for the burglary of the notes.'

'Unhappily, I know that,' French smiled. 'I suggest, again without any proof, that Swinburn was looking for something – something that he thought might give him away. I suggest he found the notes unexpectedly and thought if he took them it might tend to fix suspicion on Weatherup. I suggest that this was an afterthought and not part of the original scheme.'

'That's likely enough, inspector. But what could Swinburn have been looking for?'

French shrugged his shoulders. 'There again I made a guess – which again I couldn't prove. I thought that Weatherup, knowing Swinburn was a murderer, would scarcely risk dealing with him without some safeguard. I put this forward for what it's worth. I suggest this safeguard took the form of some kind of sealed document and that Weatherup told Swinburn that he had given it to Morley to keep and to be opened in the event of his, Weatherup's, death. He had not done anything of the kind; I asked Morley. But I suggest he bluffed Swinburn into thinking he had, and that it was to recover this documentary evidence that Swinburn broke open the desk.'

'Likely, but unproven?' Heppenstall smiled.

'Yes, sir, but I'd remind you that we hadn't to prove what the desk was broken open for. We had only to prove that Swinburn killed Weatherup, and that was established beyond possibility of doubt.'

'That's quite true,' Heppenstall admitted. 'Well, inspector, it only remains for us to congratulate you and the super and Inspector Appleby. I don't know when I've heard a better reasoned case. What do you say, Byng?'

Byng said the proper things in the proper manner. 'By the way, French,' he added, 'here's a point. Shall I call you in my book Inspector French or Chief-Inspector French?'

French, highly delighted, explained that his leg would come off if pulled too hard, and the meeting terminated.

MURDER OF A LADY

Anthony Wynne

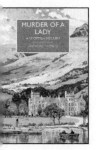

Inspector Dundas and gifted amateur sleuth Eustace Hailey tackle a locked-room mystery in a Scottish castle.

DEATH ON THE RIVIERA

John Bude

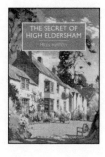

Counterfeit currency—and murder—darken the sunlit glamour of the Riviera. Detective Inspector Meredith needs to keep one step ahead.

MURDER IN THE MUSEUM

John Rowland

The murder of an academic in the British Museum brings together Inspector Shelley and mild-mannered museum visitor Henry Fairhurst.

THE SECRET OF HIGH ELDERSHAM

Miles Burton

When a pub landlord is stabbed, Detective-Inspector Young calls on "living encyclopedia" Desmond Merrion to help uncover the secrets of the village.